RACHEL CAINE is the international bestselling author of over thirty novels, including the *New York Times* bestselling Morganville Vampires series. She was born at White Sands Missile Range, which people who know her say explains a lot. She has been an accountant, an insurance investigator and a professional musician, and has played with such musical legends as Henry Mancini, Peter Nero and John Williams. She and her husband, fantasy artist R. Cat Conrad, live in Texas with their iguana Pop-eye, a mali uromastyx named (appropriately) O'Malley, and a leopard tortoise named Shelley (for the poet, of course).

www.rachelcaine.com

The Weather Warden series

Ill Wind
Heat Stroke
Chill Factor
Windfall
Firestorm
Thin Air
Gale Force
Cape Storm
Total Eclipse

The Morganville Vampires series

Glass Houses
The Dead Girls' Dance
Midnight Alley
Feast of Fools
Lord of Misrule
Carpe Corpus
Fade Out
Kiss of Death
Ghost Town
Bite Club
Last Breath
Black Dawn
Bitter Blood

Morganville Vampires Omnibus:
Glass Houses, The Dead Girls' Dance, Midnight Alley
Morganville Vampires Omnibus:
Feast of Fools, Lord of Misrule, Carpe Corpus

The Revivalist series

Working Stiff
Two Weeks' Notice

Firestorm

WEATHER WARDEN
BOOK FIVE

RACHEL CAINE

Allison & Busby Limited
13 Charlotte Mews
London, W1T 4EJ
www.allisonandbusby.com

First published in Great Britain by Allison & Busby in 2006.
This paperback edition published by Allison & Busby in 2012.

First published in the USA, in 2006, by ROC,
an imprint of New American Library,
a division of Penguin Group (USA) Inc.

A CIP catalogue record for this book is available from
the British Library.

10 9 8 7 6 5 4 3 2 1

ISBN 978-0-7490-1228-1

Typeset in 11.5/15.75 pt Sabon by
Allison & Busby Ltd.

The paper used for this Allison & Busby publication
has been produced from trees that have been legally sourced
from well-managed and credibly certified forests.

Printed and bound by
CPI Group (UK) Ltd, Croydon, CR0 4YY

For Jenny Griffee,
NaNoNov winner of 2004,
who provided a hell of a good idea
for a new class of magical being,
not to mention a slam-bang character.

Previously . . .

My name is Joanne Baldwin, and in case you haven't been keeping up with current events, we're in big trouble. The world, I mean. As for me, I've been in trouble since . . . well, always . . . but this is big. The Wardens – the folks who are supposed to be protecting all of you from the dangers of raging fires, floods, earthquakes, and natural disasters of all kinds – have been compromised. Slowly but surely, they've lost their way and become corrupt and ineffective.

I used to be one of them, until I acquired a Demon Mark and fell in love with a Djinn, but that's another story altogether (*Ill Wind*, actually, if you're taking notes). The point is that now, the Djinn – who should be the allies of the Wardens – aren't playing by the rules that have held for millennia. A Djinn named Jonathan set up those rules, and now that Jonathan's gone, all bets are off.

And the Djinn's new leader? My lover, David. What that bodes for a stable relationship is still up in the air, but confidentially? I'm worried.

The human race has one chance to keep its place at the top of the food chain: make peace with the Djinn, and that means somehow, some way, making peace with the Earth itself. Which ain't gonna be easy, because Mother Nature is pissed off.

And apparently, I may be the only one able to do something about it.

Lucky me . . .

Chapter One

I was thinking that the Wardens needed a new motto. The old one, the one on the seals on my diploma, was *Defensor Hominem*, Latin for 'Defender of Mankind,' but sometime in the past twenty-four hours, I'd become convinced that I had a more appropriate motto: *We're So Screwed*.

Yeah, that pretty much covered it.

'Duck!' I yelled as another piece of debris came flying towards us, and grabbed for whatever order I could manage in the chaos of the weather around us. Not the easiest thing in the world, considering that the whole eastern seaboard's system had been destabilised by a gigantic killer supernatural storm – now mysteriously vanquished, through no doing of mine – and all kinds of random, unpleasant, potentially fatal problems were presenting themselves.

Currently, those included a rather large and very

aggressive tornado ploughing its way across some unoccupied farmland and tossing pieces of broken fence ahead of it like shrapnel.

Cherise – my travelling companion, mainly because she had a kick-ass fast Mustang and I needed wheels – squeaked and hit the dirt, covering her pretty blond head with both hands. I remained standing. It wasn't heroism, exactly, more that I didn't want to dirty up what remained of my clothes. I think about things like that during the more garden-variety apocalypses.

This is what happens when someone like me – a Weather Warden – stops for a bathroom break in the middle of a crisis. And dammit, I hadn't even gotten bladder relief out of it. I had a very personal reason to hold my ground: the tornado was threatening to flatten the only roadside public restroom in forty miles.

I reached out for the wind currents and grabbed hold of the ones that would do me the most good. A sudden gust of wind, generated by a big push of heat in the right area, deflected an oncoming piece of fencepost – a nice big chunk of jagged wood, the size of a fire hydrant – off to the side, where it smacked into an unlucky wind-lashed tree, which it uprooted with a crash. Dirt flew, adding to the general chaos and mayhem.

I studied the tornado, ignoring gusts that tried to push me over; I was standing in a bubble of more or less calm air, but the wind was getting through in fits and spurts. Whatever good hair day I'd been having was a distant memory. We were into the scary fright-wig territory now.

Yes, I worry about things like hair, too. Probably more than I worry about world peace, mainly because at least I can usually control my hair.

Unable to do anything about my ruined look, I focused on the tornado. They're relatively fragile things, for all the scary woo-woo attitude and screaming freight-train soundtrack. Oh, they're terrifying enough if you don't have the power to do anything about them, but luckily, I was well-equipped for this particular challenge. The twister reeled like a drunken top, right, then left, and headed straight for me with fresh enthusiasm, chewing up crops as it went. I hate it when they come straight for me. What did I ever do to them?

Cherise looked up through the gate of her fingers and shrieked, then went back to hiding her eyes. I ignored her and let myself slowly slide out of my body and up into that strange state – partly mental, partly physical, all weird – that the Wardens refer to as the aetheric plane.

It was only one of several planes of existence, but it was the highest one available to me as a human being (even one with, finally, a working set of weather powers). The world took on strange neon swirls, candy-coloured sparks, and currents of power. The landscape altered around me into unknown territory.

The tornado was a glittering silver funnel, physics

in its most potentially deadly form and given an instinctive menace, like a baby cobra. Fully as deadly as the more mature version, but with less experience. I had to step in before it learnt where and how to strike.

I waited another few seconds, reading the patterns, then reached deep inside of the eye of the tornado and rapidly cooled the air into a heavy, sluggish mass. The energy exchange bled off in the form of a sudden burst of cable-thick lightning that snapped from the low-hanging clouds, and the wall of the tornado expanded and lost its coherence. In seconds, it was a confused mass of wind, moving too slowly to form much of a threat. It dropped its load of debris and wandered off at an angle, swirling petulantly.

'OK,' I said to Cherise as I sank back into my body and the comfortable solidity of three-dimensional space. 'You can get up now. Show's over. First one to the bathroom uses all the toilet paper.'

She didn't seem inclined to believe me. I waited a few seconds, then reached down and grabbed her elbow to haul her upright. She looked around, breathless.

'Wow,' she said. 'OK, that was intense.'

'Oh, I don't know. The hurricane was intense. This was just annoying.'

'Jo, trust me on this one: Everything about what's happened since I met you is intense. Does this happen to you a lot?'

'You'd be surprised,' I sighed. 'Seriously. Bathroom, or you're going to be buying new seats for the Mustang.'

We dashed off for the grubby-looking toilets. They were predictably scary, but I didn't care. It was a very happy few minutes, and if you've ever been stuck on the road without bathroom facilities for several hundred miles, you'll know what I mean.

We arrived back at the car at the same time. I held out my hand for the car keys, and a silent battle of wills ensued, but then Cherise had been driving the last stretch and what was she going to do? Argue with a woman who'd just stopped a tornado in its tracks? She dug them out of the pocket of her low-rise jeans and tossed them over.

'I'll try to keep us in the clear from now on,' I said.

'I'd tell you not to scratch the paint, but—' Cherise rolled her eyes. Yeah, the hurricane and ensuing sand blasting had pretty much taken care of ruining the shiny finish. But the Mustang still ran, and that was the important thing.

While I'd been asleep, she'd put the top up on the car – sensible, with the intermittent rain – but I pressed the buttons to fold it back again. I wanted as much of a 360-degree view of the sky and surroundings as I could get. My version of a Doppler system.

I eased into the comfy seat of the Mustang – candy-apple red, a yummy little treat of a car, or at least it had been before I'd gotten hold of it – and adjusted the seat for my longer legs as Cherise slid into my vacated shotgun position. Not that we had a shotgun. Though thanks to recent events, I'd have been more comfortable if we had some kind of arsenal beyond our wits, good looks, and a turbocharged engine.

I had my work cut out for me as we eased back into gear and tore at top speed along I-295. The storm systems just kept piling up – there was a new supercell forming off the low-pressure system in Georgia, and it was bound to head our way. That wasn't good physics, but it was the way my generally crappy luck ran these days.

'That was a good trick with the tornado, Mom,' said a voice from the backseat. Formal, female, and a little awkward. I jumped in surprise, and then I focused on a face in the rearview mirror that was eerily similar to my own, except for the eyes. Mine were plain blue. The ones staring back at me were an interesting shade of ruddy gold – I don't mean amber; amber's a human colour. This was amber on acid. Amber taken up to insane saturation levels.

In short, the eyes were Djinn. And they belonged to my daughter.

They widened. 'Did I frighten you?'

'Frighten?' I shot back. 'Why should I be frightened if somebody pops out of nowhere into the backseat of my car? Let's see, half the Djinn are trying to kill the Wardens, and at least some of the Wardens are infected with Demon Marks, and let's not forget the weather's all screwed up . . . oh, and the Earth's about to wake up and destroy humankind. You know what? Being a little frightened is a pretty laid-back response, all things considered, and yeah, next time? Knock.'

She smiled. Tentatively, as if she was still translating all of that into Djinn-speak. I felt an immediate stab of guilt; the poor kid had been alive for all of not-even-a-day. She seemed to lack the one characteristic that was common among all the Djinn I'd ever met: smugness. I'd thought it came coded in Djinn DNA, along with pretty eyes and the cool ability to pop in and out of existence at will.

'Although,' Imara ventured, 'you could have done it more efficiently. Do you want me to show you how?'

'Not right now,' I managed to say between gritted teeth. 'Any guidance you can offer beyond second-guessing my lifesaving abilities?'

She looked injured. So I wasn't good at this mom thing. I was still trying to get my head around the idea that the child I had carried inside me – and it wasn't a normal pregnancy, by any stretch of the imagination – had all of a sudden sprung up fully adult, with her own set of emotions unrelated to my own.

'Sorry,' I said, more softly. 'Imara, do you know anything? Anything about—' *David, oh God, I'm afraid for you. And I miss you.* '—about your father?'

She shook her head, holding my eyes in the mirror. Djinn, unlike human beings, spring out of death, not life. The greater the death, the greater the Djinn – that's the rule. Djinn don't like to acknowledge that a lot of them have very human histories behind them, but it's an indisputable fact. David – Djinn and lover and father of my child – had told me months ago that in order for our child to be born, it would mean he had to die. That was the normal order of things, in the Djinn world.

Only something strange had happened, and another death – a greater death – had stepped in to give my child life. David was still alive.

Just not himself, exactly. He'd become . . . different.

'Mom,' Imara said. 'Are you all right?' She waved a graceful hand in front of my face, which I impatiently swatted away and focused back on my driving. 'I apologise,' she said, and withdrew back into a dignified sitting position. 'I thought you were in some kind of distress.'

I can't describe how it feels to hear that word. *Mom*. Oh, I'd gotten comfortable with the idea of being pregnant, but being a mother was a whole different thing – especially mother of a grown young woman who dressed better than I did. I consoled myself that she wore couture because she was Djinn, and able to conjure up whatever clothes amused her, and plus she hadn't been through a hurricane. And a tornado. And a *very* long drive.

'I was thinking about your father,' I said. Which was an admission of distress in itself.

'He's all right,' she said, leaning forward and laying her forearm across the top of my seat. 'I would know if he wasn't. I just don't know where he is or what he's doing.'

Cherise was watching all of this with bright, feverish eyes. I had no idea what she was making of it. Knowing Cherise, probably something very interesting.

'Should I go find out?' Imara asked hopefully.

'No!' I yelped, and grabbed her wrist. She looked startled. 'You stay put. I want you where I can keep my eye on you.'

She gave me a mutinous look. Why hadn't my own mother traded me in once I'd hit puberty? I remembered giving her loads of mutinous looks. It was hugely annoying from this side of the maternal fence.

'I'm serious,' I said. 'The last time we saw any of the other Djinn, they weren't in the best mood ever. I don't want you running into trouble. I can't bail you out of it. Not against David.'

I tried to sound as if dealing with this, and with her, was all in a day's work. Probably didn't succeed, judging from the smile she gave me. It wasn't my smile. It was entirely her own, with a little lopsided quirk on one side.

'I'll stay,' she said. 'Besides, you may need me next time, if the weather gets worse.'

Cherise blurted out, 'Next time? Does there have to be a next time?'

'Not if I can help it,' I said firmly, and pressed a little more speed out of the accelerator. The cool, damp air streamed over my skin like the ghost of rain. I could have done with a more substantial sort of shower, the kind that came with shampoo and soap, but this did feel good. There was heavier weather up ahead, but we were in a clear area for the time being. I could arrange for it to stay with us, at least most of the way. 'Cherise, you'd better get some rest.' She needed it, poor thing. She'd been too crazed to sleep before, so I'd let her take over after we were a few hours out of Fort Lauderdale, and then again seven hours later. She'd barely closed her eyes since, and now she was starting to show the effects. Cherise was a perky, gorgeous thing, all tanned and toned in the best tradition of Florida beach bunnies, but there were telltale dark circles under her eyes. (She'd actually been a bikini model. And the 'fun and sun' girl back at the podunk, fourth-rate television station that had employed us both in Florida. I didn't like remembering my job, but it hadn't involved a bikini. Except that once.)

Right on cue, Cherise yawned. 'How much longer?' she asked. Actually, she said, '*Ow uch onger?*' but I got the point.

'About another four hours,' I said. 'I'll wake you when we get close.'

She yawned again and wadded up a blue jean jacket to serve as a pillow against the window, and in less time than it took to whip past six billboards, she was sound asleep. I thought about turning on the radio, but I didn't want to wake her.

'So,' I said, and looked in the rearview mirror. My daughter met my gaze, lifting her eyebrows. There was something of David in the expression, and I felt a sad little stab of recognition and longing.

'So,' she replied. 'This is strange for you, isn't it?'

'Little bit, yeah.'

'Would it make it better if I told you it was strange for me, too?'

'It might,' I said. 'You're sure you can't tell what Dav – what your father's up to?'

Her eyes took on a distant glitter, just a second's worth, and then she shook her head. 'No. I can't tell. He's shut me out. They've all shut me out.' She sounded wistful. 'I think he did it for my protection. This way *she* can't get to me.'

She, meaning Mother Nature. The Earth. One very ticked-off planet, who was coming slowly out of an eons-long slumber and wondering blearily what the hell had happened with the human race while she wasn't looking. After all, in the tradition of surly teens everywhere, we'd taken the opportunity to throw loud parties and trash the place while she'd been out. It's not nice to fool Mother Nature. It's even worse to fool *with* her.

I focused back on Imara. 'So . . . you're not connected to the Earth? The way the rest are?'

She looked away, and after a few seconds I realised that she was embarrassed by what she was going to say. 'It's a little like hearing music coming from the car next to you – you can hear the bass notes, but you can't make out the tune. It's not all Father's doing. There's a lot of you in me, and it holds me back.' Her eyes flew back up to meet mine, stricken. 'I didn't mean—'

'I know what you mean,' I said. 'I'm a handicap.'

Even though I was, of course. I'd worked out fairly quickly that Imara wasn't fully Djinn . . . Right now, that was an advantage, with the other Djinn more or less susceptible to control by the waking Earth, and pretty much unreliable in the free-will department. But what did it mean for her, long-term? How would she be accepted by the other Djinn? And what would happen if – God forbid – she ever had to go up against them in a real battle?

I couldn't think about that. I couldn't stand to imagine her going up against someone like Ashan, who had the morals and kindness of a spider.

She was watching me steadily with those bright, inhuman eyes. I had a cold flash. 'Can you tell what I'm thinking?' I asked.

Her eyebrows rose. 'Will it make you angry if I say yes?'

'Yes.'

'No.'

'You're lying to me.'

'Why would I do that?'

'You really are David's child, you know that?'

She smiled. 'He really loves you, you know. I can feel that, too. It's the warmest thing in him, his love for you.'

'I thought you said he'd cut you off.'

'He has. But short of killing me, he can't cut me off completely.' She shrugged. 'He's my father.'

I felt my throat heat and tighten, and tears prickled my eyes. I swallowed and blinked and drummed my fingers on the steering wheel. 'Right. So, am I doing the right thing here? Heading to New York?'

In the absence of any other ideas, I was heading for the relative safe haven of Warden Headquarters, where those of us who'd survived the last few days were sure to gather. All hell had broken loose among the Wardens, with wholesale mayhem from the normally compliant and subservient Djinn. I just hoped that I wouldn't be coming back to find . . . nothing. The last thing I wanted was to be the last Warden standing, with the Earth waking up and Djinn running crazy. Granted, it would be exciting. It would just be a very short story, and a very ugly ending.

'I don't know if it's the right thing to do or not,' my daughter replied solemnly. 'I'm only a day old.'

Great. I had no idea whether I was doing the right thing, I had a smart-ass immortal kid, and Cherise for a wingman.

Yeah, this was going to end well. No doubt about it.

Four hours later, it was dark and I was exhausted. Twenty-two hours in a car, even a Mustang, will do that to you. The Mustang purred around me like a contented tiger. Not the Mustang's fault that I was so tired that I wanted to weep, *or* that my world was falling apart, or that I was driving where my head sent me instead of my heart. My heart was back in Florida, where I'd last seen David. Where I'd last seen my sister Sarah, who was now officially a missing person, last seen being carried off by a British madman named Eamon. (I'd made use of my cell phone to report the abduction to the FBI. If that didn't screw up whatever escape plans Eamon had made, I couldn't imagine what would.)

Nope. None of it was the Mustang's fault. I liked the Mustang just fine. I was wondering how exactly I could arrange to get it as a permanent lease, once it was repainted, of course.

The Mustang's real owner stirred and smacked her lips the way people do when they wake up with monster morning breath. Cherise blinked at the pastel wash of late-night lights as we came out of the Lincoln Tunnel, and she stretched as we cruised to a halt at a stoplight a few blocks later. Guys in cars all around us watched, even though Cherise wasn't at her well-groomed best at the moment. Some girls just have it. Cherise had so much of it, the rest of us needed time-shares just to get by.

'Nurgh,' she said, or something like it, then dry-rubbed her face and threw back her hair and tried again. 'Whatimesit?' Or a mumble to that effect.

'Almost one a.m.,' I said. Since we'd travelled directly up the eastern seaboard, the Mustang's dashboard clock hadn't been fazed by our twelve-hundred-miles-in-just-under-one-day jaunt. I eyed it with the numbed disbelief of someone who couldn't quite fathom where all the hours had gone. Straight into my ass, it felt like. 'We should be there soon.'

Cherise turned and peered over the leather seat at Imara, who was stretched out like a cat over the backseat, comfortable and indolent. 'Oh. You're still here?'

'Obviously.'

'I was kind of hoping you'd gone back to the mother ship by now.'

I smothered a chuckle. 'Cher, she's not an alien.'

'Right,' she said. 'Not an alien. Glowing eyes, disappears at the drop of a hat. But not from another planet, got it.' Cherise, needless to say, was a fervent devotee of *The X-Files* and alien invasion stories in all shapes and Jerry Bruckheimer sizes. She had a little big-headed grey alien tattoo to prove it, right at the small of her back. 'Is Pod Girl going with us all the way?'

Imara raised a single eyebrow, in imitation of either everybody's favourite Vulcan, or at least a popular former wrestler. 'Going all the way? Is that a euphemism for something else?' she asked.

'Honey,' Cherise said, 'you're not that cute. Well, OK, maybe if I was really drunk and your eyes didn't glow, but—'

'Hey!' I snapped. 'That's my kid you're talking

to.' And besides, my kid was pretty much the spitting image of, well, me. So I was a little weirded out. 'Are you going with us, Imara?'

She looked frankly astonished. 'I have a vote?'

'Of course.'

'Then I'll go with you. As a dutiful child.' She still looked too grave and self-contained, but I could see a twinkle of humour in there, buried deep.

Cherise responded to that with a dubious snort for both of us. 'Whatever. So, tell me again where we're going?'

'You remember how I told you about the Wardens?' I asked.

'Organisation of people like you, with all kinds of superpowers, who control the weather and stuff. Speaking of, weren't we in the middle of a hurricane that was about to kill us about twenty-four hours ago? If you could control the weather, what was up with the hundred-mile-an-hour winds? I meant to ask earlier, but I was, you know, dealing with my trauma.'

'It's not as easy as just waving a hand!' I protested. 'And anyway, I wasn't supposed to interfere right then. – Oh, fine. Maybe I was having an off day. In answer to your original question, we're going to my office. Warden Headquarters.'

'In New York City.'

'Midtown, to be exact. First and Forty-sixth.' She had a look of incomprehension. 'In the UN Building.'

Her expression didn't change.

'You have heard of the UN, right? United Nations? Bunch of guys who get together, talk about world peace? . . .'

Imara murmured, 'Even I know what the UN is, and I really *was* born yesterday.'

Cherise shot her a dirty look. 'Shut up! I know what the UN is!'

'Sorry.'

'But . . . the UN controls the weather? Because I thought they were all about that whole world peace thing.'

I reclaimed the conversation from the bickering – ah, children. 'No, they don't control the weather. They lease office space to the Wardens, who do.'

Cherise didn't bother to say, 'You're insane,' but the expression on her face was pretty clear, and considering this was coming from a girl who half believed aliens had abducted Elvis, that was special. She even edged a little bit more towards the passenger-side window. I was wishing that I'd left Cherise at any of the various petrol stations we'd blown past along the way, but it would take only one unhappy phone call from her claiming I'd stolen her car to end my trip real quick. Hadn't seemed prudent, given the priorities.

'You weren't kidding,' Cherise said, studying the building as we got closer. 'We really are going to the UN. Is it even open?'

'Trust me, the Wardens never close.' My whole body ached, and I really, really needed a shower. I'd scrubbed cleanish in a truck stop restroom a lifetime ago, because I just hadn't been able to stand it anymore, but I wasn't what you might call business-meeting ready. My eyes ached and watered from the glare of streetlights. I was grateful that at least it wasn't full daylight. That would have been much, much worse.

I made the turn to the special security-controlled parking garage, which was locked up like Fort Knox. There was a scanner on the driver's side. I rolled down the window and extended my hand. A green laser jittered over my exposed skin, and the door silently rolled up. I gunned it, because in seconds the door reversed course and began its downward journey. Down a corkscrewing Habitrail of a parking ramp, to a floor marked only with the sign AUTHORISED PARKING ONLY. I was authorised. I slid into the first available parking slot.

It worried me that there were so many parking spaces unoccupied.

'Come on, we have a special door.'

'We do? A special door? Cool.' Cherise scrambled out of the car. Imara emerged after her, elegant and tall, tossing long black hair back from her face as if she were ready for a photo shoot. I decided she didn't look like me at all. I'd never looked that glamorous. Well, I'd never *felt* that glamorous, anyway.

There was supposed to be a special guard on the special door. There were certainly a special-made guardpost, and as far as I knew it was supposed to be manned 24-7. Only nobody was there. Maybe the guard had gone for a call of nature, but I doubted it. I tried the steel door to the hut. Locked. Lights glowed on panels inside, but the windows were covered with steel mesh. That left us standing in a hot white wash of light, looking suspicious. I looked around, and sure enough, there was a surveillance camera – as ubiquitous as houseflies in the modern world. I waved, then turned to the door again.

'There's no lock or handle,' Cherise said. 'Don't they have to open it from in there or something?'

'Or something.'

I held up my hand and concentrated. A faint blue sparkle moved across it, lighting up the stylised sunburst that was the symbol of the Wardens. It was magically tattooed into my flesh, and it couldn't be faked.

I ran it across a scanner inset next to the door. I waited, but nothing happened. If there'd been crickets around, they would have been chirping. I sighed, looked at Cherise and Imara, and shook my head. I ran a hand through my tangled hair and pushed it back from my face, back over my shoulders, and wondered what my chances were of bluffing the regular UN guards into granting me admittance.

I didn't wonder very long. They'd raised paranoia to an art form around here, and for very good reasons.

'Right,' I said. 'I guess we'll have to wait until someone decides that we look safe.'

'Yeah, and when will that be?' Cherise asked, with a significant look at our generally less than presentable turnout, Imara notwithstanding.

The door let loose with a thick metallic *chunk* and swung open about a quarter of an inch.

'Now.' I grabbed the edge and moved it wider. It was heavy. Bombproof, most likely. I ushered the girls inside, grabbed the inner handle, and pulled it tight behind me as I entered the building. The lock engaged with a snap and hum of power.

'Um . . . Jo?' Cherise sounded spooked.

When I turned, there were two people standing in the industrial concrete-block hallway facing us. Both were in blue blazers with a logo on them – UN Security – but with the additional graphic touch of the sun-shaped Wardens' symbol pinned to their lapels. Man and woman, both tall and capable-looking. I didn't know them.

I'd seen guns before, though, and they had two great big pistols pointed right at us.

I put my hands in the air. Cherise followed suit, fast, and laced her hands behind her head without being asked. Too many episodes of police shows, I was guessing, or some indiscretions that I didn't want to know about.

Imara didn't raise her hands at all, just looked at the guards with those ruddy-amber eyes and raised her eyebrows, as if they amused the hell out of her.

'Djinn!' the woman in the blazer yelled to her

partner, and took a step forward to get an angle on Imara. She had a nice two-handed shooting stance, and a voice hard enough to shatter diamond. Her eyes darted rapidly from Imara to Cherise, and then landed on me. 'Warden, put your Djinn back in the bottle. *Now!*'

I looked at Imara, wide-eyed. She looked back. 'Back in the bottle,' I said. I didn't own Imara, and she wasn't bound to a bottle anyway, but she was bright enough to realise that this might not be the time to debate the issue. She misted away, off to someplace safer, I hoped. The Wardens were a little paranoid these days. Love me, hate me, want to kill me . . . it all depended on the mood of who I was talking to, or so it seemed.

But I understood their paranoia about Djinn. I'd seen the change come over David, on a beach in Florida, and it had terrified me in ways that I'd never thought possible. Nothing more frightening than seeing someone you know, someone you love, go mad.

I focused on the two guards and tried for a wan, friendly smile. 'OK, no problem, right? Djinn's in the bottle. You guys know me. Joanne Baldwin? Weather Warden? I'm here to see Paul Giancarlo.'

Whether it was my name or Paul's, something made the two guards exchange a look and relax. They didn't holster their weapons, but they didn't look actively menacing anymore, either. And they pointed the barrels vaguely towards the floor.

'Baldwin,' the man repeated. 'Right. We've been expecting you.' He was a tall fellow, thin without being skinny. The physique of a basketball player under the wool jacket, white shirt, and conservative tie. 'Follow us,' he said, and turned to walk down the hallway.

I shrugged and followed, Cherise obediently hurrying along with me. I hoped I hadn't dragged her into the middle of something really, really bad. I had to believe the Wardens wouldn't hurt her. They treated normal people with kind, despotic benevolence.

They only ate their own.

Well, even if they tossed her out on her ear, she'd be OK. Cherise would survive. She was the kind of girl who could stand on a New York sidewalk looking helpless, and in under thirty seconds, a dozen guys would dash to the rescue.

We went to the back elevators, which were operated by key card; my minders kept exchanging significant glances, but I didn't think I had much to fear from them. Wardens were never really unarmed, of course, and for the first time in a long time, I was feeling strong and confident. If this turned into a straight-out fight, I was willing and able to oblige. Provided I could get Cherise out of the line of fire – and in Warden terms, that was literal.

The elevator rose up smoothly and deposited us with a muted ding at our destination. The doors opened . . .

. . . on a floor I didn't recognise. One that looked

like it was under construction, only construction would have been orderly, at least. No, this was under *de*struction. Panelling in splinters, pictures reduced to smashed frames and piles of glittering glass. Puddles of dark liquid that I really didn't want to examine too closely in the emergency lighting. I'd been to this place recently, and I hardly recognised it at all. It had been a hallowed, hushed centre of power.

Now it was the gruesome aftermath of a war zone.

'Oh my God,' Cherise murmured behind me, and edged carefully around a pile of splinters and glass that had once, I remembered, been a huge photo of the senior management of the Wardens.

'Watch your step,' our male guard said, and ducked under some low-hanging grids dangling from cables. 'We're remodelling.'

The dry gallows humour didn't thaw out the cold shock in my stomach. 'What the hell happened?'

The woman shot me one of those looks. The kind a mother uses when she's out of patience with a child's bullshit. 'Guess,' she snapped.

It hit me with a vengeance. They'd had a visit from some very motivated Djinn. Hence, the panic over Imara.

I kept my mouth shut as we moved slowly around obstructions to the conference room about halfway down the hall. On the way, I spotted the big marble shrine to Wardens who'd died in the line of duty. It was only lightly chipped, and my name was still on it. I supposed, with all of the furore of the last few months, they hadn't gotten around to chiselling off the writing. Or maybe they just figured my death was inevitable, and why waste the effort . . .

'In here,' the guy said, and pointed through the open conference room door. I say 'open,' but it was more of a 'missing.' Sharp fresh-bent hinges sticking out from the wall, no sign of the doors themselves.

The room was lit with emergency lanterns and chemical lights, the kind the Wardens recommended for use in hurricanes and tornadoes. It gave everything a post-apocalyptic glow – splintered heavy furniture, a blizzard of paper scattered over the floor, dark splashes on the shredded carpet.

The surviving Wardens were gathered around the splintered conference table. I counted heads. Nineteen. I made an even twenty.

I remembered the hundreds of Wardens who could have been here, *should* have been here, and felt a sick jolt in the pit of my stomach.

'Jo.' Paul Giancarlo – my old friend and mentor – looked as bad as the room. He was a big guy, well muscled, but he was looking terrifyingly banged up as he limped towards me. I met him halfway in a hug that was careful on my part, desperate on his. He was bandaged around the head, dark hair sticking up in thick unruly clumps on top, and his skin was pasty yellow. He had Technicolor bruises over half his face. 'Thank God you're OK.'

His pupils were hugely dilated. Pain medication. He was doped to the gills.

I let go and stepped back, and our fingers wrapped tight. He wasn't Lewis, and our various powers didn't amplify and rebound; I felt little to nothing from him, hardly even a whisper. Drugs could do that, but this was something else. He'd drained himself to dangerous levels. I knew how that felt. I'd done it myself, more than once.

'I wish I could say the same about you,' I said, and his big hand tightened around mine. 'Paul. What happened here?'

'They went crazy,' he said, and closed his eyes for a second. 'What the hell do you think? Not a damn thing we could do, except try to keep them off of us. Too many Wardens died. Way too many.'

I felt cold, imagining it. Djinn were like tigers, I'd always thought: beautiful and sleek and deadly when out of control. And this had definitely been way out of control. I remembered David, back on the beach in Florida – David, who would never have willingly hurt me – coming for me with his eyes glowing red. I'd have died there, if it hadn't been for Imara. And that had been open ground. In an enclosed space like this, no place to run . . .

'We couldn't stop them,' Paul finished softly. 'We lost—' He looked momentarily stunned, trying to recall a number.

Down the table, a quiet voice supplied, 'At least

thirty. We're lucky we have as many here as we do.'

'Lucky?' A half-whisper from a battered young man I didn't recognise, with the solid hum of energy that usually tokened an Earth power. 'What part of that was lucky, man? I saw people – I saw friends just ripped in half—'

Paul sighed. 'Yeah, kid, I know. Easy. We're going to get through this, OK? Jo, this is pretty much everybody we could pull in that we could reach. Got more on the way, but it's going to take some time to figure out who's still alive and able to help. Plus, we can't yank everybody out. We need them on the ground, especially now.' His gaze fell randomly on Cherise, and stayed. 'Who's this?'

'Cherise. She's a friend.' After a hesitation, I had to clarify, 'Not a Warden.'

He looked completely pissed off. 'What are we running here? A tour group? Get her the hell out of here!'

I looked at Cherise. She was dead scared and didn't know where to look but she especially didn't want to look at the puddles of dried blood on the carpet or the silent, staring faces of the Wardens. 'Cher, why don't you wait in the hall?'

'Hell no,' she said. 'I've been to the movies. No way am I splitting up in the scary place. C'mon, Jo, I want to stay with you. Please?'

She had a point. No telling what kind of dangers were still lurking around the corner. I turned back to Paul. 'She stays,' I said. He glowered. 'Paul, she stays. We don't have time to screw around with who's allowed in the cool kids' room when the house is on fire, right? Just pretend she's an intern or something.'

That wouldn't be too hard. Cherise was looking more and more like an out-of-her-depth undergrad.

'So what do we know?' I asked, and slid into an empty chair. Cherise hastily took the one next to me. I scanned faces around the room and saw about twelve I recognised. Way too many were missing, I had to hope they were still somewhere out there, doing their jobs. I exchanged quick nods with the people I knew.

'We started losing contact with Wardens all over the country about three days ago. Started with just a few, but it spread like wildfire,' a lean, weathered woman of about forty said. 'It took us a while to understand that they were being attacked by Djinn. No survivors until they came after Marion.'

I glanced down the table into shadows, alarmed. I'd seen Marion . . . Yes, there she was, half-hidden near the end. Marion was an Earth Warden, and her skill was healing, but self-healing was a chancy undertaking at the best of times. She looked terrible. I exchanged another nod with her.

'Marion, I'm so sorry. Your Djinn—?' I didn't know how to finish that question, because Marion and I knew things about each other that really weren't suited to sharing with a table full of strangers. Such as, I knew that Marion had taken enormous risks to recover her lost Djinn, not so very long ago, and it hadn't been out of selfless duty; she and her Djinn were lovers. That fell under the 'forbidden tragic love' section of the Warden code, even under normal circumstances; I just didn't know for certain how tragic it had turned out this time.

She took me off the hook. 'My Djinn helped me take out the two who came to – to *free* him. Then he asked me to put him back into his bottle. I did, and sealed it.'

'First good advice we had,' Paul said. 'We've been getting hold of every Warden we can find and telling them the same thing. Get your Djinn safe and seal the bottles until we know what the hell's going on. You got anything, Jo?'

I stretched my hands flat on the scarred wood surface. 'Afraid so. Here's the deal. The Djinn were serving us only because of an agreement made a few thousand years ago between the first Wardens and the most powerful Djinn in the world. His name is – was – Jonathan.'

Silence, and then . . .'Kind of a modern name, isn't it?' Cherise asked. 'Jonathan, I mean. Wouldn't he have an Egyptian name or—'

'Cherise. This is my story. You talk later. The thing is, once Jonathan made the agreement, which was supposed to be temporary, the Wardens didn't keep their end of the bargain. They didn't let the

Djinn go once the emergency was past all those thousands of years ago. There was always some disaster or another to serve as an extension on the contract, and then they didn't even bother making up excuses. Some of the Djinn have had enough of waiting for the Wardens to grow a conscience, and the Wardens forgot that any such agreement ever existed. So the Free Djinn—'

That term caused a rustle of throat-clearing and shifting in chairs, and the inevitable interruption. 'There aren't any such thing as—' someone began to declare, in much the same way people once insisted the world was flat.

'Yes there are, Rosa.' That was Marion, and her tone was surprisingly sharp, coming from a woman who was normally so level and soothing in manner. But then, we'd all had a damn hard few days. I could see that it might be difficult to suffer fools with the same level of grace she usually displayed.

'Continue,' Paul said, watching me.

I swallowed, wished in vain for a drink of water, and got on with it. 'So some of the Free Djinn started killing Wardens, trying to free their brethren, as well. But some didn't agree with that tactic, so there was fighting in the Djinn ranks. Jonathan—' What the hell *had* happened to Jonathan? Something catastrophic. 'Jonathan died. And when he died, the agreement between the Djinn and the Wardens, the one that kept them under our command, that went sideways. We don't own the Djinn anymore. Not as of the moment he stopped existing.'

Paul's face went a paler shade of scared. 'You mean, they're no longer under our control *at all*?'

'Yes, that's what I mean.'

'Well, that's just great. You drove all the way from Florida to tell me we're dead?'

'You want me to go on, or what?' I glared back. He finally closed his drug-glazed eyes and nodded. 'Right. Well, we've always thought we were fighting the planet, one on one. A fair contest. But I have to tell you, it isn't fair, and it isn't even a contest. She hasn't even been *awake*.' Inarticulate noises of protest and denial. I ignored them. 'She's not even concentrating on us at all. We're like little mosquitoes she's been swatting in her sleep.'

Paul's face had drained of what little colour he had. 'Jo—'

'Hang on, I'm still getting to the bad news.' I sucked in a deep breath, then blew it out. 'She's starting to wake up. Once she does, she can control the Djinn absolutely, and that means we'll face a thousand times the power we did before. Maybe worse than that. And without any help from the usual sources.'

He looked glassy-eyed. 'Was that the bad news? Because for fuck's sake, don't tell me it gets worse than that.'

'Yeah, that was it.'

He didn't say anything. The silence ticked off, one

cold second at a time, until Marion murmured, 'Then that would be the end of it.'

Paul looked up sharply. 'I'm not throwing in the towel, and you're not either,' he snapped. 'Jo. What else you got for us? Anything on the plus side?'

'I may—' I edited myself carefully, well aware of the way this might go. 'I may know of a Djinn who can still help us.'

'I'm the guy in charge of handing out life preservers on the *Titanic*. Anything you got that can help, let's have it. I mean, we're talking about Band-Aids on a sucking chest wound, but—'

'I don't know if this Djinn has the ability to do much,' I said quickly. It wouldn't do to get anybody's hopes up, and I wasn't even sure where Imara was, or what she was up to. 'But I'll check into it. Maybe we can get some intelligence about what's happening to the Djinn without too much risk. Meanwhile, we have to get off our asses. We're powerful in our own right, but we've been relying on the Djinn for too long. You need to get all hands on deck, make them quit playing politics and doing under-the-table deals. Put them to *work* for a change.' I bit my lip, debating, and then continued, 'And get the Ma'at on board. The Wardens got lazy, using the Djinn to help them. We have to learn a whole new way of doing things. The Ma'at can help.'

There was another stir of resistance. Not denial – this was confusion. Marion knew about the Ma'at, and I'd presumed she'd reported everything to Paul, but surprise . . . he wasn't looking like he recognised the name, and neither did anyone else. I shot Marion an alarmed, semi-desperate glance. She raised an inscrutable *you're on your own* eyebrow.

I tried for a calm tone. 'I thought you knew, Paul. The Ma'at. I guess you'd call them a rival organisation, who can raise up powers that can influence the same things we can. I met them in Vegas.'

'Rival organisation? Vegas?' Paul's face went from white to an alarming shade of maroon. 'Vegas? *You're telling me you knew about all this months ago?*'

Well, crap, I'd *quit*, hadn't I? Why would I have narked on the Ma'at, at that point? 'You guys weren't exactly keeping the communication channels open, you know! The Ma'at aren't as powerful as we are. OK, to be honest, I don't know how powerful they are, but I know they're not as widespread. Still, they have a different approach. They might be able to help.'

'Are you working for them?'

'What?'

He surged to his feet and leant on the table as the other Wardens exploded into babbling argument. 'Are you working for them? Is that what this is? You get inside and kill off the rest of us? You bring this Djinn along with you to finish the job?'

'Paul—'

'Shut up. Just shut your mouth, Jo.' He upgraded

the shout to a full-out bellow. 'Janet! Nathan! Get in here!'

That brought in the two guards, who'd been hovering politely out of sight around the corner. Paul gestured towards me. 'Stick this one in a room while we talk this over. Do *not* let her sweet-talk you, and do *not* let her leave. If she tries anything, you've got my permission to shoot her. Someplace painful but non-vital. Got me?'

Cherise whirled around, eyes wide. 'They're *arresting* you?'

'Looks like,' I said. I was feeling a tight flutter of panic about it, but there was no point in showing that to her. She couldn't help. 'It's OK, Cher. You go back to the car and head for home. I'll be all right.'

'Oh, hell no. I'm not leaving you like this!'

'You are,' Paul said flatly. He nodded the two guards towards Cherise. 'Escort the lady out first. Nicely, please.'

It was going to be nice until Cherise grabbed Janet's hair and kicked Nathan in the balls, and then it got a little ugly. Cherise fought like a girl, which meant she fought dirty. There was screeching. Nathan finally got her wrists pinned, and Janet – pink-cheeked and disarranged – looked like she wanted to do some hair-pulling herself, but she restrained herself with dignity.

The table full of Wardens looked on, wide-eyed.

Cherise continued to struggle even after they had

good hold of her. I went over to her, put my hand on her shoulder.

'Cherise, stop it! I'll be all right,' I promised her. 'Trust me. Go home. This isn't your fight.'

I was right, and I was lying, of course, because it was everybody's fight now. It was just that the regular folks, the ones who were going to be mowed down by the uncounted millions, couldn't do a damn thing about it. You can't fight Mother Nature. Not unless you're a Warden. And even then, it's like a particularly brave anthill taking on the Marine Corps.

She didn't say anything, just stared at me. Hair cascading over her face, half-wild, completely scared. I'd done this to her. Cherise had been a comfortable, self-absorbed little girl when I'd first met her, and I'd dragged her into a world she could neither understand nor control. Another stone on the crushing burden of guilt I was hauling around.

'Go home,' I repeated, and stepped back. Janet and Nathan escorted her to the door – carried her, actually, since she was such a tiny little thing. Her feet kicked uselessly for the floor, but they each hoisted her with an arm under hers, and out she went.

'Jo, dammit, don't do this! Let me help! I want to help!' she yelled. I didn't move. Didn't reply. 'Hey, you jerk, watch the shirt, that's designer—'

And then she was gone, and it was just me and a room full of Wardens, and it wasn't the time to be picking any fights. Besides, I wasn't fool enough to believe anybody else would jump in on my side.

'You really going to lock me up?' I asked Paul. He gave me a stare worthy of his mafioso relatives. 'I could take down a bunch of you, you know,' I said. 'On my worst day, I could still take at least three of you if I had to. And no offense, but this isn't shaping up to be *my* worst day. For a change.'

'Yeah, go on, you're making me *not* want to lock you up, with a speech like that,' he said. 'I know you could take any of us except Lewis; you always could. And when did you figure all that out, incidentally?'

'Started to a couple of months ago,' I said, and shrugged. 'So. You want to fight, or work together to help people survive this? Because I'm not going to play the traditional who's-on-top and who-can-smooch-the-most-ass game anymore. I'm not letting you stick me in some cell and pretend like this is all my fault and it'll all go away if we hold a tribunal and assign some blame. And most of all, I'm not going to sit back and let people die.'

'You'll do what we ask you to do,' said Marion, and rolled out from behind the table. Rolled, because she was in a wheelchair. I made a sound of distress, because I didn't realise how badly she'd been hurt – worse than Paul. There was something terribly misshapen about her legs. Marion was middle-aged, but she looked older than that now; lines grooved around her eyes and at the corners of her mouth, lines of pain. Even her normally glossy black hair looked dull and tangled, but I supposed that personal grooming probably wasn't on anyone's top ten to-do list at the moment. 'This isn't the moment for personal heroics, and you know it. The Wardens need to pull together. That means someone has to lead, and the rest of us have to follow. Including you.'

'Following's never been her strong suit,' Paul said morosely. 'In case you haven't noticed. And she can probably kick your ass, too, these days.'

'Paul,' Marion said with strained patience, 'perhaps we should stop discussing whose asses would be hypothetically kicked, and talk about what we're going to do to stop the bloodshed.'

'Somebody needs to contact the Ma'at,' I said. 'I'm not their favourite person ever, but at least I know some names. How's that for cooperation?'

'Hand them over to Marion,' Paul said. 'You're done here until we can check you out and find out who these people are. Marion?'

Marion, always practical, reached into her plaid-blanketed lap, and pulled out a pad of paper and a pen. I recited the ones I could remember. Charles Spencer Ashworth. Myron Lazlo. Told the Wardens about their lair in the lap of the Sphinx out in Las Vegas.

She exchanged a look with Paul, and he shrugged. 'Check it out,' he said. 'You, Jo. You're going to spend a little time contemplating how bad an idea it was to keep that from me.'

'Oh, come *on*, Paul. We don't have time for this bullshit.'

'Sorry,' Marion said, and pulled something else out from under that plaid lap blanket. An automatic pistol. It looked like one of the same police-issue models that Janet and Nathan had been sporting. 'But he's right. First, we establish contact with the Ma'at, and then we decide what to do with you. Don't worry. It probably won't take all that long, and you look as if you could use the rest.'

I felt a cold chill at how close she'd probably come to putting a bullet in me, just on general principles. I'd been shot in the back before, in this very building, as it happened. Not an experience I was looking to repeat, especially since David wasn't likely to show up again to help me out.

I slowly put up my hands.

She shook her head. 'I'm not going to shoot you,' she said, and put the gun back in her lap, though on top of the blanket. 'For one thing, the recoil is murder on a broken arm.'

'Glad your priorities are straight.'

'Up,' she said. 'I'll show you someplace you can wait in comfort.'

I looked over my shoulder when I reached the splintered doorway, and saw something that I'd never really seen before in a group of Wardens: fear. And they were right to be afraid. In all the history of the Wardens, stretching through the ages, nobody had ever faced what we were facing: a planet that was about to wake up and kill us, and Djinn who were going to be more than happy to help.

I wondered if this was how the dinosaurs had felt, watching that bright meteor streak towards the ground.

Chapter Two

I spent some time in lockup lying on a clean hospital bed, humming popular songs, and trying to imagine what the new Wardens' seal should look like. I was currently going with a shiny circular motif, with the new motto of *We're So Screwed* running around the outer edge, featuring a graphic of a nuclear mushroom cloud in the centre. A gold seal, probably. Gold goes with everything, even an apocalypse.

Bored with mental graphic design, I got up and wandered around, taking stock. The infirmary was mysteriously intact. Crisp, clean, no sign of struggles. Maybe it had been empty. Djinn wouldn't have wasted time vandalising; they'd been out for blood, and they were nothing if not focused on the mission.

Which would have been removing any humans who might pose a genuine threat to them later. I wondered if it had been David's bunch, acting under the red-eyed influence of the Earth. Or if it had been Ashan's little merry band, coming after Wardens just on general principles.

Either one would have been horrific, in these close quarters. I didn't want to imagine it, but the images kept springing up when I closed my eyes.

Eventually, not even fevered imagination could hold off exhaustion, and I surrendered to a need to be horizontal. I pulled a waffle-weave cotton blanket up over my aching body and wished – again – for a shower. I was too tired even to take off my shoes, much less undress, although these clothes needed to be burnt, not just laundered. I stank to high heaven, and was ruining a perfectly good bed, but as soon as I closed my eyes, all those concerns slid away like oil off Teflon.

I was asleep so fast, I had no time to realise it was happening, falling into a soft-edged darkness that wrapped warm around me, falling without fear and without limit . . .

. . . and then, without any sense of transition, I was sitting in a nice, comfortable living room with a fire roaring in the hearth. Curled up like a cat on a soft cotton-covered sofa, my head against the pillowed armrest, covered with the same blanket I'd been using in the infirmary.

'Hey, kid,' said a low voice. I blinked and focused across the room.

'Jonathan?' I asked, and slowly sat up. 'Am I—? Aren't you—?'

'Dead?' the mack daddy of the Djinn supplied, and popped the tops on two brown, label-free bottles of beer. He held one up, and it floated towards me. Heavier than I expected. I nearly fumbled the bottle when I grabbed it out of the air. Cold. It felt heavy and real.

'Aren't you? Dead?' I asked.

'Yeah, well. Kinda.'

I blinked again and sipped the beer. Seemed like the thing to do. Jonathan looked exactly the same as he had last time I'd seen him: human, tall and lean and whipcord-strong. Tanned. He was wearing khaki pants and a loose off-white T-shirt, not tucked in, and his booted feet were crossed at the ankles. He sipped his beer, unsmiling.

I put my bottle down on the polished wooden coffee table after shoving aside issues of magazines in languages that I didn't recognise to make room for it. 'You're dead,' I repeated. 'So why are you in my dream?'

He raised the bill of his olive drab ball cap with one finger. 'Good question. Morbid, isn't it?'

'What?'

'Dreaming about dead people. Creepy. You ever see a therapist about that?'

'I'm not—' Even in dreams, I couldn't win an argument with him. Even when he was dead. 'What are you doing here?'

Jonathan took off his cap, tossed it towards a coat-tree (and missed), and leant forward with his elbows on his knees. He met my stare. That was a frightening thing. Dream or not, he had the exact same eyes – dark, lightless, limitless, filled with an infinity of things I could never understand in my short human lifetime. Stars were born and died in those eyes. 'I think the real question is, what are *you* doing here? This is the end of the world, kiddo. Or the beginning. Tough to tell the difference. It's all one big turning circle, and where we are depends on who we are.'

I clutched the blanket closer. 'I – don't understand.'

'Yeah, didn't figure you would. But I thought I'd give it a shot.' He took another swig of beer, but those inhuman eyes never left me. 'Take a look outside.'

I rose, dragging the blanket with me wrapped around my shoulders like a bulky shawl. Not that I wanted to get up from that obscenely comfortable couch, but this was a dream, and I was going to do just what he wanted me to do. No real will of my own. My hand reached out for the drapery pull, and I yanked, and the heavy maroon curtains slid back, revealing . . .

A big field of nodding yellow flowers. Blue sky. A few clouds drifting lazily over the horizon.

I turned to look at him, a question on my face.

'Keep looking,' he said. 'Little more to the picture than meets the eye.'

I narrowed my eyes, and it was like going up in to the aetheric, only I never left my body; the horizon zoomed towards me, clarifying itself as it came. What looked like a shadowy mountain range resolved into something else entirely.

Death.

I was looking at the skeletal remains of a city. Whatever skyline shape had once made it memorable was gone, so I didn't know if I was looking at Paris or New York or Dallas; it was a twisted bare mass of metal now, corroding and twisting together, being beaten down by the gentle, remorseless rain and wind. That was how the planet triumphed, in the end. With patience. With stillness.

Without mercy.

'You're getting there,' he said. 'Closer.'

And he was closer, too – across the room and standing right behind me. His hands closed on my upper arms, holding me in place against him. I didn't want to see, but it came to me anyway.

Bones. So many bones, sinking deeper into the hungry ground. Flesh liquifying and returning to the soil, bones taking longer to flake away into bleached splinters.

Bones were all that was left of humanity, I knew that. I could sense that. Nothing remained. Not a city untouched, not a family huddled in a cave, waiting out the disaster. We'd been completely, utterly removed from the Earth.

'You see?' Jonathan's voice rasped, soft as velvet against my ear. I could feel the warm whisper of his breath stirring my hair. 'It's like bowling. When the match is over, you have to return the rented shoes. Sorry, kid. Game over.'

Six billion lives, snuffed out. I wanted to fall to my knees, but Jonathan was holding me up. There was a certain lazy cruelty in the way his fingers dug into my skin.

'Don't go all weak on me now,' he scolded me. 'Bones and dust. That the way you want it?'

'No,' I said, and firmed up my knees and spine. *Weak?* I wasn't weak, and I wouldn't let him see me that way. 'So you tell me, how do I stop it?'

'What makes you think it's your job to stop anything?'

I shook free of his hands and whirled to face him. My fists clenched at my sides. *'Because you brought me here!'*

His face smoothed out, became as rigid and emotionless as a leather mask. Those eyes, God, those eyes. Fury and power and anguish, all together.

'I didn't bring you here,' he said. 'You think you're Miss Special Destiny of the year?'

'No,' I shot back, furious. 'And I don't damn well *want* to be, any more than you wanted to be – whatever the hell you are. But sometimes there isn't a choice. Right?'

'Careful. You might accidentally make some sense. Ruin your reputation.'

'You are *infuriating*!'

'Yep,' he agreed. 'It's been said.'

Arguing with him was getting me exactly nothing. I controlled my temper with a tremendous effort of will. 'So how do we stop this?' Because I was not going to sit by and let a future roll towards us that contained six billion corpses turning to petroleum under the ground.

'That's the funny thing,' Jonathan said, and stepped back. He tugged his cap more firmly in place, one hand at the back, one on the bill. 'You want to survive, you need to convince Her that you're worth the favour.'

'How?' I practically yelled it.

'You'll know it when you see it. But first you have to get yourself to the right place.'

'Which is?'

'Someplace you've already been,' he said. 'Once. Neat little place, kinda quaint. You'll think of it.'

'Don't do that. Don't go all vague on me just when I need—'

'Not my business to save your ass,' he pointed out. 'Hell, I'm kinda dead anyway. Not my problem. And you look so cute with your face all red.'

'Jonathan—' I was all out of smart-ass. '*Please.*'

He cupped an ear towards me.

'Please,' I repeated. 'Do you want me to beg?'

'Well, it'd be nice, but . . . nah. Can you sing?'

'What?'

'Sing. Notes. Usually up and down, unless you're into that rap thing, which' – he eyed me – 'I wouldn't recommend. A little too much vanilla in the ice, if you know what I mean.'

'Believe me, I have no *idea* what you mean!'

He sighed. 'Humans. No sense of what's going on around them . . .'

He stopped in mid-condescension. His face went blank again, but not as if he was trying to conceal anything this time – more as though he was entirely focused on something beyond the two of us.

There was a sound. It started as a kind of moaning, like a breeze beyond the window. It got louder. Stronger. Became an eerie tangle of whispers.

No, not whispers. Something . . . musical.

I reached for the latch on the window, suddenly desperate to hear what it was. Jonathan clapped his hands down over mine, hard. 'No,' he said grimly. 'Do it and you're dead.'

I fought him. I had to open the window. I had to *know*. I could feel it coming, and oh it was glorious and terrible and beautiful as liquid fire, and it was going to burn me to ash where I stood with the fire of creation and joy. *Spirit moving upon the earth . . .*

I clawed at the window latch, got hold of it, and yanked up.

Stuck. I screamed and battered at the window glass, but it didn't break, didn't even rattle . . .

Jonathan muttered what might have been a curse, if I'd understood Djinn, and he spun me around to face him. The whole house around us was moving, breathing. Seduced by the power of the song outside. Longing to join with it, lose itself in that joyous, terrifying chorus.

Pieces of it were whirling away. Jonathan stayed focused on my face. 'You've got to leave,' he said.

'Am I going to see you again?' I asked, weirdly calm now, drugged by the *sound*. He smiled slightly and touched his fingertips to the tip of my chin.

'Didn't see me this time,' he said, and without any warning at all, gave me a right cross that snapped my head back with overwhelming force. Pain blocked out even the screaming of that *song* . . .

I sailed backward into the dark, falling, lost in shrieking winds and wind that grabbed and tore at me . . .

The song turned into a shrill ringing in my ears.

I jerked awake on the bed in the infirmary, felt my heart racing uncontrollably, and fumbled for the clock on the table next to me. Its reassuring green glow told me that I'd been asleep for exactly six hours.

I sank back with a sigh, cradling the clock and hitting the buttons, and then realised that it wasn't the alarm going off. It was my cell phone shrilling for attention. Damn. I needed to go with a much more amusing ringtone.

I fumbled it out of my purse and flipped it open. 'Yeah?' I sounded as drugged and disoriented as I felt.

'You stupid *slag*.' I knew that rich tenor voice, sharpened now with anger. 'You called the police on me.'

I flopped back into the comfort of the pillow and threw an arm over my eyes. 'Yes, Eamon, I called the police on you. You threatened my life, tried to kill me, and abducted my sister—'

'I saved your bloody life!' He sounded livid. I could almost see the veins pulsing in his neck. 'I could've left you out in that hurricane to die, you know. I put myself out for you!'

'Yeah, you're a prince – Please tell me you're not, by the way. I mean, my opinion of British royalty isn't that high, but—'

'Shut it,' he snarled. 'Alerting the local constabulary isn't going to get your sister back.'

'Can make your life damn inconvenient, though, I'll bet.'

Silence. I could hear him breathing. I could picture him standing there, phone gripped in those long pianist's fingers. The inner Eamon didn't match the sensitive hands, though he could pretend with the best of them. Deep down, he wasn't elegant, and he wasn't cultured. He was a total bastard, and the fact that my sister had been enthralled with him – and might still be, for all I knew – made me feel more than a little nauseated.

'Look,' I said. 'I know that you expect me to be your co-star in this little drama you're playing, but I'm busy. Get to the point, Eamon. You going to kill me? Come on and get in line. I haven't got time to screw around with you.'

Silence, for a long few beats, and then, 'Is there a problem?' he asked. Which wasn't what I'd expected.

'Why do you care?'

'Because—' He paused for several long beats. 'Because what I want from you is a Djinn. If there's anything happening that affects that goal, I need to know.'

'You have no idea how much I wish I'd given you one back home, and gotten you the hell out of our lives,' I said. I remembered the bloodstains in the conference room. Not that I wished dismemberment on anyone, but with Eamon my moral high ground was somewhere about the elevation of a sand dune, and eroding fast. 'The situation has changed. I can't get my hands on a Djinn anymore. No one can.'

'Won't, you mean.'

'I don't have time to explain it to you, but even if I gave you a Djinn bottle, it wouldn't do you any good. The – the master agreement's been broken. They don't obey us anymore. And they damn sure wouldn't obey you.'

'I see,' he said slowly. 'That's . . . very unfortunate. For your sister, at any rate.'

'Where's Sarah? If you've hurt her—'

'Don't be ridiculous. Why would I hurt lovely Sarah?' That sly hint of amusement was back in his voice. 'Much more rewarding to play along with her fantasies. You'd be amazed what kind of thing that woman gets up to in the privacy of her—'

'Shut *up*!' I shouted it, heard my heart thudding in my ears, and forced myself to relax. He liked sticking in the knife. It was part of his game. No matter what he said, I'd seen the way he'd touched her, and his hands didn't lie about that, at least. He was gentle with her. Gentler than he had any reason to be. It was even possible he really liked her, as much as he liked anyone. 'Look, just let her go. There's no reason to keep her. I already told you, I can't give you a Djinn. Please. Just – let her go.'

'Are you completely sure you can't give me what I want? Because if you *are*, there's no reason for me not to put a bullet in the head of your beautiful sister, pose her in a compromising position for the delight of the tabloid media, and be on my merry way.' He listened to my furious silence. I could feel a grin coming off the phone, like radiant heat. 'I was thinking something from the oeuvre of the Hillside Strangler. Nothing like the classics.'

'You fucking son of a—'

'*I want a Djinn*. I don't care about your technical issues. You're thoroughly resourceful when you need to be – I've seen that firsthand. No, your lovely sister stays with me until you come through for me. In the meantime, she suffers whatever I see fit to make her suffer, which I promise you will get progressively worse the longer you take to satisfy me. And if I feel you haven't done your level best to get me what I want, well . . . you'll follow the breathless coverage about her bad, sad end on the news.'

My free hand was in a fist, clenched tight. I didn't remember doing it, and deliberately relaxed until the white knuckles loosened up. 'You won't get anything by threatening her. There are other things happening, in case you're not aware. Bad things. I can't just—'

'Yeah,' he interrupted. 'Dead Wardens littering the landscape, very sad, I'm devastated, et cetera. But in short, bugger your problems, darling, because *my* problems are the priority. I'll give you exactly two days to settle your little difficulties and make arrangements to get me what I want, and no tricks, or I swear to you, your sister will *not* leave a pretty corpse, are we understood?'

'Yes,' I said. 'Yes, we're understood.'

'Then it's been a slice, love, and you watch yourself. Wouldn't want anything to happen to you before I get what I want. Now, if you'll excuse me, I hear the water shutting off in the bath. I have to go do your sister.'

He hung up before I could fire off anything I'd regret later. The number was blocked, of course. I sank down on the bed again, exhausted and aching and angry as hell, with nowhere to put all that nervous dread. Not like my sister's life could count for any more than the hundreds of thousands of people who were in danger, or the millions – billions – in the balance if we didn't figure out how to make things right again.

Bones and dust, corpses turning to petroleum. Sunflowers nodding placidly over a graveyard. Had I just been dreaming? Or was Jonathan – the spirit of Jonathan, anyway – trying to tell me something important?

Two days. Not enough time. Not enough time for anything.

I felt tears coming, and choked them back furiously. I was *not* going to let that bastard make me cry, and I was *not* going to think about him standing in that steam-fogged bathroom, wiping beads of water from my sister's naked back while she smiled innocently at him in the mirror.

No, I wasn't going to think about that at all.

OK, maybe I was.

I curled up on the bed, hurled the alarm clock across the room in a satisfying crunch of plastic, and put my pillow over my head to sob out my fury and pain. That was supposed to be cathartic, but mostly it seemed to result in aching muscles, sinuses packed with fluid, and raw, abused eyeballs.

I needed to blow my nose. When I reached for a tissue from the bedside box, my fumbling fingers met warm flesh, helpfully handing one over.

I lifted my head slowly from the smothering embrace of the pillow, and gasped.

'Aren't you going to take that?' David asked. I looked down. My fingers were clenched on the tissue in his hand, but I hadn't made any move to claim it. I slowly pulled it towards me.

David was sitting in a chair a couple of feet away, watching me with his head tilted a little to one side.

His eyes were more brown than bronze, just now, lazy behind the concealing round glasses. Relaxed. He was wearing a familiar outfit of a blue checked shirt and faded jeans and battered hiking boots, and *God*, he looked good enough to eat. Relief flashed through me like a concentrated burst of lightning, and then recent history caught up to me like the following thunder. I sat up in a hurry, heart thumping so hard, I saw red spots, because my brain finally saw fit to remind me that David, about thirty hours ago, had been intent on killing me.

'Easy,' he said, and reached out to draw a fingertip over the tender, sensitive skin on the interior of my right arm. Heat and friction, real as it could get. 'It's all right. I'm myself, at least for now. Blow your nose.'

He wasn't a dream; he was here. *Really* here, physically.

I really did need to blow my nose. I did so, in as ladylike a fashion as I could, wishing all the while – mostly stupidly – that I'd had some kind of warning, that I'd been able to shower or to brush my hair or change my clothes or . . . hell. Anything.

I tossed the tissue at the trash can nearby. He gave my underhanded girly throw an assist with a wave of his finger, not even looking. Two points.

'I didn't know if you were alive,' he said softly. 'Not at first. I remembered coming after you, on the beach, and then – nothing. I thought I'd hurt you. Killed you.'

The look in his eyes – God, it made my heart break.

I swung my legs over the side of the bed. We were close enough that our knees brushed.

David leant forward, moving slowly, the way animal trainers do with skittish creatures, and he slowly extended his hand towards me. Traced the line of my cheek. 'I can't stay long,' he said quietly. 'But I want to try to protect you, as much as I can. Help you. Will you let me?'

I couldn't say no to him, not when he sounded like that. Soft and a little desperate. I stayed where I was. I didn't reach back to him, though every cell in my body screamed for me to do it; I just watched him, until he drew his hand back. He put his elbows on his knees and focused on my face with an intensity I remembered from the first time I'd met him. Had I fallen in love with him right then, at first sight? I'd fallen in lust, for sure. Lust had been no problem at all. Still wasn't. But more than that – and I only realised it now, looking back on it – I'd lost my soul to him somewhere along the way.

And I couldn't regret it. Even now.

His fingers moved together restlessly, as though fighting an urge to reach out to me again. 'You're all right?' he asked. 'Not hurt?'

'No. I'm all right.' Minus a few dozen cuts and bruises and minor aches. Nothing to speak of, really. 'What the hell happened?'

His face went still. Masklike, the way Jonathan's had been in the dream. His eyes turned dark and filled with secrets. 'Jonathan decided to play god,' he said. 'He's dead.'

I had a sudden, aching suspicion. 'Did you kill him?'

The flash of anguish, before he locked it down again, was answer enough. David had been an Ifrit for a time, half alive, preying on Djinn for his life force. Damned and doomed and broken . . . dead, in every way that mattered. He'd gone after the biggest, brightest power source available to survive, and that had been Jonathan. Driven by the basic instinct to feed, he had turned on his own best friend.

Just the way his best friend intended, the cold-hearted, calculating, manipulative bastard.

'David, don't,' I said. 'You know he wanted to die. He just – used you. Suicide by Ifrit.'

'No, it was more than that.' He swallowed and looked aside, keeping his thoughts to himself for a few seconds before he continued, 'What Jonathan was, is – necessary. Someone needs to stand where he stood. Nature abhors a vacuum.' He attempted a smile, but it looked painful. 'I was the closest Djinn to him in power, so what he was – it flowed into me. In a real sense, I've become—'

'Jonathan,' I supplied.

He looked agonised about that. Guilty. Horrified. '*No*. Jonathan was . . . special. I don't think any of us could really take his place and do the things he did. But I've become the conduit, the pipeline from the Mother to the Djinn. The only upside is that I've stopped pulling the life out of you, the way I did when I was an Ifrit. If I'd kept on . . .'

'You wouldn't have killed me.' I wasn't sure of that, but I wanted to be.

'I came damn close.' He stared at me, miserable. 'Jo. None of us can tell what's coming. I don't know if I can control this. I'm not Jonathan. I'm not capable of – staying apart from her needs, her emotions. And when I fail, we all lose.'

Nothing I could say about that wouldn't make him feel worse about it. 'Look, you told me on the beach that the Wardens need to stop the Earth from waking up,' I said. 'That would fix things, right? Give you back free will?'

'No, not really.' He was already shaking his head. 'We never have completely free will. It's not the way it works.'

'Even now that Jonathan's agreement with the Wardens is gone?'

'Even now. We just changed hands, so to speak. Went back to our original master. Mistress. You saw. When it happened – I wasn't prepared to handle it. I didn't know how to try to hold it back, and it spilt through me to the other Djinn.'

His eyes had burnt bright red, and bright red was not a colour I associated with anything good, except in fashion. Having red eyes staring at you was downright terrifying. Still, it hadn't been only the Goth-bright gaze that had unnerved me; it had been the stillness.

The sense of David having been emptied out of his own skin, stripped of individual consciousness and responsibility.

'When she's angry,' he continued, 'when she feels threatened, she can take control of me, and through me, all the others. In a sense, we're her antibodies. And if she wants to destroy you . . .'

It would be terrifyingly easy for Djinn to do it. They were predatory at the best of times. Given free rein and license to kill? Slaughter. No human could battle them directly for very long, and there damn sure weren't enough Wardens to go around anyway.

'So what are we supposed to do? It's a little late to build a rocket ship and evacuate,' I said, 'no matter what the science fiction movies like to tell us.'

That got a smile. A small one. 'Did you know, that's one of the things we love so much about you?'

'What?'

'Your stories. You remake the world with stories. I don't think you understand how powerful that is, Jo.'

'A story isn't going to fix this.'

The smile died. 'No, you're right about that.'

'Then tell me what to do.'

'No.'

'No?'

'You have to understand—'

'Well, I don't. I don't understand.'

'You're being obstinate.'

'I'm being accurate! Dammit, David, why is

everything such a riddle with you guys? Why can't you just come right out and—'

'—tell you how to destroy the Djinn?' he asked, and arched his eyebrows. 'Sorry, but I'm not quite ready to sacrifice my people to save all of yours. I'm trying to find a way that it doesn't come down to that choice. That's what Jonathan left me. Responsibility. It sucks, but that's the way it is.'

I swallowed my comeback, because there was real suffering in his eyes. 'So what can I do?' I asked. 'I can't just wait around for the final epic battle and make popcorn.'

Another smile, this one stronger and warmer. 'You never could, you know. Always in motion.'

'Damn straight. Basic principles of physics. Objects at rest tend to stay at rest. Things in motion require less effort to overcome resistance.'

'I love your mind.'

'Is that all?' I arched my eyebrows back at him, and his eyes sparked bronze.

He smiled, and then the smile slowly faded. 'We can't do this.'

Damn. The warmth inside me, barely felt, began to fade. 'Why not?'

'Because it's dangerous. You begin to trust me; I begin to think you *can* trust me. That's a very bad idea.' He stood up. 'I shouldn't have come here.'

'Then why did you?' I demanded, out of patience. 'Dammit, don't come here and look – look all perfectly hot and good enough to lick – don't just show up and tell me that I can't trust you, because I do trust you, I always have, even when I didn't have any reason to do it! *Don't do this to us*! It hurts!'

My vehemence shook him. He honestly didn't expect that outburst – I could see it in the way he drew back inside himself, watching me. The bronze glints died in his eyes, forced back. He looked like a man. A tired, vulnerable, sorrowful man. 'I want to help,' he said.

'Well, pony up, cowboy! Now's the time!'

'All right.' He closed his eyes, as if he couldn't stand to look at me while he said it. 'You can't cut the Djinn off from the Mother. Oh, there's a way, but if you do, you only guarantee your own destruction. The Earth would go mad. It wouldn't just be humanity being wiped away, it would be every living thing in the world. She would just – reset the game and start over. What you have to do is become . . . Jonathan. Become the conduit for humanity, to *her*.'

Finally, we were getting somewhere. 'And how exactly do I do that?' He opened his mouth, then shut it again. No answer. 'David, half an answer is worse than none. Tell me.'

'I hate putting you at risk like this.'

'Dammit, how could I be more at risk? I saw—' I stopped, because I intuitively knew I shouldn't tell David about the dream. At best, he'd dismiss it. At worst, it would raise false hopes that Jonathan was . . . somewhere out there. 'I'm a Warden, and I'm on the front lines already. At least give me the tools to get the job done.'

His head jerked up, and he fixed on me with such intensity that I flinched, a little. 'I'm not sure it won't kill you.'

'Well,' I said after a shaky second of a pause, 'that's a 'been there, done that' situation, and anyway it's not your choice to make, is it?'

And that was a *long* second of pause, from both of us. Precarious and painful.

'No,' he finally admitted, and squeezed his eyes closed as he thought about it. 'All right. I can't tell you *how* to do it – I'm not even sure how Jonathan did it in the first place. But I can tell you *where*.' He made a visible decision and opened his eyes. They were glowing now, Djinn-bronze flecked with ruddy amber. 'You've been there once already. Seacasket.'

'Seacasket?' I tried to remember . . . and then I did, with a chilling rush of pain and panic.

Once upon a time, I had been a Djinn, and I had been sent to Seacasket by my master (if you could call a punk like Kevin a master, which was a stretch) to destroy the town. In fire.

David had stopped me that time. And somehow, Kevin's stepmonster Yvette had known that he would. It had been the trap she set for him, to get him back in her power.

'Seacasket's special,' I said. 'Yvette knew.'

He nodded. 'It's a – thin space in the aetheric. One of two or three places in this country where a human might be able to reach one of the Oracles.'

'Oracles?' I'd never heard of Oracles, other than the ancient Greek kind. Or the software company. From the regretful look that flashed across his face, it wasn't something *any* human had probably heard before. Or that the Djinn ever intended we would.

'They don't exist here, on this plane. They're – different. And Jo, they're dangerous. Very dangerous, even to Djinn. I – can't imagine how dangerous they'd be to a human, even if you can get one to allow you contact. Which isn't likely.'

'Can't you – I don't know, introduce me?'

'It doesn't work that way,' he said. 'I wish to heaven it did, because this would already be finished and I'd have done this for you. The way I'm connected is subordinate. The Djinn are part of the body, not apart from it. Oracles . . .' He was out of words, and he shrugged. 'There's no way to describe this, really. It's not a human thing.'

I let out a slow breath. 'OK. Leaving all that on the table, is there anything you can do about all of the – the chaos out there? Weather, fire, earthquakes? . . .'

'I'll do what I can.' David leant forward and extended his hand again. This time, I took it. His skin was firm and hot and smooth, and my skin remembered it all too vividly. He was astonishingly tactile, always touching, and even as I thought it his fingers moved to my wrist, tracing my pulse. 'I want to protect you. I want that with everything in me. The idea of sending you into danger without me . . . it terrifies me. You know that, right?'

My heart began to pound. I wanted to forget all of this. The wreckage outside of the infirmary door, the dead Wardens, the destroyed agreement with the Djinn, the upcoming end of the world. *The future of bones.*

I wanted him to keep on touching me, always.

'Jonathan always thought it was a kind of insanity, Djinn loving humans,' David murmured. 'Maybe he was right. We have to face losing what we love so often, and the urge to keep you out of danger is . . . overpowering, sometimes. But now *I'm* the danger. And the truth is, you can't really trust me, from this point on. Promise me you'll be careful of me.'

'David—'

'I mean it, Jo. Promise me. I love you, I adore you, and you really can't trust me right now.'

His hand tightened on mine. Our fingers twined, and he leant closer and fitted his lips to mine.

Hot and sweet and damp, anguished and wonderful. I let go of his hand and wrapped my arms around his neck, buried my fingers in the warm living fire of his hair, and deepened the kiss. Willing him to be with me, to make this world be something it wasn't.

He made a sound in his throat, torture and despair and

arousal all at once, and his hands fitted themselves around my waist and slid me off the bed and onto his lap. My chest pressed to his, every point of contact a bonfire. Our bodies, beyond our control, moved against each other, sliding, pressing, sweet wonderful friction that reminded us what we wanted, what we *needed*. For the first time in months, we were both healthy, both whole, both . . .

. . . both too aware of what this might cost us in the end.

I don't know which of us broke the kiss, but it ended, and we pressed our foreheads together and breathed each other's air without speaking for a long time, our bodies tensed and trembling, on the edge of burning.

'You're right,' I finally whispered. My lips tasted of him. 'I can't trust you. I damn sure can't trust myself when I'm with you.'

He smoothed my hair back with both hands. 'Good girl.' He kissed me again, softly. 'Smart girl. Remember that.'

And then he lifted me, effortlessly, and set me on my feet. I got the impression he was about to leave, and panicked just a little. 'Wait! Um . . . Seacasket. I'm not sure I can find it again.'

'MapQuest,' he said. 'The modern world is full of conveniences even the Djinn can't match.'

'Do I—?' I bit my lip, and then continued. 'Do I go alone? Or am I going to have to fight my way through some kind of honour guard?'

'Take Imara,' he said. His smile turned breathtakingly sweet. 'She's astonishing, isn't she? Our child? I wish you could see her the way I do, Jo, she's – a miracle.'

Oh, I agreed. With all my heart. 'I don't want to take her with me if there's going to be any danger—'

'I have faith in you to keep her safe.'

'David, she's *two days old*!'

'What she is can't be measured in days, or years, or centuries,' he said. 'She'll be fine. Just – take care of yourself. You're the one I'm worried about.'

A slow, warm pressure of his lips on mine, and then he was gone. Not a magic-sparkle slow-fade gone, but a blip, he-was-never-there gone. Except for the manic damn-I've-been-kissed-good tingle of my mouth and the racing of my pulse and general state of trembling throughout my body, I might have thought it was all another dream.

I walked over to the mirror. I looked like hell, but my eyes were clear and shining and my lips had a ripe, bee-stung redness.

Doesn't get much more real than that.

He was right: I really couldn't trust him. Should never *ever* trust him again. But that wasn't, and never would be, my instinct, and he knew it. He was my true fatal flaw, and maybe I was his, as well.

I hoped that wasn't going to end up destroying us both, and our child with us.

If I was inclined to mope about it, I didn't have

time. There was a rattle at the locked infirmary door, and Nathan, the security guard, looked in and jerked his head at me.

'You're wanted,' he said. 'Move it.'

I cast one last look at the empty chair where David had been, and followed Nathan out.

The infirmary was relatively soundproofed, as I discovered when I went out into the hall; there was a riot outside. People yelling, screaming at each other. Tempers flaring. There were more people crammed in than there'd been before, and everybody looked stressed and confused. There were arguments raging from room to room; some idiot was yelling in the hallway that we had to uncork the Djinn still imprisoned in the vault several stories below, under the theory that we could be prepared to give them ironclad orders to protect the building and the remaining Wardens at all costs. Someone else was making the case against it, but I could tell popular sentiment was building for the supposedly simple solution.

Paul had given up, evidently. He was sitting whey-faced in a chair in the North America conference room, eyes shut. Marion was vainly shouting for order, but since she was in a wheelchair, it was hard for her to make an impression.

I went for the floor show.

I levitated myself four feet up off the stained carpet, dangerously close to the ceiling, reached deep for power, and felt it respond to me with an ease and warmth I hadn't felt in . . . a very long time. Since before my battle with Bad Bob Biringanine, in fact.

I let the power crackle around me, building up in potential energy in the air, and most of those around me noticed and backed off.

Making light – cold light, light without heat – is the biggest trick in the book when it comes to my variety of powers. Light has heat as a natural by-product of the energy release that creates it, so I had to balance the radiation with rapid dispersal throughout a complicated matrix of atoms.

I got brighter, and still brighter, until I was glowing like a girl-shaped chandelier, hovering in the hallway. Conversation stopped. In the brilliant white light, they all looked stark and surprised, and to a Warden they flinched when I released a pulse of energy that flared out in a circle like a strobe going off.

I let the glow die down slowly and touched my feet back on the carpet.

'Right,' I said. 'Let's quit freaking and start working, all right?'

Nobody spoke. Dozens of faces, and they were all turned to me – young Wardens barely out of college, old grey-haired ones who'd been handling the business of earth and fire and weather for three-quarters of their long lives. They were tough, or they were damn lucky, every single one of them.

And most important, they were what we had.

I pointed to the Warden who'd been arguing against opening the bottles – a slender little African American guy, about thirty, with a receding hairline and bookish wire-rimmed spectacles. 'What's your name?' I asked. He didn't look at all familiar.

'Will,' he said. 'William Sebhatu.'

'Will, I'm putting you in charge of the Djinn issue,' I said. 'You need to get every single Djinn bottle, empty or sealed, make an inventory, and put everything in the vault. And then you seal the vault and you make damn sure that nobody, and I mean nobody, opens up any bottles. Got it?'

'Wait a minute!' That was Will's debating opponent, a big-boned woman with a horse face and bitter-almond eyes. 'You can't just make a decision like that! Who the hell do you think you are? You're not even a Warden anymore!' I remembered her. Emily, a double threat – an Earth and Fire Warden out of Canada. She was blunt, but she was good at her job; she also had a reputation for being pushy.

'Back off,' Paul said wearily from his chair in the conference room. His voice echoed through the silence. 'She's one of us. Hell, she may be the only one who knows enough to get us through the day.' He sounded defeated. I didn't care for that. I hadn't meant to take away his authority – at least, not permanently – but Paul wasn't acting like a guy who could shoulder the burden anymore. 'Jo, do your stuff.'

'OK,' I said. I turned back to the woman, who was

still giving me the fish eye. 'Emily, you think you can make this work because you think you're smarter than the Djinn, or faster, or more powerful. You can't. You all need to unlearn what you know about the Djinn. They're not subservient. They're not stupid. And they're not ours, not anymore.'

The assembled Wardens were whispering to each other. Emily was staring at me. So was Will. I heard my name being passed around, in varying degrees of incredulity. *I thought she was dead*, someone said, just a little too loudly for comfort.

'This is stupid,' Emily finally said. 'Paul, I thought she was out of the Wardens. How does she know anything?'

'She knows because she was with the Djinn when it happened,' Marion said, and rolled closer with a brisk snap of her wrists. 'Right?'

I nodded. 'I saw it happen. We've lost control, and as far as I know, we've lost it for good. We need to face that and figure out how to go forward.'

'Forward?' somebody in the crowd yelped. 'You've got to be kidding. We need the Djinn!'

'No, we don't,' another person countered sharply. 'I barely escaped, and only because mine got distracted. Whatever's happening, we can't risk involvement with the Djinn.'

'Exactly,' I said. 'We have to rely on ourselves, and each other. Will? You up for the job?'

He swallowed hard and nodded. 'I'll get started.'

'Get some people to help you. Draft them if you have to, and don't be afraid to use Paul's name as a big stick.' I waited for some confirmation from Paul; he waved a hand vaguely. I turned to Emily. 'You're not going to give this guy any shit, right?'

She was silent for a few seconds, looking at me, then shrugged. 'Not right now. You're right. We need to stop the bleeding, and save the surgery for later.'

I was glad Emily let me push it through, because she'd be a tough opponent. Nothing weak about her, and we needed her on our side.

There was only one side, right now. The side of survival.

I faced a crowd of people, and everybody looked tired and harassed and worried. Not the faces of winners. They looked . . . lost.

'All right,' I said. 'Everybody, listen up. We've taken some serious hits, and there's no question, things are desperate. But we are *Wardens*. Wardens don't run, and they don't abandon their responsibilities. There are six billion people on this planet, and we stand up for them. We need to be strong, focused, and we need to be *united*. No more backbiting, politics, or ambition. Understood?'

'Oh, come on! Look around you. It's impossible,' someone in the crowd complained. I fixed that area with a stare that, from the way those in its way quailed, might have been Djinn-strength.

'I was just hanging in mid-air glowing like a UFO,' I

said. 'Don't tell me about impossible. We're Wardens.'

A ripple of laughter. Some of the tension fled from their faces, and there were a few nods.

'I need a volunteer to handle cleanup crew,' I continued. 'Earth Wardens, probably, maybe a couple of Fire Wardens. Get this place back in operation. Everybody else, pick a conference room and get to work triaging the crisis information. Go.'

And amazingly, after a scant second, Emily raised her hand and bellowed, 'Right! I need two Earth and one Fire for cleanup!' and the rest of them began milling around and filtering into conference rooms.

They were actually *listening* to me.

I looked at Marion, who was sitting, hands folded in her lap. She inclined her head, very slightly. Under the bruises, she was smiling.

I said, 'Somebody had to.'

'You have a gift for it,' she countered. We both looked at Paul.

He was gone. Sometime during my little speech, he'd walked away. I felt a little stab of regret and worry. I'd taken away Paul's authority again, maybe for good this time, and that was not only unkind, but also deeply unwise.

'Excuse me?' someone asked from behind me. 'Warden Baldwin?'

I turned to find a petite blond woman standing there. I didn't know her, but she was different from the others in the hallway. There was no worry in her expression, and no exhaustion. Perky, which just seemed strange. There was something else, though, that sent a ripple of unease up my back that exploded in an ice-cold shudder on the back of my neck.

The woman was just . . . *wrong*.

'Jo!' Marion's warning shout came a second too late.

The woman had a gun. Must have taken it off one of the guards. Nathan? Janet? One of the many who'd died? And now she raised it and pointed it straight at me. I froze, unbreathing. The muzzle of that damn pistol looked big enough to swallow the sun.

And she fired.

I felt it happening in slow motion – the hammer striking the cartridge, the blooming flare of explosion inside the metal jacket . . .

I *felt it*. The same way I usually felt the flare of lightning bursting out of the sky, or the swirl of air and water.

I not only felt it, but I could . . . touch it.

It didn't take much, just a whisper, and I killed the spark before it ignited the powder in the cartridge.

Click.

My would-be assassin looked baffled, then angry, and pulled the trigger again, with the same results. I smiled thinly at her, reached out, and took the pistol away. While I was doing that, Nathan, the tall security guard, pelted breathlessly around the corner. I emptied the clip out of the gun – well, it always looked cool in the movies – and Nathan took it away from me the way you'd take a semi-automatic away from a teething baby.

He also took possession of the Warden, and handcuffed her.

She still had that same eerily calm, predatory light in her eyes, and she hadn't taken her eyes off me. I recognised that starvation in her. I'd had it eating through my own veins not so very long ago.

I was staring at her, wondering how to go about handling this particular problem, when an arrival at the end of the hallway stole my thunder. Heads popped out of conference rooms, and whispers flew down the hall, contagious as the flu. 'Lewis!'

Well, well, well . . . Elvis was back in the building.

Lewis Levander Orwell wasn't looking his best, but then, who was? Rough and tired, but intact except for some livid dry cuts and scrapes that looked suspiciously like road rash, as if he'd gotten dragged over asphalt. At least a three-day growth of beard. Still, much improved from the last time I'd seen him. There was a palpable sense of relief as he walked down the hall towards us, a feeling that at last, stability had arrived. Lewis had that effect. He was, without question, the most powerful living Warden, and he was the proverbial triple threat – weather, fire, and earth powers, all in one package.

He didn't look like the big head cheese, really – tall, long arms and legs, a kind of lanky grace and an ironic smile, brown hair that badly needed a trim, a worn pair of close-fitting blue jeans and a loose flannel shirt folded up to expose the aforementioned cuts and road burns, and corded, sinewy arms. Hiking boots. Competence and authority in a handy carrying case.

A little like Jonathan, now that I thought about it.

He gave me a bare, welcoming nod, and took a good look at the imprisoned Warden, whose eyes had started glowing even more brightly at the sight of him.

'Hey, Joanne.' He nodded to me. 'What have we here?'

'Guess,' I sighed.

Lewis always did have an economy of words. He reached over and yanked down the collar of her shirt.

It was only a glimpse, but I saw it – a black tangled mass that writhed just under her skin, and then burrowed deeper, hiding from view.

Demon Mark.

I had an instant nauseating sense-memory of how that felt. How seductively warm it could feel. How the power of it pulsed so brightly in your veins. You felt like you could do anything with one of those, and sometimes, you really could.

I couldn't save her. So far as I knew, there was no way to save any of them.

'Marion,' Lewis said. 'Got anything in this building that will hold somebody with a Demon Mark?'

He didn't trouble to keep his voice down, and it sent shock waves through the assembled Wardens.

Demon Marks, like Free Djinn, weren't supposed to exist. Hell, even if they did exist, they were supposed to be dealt with quickly and quietly, off behind the curtains.

'There's a secured cell two floors down,' she said. 'We usually augment it with Djinn guards, but—'

'Yeah, that's not going to happen.' Lewis's eyes assessed those standing around, lightning-quick, and he pointed at Nathan and two other Wardens. 'You three. Go with Marion. Get her secured. Marion, we'll talk later about what we can do for her.' He watched as the parade organised itself, then put his lips close to my ear and said, 'Come with me. We need to talk. Privately.'

I stepped back and nodded, then led him around wreckage and repairs and down around the corner, to an office that had remained mostly intact. There was a junior-level Warden working on forecast maps. I evicted her with a significant nod of my head, and closed the door behind her, then turned to face Lewis.

'Senior management?' he asked.

'Mostly dead,' I said. 'Paul's on the walking wounded list; Marion isn't even that good. Morale's in the toilet, of course. I haven't seen any other faces I recognise from the higher ranks.' I stopped and looked straight into his eyes. 'We're in big-ass trouble, Lewis.'

'No kidding.' He leant against the desk and folded his arms, looking down. Hiding whatever he was thinking. 'You know about Jonathan?'

'Imara and David say he's dead.'

'Imara?' Lewis looked up, curious.

'Ah – long story. Short version, she's my daughter. Mine and David's.'

His lips parted, and his eyes widened, and I had the rare pleasure of seeing Lewis Orwell rendered . . . speechless. For a moment, anyway. 'That's – surprising,' he said, finally. 'Congratulations. Where is she?'

'Safe, I hope. Away from here, anyway; the Wardens were a little trigger-happy, and even if it isn't too likely they could hurt her, I didn't really want to put it to the test. She's—' Precious. Special. Unique. Strange. Amazing. 'She's my kid. OK, she looks like a *Sports Illustrated* swimsuit model, but . . .'

He blinked. 'I thought you said she was a kid?'

'Don't ask me how Djinn biology works. First she's a gleam in her father's eye; then she's borrowing my clothes.'

He made a low-throated sound of amusement. 'So in other words, it's been a busy couple of days.'

I gestured around at the wreckage in the office, piled like driftwood in the corners. By extension, at the chaos swirling around in the world. 'You could say.'

'Come here.'

I frowned, but took a step closer. He reached out and took my hand, then pulled me into a body-to-body hug. I relaxed against him, letting the comfort of his warmth sink deep. He needed a shower. Hell, so did I. We were well beyond little things like that. After a few seconds, I felt the surge of power building between us . . . a cell-deep vibration, like calling to like. We had harmonics, we always did have, and the one time we'd allowed it to build out of control, we'd called up storms and shattered windows.

It built so fast, it was breathtaking. Glass and steel rattled around us. I took control of myself and stepped back, breaking the circuit. I glimpsed something wild and a little desperate in Lewis's eyes, quickly covered.

'Did you feel that?' he asked. 'Looks like we're getting stronger.'

'Just the two of us?'

'No idea, I'm afraid; I could feel it happening to me, but I've always been kind of the far end of the curve.' That wasn't ego, just fact. 'Still, nothing's what it was yesterday. Not the Djinn, and not us. Maybe in breaking the contract, Jonathan reset some kind of equilibrium. Maybe the Wardens were originally a lot stronger on their own. It could be that we've been bleeding off some of our own power to feed the Djinn.'

Interesting notion. 'So maybe we don't need the Djinn after all, if this keeps up.'

'Oh, I wouldn't go that far.' He was still watching me. Warm brown eyes, always fired with a little bit of amusement. 'It's also possible that maybe you and I are a little more connected to the source.'

'Meaning?'

He stretched out a palm, and a tiny flame flickered into life, lemon-pale and growing redder as I watched. Redder and larger. Lewis wasn't watching this minor miracle; he was watching me, still with that sly bit of amusement lighting his eyes.

And then he pitched the football-size ball of fire straight at me. Not a girly pitch, either. He put some weight behind it.

I yelped, ducked, and felt the heat singe my hair as the fireball streaked past me. It hit the wall, bounced, landed in a pile of scattered papers, and ignited.

'Shit! What the hell are you doing?' I yelled, and without even thinking about it, felt blindly for the structure of the fire. Delicate as glass, strong as steel, but fragile.

I put it out. Not even a wisp of smoke to show it ever existed.

I rounded on Lewis, shocked and furious; he had his arms crossed, leaning back against the desk, and he was . . . grinning.

'What the hell was *that*?' I demanded.

For answer, he extended his hand again and called another tongue of flame. 'Put it out,' he said.

'*You* put it out! This is a non-smoking building!'

'You're missing my point.'

'No, I'm not! You're trying to make me—' I stuttered to a stop, because I realised what he was trying to do. Or, more accurately, trying to demonstrate. Hey, I never said I wasn't a little thick. 'Oh.'

I extended my hand, cupped it over his, and felt the fire's warmth spill over me. Fire is a kind of fluid, when all is said and done: plasma dynamics. It flowed over my skin, persistent and gentle, and when I opened my palm, it was burning there. A steady tongue of flame like a pilot light, red and gold and blue.

I closed my fist around it and put it out, then opened my fingers again and called fire.

It came without even a hesitation, a flutter and a sense of pleasant warmth on my skin. I stared at it, fascinated, letting it drip from one finger to another, then rolling it back up to my palm.

'See?' he asked. He sounded smug about it. 'You're Water and Fire. Interesting combination. Pretty rare, too, there's been, what? Six or seven in recent history?'

I looked up at him. 'But I never had any power over fire. Never. They tested me.'

'Was that before you died and got yourself reborn?'

I'd died in a fire, and David had brought me back, as a Djinn. Then Patrick and his lover Sara had given their immortal lives to make me human again, and in his youth, Patrick had been . . . a *Fire Warden*.

I could feel it coursing through me now, a kind of awareness that I'd never noticed before – a sense of the electricity inside the walls, like bright glittering lines. Of static hovering like glitter in the air. Of the aura surrounding Lewis himself, glorious as a rainbow.

I blinked, and it was gone. Good. I wasn't sure I

wanted to live in a world that distracting full-time. 'But – why now? I didn't feel this before—?'

'Maybe it took some time to build the power channels.' He said. 'Or maybe something else has shifted. Hell, Jo, you just gave birth to a Djinn. Who knows what's changed inside you?'

Queasy thought. 'Um, one little problem. I don't have any formal instruction for fire powers.'

'Consider it on-the-job training. And don't get cocky. You still need a third black belt to land yourself a shot at my title.'

I laughed, and in the next blink, the glitter was back in the world. I stared, mesmerised by his glow, by the revealed glory of the world around me. Beautiful and complex as a machine made of crystal. Was this how Fire Wardens saw everything? No wonder they always looked spaced out . . .

'Jo,' he said, and drew my eyes back into focus. 'We're running out of time.'

I sobered up quickly. 'We are,' I agreed. 'Not to mention manpower. We've lost who-knows-how-many Wardens, and effectively all the Djinn. I hope you're right that we're getting stronger, because we need it—'

'Damn straight,' said a weary voice from the doorway. I turned to see Paul standing there. He walked in and slumped with a sigh in the nearest unsplintered chair, visibly gathering strength to speak. Dirty pale. 'Lewis.'

Lewis nodded silently, clearly worried at Paul's state. 'Do you want me to—?'

Paul waved it aside irritably. 'I'll live, and you've got better things to do with your power than heal my boo-boos. Listen, kids, we need to decide some things.'

Lewis glanced at me, then at Paul. 'Maybe this isn't the best time.'

'It's the only time,' Paul sighed.

'You need rest—'

'No. I need to retire,' Paul said bluntly. 'The thing is, I can't handle this anymore. It's out of control, and I'm not the guy for the job. I couldn't get their attention out there earlier, Jo, and you know it. You did.'

'Not me,' I replied, and held up my hands to push the implied offer back his direction. 'I can't stay. David gave me some ideas on how we might be able to solve this without a lot of further bloodshed, but I need to do it alone.'

'Yeah? How do you know you can trust him?' Paul demanded.

I met his eyes and held them. 'I know. And I have a plan, which is more than anybody else has right now.' Well, more or less. At least, I had a place to start. Didn't seem to be the moment to worry him with details, frankly.

Paul sighed and turned his gaze to Lewis, who straightened up fast. 'Oh, no,' Lewis said. 'I'm not going to take command. That's your job.'

'Hell, kid, I inherited the damn job, and I never

wanted it in the first place. I'm a field guy. Now I'm a field guy treading water. I want you to take it, Lewis. I *need* you to take it. You're the one guy everybody trusts around here, because you're the one guy who walked away from all this rather than play the games.'

'He's right,' I said quietly. 'It should be you.' I bit my lip, because it felt like being a traitor to say so – a traitor to Paul, who deserved my support even if he didn't want it, and a traitor to Lewis, who patently didn't want the responsibility. Especially not now. 'This is what you were born to do, Lewis. We all knew it, right from the start. And – there might be something else.'

'What?' That had both of them looking at me. Paul looked as if he really couldn't stand another dangerous surprise.

'David once told me that Jonathan used to be like you, Lewis. He had all three powers. And in some way, he was more . . . connected. To the Earth. So maybe you can work on that angle.'

Paul nodded. 'The sooner the better. If the Earth wakes up, takes a good hard look at what we've been doing to her this last ten thousand years without anybody to do some explaining, there won't be enough left of us to form a decent fossil record.'

'Who says she won't like us?' Lewis murmured.

Paul raised his eyebrows. 'Do *you* like us?'

'Some of us are pretty winsome.' I could have sworn Lewis looked towards me, under those long lashes.

'Wow, thanks for the compliment,' I shot back, largely sarcastically. He gave me a look that meant he was getting a particularly interesting mental picture, probably nothing suitable for public consumption. He shook it off with a rueful smile.

'Where are you going?' Lewis asked, back on track again.

'Seacasket.'

'Where the fuck is Seacasket?' Paul cut in, eyes closed. 'Sounds depressing.'

'It was someplace I was sent when I was a Djinn.'

'When Yvette and Kevin had you?' That had caught Lewis off guard. 'That business with Yvette wasn't my finest hour, sorry. I got a little distracted—'

'Distracted?' I let out a laugh that really wasn't much amused. 'The way I remember it, you were pretty focused, Lewis. Somewhere south of your belt buckle.'

'Yeah, thanks for the memories.' He had the grace to look embarrassed. 'Anyway, I was pretty much out of commission for most of that. You want to tell us about Seacasket?'

Not really. I sat and crossed my legs, then my arms. Defensive body language. Remembering Yvette gave me a seriously sick feeling in the pit of my stomach, because I couldn't think about her slinky, skanky sexiness without also remembering how she'd looked at the end, when Jonathan had remorselessly carried out her stepson's orders and crushed her skull.

'OK.' I sucked in a deep breath. 'Kevin, Yvette's

stepson, was my master while I was a Djinn. She didn't want me. She wanted David. She had a whole kinky-sex-and-bondage thing going for him.'

'And?'

'And what?'

'Seacasket,' Lewis prompted.

Oh, I *so* didn't want to remember. 'She wanted David, and he wasn't showing up for her to claim the way she'd intended. She figured the way to get him was . . . to make him come and stop me from doing something terrible.'

'In Seacasket.'

I nodded. 'It's a little town in Maine. I didn't know why she picked it, I only knew that she had every reason to believe that David would show up to defend it. It was a trap. For him. So she could . . .' I couldn't go on. I didn't want to remember that part, didn't want to think about her getting her hands on David and doing the things she did. Lewis looked away again, as if what was on my face was too private to witness.

I'm OK with what people do in the privacy of their bedrooms, and David's not my property (in any sense anymore), but dammit, David hadn't been a willing participant, then or ever. He'd hated it. Loathed it. And she'd taken great pleasure in the rape of his will, not to mention his body. I could never stop hating her for that. Never.

'I remember something Jonathan said once,' Lewis said contemplatively. Jonathan wouldn't even give the time of day to most humans, but Lewis was no doubt on Djinn speed dial . . . 'There are other things out there. Things even the Djinn are afraid of.'

Paul was watching us the way you'd watch a tennis match, and there was a bit of a spark in his eyes again. Not quite out of the game yet. 'There's something in the Warden records,' he said. 'Early writings. Nobody thought the translation was correct. There was a reference to some kind of higher form of Djinn. Nobody's ever found any trace of one, though.'

'Think that's what Jonathan was talking about?' I asked Lewis. He shrugged.

'Don't know. I think you're right. You've got the best shot of anyone, especially if David's at least trying to help you.' He paused to look at Paul inquiringly – a formal gesture, and a kind one.

Paul nodded. 'You do work best out there, kiddo. Go do your stuff. I'll stick with Lewis, help manage things here. And Jo?'

I looked up at him, and was caught by the intent focus of his eyes.

'I don't care how into him you are, you be careful of this Djinn of yours,' Paul said. 'Don't trust him.'

'Funny,' I said, and opened the office door to leave. 'He said pretty much the same thing himself.'

The last time I'd seen Lewis, back in Florida, he hadn't been alone, and so it didn't come as that much of a surprise to run into his travelling companion out in the hallway.

Kevin Prentiss had started out a dangerous, disaffected kid with a grudge and a rogue Djinn, and had ended up a surprisingly solid citizen, at least so long as Lewis exerted a good influence on him. Lewis had appointed himself Kevin's guardian and mentor. I wasn't too shocked by that, either; he'd always been the kind to take on wounded birds and outlaws. But it was still a pretty brave thing to do, considering that Kevin's last official guardian had ended up really, really dead, and Kevin hadn't been all that sorry about it, either.

Not that I could blame Kevin. I couldn't even begin to imagine what kind of terrible life the kid – seventeen, maybe? – had had with the psychopathic Yvette before David and I had come along to receive a short, radioactive burst of that horror.

Still, the first thing I thought when I saw Kevin was that I'd never seen him smiling before, at least not like that. It was a full, charming, sweet kind of smile, one that lit up his eyes and changed his normally surly expression into something that would melt the heart of any teen angel. Oh, he still looked slacker-chic, all longish tangled hair and sallow skin and slouching body language.

But that *smile*.

One instant later, the smile made sense, because Cherise was with him.

She looked freshly scrubbed, and she was restored to her usual glossy perfection – hair artlessly tousled (but perfectly ordered), make-up flawless. She wore a tight little top that showed off a tanned midriff, and low-rise jeans that were so low, she ought to be handing out referrals to her bikini waxer. A real pocket-size bombshell, from her head to her newly enamelled toenails.

Kevin was – of course – enthralled. Cherise didn't seem to mind that, but frankly, I didn't understand why. Kevin was a bad boy, just not in the generally accepted attractive way. He was trouble in faded baggy jeans, with slouched shoulders and an attitude that sneered in the face of authority. OK, so that was exactly what most girls Cherise's age – younger than mine, OK? – found sexy. But still. *Kevin?* Cherise could have literally any guy she wanted. I was perplexed by her sudden turnaround on the issue of quality date material.

And then I thought, *She wanted to get back in the door.* Being with Kevin did the job nicely, because he wasn't accustomed to taking no for an answer, and besides, he had the long arm of Lewis to back him up. Lord, I hoped she wasn't quite that manipulative, to come on to a guy just to get an invitation back in through the front door, but I wouldn't put it past her . . .

Or myself, come to think of it.

'Hello, Kevin,' I said with a reasonable degree of

welcome in my voice. The sweetly angelic smile twisted in on itself.

'Hey,' Kevin mumbled at the floor. 'Seen Lewis around?'

'Yeah, he's in there. He'll be out in a minute.' I couldn't bring myself to the point of small talk. I mean, I appreciated that Kevin was a complete and total jerk sometimes, but it was hard to get over having been his Djinn. Even that, I could have gotten over, if it hadn't been for the stupid French maid outfits he'd forced me to wear, the better to ogle me by.

He must have taken my silence for accusation, and looked up to glare. 'Lewis brought me. I didn't just show up or anything.'

'I'm glad he did. We need you here,' I said. I meant it. Kevin had a pretty impressive talent, when he wasn't trying to be a jerk about it, and we couldn't afford to be choosing only the nice people with good personalities.

Lewis, who'd come up behind me, nodded. I could see his face out of the corner of my eye. He was standing just a little too close, and I could feel the feedback burn of our powers responding. He didn't move away. 'Kev, they could use you in the last conference room. They're talking about fire control. You can help.' He looked at Cherise, glanced over to me. 'And – you can—?'

'Cater,' she said brightly. 'Gotta feed all these

people. Bottled water, coffee, sodas, ice – I'm hell on wheels with logistics. Um, as long as somebody has a credit card to use. Any volunteers? I'm looking for something with a platinum limit . . .'

'Cherise,' I said, and reached out to take her hand. 'You really don't need to be here. You should go home. I mean it. Everything's OK.'

She studied me for a long few seconds. 'I never knew you were so good a liar,' she said. 'Everything's not OK. Kevin told me. I saw a lot of it for myself anyway. Things are all screwed up, and you people are the ones who can set them right again. I want to help.'

'You're not – look, this isn't about you. It's just that you don't have the kind of skills that this needs to—'

'Give me a credit card and phone line, I'll show you some skills. Step off my thing.' She stared me right down, turned to Lewis, and gave him the same treatment. 'Wow, you guys just don't get it, do you? This isn't your planet. It's *our* planet. And you may be all kick-ass powerful superheroes, but that doesn't mean you don't need our help. Well, my help, anyway. Because I *am* the goddess of getting food delivered, and don't you forget it.'

Lewis quirked an eyebrow and half a smile, and looked at me. I shrugged. 'Girl's got a point,' I said. 'Maybe we need somebody with a little . . . practical perspective.'

Kevin shot Cherise a thumbs-up. 'Hey, let me know

when you get the munchies ready. I could eat.'

She made a shooing motion. Kevin ambled off in the direction Lewis had indicated . . . slowly enough to assert his independence, of course. He really was a gifted kid. I couldn't exactly call him a *good* kid. Maybe he'd turn out all right – he certainly had been given the chances. But I couldn't quite get the memories out of my head of what he'd been like when he'd had power over me. What he'd been like when he'd had power over his stepmother.

He'd liked using it. Dangerous, for a Warden.

I nudged Lewis with an elbow once Kevin was out of earshot. 'You're keeping tabs on Teen Psycho, right?'

'He's not that bad.'

'Lewis . . .'

'Yes, I'm keeping tabs on him.' He sounded resigned. 'Somebody needs to. Listen, I hate to rush you, but I can handle things here. What do you need?'

'Need? . . .'

'To make it to Seacasket and check things out.' He gave me that not-smile smile. 'Fast car?'

'Oh, you think? Maybe I can borrow Cherise's. She's got a cherry Mustang that pretty much rips up the road . . . Well, it used to be cherry. I think the last drive put a few dents in it.'

'No need to do that,' he said, and dug in the pocket of his blue jeans for a set of keys that he flung my direction. I caught them out of the air.

'This better not be an SUV,' I warned. Because

Lewis had an affinity for that sort of thing. I was an on-road kind of girl.

He flashed me a full grin this time. 'How about a vintage SS Camaro? Midnight blue and black? I bought it in Jersey just for you. Somehow, I just knew you were going to need wheels.'

My heart skipped a beat.

Chapter Three

He wasn't kidding about the car. It was pretty much the Holy Grail of cars, and I had the keys.

It was parked in the secured, bomb-hardened garage downstairs – the one reserved for only the most senior diplomats and Warden staffers. Well, what with the death and destruction, there were bound to be plenty of parking spots open. It had a fabulous exotic gleam under the overhead lights, a polished sapphire hiding unsuccessfully in a field of pebbles. The conservatively styled BMWs and Infinitis looked drab in contrast, though somebody had spiced up his love life with one of those kicky little BMW Z4 Roadsters in sleek, polished silver. Very James Bond.

I ran a hand reverently over the Camaro's silky finish. It was a 1969 model, a V8 with a 396 engine – a big, boxy car, nothing really elegant about it, none of that designed-in-a-wind-tunnel slickness of newer cars. I opened the door and popped the hood, leant in for a look, and felt my heart give that extra-double-thump reserved for true automotive love.

It wasn't just a COPO – a Central Office Production Order model, which would have been cool enough. No, it was one of the rarest of the rare: a 9560 with an all-aluminium ZL-l 427. The lightest, quickest, fastest Camaro ever made. Also, the rarest and most valuable. I winced to think how much cash Lewis had laid out for this beauty. It was in perfect condition, maintained with loving care. Not so much as a scratch.

I almost hated to be taking it out into the field, where things were bound to get ugly . . . but then again, it might just save my life. Speed counted.

I closed the hood and stood there for a moment, hand on the smooth finish, feeling the latent power of the car. It wasn't a replacement for my beloved, lost vintage Mustang, but that would be like saying that Secretariat wasn't a replacement for Man O' War. It was a thoroughbred, born to run.

And . . . Lewis had bought it for me.

Huh.

I wasn't sure I liked the implications – a guy buying you a car is at least as significant as him buying you a ring, and maybe more so in my slightly skewed worldview – but then again, I needed fast transportation.

A moral quandary. I hated those. And no question, the Camaro was seductive. I could always return it, I told myself. Sell it. Pay him back later. I didn't have to think of it as some kind of down payment for something more . . . intimate.

Then again, the Camaro conjured up those kinds of thoughts, all on its own. It just had that kind of aura. Sweaty bodies and smothered cries. Somebody had gotten lucky in this car a lot.

Dammit. I opened the door and slid inside. It was as perfectly maintained inside as out. Not a speck of trash or dust in it. I closed my eyes and went up into Oversight to take a walk around it, aetherically speaking.

Oh, God, it *glowed*. There was power in this machine. It was infused with love and dreams. In the act of creation, humans gave things a kind of reality on the aetheric, even though there was no life in inanimate objects per se. Every caring act of maintenance, every brush of the cloth on the dash or the chamois over the finish had rubbed a kind of power into this car along with polish.

I'd never seen anything like it. I wondered briefly how it would have looked to my eyes if I'd still been a Djinn; I'd have been able to unroll its past like a carpet, if I'd wanted. As it was, I was willing to bet this was a one-owner car, until now.

And that answered the question of why Lewis had bought it, too. Things like this, infused with this much power and substance, were rare and precious. It would have drawn him to it.

I let out a long, pleased sigh and inserted the key in the ignition. The engine fired up with a low, raw growl, then purred so smoothly that the tiny fine vibration under my body was almost unnoticeable.

'God, you're beautiful,' I said, and ran my hand around the steering wheel. Adding my emotion to what armoured the car. 'And you know it, don't you, baby? You know it.'

I shifted gears, and it responded perfectly to me. We eased up parking levels, to the secured gate, where my ID was checked by a uniformed security guard, and then I was out. Bright – though unfocused and cloudy – day outside, and my eyes were unprepared to deal with it; I hunted in the glove box and discovered an ancient, still-cool pair of Ray-Bans that cut the glare to something less nuclear.

It wasn't a short drive to Maine, and I didn't have a lot of time to waste.

Time. Right. I felt a pulse of alarm, remembering Eamon's two-day deadline, but I couldn't do anything about that; I couldn't even begin to try. I pictured Sarah, crying and afraid, hurting. I had to believe that he wouldn't hurt her. After all, I'd seen him with her, and I knew that on some level, Eamon did care for her. He wouldn't torment her to make a point unless I was there to witness it.

It was all no good without an audience.

I hoped.

Even with the dark thoughts, it felt good to be in

the world again, and moving under my own control. I didn't think I could stand to be trapped inside the headquarters building for long, cut off from the hum of the wind and the whisper of the sea.

OK, so New York hummed more from traffic and whispered more of sirens, but it still felt good.

The Camaro prowled through traffic like a big, dangerous beast . . . not feline, the way it was built. More wolf than cat. It turned heads, except for the cabdrivers, who ignored me to the point that I had to look sharp not to add yellow paint to the Camaro's shiny finish. I couldn't afford to go up into Oversight, not in heavy traffic, but I could sense an electric crackle in the air, potential energy heavy as impending rain, but without the healing moisture. That was going to ground itself soon, and in a particularly ugly manner, if something wasn't done.

Well, the good side of things was that I no longer had to worry about other Wardens second-guessing me when it came to things like this, and for the first time in a long time, I was at full power. So as I hit the bridge and sent the Camaro loping over the water, I concentrated on reading the systems swirling overhead. They were huge, invisible tornadoes of power. Unstable. Charges clicking together in chains, whipping wildly, then breaking when the stresses got too great. This was a reaction problem. The Wardens were concentrating their forces on handling a myriad of disasters; there were bound to be consequences.

And here was a big one.

The sky was surly overhead, soggy with thick, darkening clouds that blew in from the sea. The water under the bridge heaved and breathed on its own, a secret life most of the millions in the city would never even sense, much less understand. Water had memory, of a kind. Blood had DNA, and water had a similar structure that existed only on the aetheric plane. That DNA had been badly damaged over the years, but it still purified itself, renewed itself, struggled continually against the assaults of mankind to corrupt it.

We were damn lucky, the human race. Damn lucky that the earth's systems protected us as a side effect of its own survival mechanism, because we damn sure weren't smart enough to do it for ourselves.

I considered what to do about all that restless energy upstairs. Lightning would be the most logical plan, but it was risky; it was notoriously difficult to control lightning, and discharging it around the city could cause blackouts. Blackouts caused panics. Panics caused deaths. Deaths were, after all, what I was in this to try to avoid.

Then again, there was going to be lightning, sooner or later, and it was going to be worse if nobody controlled its strikes.

I drove for two hours. That sounds like a respectable driving distance, especially in the horsepower-rich Camaro, but unfortunately, traffic wasn't exactly cooperative. Two hours later, I was still within sight of the city. I'd hoped to be well out of range before the prickling at the back of my neck told me that something had to be done, because then it would have been someone else's responsibility. I'd been hoping that some Good Warden Samaritan would jump in and have at it, but no such luck . . . not that I blamed the folks back at Warden HQ. They had something of a full plate at the moment.

I signalled and pulled over to the side of the road in a spray of gravel, emergency flashers clicking. I settled myself comfortably in the bucket seat and let myself go up to the world above, where the landscape washed away into a surreal swirl of fog and colour. Brilliant, up here, and a unique bird's eye view of a gorgeous city. Wow. New York was charged with human purpose, driven by the engine of energy transforming and growing and changing, by passions and hopes and dreams and tragedies. I couldn't see as much detail as I'd once been able to, when I'd been a Djinn, but the city was still magnificent and mesmerising, and it was tough as hell to look away.

I forced myself to focus on the job at hand, and turned my attention upward, to the disturbance.

The force patterns up there slipped like oil in water, incandescent and rainbow-coloured. Beautiful, in their own way. Scary as hell, the way they were blending and morphing and whipping together. When lines of force connected, I saw the ultraviolet zaps of enormous power being channelled.

As I reached out to try to build a stable channel for it, I felt something . . . *notice*. That was the most skin-crawling sensation I'd ever had in my weather career, a shock to the system as extreme and terrifying as channelling lightning, if lightning had a brain and an intent. *Something* was watching me. Something big. The Mother? Was that what it was like? . . .

I lost control of the chains. They broke into random turning particles again, a soup of energy boiling over. I wanted to reach out again, but something was holding me back . . . my own fear. I was a tiny little field mouse, and there was a huge eagle shadow overhead, just waiting for me to make a move. If I tried to run, I'd die – crushed, devoured, destroyed.

Something in the real world brushed my hand, then gripped it tight. I opened my eyes, surprised, and saw that I had a passenger in the car, though the doors were still locked.

David was back, and he wasn't disguised as human at all; in fact, if anything, he looked more Djinn than ever before. A whole lot of sleek gold skin on display, because he was wearing only a pair of tight leather pants and an open leather jacket, with no shirt beneath. His hair was longer, down nearly to his shoulders, and it held a vivid, metallic shine. His eyes were their own light sources. I stared at them, fascinated; they were the colour of new pennies on the edge of melting in a blast furnace.

His hand was hot enough to be uncomfortable against my skin.

'I came to warn you,' he said. He was in my space, very close. I felt the longing in him, the shivering attraction that had gripped me from the very beginning. 'You have to stop.'

'Stop what?'

'Trying to fix this. It can't be fixed.'

'You know me better than that. Or at least, I hope you do. And by the way, what's with the bad-boy makeover?'

He brushed hair back from my face. Where his fingers touched, I burnt. Figuratively as well as literally. 'You don't like it?'

'The leather? Um . . .' I'd have to have been blind and insane not to like it, not to mention hormonally bankrupt. 'Looks good on you.'

'Not as good as you would.'

Oh *God*. My pulse started fluttering and racing, and as if his heat had crawled inside me, I started a bonfire of my own. At least half my mind – the smart half – was screaming that there wasn't time for flirting around just now. Not *now*. And not in a confined space with a Djinn who might just flip out and kill me.

I wasn't sure that sex with him in this state wouldn't kill me, anyway.

'You look good enough to eat.' He licked his lips. There was something incandescent going on in his eyes, so bright, I couldn't look for long. It was as if he were staring at my naked soul.

'Um – David—' His hand slid down the curve of my cheek, traced my chin, and then his fingers trailed down the line of my throat. His index finger explored the notch of my collarbone, and then dipped lower. He hooked it in the neck of my shirt and pulled. I swayed towards him. 'What are you doing?'

'Don't you know?' he asked.

Oh boy. The energy piling up and swirling overhead. The hot crackle between us. The heat of his skin, the restless flare inside me. The sense of something . . .

Something present, up there.

Something vast, and beyond my understanding.

He leant forward, and his lips touched mine. Liquid silk, warm and soft and insistent. Whatever defences I had, they didn't exist against him; I could feel all my resolve evaporating like ice under a summer sun. His hands seemed to be everywhere, soft little touches on my face, my neck, my arms, sliding up under my shirt, thumbs tracing the undersides of my breasts . . .

I think my mind whited out for a while. When it returned from its sensory vacation, I was back against the driver's side window, braced, with my knees up and apart, and David was kneeling between my parted thighs, and I had no idea how that had happened. The rational part of my brain insisted that this was *not the time or place* but then his hand glided warm up my inner thigh and slid inside my panties, and I gasped into the hot cavern of his mouth, and my clutching fingers sank into the lapels of his leather jacket to pull him closer.

Overhead, lightning cracked the sky, blue white. Hotter than the surface of the sun. It raced from horizon to horizon, split into a million sizzling tributaries. It covered the entire bowl of the sky, as if the whole thing had shattered.

The pulse of power that shot through me was nearly as shocking as the visual. Power echoing from the sky, to David, into me.

'Whoa! Hang on,' I blurted. He pulled back, and in a way that was worse, because now I could look at him, and damn, the ruffled hair, the kiss-swollen lips, the golden skin flushed with peach . . . He could single-handedly destroy the entire concept of celibacy, worldwide.

'Stop?' he asked. He took my hands and pressed them flat against his naked chest, under the leather jacket. Solid, velvet-soft skin. Real as it could possibly come. 'You don't want to stop. You want to go, and go, and go.'

I scrambled for sanity. 'This isn't exactly the right place—'

'If you're worried about people seeing us, they won't,' he said, and his fingers were at the bottom of my knit shirt, yanking it up. Stroking flesh. I was having serious problems getting my breath, especially when he leant closer, and I couldn't stop myself from pressing back against him. We were still dressed – barely – but I was certainly in a compromised position. My skirt was already so far up, it might as well have been a belt, and he was one fast tug on my panties away from having me. Being a Djinn, he didn't even have to struggle to peel those leather pants off. He could just will them to disappear.

And oh, I *wanted* them gone. I couldn't keep my hands off him, and there was such an intensely powerful sensation, stroking my fingers down the tight leather pants and feeling him respond . . .

The sky turned white overhead as lightning laddered across, a hissing curtain of force travelling nowhere. The air smelt acrid and tasted of tinfoil. Wouldn't be long now. It would find a ground target . . .

Oh, *crap*.

I marshalled what was left of my dignity, pushed David back – not so far as all that – and when he tried to lean in again, got my bent leg in between us, my foot on his chest to hold him in place. 'No,' I panted. 'David, you told me not to trust you. And this – this isn't like you. I don't think you're – yourself.' Not that the whole new David didn't have some really, really good qualities.

'I'm more than myself. Better.' He grabbed my ankle, wrenched my foot to one side, and lunged forward to pin me hard against the door, knees apart. Vulnerable. He was far stronger than a man, not that male strength wasn't usually enough for something like this. 'You don't know what this is like, Jo, having this, being this close to her – feeling every breath of the world flowing through you – every heartbeat pounding inside—' He was babbling. Quivering. 'It's new. *I'm* new.'

'I like the old David,' I said shakily. 'Can I have him back, please?'

He froze, leaning against the glass with a hand on either side of my head. Bronze eyes swirling, inhuman, unreadable. I could barely breathe. If David wanted to take me, it wasn't like I could say no; it wasn't like anyone had any control over what the Djinn did, maybe not even the Djinn themselves anymore. And oh God, I understood what was driving him. There was wildness in the air, wild power coursing through the sky and, for all I knew, through the ground, as well. This was the consciousness of the planet, slowly coming back to itself. A living world, an organism and a consciousness so huge that the rest of us were just dust mites crawling along its skin.

Desperation was driving him. Desperation and intoxication and the need to *feel*.

I could see a pulse racing under his skin, feel the vibration of his aching, near-painful need. It was echoing inside me, every thundering heartbeat.

I dared an indrawn breath. 'David, if you love me, back off.'

He leant away, and then shifted abruptly into a sitting position, braced on the far side of the car against the passenger window. No mistaking, in that position, that those leather pants were very tight and he was, as the artists like to say, in a state of interest.

But he was sitting on the other side of the car.

And his hands were shaking.

When he finally spoke, so was his voice. 'I'm sorry,' he said. 'This is – it's – she's never felt like this before. It's – I don't know how to—' Apparently, it was indescribable, because he just shook his head in frustration and looked away. 'It influences us. Seduces us. Makes us—'

'Crazy? Horny? Aggressive?'

The relieved smile he gave me was pure vintage David. 'Yes.'

'I like to know what I'm dealing with. And dammit, I *don't* like seeing you lose control.'

'I wouldn't be over on this side of the car if I wasn't in control.' Yeah, maybe . . . barely. I could feel the tension humming inside him, a coiled spring begging to unwind. He let out a long breath and deliberately flexed his hands, then laid them on his knees. 'Thank you for reminding me.'

'Is she awake?'

He parted his lips, not in answer but in surprise. Some of the fog left his eyes, and sanity came back. The bronze swirl muted to a soft brown, sparked with metallic highlights. 'Ah,' he finally said. 'No. Not exactly. But she's – in the process of waking up. And the feelings are especially powerful right now.'

'Like a hypnagogic orgasm,' I said. He blinked. 'The kind you have right when you're in that grey area between waking and sleeping. Really . . . deep.'

'Hypnagogic,' he repeated. 'Have I told you recently how much you baffle me?'

'No. You were too busy trying to feel me up.'

'Sorry.'

'Don't be.'

David lost the slight smile he'd managed to acquire. 'The problem is, I can't tell when it's me, or when it's *her* driving me. This is – difficult.'

'You were going to say "hard," weren't you?'

'No.'

'Liar.'

'Stop distracting me.'

He was right. It wasn't a good time to be distracting him, especially not if his self-control was all that stood between the impulses he was receiving and the rest of the Djinn. That thought sobered me considerably. 'Sorry,' I said meekly. I slowly got my legs folded into something like propriety and curled them around to put my feet on the floor. Another lightning bolt unzipped the sky overhead, broad as a superhighway – this one didn't fork. It was like a solid cable of light and power overhead. Forget about the surface of the sun, that had about as much heat in it as the entire nuclear core. If it had hit a plane, there'd have been nothing left but a floating smear of ash and some raining molten metal.

'I need to do something about that,' I said.

'Not a good idea.'

'Maybe not, but I have to try something. This system's highly unstable and dangerous.'

'It's still not a good idea.'

'Right. Can you help me?'

He was working on staying human, I could tell that; his instincts were driving him in all different directions, trying to rip him apart. I watched his bare chest fill and empty of air he probably didn't even need, mesmerised by the play of light on muscles. In the next flash of lightning, he looked almost as he had the first time I'd met him. In a heartbeat, his clothes re-formed from black leather into blue jeans and a grey T-shirt, with an open blue checked shirt on top. Hiking boots. His habitual olive drab ankle-length coat.

And glasses. Round John Lennon glasses that caught the flare in flat white circles, hiding his eyes completely.

'I'll try,' he said faintly. 'I'm not Jonathan. I can't – I don't have the experience to handle this kind of thing.'

'I doubt Jonathan would have had the experience to handle this, either. You're doing fine, David. Just fine.' I had no idea if it was true, but I wanted it to be. I reached out to him. He took my hand. His skin wasn't so burning-hot – more of a muted warmth, like someone who'd just come in out of the summer sun.

'I can feel them.' He cocked his head to the side, as if listening to something beyond the constant, restless rumble of thunder. 'The Djinn. It's like being the hub at the centre of a huge wheel, all of them connected – pulling at me. No wonder Jonathan kept himself apart. It must have been easier that way.'

Fascinating as that was, I had more practical concerns. 'Can you help me bleed off some of this energy?' I made a vague gesture up at the sky just as another painful burst of lightning exploded, racing spidery legs overhead.

He took a deep breath, nodded, and twined his fingers with mine. 'Ready?'

I nodded and let go, to drift up into Oversight. David washed into an almost invisible shimmer of light and heat – the Djinn didn't show up well in the aetheric, not to human eyes, anyway. The fairyland glow of the city behind the car was different up here, but no less intense, but what dwarfed it – what dwarfed everything – was the looming power in the sky. It was weather, and yet . . . not. The swirls and frantic updrafts were caused by the power, not spawning it, and while there were fronts forming and storms on the horizon, it wasn't the engine driving this particular machine. There was something going on that wasn't immediately obvious, and it wasn't the work of any Warden, no matter how ambitious or misguided.

I reached out to try to stabilise the system.

Too late.

Lightning exploded, down in the real world,

expending immense power upward, and slamming it down like a pile driver into the ground on the other end. There was so much energy involved that it literally knocked me for a loop in the aetheric. The roar in the physical world was devastatingly, deafeningly huge.

I felt the pulse of alarm from David, and saw something happen on the aetheric that I'd never witnessed. Never heard of, either.

An enormous column of energy erupted up from the ground in a thick, milk-white stream, heading for the sky.

What the hell was *that*?

I stared at it, stricken, and willed myself to move closer. Movement happens fast on the aetheric, unless you're careful, and I wasn't careful enough. I zipped forward, realised that I was moving too fast and the stream was closer – and larger – than I'd thought, and fought to slow myself down.

That should have been easy. It wasn't.

I could feel the suction. This thing was *moving*, and I mean fast as a freight train. It looked stable, but it was really a wildly speeding column of energy erupting up from the ground and fountaining into the sky, an uncontrolled bleed as if the plane of existence itself had popped a blood vessel.

I dropped back into my body, hurtling out of the sky at a disorienting speed, landed in flesh and jerked from the psychic impact. It didn't hurt so much as leave me reeling. David's grip on my hand steadied me. I opened my eyes and looked at him. 'You saw it?' I asked. He nodded. 'What is it?'

'There's too much aetheric power in the ground,' he said. 'It's not the only fissure that's opening. Just the closest.'

'What do I do to stop it?'

He looked grim as he said, 'I don't think you can.'

'And? . . .'

'And bad things are going to happen,' he said. 'Very bad things. Look, this problem is too big for the Wardens. Too big for the Djinn, for that matter. You have to accept that you can't—'

'*No*. I don't accept that. What, you want me to just shrug and say, Oh well, some casualties are expected? You know me better than that! David, *tell me what I can do!*'

He hesitated. And he might have persuaded me that there really wasn't anything to do, that there were some things beyond my control, but right about then a lightning bolt shattered the sky and struck a light pole about fifty feet away, across the road.

The actinic flash seared across my retinas, even though I squeezed my eyes shut and turned my face away, huddling against the car door; I felt David fling himself forward, and then his hot-metal weight covered me.

I didn't need protecting, but it was nice that he had the instinct.

When he let me up, I blinked back Day-Glo smears and looked around.

The metal light pole was half melted, and it was tipping over with majestic slowness. A tree falling in the forest. I yelled and pointed. It picked up speed, groaning, and slammed down across the road with a heavy glass-breaking thump, trailing hot wires that hissed and jumped.

Missed us by ten feet.

The traffic was relatively light, but hardly nonexistent; an SUV squealed brakes and skidded sideways, banging into the fallen pole. Then a car hit it. Then another.

Then a minivan ploughed full force into the snarl of metal.

'Oh my God,' I whispered, and fumbled for my door latch. I made it out of the Camaro and stumbled across wet gravel to the road. It was littered with hot glints of broken glass, and power lines were sliding wildly over the crushed metal. The minivan barely even looked like a vehicle, and it was about the size of a Volkswagen, post-impact. Somebody's engine was still running, and a radio was blaring. Liquids dripped.

'Help me,' I said, and looked around for David.

He was gone.

I couldn't believe it, honestly couldn't. He'd *left me?* In the middle of this, when people needed help? What the hell? . . .

No time to waste in thinking about it. I climbed over a crushed bumper and got to the window of the SUV. Two college-age boys in there, steroid-pumped, looking dazed.

'You guys OK?'

Their air bags had deployed, and they both had bloody noses, but they seemed all right. One of them gave me a wordless, shaky thumbs-up as he unbuckled his seat belt.

'Get out of your car and off to the side of the road,' I said. 'Watch the power lines, they're live.'

I moved on to the next car. A woman, unconscious. I watched the snaking power lines nervously; they were coming closer, and I knew how these things went. Power calls to power. Sooner or later, they'd be drawn to me. I could control fire, but I wasn't exactly skilled at it yet, and this was hardly the final exam I wanted. Power lines were notoriously difficult to deal with, because of the continuous stream of energy.

I put that problem aside and concentrated on the woman in the car. Hard to tell what was the bigger risk – leaving her in the car or moving her. If she had any kind of spinal injury . . .

I made the hard decision and left her where she was. Somebody was screaming for help in the minivan.

The power lines suddenly swerved, blindly seeking me. I danced back out of the way, watching them the way a snake charmer watches a cobra, and edged around to the back bumper of the wreck of the van. I tried the door. Locked, or jammed. The back window was broken. I leant in to have a look.

There was a man in the driver's side, looking limp and at the very least dead to the world, if not dead in fact. The woman next to him was the one doing the screaming. She was pinned; I could see that even from the back. The dashboard had deformed and locked her into the seat like the safety bar on a particularly scary amusement park ride. Broken bones, no question about it, and a lot of blood.

No way I could get her out alone.

I eased around the wreck to the passenger side and slid along the crumpled metal, watching my feet – not so much for the glass and metal as for the power lines, which had whipped craftily out of sight.

'Hey,' I said, and risked a look into the shattered passenger window at the woman trapped there. She was middle-aged, pleasantly plump, and under normal circumstances she might have been pretty; stress and injury had reduced her face to a mask of blood and terror. She was whimpering softly, no longer screaming. Her eyes flew open and fixed on me. One pupil was larger than the other.

'Help my daughter,' she said. 'Help my little girl.'

I hadn't seen any kids in my quick survey. 'In the back?' I asked. She nodded. 'OK. You hang on. Help is coming.' I had to assume it was; when everybody over the age of ten had a cell phone, the

911 operators had probably been flooded with calls.

I tried to see into the back, but it was an inky mess, no sign of life. I needed the Jaws of Life or something. Not that I knew what I was going to do when I found her . . .

A slender black shape hissed from the shadows under the van and struck at my feet. I screamed and skipped backward, and the power line rolled and writhed at the limit of its leash. Wanting me. Wanting to ground through my flesh.

Damn, that had been too close.

Just as I thought it, I sensed another surge, this one coming from my right, and catapulted up into Oversight. The lines looked like neon whips up there, and there were at least four of them writhing around me. Struggling to reach me. I edged left. One rolled to cut me off, then lunged.

Nowhere to go. If I tried to run, I was dead. If I stayed where I was . . .

I tried, hopelessly, to break the flood of power through the metal, but I was out of my element. Badly. Worse, every elemental control I *did* have would make things worse.

I jumped. The power line hissed over the pavement under my feet, swung wide, and just as I thumped down again, coiled over on itself and came back at me.

No way I was going to avoid it twice.

I jumped anyway, and knew instantly that it wasn't going to work; I'd timed it too early, it wasn't moving so fast, and I was going to come down with both feet right on top of high voltage.

Except that I didn't.

I didn't come down at all. I hovered.

Good move, I told myself, and then realised that I hadn't actually done the deed. Somebody else was holding me up and moving me back out of the danger zone. I was lowered gently back to clear pavement.

A Djinn walked around in front of me and inclined her head in a delicate cold click of beads. She was tall, dark-skinned, with hair in delicate and elaborate corn-rows. Neon yellow clothes and matching fingernails. Eyes as hot and predatory as a hawk's.

'Rahel,' I breathed. 'Thanks.'

'Don't thank me.' She said. 'David's orders.'

The power lines struck for me again.

She grabbed them in mid-air and held them. They writhed and hissed their fury, but she didn't seem to be putting forth much of an effort to keep hold. No lightweight, Rahel. And sometimes, as much as Djinn can be, she was my friend.

'Snow White,' she said, and smiled. That had been her nickname for me from early on, a reference to my black hair and fair skin. 'You have such interesting pets. Not very polite, though.'

She looked at the power lines she held, and hissed to them in a scary-sounding lullaby. They tried to lunge for me again. I sucked in a breath and stepped back; Rahel didn't seem inclined to let them go, but with Djinn, well, you really never could tell. She might find it funny.

'They need training,' she continued, and without any warning, the current cut off in both, and they went heavy and limp in her hands. She let them smack down to the roadway next to her very lovely shoes – Casadei animal-print pumps. Too nice for the current conditions. 'Do you ever draw a normal breath?'

'Bite me,' I said. I felt giddy and slightly intoxicated. Too much happening, too fast.

She smiled. 'Not hungry. A simple thanks will do.'

'What are you doing here?'

'I told you. David's orders.' She looked around at the wreckage as she dusted her hands. 'He had to leave. You present too much of a distraction at the moment, and he felt a need to concentrate. I give you no guarantees that I will be here for long, or that my presence will be especially helpful to you. Did David not tell you that we were no longer to be trusted?'

'And yet, here you are, saving my ass,' I pointed out. She shrugged. It had the grace of water flowing over stone, utterly inhuman in the arrangement of her muscles, the way she used them. Rahel was, in some ways, the least human of all the Djinn I'd met.

And in some other ways, one of the most.

'One must pass the time,' she said. 'Eternity is long, and there are so few truly interesting people.'

I started to say something about helping me get the wounded out of the cars, but then her head snapped around so fast that beads clacked in her hair, and her birdlike eyes fixed on something off to her left, in the darkness of the grassy median.

Another white-hot spidering of lightning overhead showed me what she was looking at.

There was a child out there. Bloody. Wandering around all alone. She couldn't have been more than five – a cute little thing, long brown hair, clutching a stuffed animal of some kind.

I sensed the lightning gathering itself.

Rahel said nothing. She was tense, but at rest. She could move faster than I could, but I saw no indications she was thinking about doing so.

After all, she was a Djinn, and she didn't know that kid. It was kind of an academic notion to her, empathy.

I lurched into a run, vaulted over a dismembered quarter panel lying in the way, and made it to the damp grass. My shoes slipped. I sensed the swirling column of the rift in the aetheric, the blood of the earth boiling upward into the sky just a few dozen feet ahead of me, near the little girl. She was staggering towards it.

The lightning chains were clicking into place. I could see it happening, see the aetheric heating up with the potential energy turning to actual . . .

I tried to break the chains of electrons aligning, but

the forces at work were too strong for a single Warden.

I hit the little girl and tackled her down to the ground, covering her with my body, and at the last second I lifted myself up on my hands and knees, away from any contact points with her skin.

Grounded four ways.

Lightning slammed into me with a force like nothing else on earth. I'd been struck by it before, but I'd been inhabited by a Demon Mark then, and considerably better protected. This was like being hit in the back by a truck, but before I could register the pain, the rest of it flooded in – power, so much power it was like a small sun channelled through a narrow few nerve channels. Unleashing itself through the circuit of my body.

It lasted only a split second, maybe less, because suddenly I was yanked up, no longer in contact with the ground, rising into the air and looking down on the huddled body of the little girl I'd been trying to protect.

The circuit was broken.

Rahel had me. Her eyes were blazing hot gold, but her face was unreadable, a blank mask of Djinn indifference.

She dropped me, job completed. Life saved.

Halfway to the ground, I felt the suction of that whirling, burning column of power rising out of the earth take hold of me and draw me in.

Oh crap, I thought, and then it was too late. As I

twisted in mid-air, being helplessly reeled in like a fish on a line, I saw her alarmed, surprised face. At least I'd given Rahel a new, exciting experience.

Not much of a comfort, as I was swallowed up in a milk-white flood of power.

It was like being baptised in battery acid. It *hurt*, oh my God, it hurt, and I tried to scream, but there really didn't seem enough left of me to scream, exactly. I was coming apart, a moth trapped in a nuclear core, and nobody, *nobody* was coming to rescue me this time.

The pain kept burning until it abruptly just . . . stopped. I was still trapped in the flood of aetheric power boiling up, and for all I knew, I was being flung miles up into the sky, but I felt no sense of motion.

I opened my eyes and saw paradise, but a paradise that humans were never meant to see, a kind of opalescent waxen beauty that swept, swirled, created, and destroyed. I was in the bloodstream of creation, and it was more beautiful and more terrifying than anything I could have imagined. No wonder human beings counted for little, in the great scheme of the world. The power here – the power that was simply excess energy, bleeding off from the slowly waking entity we called the Mother – was beyond anything we could ever understand or control.

It was kind of a privilege, seeing it as I inevitably exploded into disconnected atoms.

Only I didn't do the exploding thing. I held together and gradually adjusted to the strange pressures and odd lights and disconcerting, slick flows that mimicked glass but felt silky and liquid to the touch. Nothing matched physics as I understood it. It was wildly, insanely strange and mesmerising.

I must have been the first person to see a Demon Mark in the wild.

It entered the same way I had . . . passing through the barrier, sucked into the flow. It floated in the streams, a complex and sickening structure that twisted and turned on itself, moving with an eerie kind of life. Lazily bumping from one flow to another. I'd never seen one outside of some kind of container – a bottle, a human body, a Djinn forced to take one into itself. I had no idea they could even exist like this, on their own.

Not good news.

I felt it fix on me with an atavistic shudder of horror.

As I watched, the Demon Mark was growing larger, sucking in energy and power from the aetheric flow, like a tick hitting an artery. I didn't dare hope that it would gorge until it exploded, though. Something far, far worse would happen; I just knew it would. Nothing good ever happened to me with a Demon Mark around.

It occurred to me that there was a reason the Demon

Mark might come swimming in here . . . This stuff was blood, in a sense. Lifeblood, pure, the real deal.

The blood of the Earth itself.

When these parasites were out in the regular world, they'd latch on to anything with a trace of power, trying to stay alive – Wardens and Djinn. But because we weren't the pure stuff, they inevitably mutated and destroyed us in the process of creating an adult Demon.

Wonderful. I'd worked out the biology of the Demon Mark. That was helpful.

Not.

It drifted my way.

I screamed like a little girl and started to head blindly away from the twisting, misshapen thing. Trying to move through this grey fog of power was like swimming through gelatine. *God*, I hated those monsters, hated them with a sweating, blinding passion that owed nothing at all to logic. It wasn't coming after me, not this time. It had found its own, personal paradise. Right?

Right.

Well, then, fine and dandy. I could just leave it to munch, and go on about my business . . .

No. I couldn't. If a Demon Mark was capable of hatching an adult Demon out of the imperfect fuel of a human or Djinn, then what was it going to create out of this stuff? I couldn't even bear to imagine. *You have to get it out of here*, some part of me said. The other part – overwhelmingly the majority – told the first part to shut the hell up. *What happens if it stays? If it feeds? If it swims down instead of up, gets into the – the bloodstream?*

That annoying, shrill voice of reason. Fighting Demon Marks was *not* my mission. It wasn't my fault I'd stumbled onto this problem. Nobody would blame me if I turned tail and ran.

Nobody but me, anyway.

I took a quick poll. The vote was two to one, bravery to self-preservation. I really needed to work on evening that one up, one of these days.

I needed a way to trap the Demon Mark. I had nothing on me . . . nothing but my clothes, my shoes.

Well, anything was better than nothing.

I breathlessly stripped off my shirt, braced myself, and began swimming slowly towards the floating Demon Mark.

It got uglier the closer I came, the kind of ugly that made my stomach twist and quiver, and my whole body shake violently. It didn't seem to notice me at all. It was at least twice as large as it had been when I'd seen it enter the barrier, pulsating with an unclean hunger. At this rate, it'd be knitting little Demon booties in just a couple of minutes.

Oh, I really didn't want to do this.

I threw my shirt out like a net, covered the twisting shape of the Demon Mark, and yanked the sleeves together in a knot. It wouldn't hold the thing long – maybe not at all. I began swimming for all I was worth, heading for what I thought was the nearest way out, though everything looked the same now, disorienting and endless. I kicked grimly. At least I could breathe, though the intoxicating, slightly sweet smell of this place made my head spin.

I glanced back at the shirt I was towing. The Demon Mark's black tentacles flowed out of the seams, testing its prison. It was content to stay there for now, because it was still feeding. That complacency wouldn't last.

Without warning, I fetched up against something cool and unyielding, and slapped my hand against it in frustration. I felt it give, and slapped harder. My palm stung from the impact, but it pushed at least two or three inches in.

I'd found the way out.

I concentrated all my will, all my force, and kicked.

Half of me slid through the barrier, instantly and bitterly cold and wet; I screamed in frustration, because I had no leverage to get the rest of me through. I wiggled. That gained me maybe an inch. Two inches. I pulled harder, and my left hand, and the bundle of the shirt, tumbled out into the thin, wind-whipped air.

The Demon Mark went insane when its food supply cut off, and the shirt might as well not have been there. It seethed right through the fabric with lightning speed and wrapped tentacles around my hand.

I screamed and reached for power, but what I had was useless for fighting something like this. I remembered how it felt – the sickening, invasive throb of the thing squirming down my throat. The agony as it set up its tentacles buried deep inside, feeding from me and pumping up my body's production of power, until my body simply couldn't survive.

No. Never. I don't mind dying, but I'm not dying of this.

I grabbed it with my bare right hand and threw it. Tried to, anyway, but it stuck to my skin, pulsing, changing, shifting. Crawling and writhing.

I screamed again, soundlessly, trying desperately to shake it off. I could feel it testing layers of skin, trying to find a way in. It could burrow, of course, but it was lazy and fat. It wanted an easier path.

I'm not going to make it.

'We are sealing the break!' a voice shouted, startlingly close to my ear, and I felt something haul at me with so much strength, I felt tendons creak in my joints. I slid greasily the rest of the way through the barrier, still frantically trying to scrape the Demon Mark off my hand.

Whoever had done me the favour of pulling me free let go as soon as I was out of the milky column of power. Might have been Rahel; it was hard to tell because the night was a muddle of rain, lightning, thick spongy cumulonimbus clouds piled into an iron-coloured anvil.

I hung there for an instant, and then I felt gravity take hold. I fell like Wile E. Coyote holding an ACME anvil, flailing, screaming, my hair snapping like a wet black banner behind me. I couldn't tell how far the ground was, but if the clouds were cumulonimbus, I was probably at least thirty thousand feet up. I tried to take a breath and got nothing but sharp, empty-tasting air. Too thin to sustain me. I shut out the sickening sense of the falling, the growing terror of the Demon Mark still trying to enter my body, and focused hard on gathering the available oxygen into a cushion around me. Tricky, when you're falling. You have to match the rate of descent at a molecular level, and that's not as easy as it sounds.

I scraped together enough for a breath. Not enough to cushion my fall, and I was still accelerating. I knew enough about terminal velocity not to want to experience it firsthand.

I was enveloped by a chilly mist as I entered the cloud base, and was buffeted by increasingly strong winds as the atmosphere thickened around me. I spread out my arms and legs, trying to slow myself as much as possible, and started the hard work of creating a parachute. Oh, it's theoretically possible. We'd talked about it once in a long-ago classroom, and it hadn't seemed so tough back then, when I was younger and not free-falling out of the sky.

I hoped these weren't low-lying clouds. If they were, by the time I had visibility, it might be too late . . . but deploying my 'parachute' too early would be just as bad, because the turbulence would start to rip into it as soon as I created the complex structure of fixed molecules. Theoretically, the technique I was going to use would allow the air itself to form into flexible material, and act like a gliding parachute.

Theoretically.

I gasped in another shallow breath of air and saw my left hand in another white-hot flash of lightning. The Demon Mark was still clinging to it, wet and black, seeping slowly into my flesh through the pores. Once it was under my skin, it could go anywhere. Sink its tentacles into my brain and lungs and heart. Embed itself so thoroughly that even trying to remove it would mean madness and death.

I glimpsed something shining through the clouds to my right, flaring aetheric-hot, then ice-cold; the column of power was smaller, but it was still fountaining up into the stratosphere. I slid that direction by folding my right arm in, a kind of Superman one-fisted attitude. Good thing I'd done skydiving once or twice in the past. At the time, it had just been for fun, but at least I remembered the basics of manoeuvering in free fall.

I spread-eagled again when I got close to the column. The last thing I wanted was to fall in there again. I extended my Demon Marked right hand towards the flow, enough so that it could feel the tantalising warmth.

Go on. Go for it.

It stirred and unravelled in a lazy black twist, long and sinuous. The battering of the air didn't seem to affect it at all. It unwrapped itself smoothly from my outstretched, trembling arm and reached out towards the column of power, which had started to fade and was coming in pulses like irregular heartbeats. Rahel – or whatever Djinn had saved me – had been as good as her word. The break between the worlds was starting to seal.

Timing was everything. If I waited too long, the Demon Mark would be drawn back through the barrier. If I broke off too soon, it would simply wrap around my hand again, and I could kiss my ass good-bye.

Problem was, I didn't control the timing. I just had to hope that I could sense the second that the column started to shut down.

The Demon Mark hesitated, torn between the fast-unravelling aetheric updraft and the less powerful but more certain warmth of my body.

I felt a sudden icy sensation sweep across me, and thought, *now*, and shook my hand violently. The Demon Mark broke free, and it had to make a choice.

It went for the column . . . and as it stretched its black tentacles out, the geyser gave one last, brilliant pulse, and died.

The Djinn had been successful. The energy buffet was closed . . . and I was now the only Happy Meal available.

I curled myself into a ball and dropped, thinning the air ahead of me to make it a quicker descent.

When I uncurled again, heart hammering wildly, I broke through the bottom of the cloud cover and *Oh, crap*.

Low-lying clouds.

I snapped the structure of my air chute together, and jerked to a sudden, neck-wrenching stop that turned into a slow downward spiral as the air chute's molecules – held together by desperate force of will – began to warm from the friction and spin apart.

I was still going too fast.

And there were power lines coming up.

I let the chute collapse in on itself while I was still twenty feet up, tucked and hoped breathlessly that the mud down there would be soft enough to prevent any serious injuries.

I don't remember hitting the ground, only blinking water out of my eyes and staring up at the low, angry clouds, which glowed with continued frantic flashes of lightning.

I raised my right hand and stared at it. No sign of the Demon Mark, though in all the confusion it could be just a stealthy creep away . . .

'Mom?' Imara's face appeared over mine, ghost-pale, eyes as reflective as a cat's. 'Please say something.'

'Stay still.' Another voice, this one male and as familiar to me as breathing. 'You've got some broken ribs. I'll have to fix them, and it's going to hurt.'

I blinked rain out of my eyes and turned my head. David was crouched down next to me, rain slicking down his auburn hair and running in rivulets down his glasses. He looked miserable. Poor thing.

'Demon Mark,' I said.

'I think she hit her head,' Imara said anxiously.

'No, she didn't,' David said, and reached over to wipe mud from my face with a gentle hand. 'You're in shock, Jo.'

I shook my head, spraying mud and water like an impatient sheepdog. 'No! It was feeding off the power geyser. I got it out of there, but it's still around. Watch yourselves.' Nothing Demon Marks loved more than a warm Djinn, and so far as I knew, once Djinn were infected, there was no way to cure them. 'Get out of here.'

David said, 'Imara, go.'

'But—'

'Did you hear me?' His voice was level as a steel bar. She stared at him, then at me, and then misted away.

'You, too,' I said. 'Get the hell away from here. Go.'

'In a minute. First, you need some help.'

I nodded, or tried to. The mud around me was cold and gelatinous, and I spared a single thought for just how trashed my clothes were. And my shoes. What had happened to my shoes? Oh man. I'd loved those shoes.

I was focusing on that when David took hold of my shattered arm and pulled, and the universe whited out into a featureless landscape, then went completely black.

Somebody had put my shirt back on. I hoped it was David. It was nice to think of him dressing me. Nicer to think of him undressing me, though . . .

I opened my eyes to road noise and vibration, and the pleasant daydream of David's hands on me faded away. My whole body felt like a fresh bruise. The side of my head was pressed against cool glass, and I had a wicked drool issue going on; I raised a hand, wiped my chin, and blinked away dizziness.

I was in the Camaro, and we were hauling ass for . . . somewhere. The road was dark, only a couple of headlights racing through the gloom and the wavering dashed yellow stripe to guide us. If there was moonlight, it was behind clouds. I could still feel energy rumbling in the atmosphere.

'What? . . .' I twisted in my seat – which was, fortunately, the passenger side – and looked at the driver. 'Imara!'

My daughter – disorientation still followed the thought – glanced at me. She looked pale in the dashboard lights. 'I was starting to worry.'

'Where's—?'

'Father? He was with us for a while, but he had to go. Djinn business. I think it was about the Demon Marks.' Like her father, she had the trick of driving without paying the slightest attention to the road, and kept staring right at me. 'Are you better?'

I didn't feel better. No, I felt like I'd been boiled, steamed, deboned, and thrown out of a plane at thirty thousand feet. With a collapsing parachute. David had healed my broken bones, but the remainder of it was my problem. 'Peachy,' I lied. 'How long have I been out?'

It took her a second, juggling the human concept of time in her head. 'Four hours, I think. You hit the ground hard. Father did what he could to help you. He wasn't sure it would be enough.' Her hands kept steering the car accurately, even while we took a curve. 'Are you sure you're all right?'

Something came to me, a little late. 'And how exactly do you know how to drive a car?'

Imara blinked a little and shrugged to show she didn't understand the question.

'Kid, you've been alive for, what, a couple of days? Did you just wake up knowing everything that you need to know? How does that work?'

Another helpless lift of her shoulders. 'I don't know. If I had to guess, I'd say I know everything my parents knew. So I benefit from your life, and Father's. It saves time.'

I remembered Jonathan sending me to Patrick, the

only other Djinn who'd really had to learn how to
become one from scratch – who'd been brought over
from human by another Djinn, rather than created the
old-fashioned way, out of apocalypse and death. I'd
had to take baby steps, learning how to use what I'd
been given, because David hadn't been able to transfer
that life experience to me the way he had done with
Imara.

But the idea that your daughter knows *everything*
you knew? Not very comforting. There were plenty of
moments in my life that I'd just as soon *not* share with
my offspring . . .

I pulled myself away from that, pressed my hand to
my aching head, and asked, 'Where are you heading?'

'Maine? . . .'

David had set her on the road to Seacasket, at least.
And apparently global positioning was one of the
things that she'd inherited from him.

I nodded and tried stretching. It didn't feel great.
'What about the accident? Was everybody all right?'

'Accident?' She was either playing dumb, or all that
carnage and twisted metal had meant little to her.

'There was a wreck – there was a—' A little girl.
Wandering, bloodied, scared. I'd been trying to save
her, hadn't I? My memory was fuzzy, tied up with
images that didn't make any sense of opalescent swirls
and burning and falling . . .

'I don't know,' she confessed, and chewed her lip. I
knew that gesture. It had taken me dedication to get

over the same one. She was my kid, all right. 'I didn't know it was important or I would have paid more attention.'

'Not *important?*' I let that out, accusation-flavoured, before I could stop myself. Imara turned her attention back to the road. Not to focus on her driving, just to avoid my censure.

And then she deliberately turned back, eyes level and completely alien. 'I should have paid more attention, but you should leave that behind you now. What Father's asking you to do is more important, and you can't be distracted by individual lives now.' She shook her head. 'It's also very, very dangerous, what he's asking of you. I don't like it.'

'I just got my synapses fried in a lightning strike, and then I fell out of the sky. Dangerous is sort of a sliding scale with me.'

'Mom!' She sounded distressed. Angry. 'Please understand: Whatever you've faced before, this is *different*, and you need to stay focused on the goal. I know that's hard for you, but if you worry about saving every individual, you'll lose them all. Let other people do their part. This is Djinn work, and it isn't the kind of thing humans are built to do.'

By my very nature, I wasn't good at taking in the big picture; for me, the whole world *was* that lost, scared little girl wandering in a field. Those college boys trapped in their wrecked truck. The world revealed itself to me one person at a time.

But I took in a deep breath and nodded. 'Right. I'm focused. How much longer—?'

'About seven more hours,' Imara said. 'I'll stay with you. There are things you can't do on your own. You'll need help. Father said—' She shut up, fast. *Father.* I wondered if David was as frightened by that as I was by the *Mom* thing. Or as delighted. Or both. 'Is this still strange for you?'

'What?'

'Me,' she said softly, and turned her attention back to the road. 'Human mothers carry their children inside them. They hold them as infants; they teach and guide them. I was born as I am. That's strange, isn't it?'

She sounded wistful, even sad. I'd been so busy thinking of myself and my reactions to her that I hadn't considered how odd this might be for her, too. That maybe she felt lost in a maze of human feelings she didn't understand. Wasn't even supposed to have, perhaps.

'Imara,' I said. 'Pull over.'

'What?'

'Please.'

She coasted the car to a stop on the gravel shoulder, not far from a sign that warned of curves up ahead, and twisted around to face me. It was like looking in a faerie mirror – so similar that it made me shiver somewhere deep inside. There was an indefinable connection between us that I loved and feared in equal parts.

'You look so much like me,' I murmured, and took her hands in mine. They felt warm, real, and solidly familiar.

'I am you,' she said. 'Most of me. I'm not so much your child as your clone – Djinn DNA doesn't mix well with human. So my flesh is mostly the same as yours, and my – my spirit is Father's.'

I shivered a little. How was I supposed to feel about that? And what was I supposed to say? 'I—'

'I'm not really Djinn,' she said. 'You know that, don't you? I can't do the things Father can do. I can't protect you.'

'Mothers protect children. Not the other way around.'

She tilted her head a little to the side, regarding me with a tiny little frown. 'How can you protect me?'

Great question. 'I won't know until I get there,' I said, and impulsively reached up to touch her cheek. 'Sweetheart, I'm not going to pretend that you're not stronger than I am, or faster, or smarter, or – anything else that the Djinn part of you can give. But the point is that I'll protect you when I can, and I *do not* want you to put yourself at risk for me. All right?'

The frown grooved deeper. 'That's not what Father said to do.'

'Then your dad and I need to have a talk.' What she'd said was making me curious. 'When you say you're not fully Djinn—'

'What are my limits, do you mean?' she asked. I nodded. 'Where you're strong – in weather and fire, particularly – I'm strong. I can move the way the Djinn do. But I'm bound to my body in ways they aren't. I can't change my form. I can't use other elements that you can't control, as well.' She continued to watch me carefully. Her voice was matter-of-fact, but I couldn't help but think that David and Jonathan and I had done something terrible, bringing Imara into the world. I couldn't tell if she resented the restrictions her half-blood birth had given her. If she did, that would be one hell of a case of adolescent angst.

'But,' she continued when I didn't jump in, 'even so, I am one of the Djinn. They all felt it when I was born. I'm still a part of them, if a small one.'

I stayed quiet, thinking. She might not have been able to read my mind, but she could easily read my expressions – something I couldn't do to her.

'You're worried that if you keep me with you, they could trace you through me. A weak link.'

'A little. With the Djinn so unreliable . . .' I'd seen the Djinn turn on a dime, when the Earth called; even though Imara might seem immune to that, she was clearly a lot more vulnerable than I'd like. And I couldn't hold my own against a full-on Djinn assault, not for more than a few seconds. No human could, if the Djinn unleashed their full potential.

She inclined her head, just once. A Djinn sort of

acknowledgement, fraught with dignity. 'I don't think I could protect you against them if they came in force. Do you want me to leave you?'

'And go where?' I asked.

'Anywhere. I only just arrived. I haven't even begun to learn about the world for myself.' She smiled, but it felt like bravado to me. My kid was trying to make me feel better about rejecting her.

'Imara—'

'No, please don't. I want to help you, but I understand if you can't trust me – you only just met me. You'd be crazy not to be concerned.'

I wasn't about to break my daughter's heart. Not yet. 'Let's take it slow on the assumption of mistrust, OK? I just don't – *know* you.'

'But I know you,' she replied quietly. 'And I can see that it makes you . . . uncomfortable.'

I let that one pass. 'If David can always locate you, I'm guessing you can always locate me, no matter where you are. Right? So it really doesn't matter if you're here, or learning how to spin prayer wheels in Tibet. And I'd rather have you here. Getting to know you.'

She smiled again. 'What if you don't like me?'

It was a sad, self-mocking smile, and suddenly I wasn't seeing the metallic Djinn eyes, or the eerie copy of my own face; I was seeing a child, and that child hungered for everything that children do: Love, acceptance, protection. A place in the world.

She took my breath away, made my heart fill up and spill over. 'Not like you? Not a chance in hell,' I said. My voice was unsteady. 'I love you. You're one hell of a great kid. And you're *my* kid.'

Her eyes glittered fiercely, and it took me a second to realise that it wasn't magic, only tears.

'We'd better keep moving,' she said, and turned back to start the car. 'So what do you think? Breakfast first, or apocalypse?'

She was starting to inherit my sense of humour, too. Hmmm. Breakfast sounded pretty tempting. Lots more tempting than an apocalypse, anyway.

Those hardly ever came with coffee.

Chapter Four

I spent part of the drive napping, and dreaming. Not good dreams. Why couldn't my out-of-body experiences take me to a nice spa, with David giving me oil massages? Why did my brain have to punish me? I was fairly sure that I really didn't deserve it, at least not on a regular basis.

Unsettled by the nightmares, I kicked Imara out of the driver's seat as soon as I was sure I wasn't going to drop off into dreamland without warning. I always felt better driving, and the Camaro had a silky, powerful purr that welcomed me with vibrations through my entire body as I cranked her up. She needed a name, I decided. Something intimidating yet sexy. Nothing was coming to mind, though.

As we cruised along, switching highways about every hour because heaven forbid travel on the East Coast should be easy, I found myself longing for the endless straight roads in the West and South. Maine was beautiful, no doubt about it, but I wanted to drive fast. Responsibility and panic had that effect on me. Being behind the wheel gave me time to think, and there was a lot to think about, none of it good. All of it frightening.

I couldn't stop scrubbing my hand against my skirt, trying to get the phantom feel of the Demon Mark off me. I hadn't been infected. I knew that, intellectually, but it still made my stomach lurch when I thought about how close I'd come.

We stopped for breakfast at a truck stop, and I bought a couple of pairs of blue jeans and tight-fitting T-shirts. My shoes were missing altogether, so I added a sturdy pair of hiking boots and some feminine-looking flip-flops. Best to be prepared.

I paid extra to use the showers, rinsing off grime and mud and exhaustion under the warm beat of the massaging showerhead. Luxury. I wanted to curl up in the warmth and sleep for days, but instead I toweled off, blow-dried my hair into a relatively straight, shimmering curtain, and dressed in the jeans, T-shirt, and hiking boots.

It looked appropriate for Seacasket, anyway.

Back on the road, I fought an increasingly jittery desire to meddle with the weather hanging out to sea. Storms, of course. Big electrical storms, packing loads of wind and swollen with rain; I didn't sense any lethal tendencies in the front, but those were no fluffy happy clouds out there. Black thunderheads, trailing grey veils over the ocean, illuminated from within by constant pastel flutters of lightning. It was, as storms went, nothing more than a surly kid, but it could pack a wallop if it got aggressive. Right now, it was content to glare and mutter, out there at sea. Kicking the tops off waves. That was good; I didn't need more to handle.

Imara had my taste in music. That wasn't too much of a surprise, but it was gratifying. We both belted out the chorus to 'Right Place, Wrong Time,' both aware of just how appropriate that song was in the radio playlist.

We cruised into Seacasket at just after 7 a.m.

It was one of those Norman Rockwell towns with graceful old bell towers, spreading oaks and elms. A few 1960s-era glass buildings that looked like misguided, embarrassing attempts to bring Seacasket out of the golden age. That was the only impression I had of it, because the one time I'd materialised in the centre of town, I'd come as a Djinn, with an irresistible command to burn the town and everyone in it to ashes; that hadn't given me a lot of time for sightseeing, since I'd been desperately trying to find a way to short-circuit my own Djinn hardwiring and save some lives.

The main street was called . . . Main Street. The turn-of-the-last-century downtown was still kept in good repair, although the hardware stores and milliners had long ago turned into craft stores ('crap stores,' as my sister had always dismissively referred to them) and 'antique' dealers whose stock-in-trade was reproduction Chinese knockoffs and things that got too dusty over at the craft stores. So far as newcomers, there were a few: Starbucks had set up shop, as had McDonald's down the street. I spotted a couple more fast food giants competing for attention, though sedately; Seacasket must have had one of those no-ugly-sign ordinances that kept things discreet and eye-level, instead of the Golden Arches becoming a hazard to low-flying aircraft.

There was a Wal-Mart. There's always a Wal-Mart.

I pulled into the parking lot towards the side – Wal-Mart had a crowd, of course – and idled the car for a moment, soaking in the atmosphere. When I rolled down the Camaro's window, birds were singing, albeit a bit shrilly, and there was a fresh salt-scented breeze blowing inland. The temperature was cool and fresh, and all seemed right with the Seacasket world.

Which was, in itself, weird.

Imara, in the passenger seat, was watching me curiously. 'What are you doing?' she asked.

'I thought you knew everything I did,' I said.

'Past, not present or future. Are you reading the weather?'

'Not exactly.' Because weirdly enough, there didn't seem to *be* any weather in Seacasket. Sure, the storm

I'd been noticing was still out to sea, but there was an odd energy at work in this town. Something I hadn't felt before. As if the whole place was climate-controlled . . . which wouldn't have made a lick of sense even if there had been a Warden on-site, which I could tell there wasn't. The Ma'at, maybe? I didn't think so. The Ma'at, rival organisation to the Wardens, had their own way of doing things, which mostly involved letting nature have its way while smoothing off the highs and lows of the excesses, under the theory that if you allow the system natural corrections – even costly ones – ultimately, the entire system is more stable, less prone to lethal swings.

There was a certain logic to it, and I wasn't sure I disagreed with the Ma'at in principle . . . just in practice. Because I simply wasn't cold-blooded enough to sit back and watch a disaster. I could easily prevent them from taking innocent lives. Not for a theory. It didn't surprise me that the Ma'at mostly seemed composed of older men, who'd cultivated the detachment of politicians and CEOs.

This wasn't the Ma'at, though. This felt more like Djinn work, except . . .

I turned in the seat and faced Imara. 'What can you tell me?'

She cocked her head, looking interested but not committed. 'About? . . .'

'You know what David knew, right? So? What can you tell me about Seacasket?'

She'd inherited more from her father than just knowledge; I saw that in the flash of secrets in her eyes. 'Not very much.'

'I need to know where to find this Oracle thing. You're supposed to be my native guide, kid. So guide.'

'Maybe I don't know how to find it.' She lifted one shoulder in a shrug, and kept her metallic Djinn stare straight on me. Intimidating, but it didn't hide the fact that she was being evasive.

'Yes, you do. Why are you being so—'

'Evasive?' she shot back, and ran her fingers through her long, straight black hair. My hair was curling again in the humidity. I resented her hair. Secretly. 'Possibly because this is certain death for a human to attempt, and I might not want you to die just yet.'

'If you didn't think I could do it, why come with me?'

She smiled slightly, and those eyes looked entirely alien all of a sudden. 'Maybe Father told me to.'

'Maybe you and your Father—' I reined myself in, unclenched my fists, and took in a deep breath. 'Don't make me do this.'

'Do what?'

'Test whether or not you're really Djinn.'

She smiled. 'If you're thinking about claiming me, that arrangement died with Jonathan. It won't work.'

'Something simpler than that.' I took in a quick breath. 'Where do I find the Oracle?'

'Mom—'

'Where do I find the Oracle?'

Ah, *now* she got it. And she was surprised, and pissed off, too. I saw the flare of temper in her eyes. 'The Rule of Three. You wouldn't.'

'Where do I find the Oracle?'

Three times asked, a Djinn has to answer truthfully. Of course, truth has a nearly limitless shade of interpretations; I probably hadn't framed my question closely enough to get a real answer from her, but she'd have to stick close to the subject . . . if the Rule of Three was still in effect.

Which it looked like it wasn't, as my daughter continued to glare furiously at me with eyes that were starting to remind me more of Rahel's than David's – predatory, primal, eternal. Not good to piss off any Djinn, especially now that humans had virtually no protection from them . . .

Imara abruptly said, 'It's close.'

She didn't say it willingly, either; it seemed to be dragged out of her, and when she'd gotten to the end of the sentence she clenched her teeth tight and fell back into silent glaring.

Oh, I needed to be careful now. Very, very careful.

'Where *exactly* is the Oracle? Where *exactly* is the—'

'Stop!' She threw up her hand. 'If you do that again, I'm leaving, and you won't ever see me again. Ever.'

I swallowed hard. She looked serious about that,

and seriously angry. 'I'm sorry,' I said. 'But I need information. In case you haven't noticed, this is getting a little more important than just respecting your feelings, Imara. I need to do this. It all looks fine here, but believe me, it's *not* fine out there in the big wide world. If you ever want to see any of it, you'd better help me. Right now.'

She blinked and looked away at the gently fluttering leaves of the oak tree that spread its shade over the car. A couple of kids sped by on bikes, and another rumbled by on a skateboard. Nobody paid us much attention. Wal-Mart parking lots were anonymous.

'You don't understand how it feels,' she said. 'Losing your will like that. Being – emptied out.'

'Don't I?'

'Well – maybe you do.' To her credit, Imara looked a little embarrassed about that. She had my memories; she knew the time I'd spent as Kevin's pet Djinn, forced into little French maid outfits, fending off his adolescent advances. 'All right. Just ask. But don't do it again. Please.'

'I won't if you'll answer.'

'Fine.' She pulled in a fast breath and turned away, not meeting my eyes. 'There are a few places – less than a dozen around the world – where the fabric between the planes of existence is paper-thin. Where the Djinn can reach up higher or down deeper. These are – holy places, would be the only way I know to put it. Conduits. Places where we can touch the Mother, where we can—' It wasn't that she was avoiding an explanation; she just couldn't find the words. 'The Oracle can be reached there. But Mom, don't mistake me: The Djinn protect these places.'

Imara wasn't using the words *holy places* lightly. I hadn't known the Djinn had a religion, other than generic Earth Mother stuff, but if they did, they'd have kept it secret. They'd been a slave race for so long that they'd protect what was precious to them.

Especially against intrusions by humans.

'Seacasket,' I said aloud, and shook my head. Because Seacasket didn't exactly look like the kind of place you'd expect to find exotic spirituality. Or maybe that was just because I couldn't quite imagine something spiritual sitting in the Wal-Mart parking lot. 'You still haven't told me where to go to find the Oracle.'

She looked deeply uncomfortable, and for a few seconds I thought that I was going to have to invoke the Rule of Three, even though that would break something fragile between us. 'It's not far.'

'Yeah, so you said. Can you take me there?'

'No!' she blurted angrily, and pounded the steering wheel in a fit of fury. 'It's not a place for humans. Even the Djinn sometimes get hurt there. You can't! I'm not even sure *I* can!'

Imara might know my experiences – might have been formed from parts of me – but she certainly didn't understand me on a very basic level. Oddly, that was comforting. She wasn't just a mirror image of me with some freaky-deaky eyes; she was her own person, separate from me.

And I could still surprise her.

'I'll find a way,' I said. 'You just show me the door. I'll get through it even if I have to pick the lock.'

It sounded like bravado – hell, it *was* bravado. I wasn't some kick-ass Djinn babe anymore; I hadn't been entirely kick-ass even when I'd been a Djinn (though I'd been fairly smug about the babe part). My Warden powers were back up and running, however, and if anything, they were considerably stronger than they had been on the night Bad Bob Biringanine had given me a Demon Mark, the gift that keeps on giving, and generally screwed up my life for good.

But I was still just human. Body and soul. All of which I was hoping to keep together for a little while longer, apocalypse notwithstanding.

Imara was thinking about it, I could see, but finally she just sighed. Maybe she did understand me, after all.

At least enough to acknowledge that I wasn't about to take 'no way in hell' for an answer.

She said, 'There's a cemetery in the centre of town. Which is convenient, because you're going to get yourself killed.'

* * *

In Seacasket, even the cemetery was photogenic. Norman Rockwell hadn't specialised in morbid art, but if he had, he'd have painted this place; it had a certain naïveté that begged for cute kids in adorable Halloween costumes to be playing hide-and-seek behind charmingly weathered gravestones. Or Disneyfied witches to be offering lemonade from a cauldron. It was the most wholesome cemetery I'd ever seen.

We parked on the street, near the town square, and walked across to the black wrought-iron fence. The gates were open, the paths in the place were fresh-raked clean white gravel, and the grass was almost impossibly green. Fat squirrels gambolled in lush spreading trees. Some of the dignified (and a few quirky) headstones were well-kept, and others had been allowed to grow with wild-flowers and vines. Not messily, though. Even the neglect looked planned.

Imara's steps slowed and stopped, and I stopped with her. She was staring at the ground, and as I watched, she lowered herself to a kneeling position on the gravel, both hands upraised, palms up.

'Imara?' No answer. 'Imara, where do I go?'

She was lost in prayer, or whatever it was. I waited for a few seconds, then looked around. Up ahead, there was a big white mausoleum. The name over the lintel read GRAYSON. The doors were shut.

I took a couple of steps towards it, gravel crunching briskly.

Imara's voice froze me. *'Don't move!'*

I teetered, then caught my balance and glanced around. There was nobody else in evidence. Just us, the squirrels, and some scolding birds who didn't think this was an appropriate place for us to be strolling.

'What is it?' I asked, trying not to move my lips. And then I realised that there were two Djinn standing, very silently, watching me. They blended in so perfectly, they'd been in plain sight the entire time . . . One was as pale as marble, with flowing white hair, dressed in shades of white and grey – an angel off its marble headstone, only with eyes the colour of rubies. The other one was standing under a tree, and maybe I was crazy, but I could have sworn that her skin was dappled in camouflage patterns that moved and shifted with the wind.

As if they'd gotten the same message, both the Djinn started moving towards me. Ruby-red eyes gleaming.

Imara swung her head to stare fiercely at me. 'Mom, dammit, if you're going, go!'

She put her hand in the small of my back and shoved. I lunged forward, off-balance, and then broke into a sprint. I dodged right, but the camouflage Djinn sprang forward like a tiger, snarling, and caught me with a backhanded blow across the face.

It was like slamming full speed into a metal bar. I staggered and went down, my head full of pain and fury, and some instinct made me roll out of the way just as a clawed hand slashed at my midsection.

'Mom!'

A blur hit the Djinn and rolled it away, snarling and clawing. Imara. I got to one knee, swaying, then fought my way upright. I tasted blood and spat out a mouthful on the cheerful green grass.

A heavy grey hand fell on my shoulder and spun me around. Up close, the tombstone-angel Djinn looked utterly terrifying. Remorseless, remote, and deadly.

It carried a dagger. Not metal . . . it didn't flash in the sunlight as it lifted towards me. Some kind of stone. I screamed and back-pedalled, summoning up a burst of wind to smack the thing in the chest.

It was a Djinn. It should have been thrown back, because Djinn are essentially air . . . only the air didn't come at my command. I could feel it *trying* to, but there was something else holding it in place. Something far, far larger than I was.

Imara was right. Running was a really good plan.

I was disoriented, but survival was a great motivator; I dodged through the tombstones, moving as fast as I could. Leaping over what I couldn't avoid. The iron-bar fence was ahead of me, topped with Gothic triangular spikes; no way was I vaulting that thing. I couldn't count on the wind to give me any lift, either. I had to make it to the gates.

It occurred to me that the Djinn were *playing* with me. Robbed of my Warden powers, I didn't have any reasonable way to fight. Imara was running interference, but I could tell at a glance that she was overmatched with a single opponent, much less two.

The Djinn were determined to drive us out of the cemetery, which meant that this was the place I needed to be.

I headed for the gates at a dead sprint, reversed in a spray of gravel, and yelled, 'Imara! I need a path!'

She was neck-deep in tiger-fighting, but she ripped free, flashed across the grass, and tackled the tombstone-angel Djinn into the trees. The tiger-Djinn was momentarily occupied with getting up.

I had a clear white gravel path leading to the centre of the cemetery, and I took it at a pace that would have clocked in respectably at the Olympics. Panic and raw determination gave me wings, and I flashed past the tiger-Djinn. It grabbed a handful of my hair, but not enough to stop me; I sobbed breathlessly at the agony as it ripped loose from my scalp, and I hit the doors of the mausoleum hard.

They opened, spilling me inside.

I continued to fall forward.

Kept on falling.

No way was it this far to the floor . . .

I opened my eyes and looked. I was floating in mid-air, or falling, or something – I *felt* like I was falling, but then that abruptly fixed itself, and my feet settled onto the ground. Or what felt like ground. There was no sky, no ground, and every side of the room looked exactly the same. It was dim, grey, and lit by what looked like a firepit in the centre.

Nothing else.

I waited, heart hammering, for some kind of a response. For the Djinn outside to come howling in here and chop me to screaming pieces.

Outside, I heard nothing. An ominous nothing.

This place had a sense of energy in it, something primal and deep. I tried going up to the aetheric to take a look, and for a second I thought that I'd just simply failed, because everything looked just the same.

Then I realised that the *room* hadn't changed, but that *I* was drawn in typical glowing aetheric shades and shadows. The room was somehow real on the aetheric plane, too.

I'd never seen anything like that, outside of the house where Jonathan had lived out on the edges of nowhere and nothing.

I felt a hot surge of anguish, thinking of Imara potentially fighting for her life outside, while I waited in here for . . . for what? What made me think the Oracle would even notice me, much less deign to talk to me?

Something floated lazily at the corner of my eye, a barely seen shadow, and I turned my head, frowning.

The Demon Mark.

It had followed me.

I backed off, terrified, trying to think of a single

thing I could do. Nothing came to mind. It had me cornered. There was no place to run, and certainly no place to hide, unless I planned to jump into the fire . . .

The Demon Mark floated towards me, then veered suddenly off target and plunged headlong into the fire.

I heard the fire *scream*.

I took a big step back from the open pit, heart racing. The fire blazed up a little, flickering red and orange. No discernible source. It looked, smelt, and radiated warmth like a genuine flame.

What had I done? Oh, my God . . . the fire. The fire was the Oracle, and I'd brought the Demon Mark right to it.

The screaming ratcheted up to a level that made me clap my hands over my ears. I blinked away tears. The incredible, heartrending *pain* in the sound . . . The Oracle was in trouble. Serious trouble. I had no idea what to do. I'd temporarily stymied the Demon Mark once, but twice was pushing it, and there was no handy geyser of power around for me to use as bait. The Oracle was the most powerful thing in the room.

The fire suddenly blazed up and out, fanning my face with heat; I scrambled backward and got to my feet. As I hovered there, torn between a total lack of options, a hand reached out of the centre of the flame, and flailed on the stone floor. Groping for my help. It wasn't human, exactly – it was molten, white-hot, with curved talons instead of fingernails. Where it touched the floor, stone smoked and melted. Claws left inch-deep channels in the softening granite.

The screaming ate at my soul. I had to do something. *Anything*.

The hand flailed again, fingers opening and closing in agony. It was a stupid thing to do, but I couldn't stand being the cause of this. I dropped to my knees, sucked in a steadying breath, and tried to remember what Lewis had shown me back at the Wardens' offices.

And then, before I could think of the ten thousand reasons to stop, I reached out and grabbed the wrist of that flaming, white-hot hand. The hand instantly twisted, and closed around my forearm. Talons dug in, cruelly sharp and hot as acid. I hauled, hard, and felt something pulling back, trying to yank me inside that searing fire. I could smell the greasy stink of hair starting to fry. My hair. *God*, I hated fire.

I pulled harder, with every muscle in my body, and I got the Oracle's head and shoulders out of the bonfire. It was human*ish*, if not human in form. Broad, strong shoulders. Skin – if you could call it skin – that had the burnished metallic look of a statue, but throbbed with living, swirling patterns of heat. Tongues of flame rose off of his back, his outstretched arms . . .

When he lifted his head, still screaming, I saw the Demon Mark, flailing away on the surface of his molten skin. Trying to eat through and devour him.

The Mark was turning restlessly, twisting. Where it touched him, I could see a hideous blackened patch. It seemed to be spreading. The thing was toxic to him.

If he was connected to the Mother – connected directly, in a way we mere humans weren't, and more than the average Djinn – how much more damage would this do once it got into her bloodstream? I had a sudden, sickening comprehension of just how good a deed I'd done earlier in evicting the Demon Mark from the geyser of power outside of New York.

Until I'd screwed it up here.

The Oracle was looking at me. There was a suggestion of eyes in that heat-blurred face. The scream continued, but there was even more of an edge to it now, as if he was trying to convince me.

Beg me.

I really wasn't the self-sacrificing type. If somebody had told me that I needed to voluntarily take a Demon Mark a year ago to save the world, I'd have burnt rubber to get away from the idea. But things had changed. *I* had changed. I had a daughter out there, and people I loved.

I had too much to lose to walk away and save my own skin. And besides, this was my screw-up, and I had to make it right.

I reached out and put my hand flat over the Demon Mark. This time, I did it deliberately.

I gagged at the squirming cold touch of it, but I

didn't pull away. The flames beating hot against my skin didn't burn me – I hung on to enough of my limited Fire Warden ability to manage that – but I felt the Oracle's claws raking the tender skin of my left forearm. I focused on that pain, clear and pure, and let it flow through me to wall me off from the horrible sensation of the Demon Mark squirming under my fingers.

No way was I more powerful than the Oracle. The Demon Mark ignored me. It always, inevitably went with the bigger bonfire . . .

I was going to have to do this the hard way.

I gagged at the thought, but I closed my hand into a fist around the Demon Mark – in reality and in the aetheric – and began to pull it off.

It felt cold and slimy as a handful of thrashing worms, and it didn't want to let go. It stretched like rubbery elastic, and then it came loose with a sudden, wet smack in my hands. If I hadn't kept hold of it on the aetheric, it wouldn't have worked. If I hadn't been as strong a power as I was, it wouldn't have worked, either, but the Demon Mark decided to let go of the tough-shelled Oracle in favour of a softer target.

The Oracle collapsed face down on the floor, and the saw-edged screaming came to a halt. I heard my sobbing breaths echoing in the room, and then fire exploded out around his body in a blinding white blaze, hot enough to singe my hair and drive me all the way back against the cool stone wall. I squeezed my eyes shut because it was getting brighter, and brighter, and I could still see the glow even through my tight-clenched lids. I closed my fist over the nauseatingly eager squirm of the Demon Mark. It was burrowing under my skin, sliding cold through my pores. It was happening faster this time, and the sensation was so horrible that I was weeping, sobbing, shaking with the urge to fling the thing away from me. It was like being stabbed with a wet, slimy knife in exquisitely slow motion.

I had to get rid of this thing, even if it meant losing my hand.

I banged through the door of the mausoleum and stumbled back out into the brilliant sunshine. It felt cold as ice to me, after the heat inside. I kept my fist clenched and staggered out, trying to think of something, *anything* I could do.

Lightning. It's the visual signal of an energy shift between potential and actual energy, with light and heat as the by-products. Billions of electrons have to line up in a chain for lightning to actualise, and because like draws like, a chain forming out of the sky will be drawn to a chain building up out of the ground, and when that last electron snaps into place, and the energy transfers, it has so much power that it can vaporise steel, for a fraction of a second, at least.

It *might* be able to stun, or kill, a Demon Mark . . . if I could manage a direct hit.

I pushed at the artificial tension holding the sky together overhead. The power controlling it was vast and hard-edged, but fragile. I battered at it with the strength of desperation until I felt it crack, and saw energy flare up among the gathering clouds.

Enough. More than enough.

Oh *God*, this was going to hurt . . .

In one desperate wrench, I grabbed the Demon Mark, ripped it loose, and threw it on the ground. It seemed unnaturally heavy. It hit the grass and immediately began to scuttle back towards me, moving like a spider on PCP.

It was too close, but I triggered the lightning anyway as the thing leapt for me.

You don't see it, when that kind of power hits that close to you; you feel the overwhelming burn, and for a few seconds afterward, you really can't be sure that the lightning didn't actually hit you, because the coronal effect is so strong.

So it took a few seconds for my mind to fight off the sound, light, and pressure, of the near-miss and reconstruct from the evidence what had happened. There was a tree on fire, five feet away. The top half of it was charred black, and part of it had been blown clean off. Limbs had been blown off and were still flaming on the green, green graves.

There was a smoking black hole in the grass where the Demon Mark had been. Either I'd killed it, or I'd convinced it to find an easier snack elsewhere.

My knees buckled, and I went hard to the gravel. Ouch. When I pitched forward, the heels of my hands dug into sharp-edged rock, and I saw blood spattering the pristine white stones, dripping from my nose and mouth.

I swallowed hard, and then Imara was in front of me, eyes wide, grabbing for my elbow. She looked a little worse for wear – clothes torn, a few cuts and bruises. Her eyes were terrified.

'I'm fine,' I said. My voice seemed to come faint and from a long distance out. 'Are you OK?'

'We have to go, *now*. The Djinn are angry—'

Except that apparently the Djinn were so angry that they'd . . . left. No sign of the two that Imara had been going toe-to-toe with, which was odd. Just us, the mausoleum, the trees, the headstones.

'Not yet,' I said. 'I'm not finished.'

'Mom, no!'

'Stay here.' I climbed back to my feet, swaying, bracing myself on her shoulder for a long moment before turning back to the mausoleum.

There was a Djinn standing in front of it. Not really a Djinn, though – more. Other. He was . . . beautiful. All Djinn are made of fire, at some level, but he was fire personified, fire eternal. His body could barely contain the heat and the fury, and it rippled in patterns right under his translucent skin.

His eyes were flame. His hair was smouldering red. He was the most gorgeously wild thing I'd ever seen. Terrifying and utterly sensual. He didn't say a word to me, just stared, and after a moment, he extended his burning hand towards me. I stayed still, aware that my heart was beating like a gong, that I was dripping with sweat and terror. Aware that if he touched me, I'd probably burn like oil left on a hot engine.

I'd healed the Oracle, or at least freed him from his prison. There was still a discoloured black stain on his chest, just where his heart would have been in a human, but he seemed . . . better.

He didn't touch me. He just cocked his head to one side, watching.

I heard a rustle of clothing. Imara was down on the ground, abased, hiding her face. I suspected that the Oracle wasn't someone who got out much, and when he did, he caused quite a stir.

I was too giddy to be impressed.

'Favour for a favour,' I said. 'I need to get a message to the Mother. Can you help me?'

He didn't make a sound. If I hadn't heard that tremendously awful shrieking earlier, I'd have thought he was mute.

He continued to hold out his hand. It shimmered and flickered with heat, like the surface of the sun.

'Don't,' Imara whispered. She'd raised her head, watching, but flinched again and hid her eyes when the Oracle turned his attention towards her. 'Please, don't.'

I slowly extended my hand and touched his.

Glory rolled through me, and I exploded into flame.

I heard Imara scream, and I wanted to tell her it was all right, but words were useless. Meaningless. What I became in that moment was . . . transcendent, and for an instant, an *instant*, I could feel everything. Everyone. I could feel the long, slow, sleeping pulse of the Mother. I could taste the metallic chill of her nightmares.

It flooded into me in images rather than words. Forests burning. Rivers contaminated with greasy pollution. Skies roiling with black filth. Oil-covered birds. Dead, floating fish. Butchered whales. Clubbed dolphins. Death, and death, and death. Cows screaming in slaughterhouses. Pesticides poisoning everything for miles, from the smallest insect to the largest predatory birds.

Humans, a stinking flood on the Earth, unregulated by her natural defences. Arrogant. Untouchable as a species by any but the greatest of predators . . . Earth herself.

A furious desire to bring us to heel.

No. No, we're not like that!

I tried sending a counter-message, but the poison had filtered into me, too; what could I say about that? It was true. All true. We were a plague upon the Earth, and we deserved what we got . . .

No!

I struggled to fight it back. Images of people working

together. Of groups on beaches, pouring salt water over stranded whales, struggling to keep them alive until tides could come to the rescue. Environmental specialists restoring oceans and waters, reclaiming them from pollution. *We care. We know. We try.* Laws to protect endangered species. Jane Goodall, living with her primates. National parks, carefully tended. Children nursing injured animals back to health. *We're not monsters. We're not your enemy.*

It wasn't enough. I felt it swept away in the black tide of fury coming from the other side, and then something batted at me, vast and languid, and sent me flying.

The contact between my fingers and the Oracle's broke, and I staggered backward, moaning. My clothes were smoking.

The Oracle was gone. The conduit was closed.

I had no idea what to do now. For the first time I could remember, I'd completely, utterly failed. Flat busted. I wanted to sit down against the cool marble and weep, because I felt like I'd fought so hard, and come to the end of things with nothing but exhaustion and despair to show for it.

But I wasn't much for giving up. Not for more than a few cold, lightless seconds. There had to be something else I could do, and I'd have to think of it. Figure it out.

Maybe I actually would have, if I'd had the time. The fact was that I didn't. Imara, helping steady me with an arm around my shoulders, froze. 'Oh, no.'

A man in a natty grey suit turned the corner on the street and entered the cemetery. Tall, strong, perfect posture.

Ashan. Jonathan's third-in-command, after David. Heir apparent to the throne, who hadn't gotten what he thought he deserved.

Things were definitely worse.

Chapter Five

Ashan was intimidating as hell, and he knew it; his predominant colour scheme was grey, with a little silver for highlights. As always, he looked elegantly tailored. A double-breasted suit, the colour of mourning doves. A pale grey shirt. A teal-blue tie, with eyes to match. Ashan, of all the Djinn, struck me as less than human; he gave the impression that he just wore a bipedal shape with opposable thumbs for convenience, but he gave it no more importance than that. His movements had that liquid grace that all the Djinn seemed to possess but which they didn't usually flaunt quite so openly. Even Rahel seemed more part of my world.

He walked steadily towards us down that gravel path. There were dark spots marring it. Bloodstains, all of them mine. A flaming branch was blocking his path, and he kicked it casually out of the way with so much power that it hit one of the quaint weathered tombstones and snapped it off like a broken tooth.

Imara made a low sound of terror. I pushed her behind me.

'Ashan,' I said. 'Thanks for your concern, but really, we're fine. No need to be worried.'

'Freak,' he said. 'Filthy grovelling worm. You defile the ground you touch.' Voice like nothing at all. Grey, monotone, flat. No anger, but that didn't make me feel any better. Ashan didn't need to be angry. He just needed to be awake. 'You defiled the Oracle with your stench.'

'I saved the Oracle from a Demon Mark,' I said, and watched his expression. No surprise there. 'You knew. You knew he was infected. Why didn't you come running to save him?'

'You have no right to be here.' His empty eyes flashed towards Imara. 'Either of you.'

'Leave the kid out of it. If you want to smack somebody around—'

He moved too fast for me to see, and suddenly there was a stinging agony on the side of my face, and I was on my hands and knees. He'd slapped me. A leisurely, open-handed slap. If he'd used his fist, he'd have snapped my neck. 'Do not speak to me again.'

Imara threw herself in his path. 'You're not hurting my—'

Ashan didn't even break stride. He backhanded her so hard, she left the ground, twisted in mid-air, and flew twenty feet to slam into a massive grey headstone. I watched her, horrified. She didn't move after landing.

When I looked back at Ashan, it was too late. He grabbed my throat and dragged me kissing-close. I scrabbled and scratched at his hand, but it was like trying to pry steel with your fingernails. Overhead, dark clouds scudded in from the sea, moving fast and high, as if they wanted a ringside seat for the action. I could sense a certain eagerness up there. Storms always loved to see Weather Wardens getting their comeuppance.

'You,' Ashan said with gentle precision, his lips to my ear, 'should have stayed far, far away from here. You're too late, in any case. I've told the Mother the whole filthy history of humanity. None of Jonathan's benevolent, wilful ignorance. None of David's foolish sentiment. The *truth.*'

'Truth?' I croaked. 'Or just your version?'

He was right. I should have headed the other way, fast, the minute I'd seen him turn the corner, but with Ashan, as with any major predator who has you at his mercy, it's best not to run unless you have an even shot at getting away. Bravado's the only real defence.

'You know the thing I like best about human beings?' he asked, and took hold of my right arm with his big, cold left hand. 'You break so easily.'

He pressed with his pale, white thumb. That was all. Just his thumb, and I felt the hot electric snap of a bone breaking, followed by a wet cascade of agony. I couldn't even scream. Couldn't get it past his choking hand.

His thumb moved. There were two bones in the arm, and he found the second with unerring precision. *Snap*.

My shriek came out a strangled whimper. I saw red, and stars, and I wanted to heave but I'd just choke faster. And Ashan wasn't finished with me, that much was obvious.

'Call him,' Ashan murmured in my ear. He hadn't so much as raised his voice a single degree in temperature. 'Call your pet for me. He'll save you if you call him. He won't let me kill you.'

I wanted to. Badly. But I knew all too well what Ashan was doing; he wanted David here, alone, with a lover and a daughter to try to protect. David had power – boatloads of it, inherited from Jonathan – but Ashan wasn't far behind. And he wanted David's place as the hub at the centre of the Djinn universe. He wanted to remove the only real threat to his power.

But mostly, he just wanted to do to David what he was doing to me. Terrorise, humiliate, torment.

'No.' I managed to mouth the word. I could protect David, if nothing else. His right hand flexed, and I felt my throat flex with it. It would be easy for him to kill me. Too easy.

'We'll see.' He still had hold of my arm, and now he deliberately, slowly, twisted it. I screamed again, but he'd trapped the sound in my throat where it frantically beat inside, like a bird in a trap. Red-hot wires of agony ran through me. It was like low-budget electrocution. I could feel tears streaming down my face and over his hand, and I was staring pleadingly at his blank teal-blue eyes. Looking for mercy. Looking for anything I could recognise as remotely human.

He smiled. It was the coldest expression I could imagine seeing on a face that pretended to be flesh and blood.

Somehow, I knew that the serene little town of Seacasket hadn't noticed a thing, and wouldn't. Ashan could stand here in broad daylight and pull me apart like a rag doll, and nobody would notice a thing.

Just when I thought that he was really going to do it, he dropped me. I fell painfully hard to my knees, hugged my broken arm to my chest, and swayed on the verge of passing out. My wandering eyes focused on the crumpled form near the tombstones. Imara was still down. Not moving. I felt something go still inside me. The swirling darkness that had threatened to drag me down blew away, leaving me cold and utterly clear.

I gulped back the tears and the terror, and shifted my gaze up, to Ashan.

'You know what?' I croaked. It sounded ragged, and not quite sane. 'You and me, we have an understanding. Fair game. But I don't care how badass you think you are, you shouldn't have hurt my daughter.'

The artificially calm weather of Seacasket had been shattered by the tinkering I'd done to produce my lightning bolt; I reached out, grabbed the air, and started shaking. The world was going to hell anyway, and I wasn't about to let Ashan do this. Not to Imara. Not to me.

Not without a fight.

'You can't,' he said flatly.

Bullshit, I couldn't. I was a Warden. I had the power, and the lack of conscience to go with it. I'd had a Demon Mark, once upon a time. Maybe it had rotted something inside me that should have been thinking of the big picture, I don't know, but right at that moment, I was all about the world within fifty feet, and my child lying unconscious and at Ashan's nonexistent mercy.

Fifty feet happened to include the mausoleum that held the Oracle, too.

'You started it,' I said. I continued to shake up the system. It wasn't easy, especially with agony throbbing through my body in waves, but I was making progress. There was serious instability in the atmosphere. And offshore, the storm that had been hanging back saw its shot, and started rolling in with the wind at its back. Huge black sails of clouds, belling tight in the wind. Lightning was a scimitar in its teeth, and yo ho, mateys, the pirates were coming ashore.

'Stop,' Ashan said, and grabbed me by the hair. I grinned at him. Must have been gruesome, bloody teeth, bloodshot eyes.

'Make me.' I flipped electron polarities in the air, turning and turning and turning. Locking the chain in place with a sudden furious surge of energy, grounding energy from the storm clouds. 'I don't need David to whip your punk ass.'

Lightning hissed up from the ground, down from the clouds, and he was caught in the middle.

Flesh and blood vaporised instantly, along with all of Ashan's nice couture. I was too close. I caught the corona, was blown backward into the mausoleum wall, and ended up on the ground, screaming into a mouthful of grass because my broken arm had just gone up five steps on the ten-point agony scale, to fourteen. Man, I was trashed.

But Ashan was vapour.

That didn't mean he was dead, not at all, just not manifesting properly in human form. Didn't matter much to him, in terms of hurting him in any lasting way, but I was willing to bet that it had stung. He wasn't exactly roaring right back for a rematch. I lifted my head and saw him trying to coalesce out of the mist, and focused the wind into a hard, narrow channel, straight for him. It hit him like a cannon, blasted the mist apart, and this time, he came together more slowly. Hanging back.

I didn't bother to get up as his face formed in the fog. Not flesh and bone, more of a ghost-image. Spooky. I sounded a hell of a lot more confident than I felt. 'Turn around and leave, Ashan, because I swear, the next thing I hit will mean a lot more to you than your skin.'

I sensed his smug disbelief. So I hit the mausoleum with a lightning bolt.

The world went nuts. *Really* nuts. Winds howling, lightning stabbing all over the sky in an insane display of fury, ground rumbling . . . hailstones pelted out of the clouds, the size of golf balls. A couple hit me, and if my arm hadn't already been overwhelming me with agony, that would have been serious pain.

Ashan managed to form himself into pseudoflesh – not quite human, for certain, because he was misting out just below the hips into a grey swirl of fog. He still clung to the business suit for the top half.

But he had something to say. His eyes had gone completely dark. Lightless as space.

'You'll die for that. No matter how many friends you have among the Djinn. This is a sacred place.'

'Bring 'em on,' I said grimly. 'Maybe you'd like to explain why you let the Oracle suffer like that. Unless you were just blaming it on poor old humanity. Again.' I struggled up to my knees, then somehow to my feet. It was more of a stagger than a graceful rise, but the fact I was standing was pretty much a victory. 'Guess what? I talked to her. And now she knows that you've been lying to her, you bastard.'

Which was a blatant lie, because I'd gotten zero sense she'd paid the slightest attention to me, but hopefully Ashan couldn't know that. The air was full of threat, his and mine and something else, something vast. I was guessing that Mom was telling us kids to quit, she didn't care who'd started it. Of course, *this* mom was capable of administering a smack to the bottom that would flatten half the eastern seaboard.

Maybe I'd been a little hasty, using the last lightning strike. But it had been that, or roll over and die, not something I was very good at doing.

Not with my child at stake.

Ashan just . . . vanished. Not so much a puff of smoke as a wasting away, tatters on the gusting wind. I put my unbroken hand against the wall of the mausoleum and leant for a few minutes, breathing hard, trying not to faint; my knees buckled a couple of times, but somehow I got upright. The storm was growling overhead, but when I read its pedigree, it was still a punk, not that much of a threat. I'd unsettled it, for certain, and upped it a few degrees on the dangerometer. I needed to smooth it down.

And I'd get around to it. But first, I stumbled across grass, around tilting old headstones, and collapsed next to my daughter, who was lying motionless on the ground.

'Imara?' I reached out and touched her.

My hand went through her. Not in the way that it would have if she'd been, say, consumed by little blue sparklies that seeped in from an alien dimension, but as if she was mostly vapour, held together by memory and will. She didn't move. I withdrew my hand hastily, and used it to cradle my broken arm across my chest. Damn, that hurt. I saw stars and jagged red streaks, and managed somehow to breathe through the pain. 'Imara, can you hear me?'

If she could, she wasn't giving any sign. She was in a kind of there and not-there state, lying face down on the grass. I couldn't grab her to move her, or turn her over. All I could do was call her name.

Rain pattered down, cold and hard on my exposed skin. I sat on the grass and shivered, next to my unconscious Djinn child, and fought the urge to call for David. He'd come, I knew that. But I wasn't entirely sure that it would be safe for him; if Ashan was still hanging out there, watching, this could still turn wrong.

Not that it was in any way right to begin with.

After I while, I noticed that Imara's clothes began to absorb water. I reached down and lightly touched the fabric. It had texture and weight.

At my touch, she exploded into movement, like a startled deer – up and on her feet, white-faced and wild-eyed. Scanning the skies, then the land, then focusing on me.

I wasn't sure she even remembered who I was. One thing was certain – there was so much menace coming off her that I didn't dare move. She'd have whacked me halfway across the cemetery, just the way she'd been hit, and without a doubt, it would have snapped more than my arm.

The panic cleared from her eyes. 'Mom?' She was across the intervening space in seconds, crouched next to me, reaching out. I was cold, wet, and shaking, and I was probably going into shock, if I hadn't already booked a full vacation package there.

She was speaking a liquid language, words that sounded fast and golden in my ears, and I didn't know what she was saying, but I knew it was in the language of the Djinn. I recognised it, from moments with David.

'Hey,' I said weakly. 'English, kiddo.'

She felt warm. So warm. I vaguely remembered leaning on her support as I staggered out of the cemetery and onto the street. The Camaro was sitting right where we'd parked it, looking bold and sassy through the downpour. Imara got me in the passenger seat.

It was all over. I'd failed. I'd just . . . failed.

'Mom?' Imara sounded worried as she put the car in gear and scratched gears getting us out of town. 'Mom, where do we go?'

I had no fucking idea. I turned my face away, towards the world outside. The world that was going to die because I'd been inadequate to the task of saving it.

'Find the nearest Warden,' I said. 'Maybe there's something we can do to help.'

'With what?'

I shrugged, one-shouldered. The other one felt like

ground glass had been driven into the joint. 'Whatever.' I wasn't very interested.

Imara kept casting anxious looks my way, but I didn't say another word.

I had no idea how long the drive was, but it wasn't long enough for me to come up with a decent bright idea. So Imara just followed instructions and drove me to the nearest Warden.

That turned out to be Emily, the Earth and Fire Warden who'd given me crap back at the Headquarters building. She lived in a one-dog town in the middle of Nowhere County, Maine, and when Imara coasted the Camaro to a stop on the gravel driveway, she parked it next to a mud-spattered Jeep.

The Warden was home. She came to the door when Imara knocked, stared at my kid as if she was the Second Coming, then at me like the devil incarnate.

'Oh,' she said flatly. 'They sent you. Great.'

She turned and walked into the house, not bothering to show us in. I was too sick and in too much pain, not to mention despair, to care about that. I followed her to a homey-looking living room, with one wall painted a somewhat unfortunate shade of cinnamon; Indian blankets and southwestern art lined the walls. The furniture was chunky wood, deliberately primitive. Knickknacks ran to kachina dolls and dreamcatchers.

I knew Emily vaguely. We'd never been friends, or even what I'd call acquaintances, but we'd worked on a couple of projects together, and shared a desk at the national Warden call centre before, the one Wardens use to yell for help when things turn really bad. Emily hadn't exactly been a people person then, and I doubted she'd mended her ways. Earth Wardens in general tended to be either hippies or hermits; she definitely fell into the hermit category. Apparently, the Fire Warden tendencies hadn't done much to influence her basic character.

She was wearing what she'd had on the last time I'd seen her – baggy blue jeans and a nondescript tunic top, one that stretched. Bare feet, that was the only real change. Her short-cropped hair feathered around her blunt-featured face, and the scowl looked at home on her face, worn in deep.

I sank down in a chair and cradled my broken arm closer, trying not to scream.

'Huh,' Emily said, and jerked her chin at it. 'Looks bad.'

'Thanks.'

'Wasn't a compliment. You want some help?'

'If it wouldn't put you out.'

Imara was standing indecisively a few feet away, clearly trying to get a signal from me as to what, if anything, to do. I didn't have time. Emily bent down, took my arm in her big, strong hands, and did a twist-yank thing that hurt so bad, I teetered on the edge of darkness.

'There,' she said in satisfaction. 'Hold still.'

She put her hand around the break, and I tried to obey her order. Not easy. The throbbing agony was hard to ignore, and then the sense of burning, and then the deep itching. The burning just got worse, until it felt as if I were holding my arm over a Bunsen burner. I wanted to snatch it back, but I knew better.

I'd felt this before.

It took about fifteen minutes. Emily wasn't the world's most powerful Earth Warden, though she was competent enough; when she let go, the arm felt hot and sensitive, but more or less healed.

'You're going to want to go easy on it,' she said. 'The mend's still green. Let it cure.'

'Sure,' I croaked. My throat felt horribly dry. 'Water?'

Without a word, she went into the kitchen and came back with a glass, which I drained without stopping for breath. She refilled it. I managed another half a glass before I decided that too much might make me gag.

'We don't have time for this,' Emily said. 'The fire's burning hot out there.'

'Fire?' I asked.

'You didn't come to fight the fire?'

'Not – exactly.'

Emily leant back in her big leather chair, frowning at me. It was covered in what looked like the hide of a Holstein. A little too identifiable for me to be comfortable with it. I didn't like knowing the genetic heritage of my furniture.

'Then what the hell do you want, a *meeting*?' She made it sound like the filthiest curse she could imagine. It probably was, for her. Come to think of it, I didn't much approve of them, either.

'No,' I said, and sighed. 'I just . . . You need help. I was in the area. Let's leave it at that.'

Her frown grooved deeper, and she tilted her head to one side, considering the problem of me. 'Yeah, you're going to be real useful, the shape you're in.' She shook her head. 'Not that beggars can be choosers. How do you feel?' She didn't sound like she much cared, but she was forced to ask the question.

'Better,' I said. It wasn't a lie, really. I'd been at rock-bottom earlier, now I was a quarter-inch above the ground. Everything's relative. 'Thanks for this.'

'What, the arm? Part of the job.' Emily cocked a thumb at Imara, who had settled back in a corner, watching us. 'Thought you said we weren't supposed to trust them anymore. What, you don't have to obey your own rules?'

I decided not to engage on that one. 'You don't have a Djinn, right?'

'Never needed one.' She sounded as if those who did were clearly lacking some important feature, like guts. 'She going to go nuts and kill us?'

'Well, wouldn't that be exciting?' I sighed. 'Imara? You going to go nuts and kill us?'

She thought about it. Gravely. 'Not quite yet.'

'Right. Keep us informed.'

I thought for sure that Emily would bring up the resemblance between me and Imara, but she wasn't that observant. Her eyes darted between us for a few seconds, bright but not registering any connections, and then she decided to shift the conversational ground. 'What do you know about fighting fires?'

'Pretty much what every Weather Warden knows.' From the flash in her eyes, that wasn't something that met with her approval. 'Maybe I can wing it.'

Emily was old school. She fixed me with a narrow stare. 'No, you won't wing it. I'll call up Paul and get a real Fire Warden up here.'

'I thought Lewis was—'

'I don't take orders from Lewis Orwell.' Didn't like him much, either, from the unpleasant twist of her mouth around his name. A lot of Earth Wardens didn't care for him, for some reason. I think it was because he kept showing them up. That would especially bother Emily, Miss I-don't-have-a-Djinn-because-I'm-too-badass-to-need-one. 'Look, this is my territory. There's a chain of command. Lewis isn't even part of the Wardens, as far as I'm concerned; he turned his back on us long ago. If he's what we've got for leadership these days, we're in trouble.'

'Lewis—'

She cut me off with a sharp gesture. 'And the last I heard, *you* were out of the Wardens completely.

Anyway, it doesn't matter. I'm working too hard to keep things together around here to worry about politics. So don't bother with the campaign speeches. What are my chances of getting somebody who knows firefighting from a hole in the ground out here?'

'Chances?' If I kept repeating things, she had every right to stick me in a cage and call me a parrot. 'Not too good. I think I'm what you're going to get.'

She sniffed. 'In other words, not much.'

I kept my mouth shut and shook my head. She let out a long, slow breath and sat back in her slaughtered-cow chair. I wondered if she'd killed it herself. Well, that wasn't exactly fair. She was an Earth Warden. The cow had probably died of natural causes.

'I heard a rumour there was some other organisation out there. Other than the Wardens,' Emily said. 'Any idea how to contact them?'

'Lewis was handling that. I don't know how far he got with it. How bad is this?'

'Bad,' she said. 'Real bad.'

'Then we should get moving,' I said, and levered myself to my feet. The world swam. I sat down again, and leant my head back against the couch cushions and moaned. When I tried to adjust myself to a more comfortable position, the arm stabbed a protest into my shoulder. Some Earth Warden she was. Hadn't been trying very hard, had she?

Imara was next to me, down on one knee, one long, graceful hand on my shoulder. Sending waves of warmth through me. She wasn't a full Djinn, she couldn't really heal me, just take away the pain temporarily. Still felt nice, though. Nobody turns down magic morphine.

'You can't do this,' she said. 'You need rest.'

'I'm good.'

'No.' She gave me a long, significant look from those breathtaking Djinn eyes. 'I won't allow it.'

I started to say, *Who made you the mommy?* but I wasn't about to let this degenerate into a mother-daughter squabble in front of Emily. Who was looking far too interested, anyway.

'Your Djinn there's probably right,' Emily said. 'Fact is, the shape you're in, I wouldn't recommend you take on a campfire, much less a forest fire,' she said. 'You took some pretty good knocks. A good hard impact, and you'll break those bones loose again. No help for it; it's going to hurt while it's healing.'

Clearly, she wasn't Lewis in the healing department, which I couldn't really resent. She'd helped me out when I needed it.

And then she spoilt my attempt at charity by saying, 'And besides, I really don't want to babysit you out there.'

Imara oriented on Emily like a cruise missile. 'She can do as she pleases.' Typical kid. Whatever the adult's position was, take the opposing view. Hell, two seconds ago she'd been trying to talk me out of going.

Emily barely spared Imara a glance, which was pretty gutsy, considering. 'Sure. She can please shut up while I borrow her Djinn for the duration.'

Oh, crap. I remembered Emily back at Warden HQ, arguing for the release of more Djinn from the reserves. Of course she'd be all about co-opting Imara. I should have seen it coming. Would have, if I hadn't been half-crazy with pain.

Imara growled low in her throat. 'I won't leave her,' she said.

'Not your choice,' I said sternly. 'Look, Emily, I'm low on patience, I'm in pain, and no way are you using her to fight a forest fire. I appreciate what you've done for me, but—'

'I said, I'm taking your Djinn,' Emily said bluntly. 'You don't want to make me take it to a full-on fight. You'd lose, the condition you're in.'

Imara moved, unasked, and came right up in Emily's space, close and – I was sure – burning up with menace. Emily went rigid with fear. As well she should. 'Keep a leash on her,' Emily said.

'Imara?' I asked. 'Relax. We're just talking. Aren't we?'

Emily nodded jerkily. Angry. 'Yes.'

'Then I think I'm ready to leave,' I said. 'Imara, go get the car revved up, would you?'

'I don't like leaving you with her.'

'Emily's a Warden,' I said. 'We understand each other.'

Imara didn't like it, but she threw me a warning look, and vanished.

'You can't,' Emily said flatly. 'You're not strong enough to leave.'

'Funny how that is. Your threat to steal Imara put all that in perspective.' I proved it by getting to my feet. The world did that liquid-shimmy thing, but I stayed upright and reasonably stable. 'You said you didn't have time for this, and neither do I. Good luck, Emily, whatever your crisis is right now. I'll find somebody who appreciates my help.'

'Wait.'

I didn't. I headed for the door. But when I got there, I found the handle wouldn't turn. Not at all. It wasn't the dead bolt . . . The metal was simply frozen in place.

I didn't bother to look behind me. 'Emily,' I said, 'let's not do this. I'm tired, I'm cranky, I'm dirty, and my arm hurts like hell. I am *not* in the mood to play. Just let me get out of here, and I'll pretend that you're not begging for a fight, because by God if you want one, you're threatening the right girl.'

Earth Wardens have power over growing things, living things, and also over metals and woods. The door wasn't going to open if Emily didn't want it to do so, not unless an Earth Warden with greater abilities stepped in. And it was unlikely I'd be able to blow it open, either, not without bringing the whole house down with it. Our powers weren't necessarily the kind that cancelled each other out. Imara was an ace in the hole, of course, but I hesitated to put her to use. I wasn't really interested in damaging one of the few surviving Wardens, given the current state of the world.

'Sorry,' Emily said. 'I've got some real problems here. You can be of use.'

I sighed and turned around to face her. 'OK, then, let me ask you this: How am I supposed to trust a Warden who holds back on the healing just to bogart my Djinn? Because you could have at least fixed the arm, Emily. That was a low blow.'

She went just a shade paler, but held her ground. She'd never lacked in guts . . . just brains. 'They say you're behind all this.'

'All of what?'

'Bad Bob. The rips in the aetheric. The Djinn going crazy. Is it true?'

That hit me with a cold, hard shock . . . Definitely, I'd been responsible for Bad Bob getting his comeuppance, not that many people were ever going to believe he'd actually deserved it. And David and I together had been responsible for the poisoning of the aetheric, when he'd created me as a Djinn. And as for the Djinn going nuts – well, I wasn't sure I had sole responsibility for all that, but I probably couldn't sidestep it altogether, either. If it hadn't been for my actions, and David's actions, Jonathan wouldn't be dead right now, the Djinn agreement would still be peacefully in place, and the Earth would be sleeping quietly.

I elected not to say any of that, however. I just set my jaw and stared back at her, daring her to continue.

'The fire's across the border, in Canada,' she said. 'It started small, but it's growing. The Wardens overseeing that territory are dead. Lewis says they can't spare anybody else, last time I checked. I'm on my way there, and I need your Djinn. I'm not going to apologise for doing what's necessary.'

'She's not my Djinn,' I said. 'Nobody owns them anymore.'

'Yeah. Yet you're riding around with one as your chauffeur.'

'It's complicated.'

'Obviously. And there are major population centres in the path of a Class Four wildfire. That's a little complicated, too.' She hesitated, then locked her eyes on mine. Surly and difficult, she might be, but I had never known her to be a liar. 'I need your help. It's just me and another Fire Warden who's already there. Those people need somebody to save them, and we're it.'

Truth was, I agreed with her. If I turned my back on people who actually needed saving, I was losing my way. Losing my honour. Something inside me insisted that you couldn't save humanity by sacrificing your principles.

I didn't like the way Emily had elected to do this, but I could understand why she'd mousetrapped me. She was desperate. I'd have done the same thing, in her place. Because the lives I'd save would be more important than the nebulous big picture. Maybe that made me weak. Maybe that made me unsuitable for the role of great hero. Lewis would have walked away without hesitation – with regret, not hesitation – but I wasn't, and could never be, Lewis.

'I'm not putting Imara in danger,' I said.

'But—'

'She's my daughter, Emily. My daughter.'

Emily's mouth opened in surprise, then closed. She finally, reluctantly, nodded.

'Tell me what you need,' I said. 'I'll do what I can.'

'You'd damn well better.'

'Oh, and—?' I made a gesture with my sore arm. She looked ashamed. Briefly.

'Might as well,' she said, and reached out to finish up the healing. 'You're no good to me passed out.'

Imara wasn't any too supportive of my decision to hang around and brush up on my firefighting. 'This isn't a good idea,' she said. 'You're not well. And the fire's too big.'

We were standing outside, by the car. I put a hand on the smooth, satin finish, then scrubbed away my fingerprints. 'You're probably right,' I said. 'But I can't walk away from it, either. Emily might be a bitch, but she's right. And I'm a Warden. I'm sworn to protect.'

'There are others to do this kind of thing.'

'Others who aren't here. I'm here. And it's my job, Imara.' I looked up at her, and saw the worry on her face. 'Relax, kiddo. It's not my first dance. Not my last, either. Emily's a very competent Fire Warden, and if there's a Fire Warden already working on this, I can work the weather angle. We can end this thing.'

Her eyes went distant for a few seconds, then snapped back. 'There are no Djinn,' she said.

'What?'

'No Djinn near the fire,' she said. I must have looked blank. 'Djinn are drawn to fire. The bigger, the better. They leave human form and . . . bathe in it, I guess you'd say. Renew themselves. You remember what it was like to feel sunlight in Djinn form?'

Slow, sweet, orgasmic pleasure. Yeah, I remembered.

'If the Djinn aren't coming to *this* fire,' she said, 'that means there is something else happening here. It isn't natural. And it isn't – it isn't safe.'

'Not for you,' I agreed. 'If the Djinn are staying away, I want you to do the same thing. Stay away. In fact, stay here and watch the car. Or go talk to your father, find out what we can do since we didn't exactly knock it out of the park in Seacasket. Right?'

'I'm not leaving you!'

I reached out and fitted my hands around her cheeks. Djinn skin, burning hot. 'Yes,' I said. 'You are. I need you to find out what we do next, Imara. That's very important. In fact, it's absolutely critical.'

'But—'

'Don't make me order you around.' I pulled her into a fierce, warm hug. 'Just go. I'll be all right.'

'Is it because – I know I'm not – not as powerful as I should be. As you need—'

'No!' I pulled back and smoothed hair away from her face. 'Honey, no. None of this is your fault. You're the only good thing that's come out of all this. OK?'

She nodded slightly, but I could tell she didn't believe me. My Djinn child was getting a full-on inferiority complex. More than human, less than full Djinn. That was a burden I wasn't sure how to help her carry.

'Go find your father,' I said. 'Explain to him what happened with Ashan. Find out what we should do next. OK?'

'OK,' she said, and stepped back. 'Mom . . . be careful.'

And then she was gone, blipped out without another sound. I heaved a sigh and turned to see Emily, on her porch, staring at me accusingly. I hadn't heard her come out.

'We really could have used her,' she said.

'Imara's the only Djinn in the world we can trust right now. I'd rather not throw her at every single challenge. Besides, we can handle this on our own.'

'You hope.' She looked surly about it.

'What happened to *I don't need a Djinn to solve my problems*?' I asked. 'Buck up, Auntie Em. We're going to have an adventure.'

I swear, her scowl could have fractured glass.

* * *

Imara, not being in much need of transportation, had left the Camaro sitting in the driveway. It was a choice between that and Emily's battle-scarred SUV, with a four-wheel drive that had seen hard use. We didn't, strictly speaking, actually have to go to the site of the fire; Wardens often did their work remotely. But if this fire was as dangerous as she seemed to think, then being on the ground might be the only way to react quickly enough. Fire was the trickiest of all the elements. Even more than storms, fire had an intelligence, a malevolence. A desire to hurt. The bigger the fire, the smarter and angrier it became. Bad combination.

I chose the SUV. The Camaro really wasn't the kind of car I wanted to subject to off-road conditions.

Emily lived in a tiny little burg called Smyrna Mills, which was mostly distinguished by Smyrna Street – we were out of town in less time than it took to flash a blinker, and heading south to I-95. The other Warden, it turned out, was a country music fan; I wasn't. I mostly spent the time on the drive to Houlton and the Canadian border thinking and watching the skies. They didn't look good. The aetheric was in a boil, everything disturbed; flashbulbs of power were popping all over the place as Wardens tried to deal with their local problems, but it wasn't really a local issue. It was bigger. Nastier. And it was going to get worse.

I really didn't have any business taking a side trip

like this, but I couldn't think what else I could have done. Walk away from thousands of lost lives? I'd be crawling, not walking, if I did that. And none of it would matter from that point on, because I would have lost my way completely.

As we approached the border crossing, I remembered something with a sick, falling jolt. 'Um, Em? Little problem.'

'Which is?'

'No passport.'

'What? Where is it?'

'In Florida. With everything else I own that hasn't washed away.' She was staring at me as if she couldn't believe I'd leave home without it. 'I wasn't planning on any international trips.'

She shook her head and took a quick turn-off on a narrow trail into the woods. 'Hold on.'

I grabbed the roll bar as we started bouncing along at speed through the wilderness. Four-wheeling at its finest. I had no idea where we were going, or whether Emily had the slightest idea of direction, but she didn't seem worried.

'Thing is,' she said, whipping the wheel to the left to avoid a tree stump, 'normally I wouldn't be able to slip around behind them like this, but it's chaotic right now. If they do manage to stop us, shut up and let me do the talking.'

I planned on it.

No Mounties materialised out of the trees to flag

us down. Thirty minutes of twisting back road – and no road – later, we emerged from the trees and hit Canadian Highway 2, turning north.

I lost track of our route somewhere around Presque Isle; Emily, on her cell phone, followed back roads in response to directions. We got stopped by a police blockade; whatever Emily said, they let us past. The roads got progressively more challenging on the suspension. I hung on to the panic strap on the passenger side and tried not to think about the residual pain in my healing arm.

I was feeling more than a little nervous, out here in the wilderness, and I wasn't really dressed for firefighting, either. *Someday*, I promised myself, *you'll be able to get back to a normal life. Nice clothes. Bikini on the beach. Shoes that don't have sale tags.*

I closed my eyes, but when I did, I didn't see visions of Jimmy Choos or Manolo Blahniks, but David's face, the way he'd been the first time I'd seen him. That sweet, ironic smile. The deep brown eyes, flecked with copper. Angular cheekbones just begging to be stroked.

That smile.

I missed him so much, it felt like a physical pain, brought tears to clog my throat. We hadn't had a chance, had we? So little time to know each other, to find our balance. The world just kept pushing, pushing, pushing. I wanted it to *stop*. I wanted quiet, and I wanted a place where I could be in his arms, wrapped in silence and peace.

And I wasn't sure that was ever going to happen, especially now that we were two steps from the end of the world.

The SUV hit a particularly axle-rattling bump on the dirt fire road. I opened my eyes and saw a storm cloud looming over the tops of the huge trees.

No, not a storm cloud.

Smoke. Black and thick and pendulous.

A deer bounded out of the underbrush and rushed past us, staying out of our way somehow – it looked wild and terrified. Emily slowed the truck to a crawl. Other wildlife was coming down the road – rabbits, a bear cub, a huge lumbering mama bear behind it hurrying it along. More deer, leaping ahead of the pack.

Emily braked. The fleeing animals ran under the truck, if they were small enough; the larger ones went around. The bear passed close enough to my window that I could smell the hot rank odour of her fur, and hear her heavy chuffing breath.

'We have to go on foot,' Emily said. 'The other Warden is up ahead.'

'Why can't we drive?' Because this was about as close to a big huge bear as I really wanted to get. Emily spared me an irritated glance.

'If I take it farther in, the fire could get around us, the gas in this truck could explode,' she said.

'I'm assuming you don't want to be in it at the time. Besides, I like my truck.'

The exploding part made an impression on me. I unbuckled and scrambled out of the truck, careful of my feet, but it looked like the evacuation had slowed down. A couple of late-breaking grey rabbits broke right at my appearance, and some field mice ran under the truck. No additional bears, thank goodness.

The air felt heavy and hot. There was a steady furnace breeze blowing towards us. It was a tiny tittle hint of the forces already at work – the fire, which had already been burning for hours, would have created a huge updraft, which would have shoved cooler air in front of it outward in a circle. Cooler air, being heavier, would have been forced out in concentric waves as the temperature increased. It would look like a frozen nuclear explosion, with a hot central column and the rings emanating out.

The breeze was just the forerunner of what was behind it.

Hell.

People think they understand what a forest fire is. They don't. At a certain point, fire becomes semi-liquid – plasmatic – and it behaves like liquid, becomes heavy with its own energy, rolls and floods through dry brush, consuming everything in its path. It saps every single ounce of moisture from the air, leaving it dead and dry; its own energy release whips the winds higher, spreading it like a virus. It can jump and encircle an area like an invading army before anyone can see it coming, and then the rising temperature will cook anything caught inside before the flames close in. Most people trapped in fires die of the smoke or superheated air, which cooks their lungs into leather from inside on the first indrawn breath. It's an awful way to die, suffocating, but it's still better than the fire rolling over you and burning out every nerve ending in slow, awful progression.

The only mercy fire shows is that after your nerves burn, you can't feel the rest of it. You can't feel your body being turned to cooked meat and ash. And you're probably – although not certainly – dead before your internal organs burst, and your brain's superheated liquids blow open your skull.

No, the *last* thing I wanted to do was die of fire. The very last. Even drowning would be better.

And I was starting to wonder why in the hell I'd agreed to this. Pragmatism was starting to get the better of altruism.

As if she sensed it, Emily looked at me over the hood of the SUV, mouth twisted into an unpleasant grin. 'You like doing this from a nice, safe distance, don't you?' she asked. 'Some nice conference room where you can't feel the cinders on your back.'

'If you had any sense, that's how you'd like it, too,' I said. 'But I'm not letting you do this by yourself.'

'That's sweet. You afraid for me?'

'No, but you said it yourself: There are way too many lives depending on this. This is important.' I swallowed hard. There was a sound out there in the forest, a roaring that I didn't need to be a Fire Warden to know wasn't right. Not right at all. 'Let's just get it done, if we're going to do it. I've got places to be.'

'Shoe shopping?' she said archly. My reputation preceded me. 'Fine. Watch yourself – I'm not going to have time to keep your ass out of trouble. You see a bear or a mountain lion, freeze, turn profile, and if it charges you, curl into a ball and get under the truck. They probably will ignore you, given the fire, but you don't want to run from them. They do enjoy the exercise.'

I gulped. Audibly. She smiled. I wondered if she was just needling me, but then I decided she wasn't. She'd take her responsibilities more or less seriously, out here.

'What I need from you is to hang back here and do what you can to get a decent rain going. Counteract the prevailing winds. Think you can do that?'

I could do that in my sleep. I confined myself to a quick nod, gathered up my hair in one hand and tied it back with a rubber band from my pocket. The way the wind was swirling, that last thing I wanted was to obscure my vision. Too many things could sneak up on me. Fire, for one. Or bears. The bears were worrying me. Badly.

'Take two steps to your left,' Emily said.

'Why?' I froze, staring at her. She nodded down at the ground.

There was a timber rattler gliding along the ground right by my foot. I jumped out of the way with a little shriek, hands held high. 'Snake! Snake!'

'No shit,' she said dryly. 'Trust me, she's not paying attention to you. She's got plenty of problems of her own. Not so quick a traveller as the larger critters. She'll have a job of it to try to get out of here in time, poor girl.'

I watched the snake wiggle its – her – way down the road. Emily was right; the reptile didn't pay me any attention. Good. On the plus side, now I wasn't nearly so worried about bears. Bears didn't sneak up on your feet like that.

When I looked up again, Emily was striding along the road, straight for the fire. 'Hey!' I called after her. She didn't answer. I suppose she really didn't need to answer; I knew what I was tasked to do, she knew what she was doing, and there wasn't a lot left to discuss.

Still, when she looked back, I said, 'Good luck. I'll do whatever I can.'

She had a surprisingly sweet smile, when she wanted to. 'I know,' she said. 'You're a Warden.'

I sat down on the bumper of the SUV and contemplated the sky.

The fire wasn't big enough yet to truly drive the system – weather systems are massive, full of energy of their own, and it would take a real out-of-control wildfire for that synergy of elements to take on an unstoppably deadly partnership. But the weather wasn't feeling particularly cooperative, either. The heat from the fire definitely had it feeling its oats, and the evaporation of moisture was creating low-level disturbances. Lots of cumulonimbus action forming, but it was hanging out on the fringes, getting pushed along by the warmer air of the fire. I needed to pull it in and start squeezing those moisture-rich clouds for rain.

First things first: I had to pump more moisture back into the air, keep the underbrush from drying out quite so quickly so that it wouldn't just continue to explode into flame. There was a lake five miles to the east of where we stood; I went up in the aetheric and soared across the fire, which looked like a giant twisting tangle of ghosts, twisting and mating and soundlessly screaming. On the aetheric, you couldn't feel the heat, but you definitely felt the forces at work; it translated as pressure on me, a resistance that was hard to push through. I made it and touched down for a landing – still in spirit-form. I was at the edge of a glowing, whispering fog that was, back in the real world, a nice place to boat and fish.

Ever seen one of those fog fountains? They sell them in stores now, complete with transducers that create fog from water. Simple process. All you have to do is bombard the water with ultrasonic pulses, and it breaks up into fog. Not quite without cost – six hundred calories of heat per gram of water, in terms of energy – but a nice benefit. As mist evaporates, energy exchange results in temperature reductions, too. With the humidity as low as it was in the vicinity of the fire, mist evaporation would bring down the temperature by about twenty degrees.

I started shaking up the water.

Mist began rising almost immediately . . . thick, milky tendrils off the surface of the lake. I kept it going, piling mist in layers until it was as thick as foam on a latte and as tall as a three-story building. I'd drained the lake level by quite a bit, but if the fire reached the shore, the evaporation would occur anyway, and for a lot less constructive a reason.

When I had enough airborne moisture, I sent wind to blow it towards the unburnt areas around the fire. Just a strong breeze, and I kept careful hold of it; it wouldn't do any good to send my carefully made fog right into the blaze itself, where it would be instantly zapped. No, I pushed it just far enough to layer it over the outlying underbrush, a thick wet blanket that would make it much more difficult for the advance scout sparks to take hold.

Once that was done, I shot up into the clouds. I'd long ago learnt to deal with the dizziness of altitude, but this was just plain disorienting . . . I could see the heat rising up from the twisted trauma of the forest being destroyed below me, and it came in waves of red and pink and purple, like some crazy '70s acid trip. I hadn't usually been this close. It was – different.

I decided not to look down. My business was with what was overhead, in any case.

The updraft was making inroads, getting the attention of the weather system, but it was more of an annoying dinner guest than a partner in crime so far. If I could turn the weather system against the fire, so much the better, but if I couldn't, then at least I could cut off any kind of sympathetic energy exchange that could make both more dangerous.

I lowered the temperature at the higher elevations, forcing the moisture in the air closer together. My goal was rain, but I wasn't sure if there was enough aggregated moisture to really bring it off, without feeding the process out of the ocean. That would take time I wasn't sure we had. Best to get started with what there was, then work on the supply lines to keep it going.

Even a good downpour wasn't going to put out this kind of a fire, not as well-established as it was, but it could help contain it. With a decent Fire Warden – which Emily was, as far as I remembered, in addition to being an outstanding Earth Warden – this could come to a peaceful conclusion.

If everything went right.

Of course, there was no reason everything *should* go right. Especially not now, with everything I'd grown up knowing as fact turned into rapidly shifting fiction. The laws of nature were only laws so long as nature intended them to be. And I wasn't sure where we stood anymore.

The rain started to fall – not a downpour, but a nice steady shower, anyway. It would raise the humidity and bring down the temperature, and if it couldn't douse the fire, at the very least it could soak the surrounding areas and intensify the fog layers.

It was, I decided, a pretty damn good job.

I let go on the aetheric and plummeted back down into my body, a scary thrill ride of fast-moving colours and a sense of imminent disaster that ended suddenly – and safely – as I found myself back in my body again. I sighed, breathed deep, and gagged on the taste of smoke.

And I opened my eyes and realised the trees right in front of me were burning.

'Shit!' I screamed, and slid off the bumper of the SUV. The air was intensely hot, well over a hundred degrees; my clothes were dripping with sweat. While I'd been doing all that careful manipulation, the fire had slipped up like the serial killer in the movies, and as I looked wildly around, I saw that the fire was leaping from one treetop to the next. The rain – which hadn't yet reached this spot – was doing its job; it just wasn't doing it fast enough.

The underbrush was a wall of fire that roared like a jet engine, sucking in air. I covered my head as sparks drifted down out of the sky and sizzled holes in my shirt. I smelt burnt hair. I willed my Fire sense into action, covering myself; I wasn't sure if that extended to hair, but dammit, I had way too many hair issues already. Having it scorched again wasn't going to make things better . . .

I dived into the SUV and slammed the door. As I did, fire rolled like plasma through the underbrush to my left, on the driver's side, and I realised it was going to cut off my escape route. Once I was encircled, I'd roast, then burn.

The interior of the SUV was already hot. I remembered Emily's comments about the gas tank blowing up, and bit back a curse. I concentrated on the ten feet in and around the SUV itself. I needed to build a shield of cool air. That was a little easier than you might think – cool air being heavier and slower, it was a bit of a natural barrier, and as I chilled the air by stilling the vibration of the molecules, I concentrated on a feeling of calm. Peace. Stillness.

Within the bubble, the temperature began to fall.

And then, without warning, it started moving up again. I grabbed for control of the air, but it wasn't just a fault in my concentration, it was something else.

Some*one* else.

I opened my eyes and looked around, frantic, and saw something impossible. There was a man standing in the hellish fury of the burning trees. A man on fire, who didn't seem to care that he was on fire. His hair was already gone, his skin shrivelling and blackening, but somehow his eyes were open and bright and fixed on me with purpose. He took a step out into the clearing. He left a trail of cinders and shed flesh, and there was something so incredibly creepy about it that I screamed and hit the locks on the SUV doors.

Nothing happened.

Electric. He was interfering with the circuits.

The air was heating up even faster than the blaze around me could account for, and I knew that this man, this *creature* walking towards me was responsible for it. It wasn't possible that he was still moving, with that much damage. Just not possible at all.

Imara had told me the Djinn weren't coming to this fire. So this wasn't a Djinn.

Then what was he?

He reached out to open the door. I grabbed the interior handle and braced myself in an unladylike position, both feet against the steel posts, holding tight. I felt the tug as he tried to yank it out of my grip. He might have been supernaturally alive, but he wasn't supernaturally strong. His muscles had already contracted from the heat, and his hands were blackened claws. I was sickened to see that a couple of fingers dropped off when he pulled back from the door handle.

What in the name of God—?

He was still staring at me, and against all odds, I recognised what was in those eyes. I *should* recognise it. I'd known that exultation, fury, and most especially, that power.

There was a Demon Mark in this dead or dying Warden, and it wanted an upgrade. I was the next available candidate. It would keep the body it had alive until the very last second it could, and it would come after the nearest available source of power greater than what it had.

Where the hell was Emily? Oh God, was this *her*? . . . No, it was a man. I thought. I was almost certain.

Not Emily. This thing was taller.

It circled the SUV, staring at me, and reached for one of the back doors. I lunged over the seat and hit the manual lock with a clenched fist just as the clawed, flaking hand scrabbled at the handle. Another of his fingers snapped off. I didn't waste time; I hit the manual locks on everything I could reach, then slithered over the back into the trunk area and tried to find a manual lock for the trunk lift.

Nothing.

Right about the time that I was trying to figure out what in my weather arsenal would destroy a Demon with access to Fire Warden powers, the right side window shattered. The Demon was more of a lateral thinker than I was; apparently, he'd simply thrown a rock. It lay smoking and nearly molten on the upholstery, which charred in a circle around it. I yelped and grabbed for a leather jacket in the back, wrapped the rock in the coat, and started to toss it out, then changed my mind. It made a pretty good club, sort of an oversize and really clumsy blackjack.

The Warden-zombie, trailing smoke, slithered in through the window like some disgusting man-size snake. Where skin sloughed away, his muscles were exposed. Anatomy class in live action. I gagged at the roast-pork stench and lashed at him with my makeshift blackjack. I shattered at least two bones, and gave him a good crack on the skull, but he kept coming for me, squirming. The face was a mask of charred flesh. I couldn't tell if the grin was thanks to a contraction of the facial muscles, or a look of triumph.

I turned the interior latch on the trunk and bailed out of the SUV.

Talk about out of the frying pan . . . The fire was intense, a hot orange curtain flickering on all sides of the road. No, not a curtain, a bowl – it was overhead, consuming the treetops. Rain was falling, but there wasn't enough of it; it was slowing the advance but not putting out what was already burning.

Which was about to include me, any second now.

I dropped down on the ground – not by intention. Dizzy. The air tasted thick, too hot to breathe, acrid with filthy smoke. I coughed rackingly and hugged the dirt; then I remembered what it was I was running away from and started a low crawl. No place to go. No place to hide, except under the SUV, and I didn't need Emily to tell me that the fire was going to make that a death trap in short order.

You are fire.

It came in a cool whisper, soft as mist, and for a second I could have sworn I saw the Oracle from Seacasket standing in front of me, burning and lovely. The very polar opposite of the thing stalking me.

A black claw grabbed hold of my ankle. I screamed and lunged forward – into a burning tree. Fire spilt over me.

It didn't burn me.

It just spilt over me, liquid and dripping. Oddly heavy. Where it hit the ground, it hissed and sparked and danced; grass shrivelled and blackened at its touch, but I wasn't affected.

I twisted, formed the handful of fire into a ball, and threw it at the grinning dead thing that had hold of my leg.

It exploded like napalm. The zombie-Warden let go and rolled, fighting an invisible enemy, as the flames fed on what should have been just a blackened shell anyway. What the hell was the fire feeding on? It was as dead as a burnt-out match . . .

The creature – I couldn't even think of it as human

anymore – opened its black maw of a mouth and screamed. It was alien. Other. Older.

And then it just – ripped apart. Exploded in pieces of burning meat that flew in every direction. I coughed and gagged as something spattered me, and when I looked back, something silvery blue was clawing its way free of the remains.

Oh shit, I thought numbly.

Because I was pretty sure that was an adult Demon.

And it was looking straight at me.

Chapter Six

There was a sudden blowtorch flare out of the forest, and another human figure staggered out of the inferno. Not burnt, though she was smudged dark with smoke and coughing like her lungs might blow out. Emily had looked better. Her clothes were smouldering, but she was keeping it together. Barely.

'Get in the truck!' she screamed. Her eyes skipped right over the glistening twisted form of the Demon, and I realised that she couldn't see it – that Demons, like the dark shadows of Djinn who became Ifrits, weren't visible to normal Wardens. I didn't waste my breath. Emily tried the truck door, found it locked, and cursed breathlessly. She fumbled for keys. I reached in my broken passenger window and unlocked the doors, and we crammed ourselves in. I was sitting on broken glass. Didn't care.

Emily started it up and hit reverse just as a tree began

to topple in front of us. She screamed and floored it, and the SUV slalomed, skidded, and grabbed dirt. We rocketed backward. I hoped she was watching behind us, because I was riveted to two things: the torch of a tree that was heading for the roof of the SUV, and the twisted, flickering shadow of the Demon loping after us in pursuit.

'Do something!' Emily yelled at me. She looked scared to death, and she didn't know the half of what I did.

'Do what?' I screamed back, and grabbed for the panic strap as the SUV bounced over rocks. Still moving backward at a speed that no human-operated vehicle was supposed to go, at least in that direction and in the middle of nowhere.

'Anything!' she roared.

The noise of the tree crashing towards us was lost in the constant deafening train-whistle scream of the fire, but there was no doubt that it was going to hit us. And if the truck was put out of commission . . .

I sucked in a deep breath of air that was almost too hot to breathe, concentrated, and grabbed the dashboard as I stared at the falling tree.

Come on, come on, come on . . . Updrafts. There were plenty of updrafts, no shortage of those, but they were wild and unpredictable, fuelled by an incredible outpouring of energy.

I grabbed hold of a rising superheated column of air and wrenched it free of its source, then directed it at an angle at the falling tree. Twenty feet. It was coming for us fast, and no way were we going to clear it in time. Flames all around us. Ten feet. Heading right for the roof of the SUV . . .

I let the superheated blast of air go, cooled the outer edge, and it hit the tree like a huge blunt object, hammering it off course. Not by much.

The outer blackened pine branches snapped off on my side of the truck, and the trunk crushed the underbrush just a couple of inches to the right of the SUV's hood.

Emily shot me a disbelieving look. I shrugged and took my hands off the dashboard. Left wet, sweaty handprints behind.

I couldn't see the Demon anymore. Wishful thinking made me hope that Demons weren't impervious to fire, but damn, I pretty much knew better than that. Demons were impervious to everything nature or humans could toss their way. They could be contained by Djinn, but destroyed? Probably not, once they'd achieved full form, as this one had.

We were clear of the fire suddenly. Trees swayed around us, uneasy in the looming smoke, but nothing was aflame around us. Emily had, temporarily, outrun the flames.

She slowed the SUV, stopped, and wiped her hands on her filthy pants. She was shaking all over, and black as a coal miner at the end of a shift. Eyes red and bloodshot.

'That,' she said faintly, 'was maybe a little too close.'

'A little,' I agreed. 'Nice driving.'

'Nice wind management,' she replied, and was overtaken by a series of racking, tearing coughs. Sounded painful. I leant over, put my hand on her back, and concentrated on the air inside her lungs. I oxygenated it as much as possible, then extended it into a bubble within the cab of the SUV. Couldn't do it for long, because we'd both get high and giggly, but it would help, short-term.

'What the hell just happened?' I asked, in between gasps. Emily put the SUV in gear and managed – somehow – to turn it around on the narrow road so we could drive forward instead of backward. Smoke was thick and acrid around us, blowing our direction.

'Something's working against us,' Emily said grimly. 'Don't know what it is. I thought it was another group of Wardens, but now I don't know. It's not just the typical crap you get in wildfires. You know what I'm talking about?'

I did. Wildfires were dangerous in and of themselves; they hardly needed any villains to come add complications. I still vividly remembered the big Yellowstone fire that had claimed so many lives among the Wardens, several years back . . . the one that had destroyed Star both physically and mentally. That hadn't been anything but the nature of fire and the cruel purpose of the earth.

I had a good idea of who had been messing with

the fire here: a Demon Mark-ridden Warden. And that made sense of why the Djinn had elected to stay away. The hatching of a full-blown Demon out of its human carapace was nothing they'd want to be around. David had fought a full-grown Demon, once upon a time, and I had to assume he'd won, but it couldn't have been an easy fight.

Out of nowhere, I remembered David telling me, *We are made of fire.* He'd meant Djinn, of course, and he wasn't exactly being literal, but it made me wonder. Djinn reacted to light and heat, to the transformation of energy. I wondered if Demons were the same. If they were drawn to these kinds of events to help them – hatch. If so, there might be more of them out there – Wardens with Demon Marks, moving mindlessly towards something that would finish the process of incubation. Probably they wouldn't even understand why. I remembered how it had felt when my own Demon Mark began to manifest itself in a big way . . . I'd been euphoric, almost godlike. No thought for consequences. And no sense of self-preservation, really.

I started to tell Emily about it, but then I realised that it wouldn't do any good. Even if she believed me – which was doubtful – there wasn't anything she could do about it. We were on our own out here in the wild Canadian wilderness, apparently. I missed Marion. She'd know, if anybody did, how much trouble we were all in right now.

Emily got us back to a logging road, then out to a paved two-lane road. There were police barricades flashing in the distance. She slowed and pulled over to the narrow shoulder.

'We need more Wardens,' she said. 'Weather and Fire. Think you can get us anything?'

'No idea. I'll try.' I pulled out my cell phone and dialled up the hotline number. Busy. I reconsidered, dialled Paul's personal number.

Busy.

Marion's rang, though. She answered without her typical calm assurance; in fact, she sounded downright sharp. 'Joanne?'

'Yeah.'

'Where are you?'

'Wildfire across the border in Canada,' I said. 'Long story. Look, there's a desperate need for—'

'I know,' she cut me off. 'We've got wildfires breaking out everywhere, and damn few Fire Wardens left to fight it. There's not much I can do for you guys. Do the best you can. Let it burn, if you have to.'

I cradled the phone against my chest and looked at Emily's grimy face. 'Where's this thing heading?'

Under the black oily veil of smoke, she looked troubled. 'Ultimately? I'd have to say it's making a beeline for Montreal. But one thing's for sure, it'll take out every town on the way, too. Five thousand, ten thousand homes at a chunk. If this thing isn't stopped . . .'

I got back on the phone. 'No go on the hands-off, Marion. We need to find a way to firebreak this thing.'

'I'll get Weather on it,' she sighed. It was clearly not a new refrain. 'See what you can do from there. And Jo?'

'Yeah?'

'Lewis says that there's a hurricane brewing just past Jamaica. If it forms and comes inland, we could be looking at another very bad time in Florida. There's another one right behind it that looks like it could veer to hit the Gulf Coast, or South America.'

'Is there anything that isn't going crazy?'

'No,' she said flatly. 'Large cave-in in Kentucky, several hundred miners and tourists trapped in the region. Most of our Earth Wardens are converging on that, but we've got warning signs all up and down the Cascadia subduction again.'

'So. This would be the end of the world, then.'

'We're keeping hitching posts handy for the Four Horsemen. Any luck on the Djinn front?'

'Some,' I lied. Didn't seem much point in adding my bad news to the pile. 'I'm working on it.'

'Then you'd better quit screwing around with the fire and get the Djinn back on our side,' she said grimly. 'While we've still got enough of us alive to make it matter.'

I hung up, took in a deep breath or two, and turned back to Emily.

'Right,' I said. 'Let's get back to work.'

* * *

There was a ranger station seven miles down another logging road – abandoned, since the rangers were out doing fire spotting, and had field radios with them. Emily and I commandeered the radio that had been left behind – a huge old clunker of a thing, and proof positive that upgrades weren't high on the federal budget triage scale. I tried to figure out the ancient technology. Seemed simple enough. I spun the dials to the right frequency – the Wardens' emergency frequency – and clicked the old-fashioned button on the old-fashioned microphone.

Now, if I could only remember all the codes . . .

'Violet-violet-violet,' I said. 'Anyone reading? Respond.'

Static. White noise. I looked over at Emily, who was washing her filthy face in the sink; she needed more than a little soap to get clean, but that did a fair job. She only looked like a chimney sweep now, instead of a smoke eater. As she scrubbed a second time, I clicked the button again. 'Violet-violet-violet,' I repeated. 'Respond, please.'

This time, I got a sharp metallic click, and a tinny voice that sounded about twelve years old saying, 'Hang on!'

Not exactly the approved format for responding to emergency calls, but I understood. It wasn't shaping up to be a normal day anywhere in the world, but least of all in the Warden Crisis Centre.

I waited. The voice came back, eventually, right

about the time Emily finished her third ablution. 'Name and location,' it said. Not the same voice. This one was male, authoritative, and familiar.

'Hey, Paul,' I said. 'It's Joanne. They've got you answering phones?'

'I've got damn graduate students answering the phone.

You wouldn't even believe the magnitude of the trouble we're in. Where are you?'

'I'm up at the Canada fire, with Emily. Who else is up here?'

'Canada? Fuck if I know. Hang on, let me check.' He clicked off. I knew how the Crisis Centre worked – there'd be a huge write on-wipe off board with events and Wardens assigned – usually. Today, who knew. I had the feeling that it was all just happening too fast. 'Yeah. Jo, Emily's Earth and Fire – you've got a second Fire Warden located about eleven miles away from your current position, on the other side of the fire. Gary Omah. He's not real high on the scale, by the way. Not a lot of heavyweights left up there.'

'I don't think we can count on Gary Omah,' I sighed. 'Who else?'

'Weather Warden out of Nova Scotia. That's what I've got for you.'

'Who is she?'

'Janelle Bright.'

I didn't know her, but that wasn't unusual; she was probably young, and probably lower level.

Those seemed to be the survivors, so far. Probably because they hadn't earned any Djinn, and hadn't encountered any along the way. Also, Nova Scotia wasn't exactly the crossroads of the world. She'd probably be safe enough, if she didn't make a target of herself.

But then again, there were no longer any guarantees of anything, were there?

'OK,' I said, and then remembered to click the button. 'Right, Paul, I'm going to organise this one, OK?'

'Fine by me. We're up to our necks around here. You're senior on the ground pretty much wherever you go right now. Take charge.'

Now *that* was a really scary thought. It told me more than a Weather Channel documentary just how much trouble we were in.

I glanced over at Emily. 'Um, Paul? One other thing.'

'Please, let it be something fluffy and happy.'

'Not so much. Demon.'

'What?'

'There's a Demon loose. I saw it break out of a dying Warden – Gary Omah, I'm presuming. It tried—' I swallowed hard and kept my voice even with an effort, because the crispy zombie flashbacks weren't easy to suppress. 'It tried to get to me, but I managed to fight it off.'

Paul was quiet for so long, I thought I was having

a conversation with static, and then he said, 'I can't spare anybody else to help you.'

'Make it happen, Paul. I *need someone.*'

He put me on hold. Mercifully, there was no annoying music, it was just straight static. I listened to white noise and thought about Gary Omah, wondered how he'd come in contact with a Demon Mark, wondered whether taking it on had been his own choice or an infection that had happened against his will. I couldn't afford to agonise over Gary, though. If he was the blackened, hollowed-out corpse I'd met in the forest, then he was better off dead, and I had bigger problems.

Paul came back on the line. 'Paul, I need—'

He interrupted me by covering the phone and bellowing, 'You! Yeah, you in the fucking yellow! I told you, get those people over to the *west* side of the thing, do you understand me? *West!*' The muffling came off the phone, not that it had concealed much. 'Shit. I've gotta go. Do your best. I've got to go be the first officer of the goddamn *Hindenburg.*' He was trying to sound light, but somewhere underneath I could tell he was genuinely, grimly terrified. 'At least Lewis is the one wearing the shiny hat.'

'I know,' I said softly. 'Keep bailing, buddy.'

'Jo, just get the fuck out of there. Do what you've gotta do. We can't save everybody. Not this time.'

'I can't just walk away.'

'Learn how,' he said. 'People are dying. People are

going to die. It's all just a question of how many, and how bad they go. We need the Djinn back, and we need them *now*. So you've got to stay focused. Do what you can, but *stay on mission*."

He clicked off before I could respond. I sat back, looking at Emily; she was staring out the window at the orange-coloured distance.

'I can't get anybody besides one Weather Warden out of Nova Scotia,' I said. 'They're swamped.'

She nodded. 'We're really fucked, aren't we?' she asked, like it was an academic consideration.

'Not necessarily. All we have to do is pile in the Jeep and leave.'

She gave me a bleak, absent smile.

'Yeah,' she said. 'That's likely.'

Of course, we didn't leave. We didn't even discuss it. We just went to work. I spent time up on the aetheric, trying to move weather patterns around and layer cooler air over what was increasingly a troubled system. The fire was generating enormous amounts of heat, and that heat was affecting the already-unstable weather. It kept sliding out of my control, finding ways to twist back like a snake trying to strike. Lightning, for instance. Just when I thought we'd gotten things contained at a reasonable level, the energy began churning around and creating vast random pulses. It had to go somewhere. I deflected most of them as sheet lightning, or sent the energy flaring across the sky instead of down to earth, but it only takes one, sometimes.

And one slipped through, hit a giant pine, and ignited it like a torch.

Beginning of the end.

'Emily!' I yelled, and pointed. She was busy trying to contain the forest fire itself, but this was a second front, and we couldn't afford to let it get busy at its job. I shot up into the aetheric and looked for the other Weather Warden who was supposed to be helping us. Janelle. She was a weak spark indeed, barely glowing up on the aetheric; she was, I sensed, exhausted. Whatever was going on in Nova Scotia, it wasn't good. She was working the systems from the back, which was about all she could do, with the strength she had at hand. I wasn't about to push her for more. We were all redlining our limits today.

I caught sight of something in the aetheric. No, *caught sight of* wasn't exactly accurate – I sensed something, although everything looked just about as normal as an unsettled higher plane could look . . . The fire was a gorgeous lavalike cascade of colours, pouring out over everything in its path, but there was something going on that didn't belong. I couldn't pin it down, exactly. I just knew something wasn't right.

Then the fire arrived at the first human structure, a luxurious hunting lodge that was, luckily, empty of inhabitants, and set to work industriously licking at the propane tanks in the yard as if it had made straight for them.

That hadn't been a natural progression. That had been a *choice*.

'Crap,' Emily said from her post at the window. She sounded matter-of-fact, but she was pale and shaking with strain. I didn't have an up-close-and-personal relationship with fire – well, not until recently – but I understood that the stress of being a Fire Warden was unique. I could see that she was caving under the pressure, and there was nothing I could really do to help. I had my hands full already; lightning was jumping around in that storm, struggling to find new targets. My newly discovered Fire powers were too raw to be of any real use in a situation like this. Fire Wardens, even more than Weather, needed fine control.

I had no idea how long it had been since my call to the Crisis Centre; time is funny when you're in the middle of something like this. It can make minutes crawl, and hours fly; there wasn't a clock in easy view, and I was too busy to consult one anyway. Any little slip in my attention meant the fire gained new ground against the rain I was directing over it. Janelle, my remote support, was weakening further; she wouldn't be able to last long, and when she was gone, the weather system would swirl out of control out to sea, and the winds whipping in would spread this fire far and wide. I remembered how it had happened at

Yellowstone, the day Star had gotten burnt. The day so many Wardens had paid the price. Once a wildfire took control, it would be coming after anything and everything it sensed might be able to fight it.

This one was right on the edge. You could feel it *thinking*, and, boy, not nice thoughts, either.

The propane tanks at the hunting lodge blew with movie-spectacular effect. It bloomed white-hot at the centre, curling yellow petals towards the sky on a stem of black smoke.

The deafening roar rattled the glass a couple of seconds afterward.

It was warm in the cabin. I realised that I was sweating, and it occurred to me to take a look around; we'd been staring out the front window at the advancing blaze working its way up to slop towards us, but it was still a good half a mile away and moving slowly, thanks to the rain I continued to pour on it.

But I hadn't checked *behind* us.

I stayed where I was in the real world and turned on the aetheric plane to take a look.

Oh, lord.

It was advancing like a lava flow, rolling *down* the hill; it had crested the mountain, and was eating everything in its path. No wonder it was hot inside the cabin.

The fire had outflanked us.

We were trapped.

'Em!' I yelled. She didn't answer, transfixed on

what was going on in the front window. Focused to an extent that was going to get her killed. This was why Fire Wardens died so often; fire could turn so fast, and it required so much concentration. I lunged over, grabbed her by the shoulders and shook her, hard. Her eyes rolled back in her head. She collapsed against me, heavy and loose, and I had to let her slide down to the floor. If she was unconscious, not just entranced, we were *so* screwed, because the fire would lunge straight for this cabin like a tiger for a staked-out goat. Like called to like, power to power, and fire didn't like being caged.

I grabbed Emily under the arms and began dragging her across the dusty wood floor to the cabin door.

Oh my God. This wasn't happening. It couldn't happen this fast . . .

I felt a wave of heat across my back, and heard glass shatter; the back window had just blown out. I gritted my teeth and heaved – dammit, why couldn't I get some willowy little girl who was easy to rescue? – and Emily's workboot-clad feet scraped another two feet of board on the way to the door. I was seeing stars. My pulse was hammering, and the air I was sucking in tasted burnt and hot and nearly unbreathable.

The cabin was burning. Smoke was flooding in, heavy and black. I tested the doorknob and found it not quite burning hot, so I grabbed it and yanked. The door flew open, letting in a wave of hot air thick with smoke. I crouched down low and grabbed Emily's heavy form under the arms and started pulling. There were four steps to the ground. I wasn't too careful about how gently I was pulling her down them, and then I had to dump her in a heap on the gravel as I opened the back door of the SUV. Her turn to suffer being scraped over broken glass, but I figured she'd rather that than the alternative.

Fire took hold of a tree on the left side of the ranger station with an unholy bright-blue flare and snap. Sap exploding. Everything was superheated, ready to go up at a spark. My clothes were drenched with sweat, plastered to my skin as if I'd been swimming, but I was shivering; the intense heat was evaporating the sweat too fast. I needed water. Badly. The inside of my mouth tasted like dirty cotton, and I was feeling light-headed. I couldn't smell anything anymore; it was all just the same overwhelming smell of things dying.

A hugely antlered buck burst out of the burning forest, plunging past me, head down, blind with pain and terror. No way I could help it. I wasn't even sure if I could help myself.

I shoved Emily the rest of the way into the backseat of the SUV with the strength of the truly desperate. I turned to glance behind me, like Lot's wife, and saw the eeriest, most beautiful thing: fire flowing like heavy syrup down the hill, sliding over every charred, twisted thing its path. This was fire at its most elemental, its most powerful. No wonder Emily had collapsed, if she'd been trying to hold this back.

The stuff was going to roll right over the ranger station, and then right over us.

Cinders blew in my face. I slapped sparks from my clothes, jumped in the driver's seat, and started the truck. The situation called for a fast exit, and I gunned the engine, fishtailed on the loose gravel, and then found enough traction to leap forward down the bumpy fire road.

I was going too fast for the terrain. Gravel banged and rattled on the windshield and grille, and the suspension bounced me around like a toy inside the cabin. Emily was a rag doll in the backseat. The temperature inside the car was like a kiln, and I tried to pull in short, shallow breaths to spare my lungs. I could barely see ten feet ahead, as black smoke swirled across the road, but I kept my speed up. No time to slow down.

In my rearview mirror, fire was flowing down the road like lava.

'Damn, damn, damn,' I chanted, and reached for anything to hold it back. I was nowhere near the calibre of someone like Emily or – hell – Kevin. I managed to slow it down, just a little. Or maybe it just did that on its own. Hard to tell, with the chaos on the aetheric.

I broke out of the smoke into a temporary little clearing – green trees swaying with agitated winds, not yet on fire. I wiped sweaty palms on my shirt and firmed up my grip on the wheel, and hit the gas . . .

. . . and a massive – and I mean *massive* – tree

toppled over across the road, slamming down with pulverising force about ten feet from the battered hood of the SUV.

I screamed and hit the brakes. Felt the thump as Emily's limp body hit the back of my seat and fell into the floorboard; she made a weak moan, so at least she was still alive. The SUV fishtailed, tried to yaw left, and lurched to a halt.

Oh *fuck*.

I turned frantically to look behind. The advancing fire was moving fast again, leaping from tree to tree like some demented flaming Tarzan. I felt the heat notch up inside the car.

We were going to die. If we were lucky, we'd expire of the smoke first, but I didn't think the fire was feeling especially generous about it . . .

I ducked my head as the tree to my left caught with a bubbling, hissing snap of pine sap combusting. Smoke clogged my throat. I coughed and slid sideways to try to find some clean, breathable air. Panic made it hard to do anything Wardenish with the situation; my body was acknowledging imminent death, and it had no time to spare for rational thought.

I tried to breathe, but it was too hot, and there was a dry, hot, sere blanket pressing down on my mouth and nose and I *couldn't breathe* . . .

And then, I felt a breath of fresh, cool air, as if somebody had turned on the biggest air conditioner in the world. I sucked it in with a gasping whoop, coughed, and kept breathing as I forced myself back up to a sitting position.

David was standing in front of the truck, arms spread wide, coat flared out like wings. He looked fragile, standing framed by a curtain of fire, although I knew he wasn't. He reached out and rested his hands lightly on the hood, staring in at me through the haze of cracks in the glass, smoke, and dust.

Cool air filled the cabin of the truck. Sweet and pure as an early spring morning. Except for the surreal roar of the fire outside, we could have been parked for a picnic.

David gave me a faint, unreadable smile, then straightened up and walked over to my side of the vehicle.

'We don't have a lot of time,' he said. Master of the obvious, he was.

'What the hell are you doing here?'

'Other things,' he said. 'Surprisingly, I don't spend all my time following you, but then, I didn't think I had to. Imagine how surprised I am to see you in the middle of this. Have you lost your mind?'

'You can psychoanalyze me when we're not getting burnt alive,' I gasped. 'For now, could you just help us get out of here?'

'I will. Once I move this tree, *don't stop*, whatever you see. Understand?' He reached in and traced a finger down the side of my face, a hot sweet touch that ended too soon. 'Go now. Time's short. I'll yell at you later.'

'But—' I gestured helplessly at the gigantic felled tree in the way.

He walked over, and grabbed a fragile little twig of a branch that should have snapped off in his hand the second he pulled on it.

Instead, he picked up the entire tree, like some balsawood stage prop. Only, clearly, it was the real thing, heavy and groaning, shaking dust and splinters as he hauled it around like a toy. He casually dragged it in a quarter circle, like a gate on a road, and dumped it along the side in a thick crash of pine needles.

'Go!' David shouted. 'Don't stop!'

I gunned it. The SUV's tires flailed for purchase, caught, and rocketed us forward. As we passed David, he reached out to touch the truck, just a brush of his fingers across the finish.

The broken and cracked glass healed with an audible, singing crack. I couldn't tell about the other damage, but I was willing to bet that Emily was getting her SUV back in like-new condition.

And then he was gone, a dot in the mirror, vulnerable and fragile next to the rising giant fury of the forest fire, standing in front of the oncoming flood of plasma and flame.

I was shaking all over. Too much information, delivered wrapped up in too much personal death-threat, to absorb all at once. At least I'd seen David for all of thirty seconds. That was something . . .

Yeah, I'd seen a Demon hatch out of a crispy-baked Warden, too. And been attacked by a burning zombie.

I wished I could say that it was an exceptional day.

'What happened?' a hoarse voice asked at my ear. I screamed, took my foot off the gas, and then jammed it back on as my forebrain caught up with my instincts. 'Sorry. Scare you?'

Emily. She was sitting up, looking weary and smoke-blackened and red-eyed, barely better than something from a horror movie herself. Clinging to the seat for support.

'No,' I lied. 'Are you OK?'

'Fuck no, you've got to be kidding,' she said, and let herself drop back against the seats. 'Is it out? The fire?'

I checked the rearview mirror. The whole sky was red and black, a churning fury of destruction.

'Not quite,' I said bleakly.

'It's only a couple of miles from Drumondville. We have to—'

'No,' I said flatly. 'It's enough, Emily. We can't do any more.'

She lunged upright, grabbed the back of my seat, and thrust her face next to mine. I got an up-close look at her red-rimmed eyes, furious and brimming with moisture.

'There are *people* out there! People who are going to die! We're *Wardens*! You can't just *leave*!'

I knew that. I felt it inside me, the same desperate yearning to make everything right, set the crooked straight, save every life and fix every broken thing in the world.

I turned my stare back to the bumpy road, blinked twice, and said, 'Sometimes you have to let it burn, Emily.'

She stared at me in disbelieving, weary silence for a few seconds. 'You cold-hearted unbelievable bitch,' she said. I didn't answer. I kept driving. She was too weak to try to take the wheel from me – hell, she was too weak to be sitting up for long, and she proved it by letting go and slithering back down to a supine position on the backseat. When I looked in the rearview, she turned her face aside, but there was no mistaking the startlingly pale tracks of tears on her dirty face.

'They were right about you,' she said. 'You should have been neutered when we had a chance. You don't deserve to be a Warden.'

I felt her words like a blunt, cold knife shoved right under my heart. If she'd been trying to rip my guts out and decorate the truck with them, she couldn't possibly have done a finer job. Since the night I'd fought for my life against Bad Bob Biringanine, the surly but beloved old codger of the Wardens, I'd been persona non grata in a big way. The black sheep of the family. Blamed for everything, and praised for nothing.

But I was a Warden, dammit. I loved the sky, the sea, the living air around me in cell-deep ways that only another Warden could ever understand. I wanted to help people so much that the impulse ached inside me. I was a Warden, and the Wardens loved the world. But it was strictly a one-way love affair, and we forgot that, the closer we got to our duties.

'Bitch,' Emily mumbled distantly. She was sliding into unconsciousness again, or sleep. Too tired to be angry. I turned on the radio, glided it over to a station that had some decent music, and kept it on for the rest of the bumpy escape from the forest to cover up the quiet, uneven sounds as I gulped back tears.

The SUV growled to the top of the ridgeline, and I had a spectacular view of the inferno of the valley behind us, and what lay ahead.

'Oh *no*' I whispered, and the tears finally broke free.

David had warned me. *Bad things.*

There were dead people lying in the road.

The only ones standing were the Djinn – four of them. They were crouched among the dead, studying bodies with varying degrees of disinterest. I jammed on the brakes, remembered what David had said as the Djinn began to turn towards our Jeep.

Don't stop, whatever you see.

I didn't recognise any of these – two males, two females, at least in appearance. Two of them looked very young, almost childlike. One of the male Djinn had a burly, weightlifter-type look. The remaining female Djinn could have sat for a portrait of a Pre-Raphaelite angel, minus the wings . . . unbelievably, radiantly beautiful.

She was the coldest one of all.

All this went through my mind in a second, and then I hit the gas. The Jeep raced forward. I felt the engine sputter and realised, with a chill, that the Djinn were capable of stopping it dead. David had done it to me, once upon a time. Only not with such a deadly motivation.

Don't stop.

I formed shells of pure air around the spark plugs. The engine sputtered again, caught, and surged, rocking from side to side on the rough road.

'What's happening?' Emily had decided to speak to me again. I didn't have time to answer. I felt her pull on the back of my seat as she hauled herself upright. 'What – What the hell? . . .'

She screamed in my ear as all four of the Djinn – *all* of them, moving in concert – stepped into the road, blocking us. The kids in front.

Don't stop. No matter what.

I closed my eyes, sucked in a panicked breath and held it. And kept the Jeep hurtling towards them at speed.

'No!' Emily shrieked, rattling my eardrum, and I felt the wheel wrench as she grabbed it over my shoulder and twisted, hard, to the right. I lost my grip. The wheels lost the road, bounced over ruts, lost purchase . . .

We rolled over. All the way over, in torturously slow increments, as the world spun in a complete 360. The Jeep bounced and groaned as it settled back upright on its springs again.

So much for Emily's SUV being good as new.

'You *idiot*' I yelled, and cranked the key. Nothing. Whether it was the crash, or the Djinn, the truck wasn't going anywhere. I wasn't hurt, but I was scared, and my personal terror level got elevated as the driver's side door was wrenched open.

Angel Djinn stood there, staring at me with pure white eyes. Her skin was a delicate, inhuman silver, and her robes like alabaster silk blowing in an unfelt breeze. She had dark, waving hair that cascaded in luxurious waves over her shoulders, past her hips, down to trail the ground and her bare feet.

She reached in, grabbed my seat belt, and ripped it loose with a single tug, then grabbed my arm and dragged me out. Slammed me up against the fender of the Jeep in a flurry of dust and held me there, with her hand poised over my heart.

We froze that way. I didn't dare breathe. She didn't need to. Her head slowly tilted to one side, then came back upright again. I was reminded of the deliberate targeting movements of praying mantises.

'You stink of it,' she whispered. I could hardly understand her; her accent sounded odd, antique, as if she hadn't bothered to speak to a human in hundreds of years. 'Filth. Reeking filth.'

Next to her shining perfection, that's pretty much what I felt like, too. But I knew what she was sensing – the two Demon Marks I'd had on me in the past twenty-four hours. Not to mention the Demon that had been chasing after me like a freight train back in the forest, lighting trees on fire as it came.

But I'm not one to take that kind of thing lying down. 'Do I *have* a Demon Mark?' I demanded. Not that you should demand anything from a Djinn who's just participating in the slaughter of about – my brain whited out at an attempt at the number. Upwards of fifteen people, at least.

'No,' she said, and did the head-tilt back and forth again. Maybe I was like a Magic Eye poster, and she was trying to see the Statue of Liberty hidden inside me. She dropped her hand back to her side. 'You may go.'

She abruptly turned and glided around the Jeep, over to the other side, where Emily was leaning against the door. Emily promptly scooted over to my side of the car and rattled the handle. Stuck. *Stay there*, I mouthed. She ignored me, of course. But to be fair, maybe she couldn't see me. The window was fractured into a fine latticework of cracked safety glass.

'Excuse me,' a polite voice said, and before I could flinch, much less grant pardon, I was picked up and set gently off to the side by the big male Djinn, who had dark cocoa skin and black eyes, and a whole lot of long pale hair that was tied into a ponytail at his back. He was dressed in more conventional styles than Angel Djinn – blue jeans, a chambray work shirt in fashionable (and daring) light purple. He misted out at the knees. It didn't seem to bother him.

I stumbled on gravel when he let go of me. He reached over, grabbed the handle of the back door of the SUV, and removed the door, handle and all. He set it gently aside, next to the one Angel had dismembered, and leant in to grab Emily by the scruff of her shirt. She screamed and fought, but it was a little like a puppy fighting a wolfhound, only not so equal. 'Shhhhh,' he told her, and held a finger to her lips. She went instantly still, and white as bleached paper. 'Good girl.' He set her on the ground and stepped back, still holding her by one arm in case she might decide to sprint for it.

Angel glided back, barely touching the ground. Her feet looked as if they'd never encountered dust, much less rocky, tough ground.

She held her hand over Emily's heart.

Head-tilt. It stayed frozen in one spot for longer than I liked, and then slowly came back upright.

She moved quick as a tiger, fingernails forming into silver claws, and ripped Emily's shirt open over her heart. Not just the shirt. The jog bra was a casualty, and Angel hadn't been too careful about the skin, either.

Under the pale flesh and the claw marks and the vivid red blood, I glimpsed a tangle of black racing out of sight under her skin.

'No,' I whispered. 'Oh, no. How—? When—?' Because I knew for a *fact* that Emily hadn't been infected when we'd left her house. It had to have happened in the woods, when we'd been separated.

The damn Demon Mark was still following me, and when it hadn't cornered me, it had gone for Emily.

Emily's jaw worked nervously, and she looked at me as she fumbled the shreds of her shirt back together.

'It is early,' Angel said. She was unquestionably the Djinn in charge here. The two who looked like kids – a matched set, boy and girl twins dressed in identical T-shirts and sloppy corduroy pants, with tangled brown hair – looked at her with a kind of unquestioning worship. The polite male Djinn, too. 'Do you want this one?'

She was talking to me. To *me*. 'Do I – uh – what?'

'Do you want this one?' she asked slowly, sounding out each word with heavy care. When I looked blank, Angel turned to the male Djinn holding Emily's elbow.

'Do you want us to take the Demon out of her,' he translated. 'It's still early. We can do it.'

'Um . . . will it hurt her?' Stupid question. Of course it would. But it would hurt her a lot worse to keep it. 'Never mind. Yes. If you can.'

He nodded, took a glass bottle from a leather bag at his side, and handed it to Angel. She opened it carefully and held it in her left hand.

'Don't move,' she said to Emily, and plunged her right hand into her chest.

Emily shrieked. I think I must have, too. I know I lunged forward, or tried to, but suddenly there were arms around me from behind, although all the Djinn were in front of me.

'No, love.' David's whisper in my ear. 'This has to be done.'

I spun to look at him. Emily was making terrible, agonising noises, and there were dead people on the ground, *dead people* . . . 'You killed these people?'

He looked tired. Shadows in those normally bright eyes. 'It had to be done.'

'*You* killed them?'

He shook his head. 'Let's not do this. Not now.'

'Why didn't you want me to stop, if you didn't know this was going on?' But I knew. He must have sensed the lingering presence of my encounters with Demon Marks on me, just as Angel had. He'd been afraid that they'd just assume I was one of the infected. 'God, David, how could you do this? These were Wardens.'

'Wardens have always passed their infections on to Djinn, and we could never fight back. Now we can.'

'So it was them or you. Is that it?'

His eyes held mine, steady. Flecked with amber and full of regret. 'Yes. Them or us. And don't tell me the Wardens haven't done the same. Don't tell me that *you* wouldn't if it came to it.'

'Slaughter fifteen people like sheep? No, David, I—' Emily's tortured moans suddenly cut off with the sound of flesh hitting the ground. I spun back towards her, and saw her being picked up from her faint by the big male Djinn, who placed her back in the SUV's passenger side. He removed that door, too, and the back one, as well. Evidently, he liked symmetry.

I rushed to her side and pressed my fingers to her throat. A nice, steady pulse. She moaned weakly and opened her eyes. Bloodshot and unfocused, but it looked like she'd live.

'They were on their way to the fire,' David said grimly. 'Fire that would have accelerated the Demon Marks and hatched out more than we could handle at one time. We had to stop them before the Demons emerged, and it was too late to remove them safely. We didn't have a choice.'

'We could have done something!' I shouted, rounding on him. He didn't back up. 'We could have put them in a cell, in a hospital, anything but killing them and tossing them out like yesterday's trash! You don't have the right, David!'

'No!' he shouted back. 'I have the *responsibility*! Now, if we've taken enough of a guilt trip, I have a fire to stop.'

He whirled and stalked away, coat flapping in the hot wind behind him. I scrambled after, heart pounding in a bloody, loud fury in my ears. I grabbed his arm, felt heavy wool and the flex of muscles, and dragged him to a stop.

'David!'

He turned, and his expression . . . Ah, God. The

agony was heartrending. 'There's nobody else to make these choices. You know.'

I did. I remembered all the times that I'd run screaming from the burden of hard choices. Even this time, I'd let myself get distracted from the mission by the opportunity to earn myself a little feel-good glory. It was Emily's job. It hadn't been mine. I'd come out here with good intentions, and hell lay at the end.

'This whole thing won't stop,' I said. 'It won't stop until we're all dead. Right?'

For answer, he reached out and folded his arms around me, holding me. He smelt of smoke and sweat, real and human, and I wanted nothing but to be somewhere else with him, somewhere free of chaos and responsibility. Somewhere I could hold him against my skin, and we could wash each other clean.

If we could ever be clean again.

'I know you didn't kill them,' I whispered against his neck.

'I'm responsible,' he said again, and his lips touched the sensitive skin below my ear, a delicate benediction. 'That's all you need to know.'

Lewis and Paul would shrug it off; fifteen more dead Wardens? A tragedy, sure, but we'd already lost more than we could count. And Demon-infected Wardens weren't an asset to anyone. I knew all the logical reasons, and none of them touched the black, oily guilt that continued to seep into my heart.

I took a deep breath and pulled back enough to

look him in the eyes. 'Where are these things coming from? What do they want?'

For a second he didn't react, and then his pupils narrowed as he comprehended what I was asking. 'The Demon Marks? They're destined to produce adult Demons. They reproduce at will, once they hatch. The Marks – the eggs – are drawn through rips in the aetheric, and they're pulled to the nearest source of power. Djinn or Warden.'

'Is that all?'

'No. They're drawn to us because we're part of *her*, in greater or lesser measure. What they want – especially the adults – is to get to the Mother.'

'Like I do.' Oh, the irony.

'Not . . . like you do,' David said slowly. 'If they can get to a place where she's vulnerable, they could kill her. Demons are a disease, Jo. And we have to fight them however we can, especially now. She's vulnerable. And she's hurting.'

'The Oracle. The one in Seacasket. He was infected with a Demon Mark—'

'What?' He pulled back, completely back, eyes wide. 'No. That isn't possible.'

'I – I think it might have been my fault. I got it off him, but I don't know how much damage it did first.'

His face went stiff and blank. 'I have to go,' he said carefully, with exquisite care. 'Don't – don't go back to the Oracle. Don't try.'

'But—'

'If you go back,' he said tonelessly, 'I'll have to kill you. Don't even think about it.'

I swallowed hard. He'd shifted from the warm, comforting lover to the leader of the Djinn, and the change was terrifying. 'Then what do I do? David, you're the one who said—'

'I know what I said. But it's out of my hands now. And yours. Go home, Jo.'

I stood there, stunned. He walked away, towards the fire.

One of the other Djinn was standing next to me – the big one, his pale white ponytail fluttering in the wind. He raised an expressive eyebrow.

'You can go,' he said.

Something occurred to me, late and hard. 'I forgot – there's a Demon down in the fire—'

'We know, love,' he said. 'That's why we're here. Go.'

When I didn't move, he just picked me up and effortlessly carried me back to the SUV, and plumped me into the driver's side. This time, the engine started with a throaty roar. I looked over at Emily, who was firmly buckled in, and fingered the shredded remains of my own seat belt.

'Oh, sorry,' he said, and reached in to touch it with a fingertip. It knitted together with dizzying speed. Good as new. He solicitously buckled me in and patted my shoulder. 'You do what he says, now. You go home.'

I hardly even remembered driving away. I remember staring into the rearview mirror, at the smoke and flame and the battlefield of dead Wardens, until the next hill hid it all from view.

I cried for a while. Tears of fury and anguish and bitter, bitter disappointment. Disappointment in myself, mostly. If I'd stayed in Seacasket . . . if I'd gone back instead of going into the fire with Emily, maybe things would be different. Maybe those fifteen Wardens wouldn't be dead. Maybe . . .

Maybe it would all be the same, only I'd be dead, too. No way to second-guess it. I knew only that the path I was on wasn't the right one, not at all.

Emily continued to sleep, and snore, as I piloted the broke-down Jeep back down dirt roads, heading for civilisation.

The first sign of which was a paved road, black and level, at right angles to the road I was on. I turned left.

It's so strange, how quickly you can go back to normal life. The first shock came as the tires of the SUV hit blacktop. The sudden lack of vibration felt weird and unnatural, and for a second I had a nightmarish vision of myself as a backwoods four-wheeling fanatic like Emily, wearing oversize work shirts and thick-waisted jeans and clunky steel-toed boots. With a collection of trucker gimme caps.

Behind us, the forest fire was a lurid red fury, pouring blackness into the clouds. I felt sick, remembering how I'd left things with David. It already seemed more dream than reality.

I wiped tears from my grimy cheeks and thought longingly of a shower. A long, hot shower, followed by a deep, drug-induced sleep.

Paved road or not, I still had a half mile or so to go before we reached the actual highway. Not out of the woods yet. The fire had turned back, consolidated itself – fighting the Djinn now, instead of the Wardens. It might give us just enough breathing space.

Home. Where was home? Sure, I'd drop Emily off at her house, but where did I belong? Back at Warden HQ, helping Lewis oversee the end of the world? Back in Florida, salvaging whatever was left of my apartment after the big storm, and waiting for the next one to hit?

My home was David, and I couldn't be with him.

I fought the tears again – self-pitying bullshit tears, and I wasn't going to give in – and decided to go with the one-crisis-at-a-time theory. First, get Emily home. I'd saved her, at least. That was something. Not much, but something.

From the backseat, Imara said, 'Where are you going?'

I yelped and flinched, and the Jeep veered wildly, tires squealing. I got it under control again and looked behind me in the rearview. Imara was sitting there, black hair blowing liquidly in the wind.

'Isn't this supposed to have doors?' she asked.

'Upgrade,' I said hoarsely. 'Where were you?'

'Trying to get help.' She closed her eyes and rested her head against the upholstery. 'I ran into Ashan. I wasn't very successful.'

'Help,' I repeated. 'Wait, Ashan! . . .'

'I'm fine. It doesn't matter,' she said. 'But at least you're safe.'

I laughed. It turned into a racking, smoky cough and ended up in a sob that I controlled with an effort. 'Yeah. Safe,' I said. 'How's the fire doing back there?'

She didn't even open her eyes. 'Father and some of the other Djinn are there, trying to hold it, but it's hard. The Mother's . . . I suppose the closest description is that she's having a nightmare. He's trying to shelter the Djinn from it, but it's getting stronger. He won't be able to keep it from them indefinitely.'

'A nightmare,' I said. 'About what?'

Her eyes opened. Amber-brown. Very human. 'About humanity.'

Sorry I asked. I remembered the dead Wardens, the suffering on David's face. My responsibility, he'd said. If he'd been trying to hold the Djinn back from whatever bad vibes the earth was trying to send out, maybe he'd slipped. Lost himself.

Maybe I was still trying to make excuses for him, and it had been a cold-blooded choice. Lewis had warned me, not so very long ago, not to underestimate the alien nature of the Djinn. Even the ones I loved.

Of course, the same could be said for people . . .

'You're thinking about Father,' she said. 'Right?'

'Why do you say that?'

'You look sad,' she said quietly. 'He'd hate that he makes you sad.'

Oh, *dammit*. I was going to cry, wasn't I? No. I wasn't. I gulped enough air to make myself belch instead. 'Are they going to be able to contain the fire?'

'Yeah,' she said, and looked away. 'But there's something else in there. Something bad.'

Tell me about it. 'Don't worry about your father – he's fought bad things most of his life.'

'I know,' she whispered. 'But it's all falling apart, Mom. Why does it have to happen just when I—?'

The second she's born, the world starts to collapse. I bit my lip, furious with Jonathan suddenly; this was too big a burden to give any kid. Even a Djinn-born one. 'It's going to be OK,' I told her.

'I know,' she said. Wind whipped her hair over her face and hid her expression. 'I trust you.'

I didn't answer. Couldn't. My throat had locked up tight, fighting the tears. Deep breathing helped, and concentrating on the flashing yellow centre stripe. Freeway up ahead, and a battalion of flashing emergency lights. I slowed for a barricade. Since there was an exodus from the fire, it didn't appear passports would be an issue. The Mountie manning it nodded to me and moved it aside, and then we were out, racing into the clear day.

Free.

* * *

I dropped Emily at her house. She woke up halfway home and subjected me to a foul-mouthed inquisition; she didn't remember anything past her collapse at the ranger station, as it turned out. Convenient, that. I didn't have to answer questions about the Djinn, or the Demon Mark, or any of that crap. She looked ill, but intact, and when I offered to keep her company, she brushed me off as rudely as ever.

The fire was down to normal size, up north, according to the radio, which blamed it on a lightning strike and credited the brave Canadian fire patrols for containing the blaze. No mention of fifteen dead bodies littering the landscape. I wondered if David had cleaned up after his hit squad.

'Where now?' Imara asked. She was behind the wheel of the Camaro when I arrived, and I was too tired and too sore to argue with her.

'Back towards Seacasket,' I said. She gave me a long, frowning look. 'I know. I said *towards*, not *to*. I just need to think for a while.'

'I'm not taking you back there,' she warned, and put the Camaro in gear. 'Father doesn't want you near the Oracle.'

Having a Djinn driver was pretty damn sweet, I decided. For one thing, she was fully capable of opening up the car to its fullest potential, and simultaneously hiding it from any observant highway patrol cars. The Camaro loved to run, and some of its joy bled off into me, easing the ache in my guts. I closed my eyes and let the road vibration shake some of the despair away.

I must have dozed off; when I opened my eyes again, the car was downshifting, and Imara was making a turn into a parking lot in front of a roadside motel. 'What's this?' I asked.

'You could use a shower,' she said.

I winced. 'Tact, Imara. We'll discuss it later.'

'I'm sorry to be blunt, but you need a shower, and real sleep. Also, this is as close as I can take you to Seacasket without attracting Father's attention.'

I hated to admit it, but the kid wasn't wrong. I sniffed at myself. Ugh. I did reek.

I sent Imara in to get the room – one look at me, and they'd promptly light up the NO VACANCY sign – and lounged against the dusty hood of the car, waiting. She came out dangling a clunky-looking key, the old-fashioned metal kind with a diamond-shaped holder blazoned with the room number. Four was my lucky number, at least today.

While I was in the shower, shampooing for the third time, Imara knocked on the door and shouted, 'I'm going to get you some clothes!'

By the time I'd rinsed off and strolled out of the heat-fogged bathroom, she was gone. I curled up under the covers and flipped channels on the TV. The news was full of bad stuff: fires, earthquakes, storms, volcanoes. Europe was locked in a sudden, unexpected deep freeze. India was facing floods. So was South America.

I turned it off and remembered the Oracle. I'd come

so close . . . so close. Wasn't there anything I could do, anything at all? I remembered the rich, dizzying, overwhelming sensation that had come over me when I'd been holding his hand. It reminded me of the on-rushing music of my dream, when Jonathan had told me to leave.

I could almost hear it again, washing through me. Wiping every thought from my mind in a white, overwhelming rush. Floating . . .

There was someone with me in the room. I hadn't heard the door open, but I sensed a presence. Imara was back, I thought, and opened my eyes.

Even in the dark, I knew that wasn't Imara.

'Hello, love,' Eamon said. He was right next to the bed, leaning over me. Even as I tried to roll, he grabbed me by the shoulders and pinned me down.

'Hello, Eamon,' I said. I sounded calm, no idea why, because my heart was rattling in my chest like dice in a shaken cup. I was having an out-of-body experience, or I knew I'd have felt something more than this ringing, empty amazement. Shock, I guessed. And fear. 'How'd you find me?'

'GPS in your cell phone,' he said. 'The wonders of modern technology. Turns out that it isn't just for law enforcement anymore.' His hand slid down my bare arm. 'Are you naked under there?'

'Fuck you,' I gasped, and tried to wrench away. No luck. He was a wiry bastard, and when I reached for power to even the score, I felt a hot, wet sting in my bicep. I flinched, but it was too late; he'd emptied the contents of a syringe into me with a fast shove of the plunger. Something heavy and sickeningly warm raced up my arm, into my neck.

'That should keep you from doing any parlour tricks,' he said, and flicked on the bedside lamp. He looked only a little battered from our adventures in Florida – God, it hadn't even been long enough for his cuts to fully heal – but he was his usual natty self, dressed in a cool marine-blue shirt that looked fresh and crisp. Khaki pants. A dressed-down look, for Eamon, but fully complimentary. His hair was still a little too long, but I didn't let that friendly boy-next-door look fool me. No matter how limpid and sweet his eyes and smile might be, there was something deeply disturbing inside this man.

'There we go,' he said soothingly, and he blurred out of focus again. No amount of blinking would help that. The warmth was stealing through my chest now, down my legs, up into my head. Such a nice, safe feeling. 'You're all right, love. Just relax. No worries at all.'

His voice was so soft and soothing, and I wanted to believe him. I knew better, but it was almost impossible to resist that kindness.

'Sarah,' I managed to mumble. The world had turned into a candy-coloured swirl of shapes. Strange tastes in my mouth. 'Where?'

'Sarah is very safe, Joanne. You don't need to worry

at all about your sister. I wouldn't hurt her.' His laugh was dry and mocking. 'Well. Not without giving you the chance to make good on our agreement first, of course.'

I tried to say something, but my tongue was as thick as folded felt. I felt his hot fingers touching my neck, feeling my pulse, and then saw a bright hurtful glare as he lifted one eyelid. The room was doing a slow, graceful swirl.

'Excellent,' I heard from a great distance. 'A nap will do you good.'

When I woke up in the dark, my mouth felt like a litterbox some cat owner had neglected for a month.

I was tied down, as I discovered when I tried to sit up. Ropes around both wrists. My ankles were tied together, but still anchored to something that felt rock-steady. I jerked at my bonds a few times, but got nothing but a steady rasping pain in my wrists for my trouble.

I felt dull and sick, and for a long few moments I didn't remember anything about how this had happened. It came back in flashes. Fire rolling down the road like flaming syrup. David. Dead Wardens.

Eamon.

A light flicked on across the room – a low-wattage bulb, barely enough to throw a yellow circle a couple of feet – but it burnt my eyes. I winced, closed them, and then deliberately forced them open again. I wasn't in my room any longer. In fact, I doubted I was even in the same motel.

Eamon was sitting in an armchair next to the light, which was a standard-issue sort of thing with a lopsided paper shade. He wasn't an intimidating presence, generally; tall, lean, with pleasantly shaggy hair and a neat beard and moustache that gave some softness to his angular face. His hair was a colour trapped somewhere between brown and blond, and although his eyes looked dark at the moment, I remembered them as that smoky colour between blue and grey. He was, in a word, cute. Older than I was, but not more than ten years at a stretch.

In some ways, his hands were the most striking thing about him. Long, restless, graceful hands that should have been doing something artistic, like music or sculpting or neurosurgery. He took good care of them. His manicure was better than mine.

'How long?' I asked. My sense of time was screwed.

He tilted his head slightly, watching me. He looked a little surprised, as if that wasn't the first question he'd expected me to ask.

'An hour,' he said. 'By the way, congratulations on your escape from certain death back at the fire. That was exciting.'

'You were following me.'

He shrugged. 'I'm not that energetic about it. I was tracking you. I only saw a bit towards the end.'

'Why?'

Ah, that was the question he'd been expecting. He smiled. A sweet smile, with a loony's edge. 'I had a strange idea that you weren't going to be looking after my interests,' he said. 'Seemed like a good idea to keep my hand in.'

'Well, you've made your point. Very scary. Now let me go.' It *was* scary. I was starting to sweat again, and I really didn't like the ropes sawing into my hands and feet. The threat was implicit and precise, and the ease with which he'd handled me was frightening. He'd had a lot of experience at this abduction thing.

'Have I?' he asked. It was a neutral question, but I sensed the menace behind it. 'Love, I haven't even started making my point with you. I warned you before. I need a Djinn, and I need it now. I'm not going to wait politely while you take care of your own affairs. You satisfy me first. Now.'

There was a double entendre there that I was quite sure was intentional.

'I'll kill you,' I said. 'I'll kill you if you—'

'I'm not that crude,' he interrupted. He hadn't really even moved since turning on the light, except for tilts of his head; his hands were limp on the arms of the chair. 'I'm not Quinn, you know.'

He knew. Quinn had told him what he'd done to me. Fury boiled up inside me, hot as plasma, and I didn't know how to deal with it. I'd never told *anyone*, not about what had happened to me in that darkest place, but Quinn had been shooting off his mouth to Eamon. Laughing about it over beer and chips, or whatever it was those two bastards did for fun besides tormenting others.

'No,' Eamon said quietly. 'He didn't tell me. I guessed. I wouldn't have done that to you, you know. There wouldn't have been any point. I keep my business and my pleasure completely separate.'

He knew me way too well. I closed my eyes and focused on controlling my breathing. I needed calm, and I needed to have full command of my powers. Weather and Fire. I was tired, and I was waterlogged with drugs, but dammit, I wasn't going to take this. Not from Eamon.

'Yeah, but you've still got me tied up on a bed,' I said. 'Do the words *sexual predator* mean anything to you, Eamon?'

'Mmm. Fifteen to twenty-five, by the laws of this particular state, I believe. If I don't kill you. If I do, of course . . . does Maine have the death penalty? I'm afraid I can't keep track, as often as you people change your minds about cruel and unusual.' He sounded bland and unworried. 'You'll notice I tied you with your legs together. I could have done anything I liked. For that matter, I still could. You should be a little more polite.'

That edge showed for a second, naked and glittering as a knife. Eamon was a Halloween candy bar full of razors. He terrified me on some level that I couldn't even fully understand.

'Somebody's going to come looking for me,' I said to him. That got a stir from him; he sat forward, elbows resting on his knees, and tented his hands with his fingertips resting over his lips.

'The girl?' he asked. 'The one who looks so remarkably like you that I had to ask Sarah about younger sisters, cousins, et cetera? I had to conclude that she was a closer relation. Daughter, I think. Very, very pretty.' He smiled, and it was an expression that curled my stomach in on itself. 'And since I've fairly comprehensively established that there's simply no way you could have conceived and delivered a child without there being some kind of record of it, she's something else. Something . . . unusual.'

I stopped breathing, then forced myself to start up. Calm and casual, that was the only way to do this. 'I'm not old enough to have a grown daughter.'

'Please, don't force me to be ungentlemanly about it. You're more than old enough. But I think I can assume this is something else. Something to do with your handsome young Djinn boyfriend, for instance, and the desire of all living things to reproduce.'

'You're crazy.'

'Very likely.' He nodded. 'But your daughter is Djinn, and I want her. Need her, actually. I promise to return her unbroken, if that will help.'

There were lots of answers I could have chosen from, but the most primal one boiled up first. 'Touch her and I swear, I'll rip you apart, Eamon.'

'I believe that,' he agreed. 'I don't think I've ever met anyone quite as capable of violence as you, Joanne. You disguise it well, but there's nothing light in your nature when you're at the sharp end. I like that about you.'

'I mean it!'

'Oh, I spotted that right off,' he said, and suddenly he was standing. He moved that way, unexpectedly, and my heart did a funny little jump as he crossed the short distance to the bed. He stood over me. There wasn't so much light over here, and he was blocking out most of it. I couldn't see anything but a pale oval for a face, and the darkness of his body.

The bed creaked as he sat down next to me.

'I love your sister,' he said. Talk about things I hadn't expected . . . I kept my eyes on his unseen face. 'That is very annoying, you know. I hadn't planned on feeling anything for her, beyond the occasional gratitude for being a good fuck—' He smiled at my animal noise of protest. 'She's a good woman, Sarah. And she believes that I'm a good man. No doubt that bubble will burst soon, but I'd like to keep the fantasy intact awhile longer. She makes me feel—'

He fell silent. I didn't interrupt his thoughts.

'Well,' he said, finally. 'She makes me feel well.'

No question, Eamon was sick on some level I didn't even want to understand. 'Don't hurt her.'

'I don't want to. But I'm afraid that's really up to

you at this point, and your daughter. I've told you what I need, and it's up to you how it gets provided to me. I've made the request nicely—'

'You abducted my sister!'

'Rescued, actually.'

'You *molested* her!'

'Yeah,' he admitted cheerfully. 'I did, a bit. Sorry about that. Can see how that might rot the trust between us to some extent, but love, I was trying to emphasise to you the seriousness of the situation. Which has, I could point out, become even more serious. So *I want my bloody Djinn or I will crush your fucking throat.*'

The last was snapped out in tones that made me cold inside. Before I could draw breath, his right hand was around my neck.

I wanted to scream, but nothing came out when I opened my mouth except a choked gagging sound. He was an expert at it. He choked me just hard enough to lock the scream in my throat and make it unbearably painful to breathe. The darkness began to spark with fireworks. Oxygen deprivation. He kept holding my throat, steady and sure, and then suddenly the pressure was gone. His hand stayed, loose and cool against my burning skin, and I whooped in a convulsive breath.

'Scream and I'll kill you,' he said. It was a whisper, and it was against my ear, and he sounded utterly serious about it.

I didn't scream. I concentrated on breathing and marshalling my powers. It wasn't working. The drugs coursing through my system were interfering with my concentration and control; he must have done some research. These must have been similar to the drugs that Marion and her team used to sedate Wardens who'd proved dangerous.

I couldn't get enough power together to light a match, much less fry Eamon the way he deserved.

'I'm presuming you don't have some other Djinn in your handbag, ready to give me,' he said. 'No, don't speak. Shake your head yes or no.'

I indicated no, silently. His fingertips moved slowly down the column of my throat to the notch of my collarbone, then back up. Stroking.

'Then I'm afraid it's your daughter I will require,' he said. 'Cross me, and I'll kill your sister and cut my losses. No warnings. I'll just phone you up and let you listen while she dies, all right?'

I managed to croak out some words. 'I thought you loved her.'

'I do,' Eamon said. 'I'm afraid that doesn't change anything.'

His fingers trailed down into the open valley between my breasts. I didn't dare move. There was a tension in him that I couldn't quite understand, but I feared it. I wasn't sure he was quite in control of what he was doing.

'You and your sister,' he sighed after a few silent

seconds. 'I can only imagine what you'd be like together.'

Ewwww, that was an image I could have done without. I gritted my teeth and fought the urge to spit at him.

'Take your hands off me,' I said. I wasn't sure how it would come out, but it sounded cool and controlled and furious. Not edged with panic, which was a miracle.

He covered my mouth, and in one swift motion, he swung a leg over me and straddled me. I felt a hot surge of utter despairing terror, a flashback from other times, years ago, when I'd been out of control and utterly lost, and it was only at the last second that I realised he hadn't untied my ankles, and I was relatively safe from the traditional kind of assault.

But then, Eamon didn't strike me as a traditional kind of rapist, either.

'Shhh,' he whispered, and I froze as the sharp edge of a huge knife pressed against my throat. 'Say hello to your daughter and tell her not to be stupid.'

Imara? I gasped and blinked, and saw her face in the darkness, pale as snow. She was crouched in the corner, wild and feral as an Ifrit. Her eyes blazed hot gold.

'No,' I croaked out, and waved one bound hand ineffectively. 'Don't, Imara.'

'That's excellent advice. It takes one little slip to end your mother's life.'

No answer. No move from Imara. She just waited, staring, patient as a lion. Eamon's hand was trembling, just a little.

'I just want to establish the ground rules,' he said. 'First off, I'm keeping this knife in place until I have a clear understanding between us, all right? The drug that I injected in Joanne is toxic. Slow, but sure. I have the antidote. Not on me, of course. Do what I say, and everyone comes out of this alive and happy.'

'Mom?'

'I'm OK,' I said.

'No, in point of fact, you're not,' Eamon said. 'As I was saying. And if your offspring rips my heart out, you'll be buying burial plots for two, because your sister won't survive the day, either. I gave her a little shot, as well. Insurance. Now that we're clear about the cost of vengeance, I'm going to remove the knife from Joanne's throat, and you're going to be a very good little Djinn, aren't you?'

Imara's lips pulled back from her teeth in a snarl, but she didn't move. Eamon leant back, then slipped off me with a creak of bedsprings. He used the knife on the ropes, quick slashes, and I rolled over on my side. I felt hot and sick. Drugged. Too drugged to do much. Eamon patted me on the shoulder. 'There, there. You'll feel better – well, if you make me happy. If not, you'll slip into a coma and die.'

Imara was up on her feet in one fluid motion. Her hands were at her sides, but I could see the gleam of claws, and threw her a warning shake of my head. 'He gave me a shot,' I said. 'Can't – just wait. Wait.'

Eamon hauled me to my feet. Cold air hit my skin, and I remembered with a bleary shudder that I was naked. He barely glanced at me, just shoved me forward into Imara's arms. 'Get her dressed,' he said. 'Don't think of trying anything tricky. If you cooperate, we'll be saying our fond farewells in just a little while.'

'Mom?' Imara sounded scared, and pissed as hell. 'Should I kill him?'

Funny, I'd been blaming David for murder in the name of self-preservation just a little while ago, hadn't I? But if I hadn't had Sarah's life depending on this, as well as my own, I'd have cheerfully watched Imara de-bone the bastard right in front of me. Flexible ethics. The key to a happy life.

'No,' I said. 'Not yet.'

She opened up a bag that was lying on the floor behind her. Clothes. Nice ones. Silky, formfitting underwear. A silky pair of grey microfiber pants. A pull-on black velvet scoop-necked top.

And a pair of elegant black shoes, sculptural and spike-heeled.

'Manolo,' my daughter said. 'For moral support. There's a more practical pair underneath.'

The other pair was Miu Miu flats. I swallowed hard and slipped them on. Perfect, of course. I kissed Imara on the cheek and smiled at her. Weakly.

'I'll kill him for hurting you,' she said.

'Maybe,' I agreed. 'But for right now, let's just see what he wants.'

'What he wants,' Eamon said from where he reclined on the bed, 'is to get your lovely bums out of here and into the car. Shall we?'

I nodded. The room did a greasy, unpleasant spin, but I hung on.

'Fine,' I said grimly. 'The faster we can get you out of our lives, the better I'm going to like it.'

'Ah,' he sighed. 'Just when we were starting to bond.'

Chapter Seven

He'd said a couple of hours. Actually, in most cars it would have been about four; in the Camaro, with Imara behind the wheel, it was closer to two.

No small talk. I sat in the backseat, with Eamon; he had his knife out and tapped the flat of it restlessly against his knee. I felt sicker than ever, my head pounding so hard that I started to worry about an aneurysm. Resting my left temple against the cool window glass seemed to help. A little.

I roused to find that Eamon was taking my pulse. He seemed competent enough at it . . . He looked up when I tried to pull away and held on. 'How do you feel?' he asked.

'Like I'm dying.'

'I can give you something for the headache.'

'The last thing I want is you medicating me. Again.'

He shrugged and went back to tapping his knife.

Imara was watching us in the rearview mirror. I nodded slightly to let her know I was all right.

The rest of the trip was conducted in tense silence.

We arrived in Boston just after dark, and Eamon gave directions in terse, single-turn increments. I had no idea where we were going, and it was a bit of a surprise to pull up in the parking lot of a huge granite building. I'd been expecting some deserted warehouse, some place where his sleazy business – whatever it might be – could be conducted in private.

This was a hospital.

'Out,' he said to me, and prodded me with the point of the knife when I didn't move. Imara growled, low in her throat. 'Let's all behave nicely. We're nearly done, you know. I'd hate for you to screw it up now.'

I got out of the car and had to brace myself against the cool finish. Oh, *God*, I felt sick. Nothing in my stomach, or it would have been on the pavement. Imara took my arm, and Eamon slid the knife into a leather sheath that he concealed in a folded magazine.

'Right,' he said. 'After you, please.'

We went in through the front door, just another concerned little family crowded together for support. All hospitals look pretty much the same; this one had a lived-in feel despite the constant application of astringents and floor wax. Lots of people in scrubs walking the halls, which were decorated with soothing framed prints. I barely noticed. I was too busy thinking about whether or not, since I was in a hospital, I should start shouting for help. The fact that the knife was still in Eamon's possession was a cause for concern, though. He could hurt innocent bystanders.

And would.

'Easy,' Eamon whispered in my ear, as if he'd sensed my inner debate. 'Let's not get tricky, love. On the elevator, please. And push six.'

A long, slow ride. It was just the three of us. I calculated the odds of whether or not Imara could take him before he could stab me, and I could see she was doing the same math problem. She slowly shook her head. Not that she couldn't take him – she could – but that she didn't think it was a good idea.

Neither did I.

The doors dinged open at the sixth floor, and there was another long, clean hallway. Deathly still. We moved down it, and as we came even with an inset nurse's station, the woman on duty looked up and smiled.

'Eamon!' She looked ridiculously happy to see him. Did she not have any idea? No, of course she didn't. He was turning on the charm for her. 'You're coming kind of late. Visiting hours just finished.'

'Sorry,' he said. 'My cousin and her daughter got held up at Logan. Is it all right—?'

'Logan? That figures. Sure. Just don't stay too long, OK?' The nurse gave us an impersonal smile, half the wattage she'd reserved for Eamon. She focused in on me, and frowned a bit. 'Poor thing, you look done in. Long flight?'

'The red-eye from hell,' I said. Before I could say anything else, like *Call the police, you idiot*, Eamon hustled me onward. 'All right, what is this?' I hissed. 'Why are you taking us to a hospital?'

'Shut up.' He pressed the magazine in my side. Sometime when I'd been distracted he'd slid the knife free, and it pressed a sharp reminder of his intentions into me. 'Six doors down on the right side.'

Some of the doors were shut, with medical charts in the holders out front. The sixth one was propped open. Eamon gestured the two of us to go first, outwardly polite, inwardly measuring the distance to my kidneys. I stepped in, wondering what kind of trick he was about to play.

None, apparently. No gang of scary people lurking in the corners – not that they'd have been able to do so, in such a small, clean, brightly lit room. Nothing to hide behind. Just some built-in cabinets along the walls, a hospital bed, and the woman lying in it.

Eamon closed the door behind us. We stood in silence for a few seconds, and I stared at the woman. She was maybe twenty-five – it should have been a pretty, vital age, but she was pallid and loose and limp, her skin a terrible sickly colour. Her hair looked clean, and carefully brushed; it was a medium brown, shot through with blond. Her eyelids looked thin and delicate and blue, veins showing through.

I waited, but she didn't move. IV liquids dripped. There was a tube down her throat, and a machine hissed and chuffed and breathed on her behalf.

I opened my mouth.

'You're about to ask me who she is. Don't.' Eamon gave me a bitter, thin smile. 'Just fix her. You don't need to know anything else.'

'Pardon? Do what?'

The smile, thin and bitter as it was, faded. 'Fix her. Now.' He enunciated it with scary clarity. He transferred his stare to Imara, who frowned and glanced at me. 'Don't even think about saying no, love, or I'll do things to your mum here that not even a hospital full of surgeons can fix.' He grabbed me with his forearm around my throat, pulling my chin up, and set the knife to my exposed neck. I stood on tiptoe, fighting for balance. Fear gave me a sudden bolt of clarity, but there was nothing I could do or say, not like this. Too risky.

I had to trust Imara.

She slowly extended her hand towards him. Graceful and supplicating. 'Sir, please understand,' she said. 'You didn't have to do it this way. If my mother had known what you wanted, she would have tried to help you without the threats.'

'Maybe. Couldn't take that chance, though, could I? But still, here we are, and since you're suddenly taken all warm and fuzzy, go on. Do your good deed of the day.'

Imara slowly shook her head. 'I'm not – like that. I can do only a few things. I can't heal. Certainly not something as grievous as this.'

His arm tightened, compressing my throat. I made a muffled sound of protest and teetered on my toes.

'Please! If I could save this woman, I would, but I'm not *capable*, don't you see?'

'Then go get someone who can.'

'There *isn't* anyone who can, not among the Djinn or the Wardens. There are rules, and they're larger than your desires or your needs. I'm sorry.'

I couldn't see Eamon's face, but I couldn't imagine that cold, crazy man was letting that be the last word. He didn't have a ready comeback, though. I felt a tremble go through him, and the knife dug just a bit deeper into my skin.

'All right!' Imara said sharply. 'Don't hurt her! I'll try.'

She put her hands on the woman's face, turning it gently to one side so that it faced towards me and Eamon. I thought I saw the translucent eyelids flutter, but nothing else happened. The frail chest rose and fell under the pale nightgown. IV fluids dripped.

And then, with the suddenness of a horror movie, the eyes flew open. Blank and clouded, but open.

The eyes of the living dead, nothing in them at all.

I felt Eamon's reaction through the connection of his arm, a shudder that might have sent him reeling if he hadn't kept hold of me. Which he did, for a blank second, and then he shoved me away and lurched to the bed. The knife fell to the floor, forgotten, and Eamon bent over the woman. 'Liz? Can you hear me?'

Her eyes rolled back in her head, and Imara let go as the woman's body went into a galvanic spasm, practically leaping off the bed. Convulsions. Bad ones. I looked at Imara, speechless, and she looked as shocked as I did.

'I told you,' she said. 'It's forbidden.'

Eamon turned on her with the speed of a cobra. 'No. You're holding back. Wake her up.'

'I can't.'

'Wake her up!' he shouted, and turned to pick up his knife. 'I need five bloody minutes! Five!'

'I can't give it to you. I'm sorry.'

'You're going to be!'

He rounded on me, and Imara reached out and knocked the knife out of his hand. It skidded across the floor in a hiss of metal, and bumped into a pair of shoes that had just manifested out of thin air.

I blinked away confusion and focused. Even then, it took me a few long seconds to recognise that David had come to our aid.

He bent down and picked up the knife. 'Looking for this?' David's voice was reduced to a velvet-soft purr. The shine of the knife turned restlessly in his hand, over and over. 'It has Joanne's blood on it, I see. Do you really think that was a good idea?'

Eamon froze. The woman on the bed stopped her

galvanic spasms and went completely still again. Her eyes were half-shut.

'Yours?' David asked, and pointed at the bed with the tip of the knife. He looked – cold. Perfect and cold and furious, but absolutely self-contained. Rage in a bottle.

'Mine?' Eamon sketched a mad sort of laugh. 'What the hell would I do with a girl in a coma? Other than the obvious, I mean.'

I remembered Eamon's taunts and hints, dropped all the way back when he'd revealed himself to me as the bastard he truly was. Drugging my sister. *I like my women a little less talkative and more compliant, in general*, he'd said. The possibilities nauseated me, together with the fact that the nurse outside had recognised him by name, as a regular visitor.

I took a step backward, until the wall was at my back. Felt good, the wall. I needed the support. My legs had gone cold, pins-and-needles cold. My balance insisted that the room was pitching and rolling like the deck of a sinking ship.

David exchanged a look with Imara, a nod, and she dropped her gaze and moved out of his way. Nothing standing between him and Eamon now. I saw Eamon register that, and lick his suddenly pale lips.

'Hang on a minute, mate,' he said. 'I know it looks bad, but the truth is, I only need to wake her up for a couple of minutes. Less, even. Just long enough to say my good-byes and—'

'Don't lie,' David interrupted. The knife kept turning in his hand, drawing my eyes as well as Eamon's. 'You have a reason, and it isn't anything so sentimental.'

Eamon's eyes narrowed, and I could see him trying to decide whether or not he'd be able to take the knife. He couldn't, but there was no way he'd be able to judge that for himself. I hoped he'd try. I really did.

'All right,' he said. 'Nothing so saccharine. We were partners. She took possession of a certain payment, and she didn't want to share. I need to make her tell me where she hid the money.'

'Still not true,' David said. His eyes were terrifying – flames swirling around narrowed pupils. 'I want you to speak the truth, just once before you die.'

'You don't want to kill me, old son. I'm the one with the antidote for your girl's poison, and unless you want to see her in a hospital bed next to my beloved Liz here—'

David moved in a streak of light, and suddenly he was pressed against the other man, chest to chest, bending him over the hospital bed in a backbreaking curve. His right hand was locked around Eamon's throat, and his left . . .

. . . his left held the hilt of the knife he'd buried deep in Eamon's side.

Eamon's eyes widened soundlessly.

'That,' David said, 'is a fatal wound. Feel it?' He moved the knife helpfully. Eamon tried to scream, but nothing happened. 'Shhhh. Nod if you believe me.'

Eamon shakily nodded, throat still struggling to let loose his terror.

'Good.' David pulled the knife free in a single fast rip. No blood followed, and there should have been fountains of the stuff. 'I'm holding the wound shut,' David said. 'But the second you disappoint me, little man, the *instant* I think that you're mocking me or even thinking about harm to my family, that ends. I watch you bleed your life away in less than a dozen heartbeats. Understand?'

Eamon nodded convulsively. He was paler than the woman on the bed.

'Now, you're going to get the antidote,' David said. 'Which I imagine you have hidden somewhere in this room. You're going to give it to Joanne, and then you're going to go and give it to her sister.' He let go of Eamon's throat. 'Move.'

Eamon edged out of the way, one hand pressed trembling to his side. Too terrified to move quickly. David watched him with glowing metallic eyes, and Imara did, as well.

I made some sound of effort, trying to straighten up. David had his full attention on Eamon, and his knuckles were white where he gripped the knife. I remembered Imara saying that he was fighting off the influence of the Mother, and how difficult it was. I wondered what would happen if he succumbed to that here, in a building full of innocent and helpless victims.

Not for me. Please, not for me. I tried to send him the message, but I had no idea if he was listening. His attention was completely riveted on Eamon.

Eamon, meanwhile, was moving – slowly, carefully, with a hand pressed hard to the place the knife had gone in as if he could hold his life in with it. He walked to a wooden cabinet and dragged a floral suitcase – clearly a woman's – from a narrow cubbyhole. He opened it and took out a bottle filled with clear liquid that he held up in one shaking hand. His hair was plastered to his face in wet sweaty points, and I could feel the rage and fear coming off him.

'I hope we understand each other,' David said. 'If Joanne dies, I take you apart. Slowly. I can show you things about pain that you've never even imagined. And I can make it last for an eternity.'

Eamon, if possible, paled even further. He tossed him the vial. David effortlessly snatched it out of the air without moving his gaze from the other man's face, and held it out. Imara took it and looked uncertain.

'Syringe,' Eamon said. Imara ripped open drawers in the cabinet by the sink and came up with a syringe, which she filled from the vial.

She crossed to me and hesitated again. 'I – I don't know how to—' She did. I knew, and she knew everything I did, but it was comforting to know that there were still things that could make my daughter flinch.

'Vein or muscle?' I asked.

'Muscle,' Eamon said.

I took the syringe out of Imara's hands, jammed it into my thigh, and depressed the plunger. Whatever it was in the hypo, it went in ice-cold, tingling, and then turned hot. It moved fast. I gasped for breath as I felt it move through my circulatory system. My lungs felt as if I'd sucked on liquid nitrogen, and I got an instant, mind-numbing flash of a headache.

Then it was done, and I felt . . . clearer. Not well, by any stretch. But better.

For the first time, David looked at me directly. I gave him a shaky nod as Imara helped me up. 'I'm OK,' I said. 'Now, can you – help her? None of this is her fault. She doesn't deserve to suffer for it.'

David looked baffled for a second, then turned his attention to the woman lying on the bed. He crossed to look down at her, and put his fingertips on her forehead.

And then he said, very quietly, 'There's nothing there to help.'

'No,' Eamon said, and lunged forward over the bed, one hand still clutched to his side. 'No. She opened her eyes—'

'Imara opened her eyes for her,' David said. 'The mind that was inside her is gone. She's been gone for years.'

Eamon's face turned into a rigid mask, with a red angry flush across his cheekbones. 'No. She's there. I told you, I need five minutes—'

'Her brain is dead, and her soul is gone.' David looked up at him, then at me. 'This is why you wanted a Djinn. To heal her.'

Eamon said nothing. He'd taken the woman's limp hand in his, and he was holding it. For any normal person, it would have been horrible, coming here, holding her warm hand, knowing on some level that it was just a lie her body was telling. I wasn't sure what it was for Eamon. I wasn't even sure why he cared so much. Both his explanations had been lies, David said. So what was the truth?

'You said you had a time limit,' I said.

'Her family's turning off the machines,' he said. It was barely a whisper. 'Tomorrow. Brings new meaning to the term deadline, doesn't it?'

He laughed. It was an awful laugh, something wild and dangerous and mad. Not a good man, Eamon. Not a sane man. But there was something in him, some overwhelming emotion driving all of it.

'How did it happen?' I asked.

'Why would you care?' he asked, and brushed the glossy, oddly healthy hair back from her pale, dry face. It had to be about money, didn't it? Cold, hard cash. Because I didn't want to believe he was capable of love and devotion – it made things far too complicated.

'You did it to her, didn't you?' Imara suddenly asked.

Eamon transferred that feverish stare from the woman to my daughter. 'Bugger off.'

'Imara's right. She was just another victim, wasn't she? Only this one up and died on you.' My voice was shaking, and I could feel the rest of me trembling along with it. 'You got carried away, playing your little games.'

He laughed, and looked down at the woman. 'You hear that, Liz? Funny. Just another victim.' He shook his head. 'Liz and I – let's just say we had a professional relationship. And she violated some professional rules. Things went wrong.'

I was never going to understand him. Nothing he said matched to what his body language said. The slump of his shoulders, the trembling in those long, elegant hands – that all spoke of grief, real and bone-deep grief.

David hadn't said anything. He was watching Eamon with the same intensity, but the incandescent rage had died down a bit.

'You going to kill me now?' Eamon asked. 'Give me a colourful end to a bad career?'

'No.' David shrugged. 'I healed the wound. You'll be fine so long as you don't make any sudden movements. Or come after my family again. If you do that again, I *will* kill you.'

My family. That struck me deep.

'You can all go to hell for all I care,' Eamon said, and reached across to rest his hand on top of the respirator that breathed for the woman on the bed. 'I didn't poison your sister, by the way. She's the one bright thing in my life. I didn't—' He fell silent.

'If you really think that, then let her go,' I said. 'Just let her go.'

'Oh, I already have. I left her a note. I told her I had to go back to England. She'll come crawling back to you any moment now. Now *bugger off*, all of you!' The last came with a viciousness like a thrown razor.

David looked down at the bloodstained knife he was still holding, and casually broke the blade of it in two with his fingers. He tossed the remains in the trash.

And then the three of us – Imara, David, and I – left the hospital room.

As the door hissed shut behind us, David took me in his arms, and I melted against him. Into him.

I didn't ask, but David knew what I wanted to say. 'I really couldn't do anything for her. There are limits.'

I kissed the side of his neck. 'I know.'

'I leave you alone for five minutes—'

'It was more like days.'

He growled lightly into my shoulder. 'You're impossible. And I have—'

'Responsibilities,' I murmured. 'I know you do.'

He let go.

'What about him? Eamon?' Imara was standing straight and tall, hands folded, watching the two of us. My daughter's face was a mirror of mine, at least in form, and in this instance I suspected she was a mirror of my expression, too. Compassion mixed with wariness. Eamon was a wild animal, and there was no telling what he'd do. Or to whom.

'If that demonstration didn't frighten him off, then the next step is to kill him. Not that I'd mind that.'

My thoughts were on other things. 'The woman – Liz – was she his victim, or his partner?'

'I don't know,' David said. 'I only know that Eamon never once told the truth about her.'

Imara said, 'Yes, he did.'

David turned to her, surprised.

'When he called her 'beloved Liz.' He meant that.'

At the nurse's station, an alarm began to sound. The nurse jerked to attention, checked a screen, and hit a button, then rushed past us . . . into the room we'd just exited.

'Let's go,' David said.

'Is she—?'

'Go.'

'Did Eamon—?'

He held the door to the elevator for me, head down, staring at his shoes.

'Oh God, David, did *you*—?'

He didn't answer. Neither did Imara.

On the way to the lobby, I called Sarah's cell phone. She was crying when she answered. 'Jo, oh my God –

Eamon – Eamon left me a note – I thought – I thought
he really loved me—'

So. He wasn't entirely a lying bastard, after all.

'Sarah?' I said gently. 'Stay there. I'm coming.'

He hadn't exactly stinted her on accommodations.
Sarah was registered at a downtown Boston hotel in
her own room, a luxurious suite that came with a
panoramic view, a fabulous king-size bed, and its own
monogrammed robes.

I knew about the bed and the robes because
when we arrived, Sarah was curled up on the bed
sporting the robe, clutching a tearstained note in
one hand and a generous wad of tissues in the other.
She looked like hell, but she didn't look sick. I still
felt achy in places, but I knew that was a legitimate
price to pay for what I'd avoided. Eamon really
would have killed me.

And my sister was weeping herself sick over him.

After parsing some of the hitching, half-understood
things she was mumbling, I came to the conclusion that
she'd consulted the liquor cabinet for some comfort,
too. Great. Drunk, maudlin, and irrational. Sarah's
best day ever.

I rolled my eyes at David, who had the grace to turn
to look out the windows at the rain streaking the glass.
Imara grinned. Together, my daughter and I escorted
Sarah to the bathroom, where I dumped a cold shower
on her to help with the sobering up (and yes, it was

more than a little fun, too), and helped her get herself together. Eamon had provided plenty of tools, from high-quality make-up to shopping bags from half the high-end clothiers in Boston.

My sister should have been a model. She had the rack for it, and the elegant bone structure. Where I was round, she was straight, flat, and lean. Her hair still retained the delicate cut and highlights that I'd helped her put in – God, had it only been a week ago? I decided to forgo the mascara. As much as Sarah continued to sniffle about her latest romantic disaster, it was bound to be a wasted effort.

'I was so worried,' Sarah suddenly said as I applied blusher to her pale cheeks. I stopped, surprised. 'I didn't want to leave you, Jo. Eamon said – he said you'd gone back to get your friend.'

I nodded. 'I did.' He'd basically left me to fend for myself in a hurricane, but he'd cut me loose, at least. Had to give him points for that. 'I'm sorry. It took me a while to catch up to you.'

She studied me from bloodshot eyes, getting more sober by the minute. 'Were you? Catching up to me? Or were you really looking for Eamon?'

I applied myself to the make-up with an effort. 'Looking for you, of course.'

'Jo.' She stopped my hand with hers. 'I know he's a bastard. But there was something about him – you understand?'

'I understand that you were married to one jerk,

and you just fell for another one,' I said. 'But in this case, I can't really blame you. He put on a good show. Even I believed it for a while. So I think I'll have to forgive you for this one.'

That was what she wanted to hear. I saw the flash of relief in her eyes, and then she hugged me. A warm cloud of Bvlgari Omnia embraced me, too. She'd put too much on. She always did.

I hugged her back fiercely. 'Come on,' I said. 'Let's get packed up.'

It didn't take long. Everything she owned, Eamon had bought for her; like me, she'd had to flee Fort Lauderdale with nothing but the clothes on her back. Even her suitcases were new.

And designer.

Some refugees just are born to land on their expensively manicured feet.

'What am I going to do with her?' I sighed to David as we leant against the wall and watched Sarah fill the third Louis Vuitton bag with toiletries and shoes. I was considering knocking her over the head and stealing the suitcases. Eamon had excellent taste.

'She shouldn't stay here,' David said. 'If he comes back, I'm not sure she wouldn't—'

'Oh, I'm sure she *would*. Eagerly. Eamon could talk her into anything, and you know it.'

'Then you'd better send her someplace safe.'

'And where would safe be, exactly?' I asked. He folded his arms and stared at the carpet; there really wasn't a good answer to that, and he knew it. 'I've used up my favours. I have no other family to ship her off to—'

'Actually,' Imara interrupted, 'you do.'

We both stopped to look at her. A flash of lightning outside the windows illuminated the humour in her smile.

'I'll take care of her,' she said. 'If you're about to jump back into trouble, you can't keep her with you. She'd slow you down.' Imara's golden eyes sought David's for a second. 'So would I, as a matter of fact.'

'Imara—'

'You have to take her,' she said to her father. 'You have to take her to see the Oracle, and you know you do. I can't go. I'd just be in the way.'

He reached out and brushed her hair back from her face, a gesture I'd felt a thousand times from him. Tenderness incarnate. 'I need you to go to the Ma'at,' he said. 'Take Sarah, and get on the first available plane to Las Vegas to make contact with them. Tell them that we'll meet them in Phoenix.'

'Phoenix?' Imara and I blurted it together.

'I'm not taking you back to Seacasket,' David said. 'That way is – well, it's just not possible. We have to go to the other access point where you can reach the Oracle.'

'Phoenix,' I repeated. 'David, that's a long, long way.'

'Yes,' he agreed blandly. 'Imara, get Sarah on the plane. Jo—'

'You two should get some rest,' Imara said with an utterly bland expression. 'The room's paid up for the night.'

There was a storm, of course. There's always a storm in my life, and this one was big and nasty and intent on harm. I did what I could, in concert with the other two Wardens still alive in the vicinity to help – two hours spent in front of the plate glass window, watching the clouds, reading the weather patterns and gently herding it where it needed to be. David didn't help me with the weatherwork. I think he knew I needed to do this myself, feel that I was at least being useful in some small way.

When I came back to myself fully, he was holding me from behind, arms around me, and I was leaning back against his chest.

'Why aren't you crazy?' I asked him wearily.

'Excuse me?'

'Crazy. Red-eyed, bugged-out crazy. Why isn't *she* controlling you?'

'She isn't awake.'

'Could've fooled me.'

David let out a slow breath that stirred my hair. 'She's still dreaming, Jo. When she wakes up . . . it will be worse. A lot worse. Unless something happens to change her mind about humanity.'

'Ashan took care of all that. He's been whispering sweet nothings in her ear for years, I'd be willing to bet. Maybe centuries. Nothing I can do or say will counteract that.'

David kissed the top of my head where I was curled against him, and he stroked my hair. It was a familiar ritual. My curls relaxed under his touch and smoothed into a silk-soft curtain. I'd never realised how intimate that was, how . . . caring. He felt so strong when I leant against him. So solid and immediate and real. 'Don't underestimate yourself,' he said. 'You stopped me in my tracks the first time I saw you. She has to love you.'

I was overwhelmed by how much I missed him. Such a girly thing to do, but I couldn't help it; I turned my face to his chest and began to sob. Abjectly, silently, near-hysterically. My whole body trembled with the force of it. I didn't want to be doing these things, risking these things; I wanted to forget the feeling of dread and terror and helplessness that Eamon had buried inside me like a broken-off knife. I wanted to take David home and live in peace. For heaven's sake, just *live*.

He understood why I was crying, I guess, because he didn't speak. He just held me, stroking my hair, and let me cry. There were advantages to having a lover older than recorded history. He knew when to be quiet and just let me get on with it.

Once the storm had passed, I felt weak, feverish, and not very much better. My eyes were scratchy and swollen, and I needed to lie down and curl up in a ball for about, oh, a week. Next to him. Holding him.

'I'm sorry,' he said, and let me straighten up when I tried to pull away. 'You didn't ask for any of this. You never did.'

'Damn right.' I took a handful of tissues from the box that Sarah had been using before me, and used them to wipe my face, blot my eyes, and blow my nose. David watched with nothing but compassion on his face. 'I was going to ask *why me*, but I don't think there's really a very good answer for that.'

'The stronger the shoulders, the larger the load,' he said. It sounded like an aphorism, but I didn't know it. 'You're strong, Jo. Stronger than most humans I've ever known.'

'Great. My boyfriend thinks I'm a Clydesdale.'

He smiled. 'I think you're a goddess.'

'Sweet,' I said, and honked my nose, 'but goddesses don't cry in their beer about crap like this, do they?'

'How many goddesses have you ever met?'

I didn't want to ask how many *he'd* met. Sounded like a discussion of former girlfriends that I didn't want to have right now. 'How long can you stay? With me?'

'I don't know.' Oh, hell, I didn't want him to be honest about it. Men. Why don't they ever know when to slide in the comforting lie? 'Like you, I'm doing this from moment to moment. On instinct.'

'Yeah, but at least your instincts are honed by a few millennia of experience. Mine, they're finely calibrated by a few years of screwing up.'

That got a cute little smile from him, with raised eyebrows, and nearly revealed a hidden dimple. Ooooh. I blotted my tears again, to keep him in focus.

'Close your eyes,' David said.

'Why?'

His eyebrows quirked. 'Don't you trust me?'

Unarguable. I closed them, although it deprived me of the sight of him, which was a big minus. The sandy itch of post-crying swelling was nearly unbearable . . . until I felt the light, silky stroke of his thumbs across the lids.

And then the itchy, swollen feeling was gone.

I sucked in a startled breath and discovered that my bloated sinus passages were fixed, too. Nice. The ache in my temple also vanished.

The vague heavy ache of the after-effects of Eamon's drug were gone, as if it had never existed.

I opened my eyes again and looked straight at him. His smile kindled into the kind of fire you get at the heart of a nuclear power plant. The look melted me into a little radioactive puddle. Figuratively. But I wasn't entirely sure he couldn't do it literally, as well.

'You bastard,' I breathed. 'You could have just zapped Eamon's poison right out of me, couldn't you?'

'I wanted a hands-on approach. And I wanted him to clearly understand that we were not the people he should want to play with.'

'Oh, I'm pretty sure you got it across to him.' I put a hand on the warm plane of his cheek and let my fingers glide down the warm skin, rough with just a hint of beard. David might be wearing human form as a kind of disguise, but he was thorough about it. He understood the delight of textures.

'We can leave in the morning,' he said. 'Imara's right. You need the rest.'

I didn't want rest. All I wanted was a bed, a lock on the door, and David. It was irresponsible, it was dumb, and I didn't care. I was exhausted with the strain of giving up what I wanted for the sake of . . . everyone else.

The weather was distracting me. I got up and yanked the cords on the curtains to whip them closed.

His hands slid around me from behind before I could turn around again. They wrapped hot around my stomach and pulled me back against his body. His head dropped forward, pressed against mine, and I felt the shuddering breath that went through him. As if he wanted to weep the way I had, but men – even male Djinn – didn't do that kind of thing. He pressed his lips to the back of my neck instead. His voice, when it came, was rusty and low. 'I hate this,' he said. 'I hate seeing you hurt. I want to keep you safe, and I can't. I can't even keep you safe from me.'

'You have.'

'So far.'

'You will.'

'Maybe.' He loosened his hold on me and let me turn around; his hands settled on my hips and pulled me closer against him. 'I wish you'd never met me. You'd have been—'

'Dead,' I finished for him. 'You know, because you saved my life. A few times.'

He shook his head. 'You might not have been in danger if it hadn't been for me.'

'Not everything's about you. Or the Djinn,' I said, but I said it gently, because I hated to imply he wasn't the centre of the universe, and kissed him to let him know not to take it personally. It was a nice, long, slow kiss, and it felt like we were melting into each other. Tension flowed down my back, out through my feet, and left me in a deliciously languorous state of bliss. Without breaking the kiss, David walked me back a step, then another, until the bends of my knees collided with the bed. I wavered, then let myself fall; David let go long enough for me to writhe fully onto the bed, and then he just stood there, looking down at me.

'What are you looking at?' I demanded. I got a beautiful smile that held just a tinge of sadness.

'You,' he said. 'I just want to remember this.'

He shrugged off his olive drab coat and let it fall in a heavy thump to the carpet. Underneath, he was wearing a blue-and-white shirt and a pair of khaki cargo pants.

'Your turn,' he said.

'We're taking turns?'

He shrugged. There was a sinful glint in his eyes. 'One piece at a time.'

I didn't have a coat. I considered, then kicked off my shoes. That got a raised eyebrow. He retaliated by stripping off his own, socks included. I loved his feet. Long, narrow feet with a high arch. Baby soft, because the Djinn had no use for mundane things like calluses. Every inch of him was perfect, I recalled. Warm and velvet-soft and perfect.

I was igniting inside like an oil-soaked rag on a bonfire.

'Shirt, please,' he said. The word was almost a purr in his throat. 'Slowly.'

I made a production out of it, arching my back to slide it off over my head, shaking my newly straightened hair until it fell like black satin over the lace of my bra. David's expression was closed and mysterious, his eyes narrowly focused on the rise and swell of my breasts, the way the lace curved down and away from the skin.

I propped myself up on my elbows, making sure he got a good, long look, and gave him a slow smile. 'Your turn,' I said. 'Shirt.'

He went to it with a will. I watched the flicks of his fingers, the way the fabric slid away to reveal burnished skin, and swallowed hard. When the last button fell loose, I had a good view of his flat abdominals, and that sexy shadow of hair that was just barely visible at the waistband of his pants. They rode low on his hips, as if they wanted to come off.

Silence. He was watching me. I was watching him. 'You first,' I murmured.

He gave me a slow, completely wicked smile, and unbuttoned his pants, then let down the zipper. As the fabric slipped down his legs to puddle on the floor, I let out a slow held breath. He was perfection and flame made flesh, and oh God, how I adored him.

'You cheated,' I accused. 'What happened to the underwear?'

'Got impatient,' he said, and then my remaining clothes began to mist away, turning into cool wisps of smoke that made me shiver in delight. The bed creaked as he put one knee on it, looking down at me. 'I do that sometimes, with you.'

'Bet you say that to all the mortal girls.'

His eyes met mine, and for a second they weren't Djinn eyes, they were *David's*, and I saw the man he'd once been all those millennia ago before the fires had turned him into something else entirely.

'No,' he murmured. 'I don't.'

He had great hands. Incredible hands. They glided up my sides, skimmed over my breasts, cupped them in heat. Caressed my nipples until I was biting my lip and making whimpering noises of need.

And then his hand slid down between my legs, and my mind exploded in a haze of bliss so strong that it seemed to dissolve the world in opal swirls. Every muscle in my body convulsed, held, trembled and kept on going, and my thighs trapped his hand in place. It seemed to last forever, and just as I began to slip back into the mundane, he moved and did something else and *oh God*, it started again.

It felt like hours. Maybe it was hours, slow and hot and torturously wonderful, before he finally succumbed to temptation and slid inside me, melting us together into a mindless, perfect union. It felt so good, so right, and I wanted to move, wanted him to move . . . but he didn't. He stayed still, buried deep, and our eyes locked together in fascinated wonder. I could feel the energy running through him, hot and wild. The same energy that had overtaken him outside of New York, in the car, but he understood how to channel it better now. How to bend it to his will.

'Let go,' I whispered, and his lips parted in a gasp, and the light in his eyes brightened. 'There's such a thing as too much control.'

He'd made love to me so many different ways, and this was yet another – frantic, wild, tender, dangerous, sweet, and utterly open. Like the weather pounding at the window and crackling in my nerves, he was unstoppable. When the pleasure peaked, it was like a tidal wave carrying me to the sky, where I shivered into stars and fog.

I clung to him, exhausted and shining with sweat. Panting as it passed. He collapsed with me in a tangle of arms and legs. Our hands were clasped together, still trembling from the force of the aftershocks. David's eyes were closed, and his face was – momentarily, at least – relaxed and peaceful. I studied it with the intensity of someone planning to do a portrait, the way the shadows defined his angles, the way his eyelashes feathered, the way his cheekbones demanded to be caressed.

'I need to tell you something,' he said with his eyes still closed. His voice was unsteady, his breath coming quickly.

I didn't feel any steadier. 'So long as it's not goodbye.'

His eyes flew open. 'I'm not that cruel, am I?'

'No.' I kissed the point of his chin. He made a lazy sound of pleasure, so I kept on, nuzzling his neck. He smelt clean and hot, with just a hint of musk. Lovely. 'Well, sometimes. But believe me, I know when a guy's getting ready to hit the door. That was *not* good-bye sex. That was *whoa, hello!* sex.'

His arms went around me and rolled me on top of him. Breathtaking, the strength he had. The control. The precision. His skin was hot and damp and wonderful to touch. 'Anyone who's ever said good-bye to you is a fool.'

'Well, *obviously*. Your point?' I was playing, but some part of my brain was arguing with me. It had been shut up in the basement while the rest of me had gotten what it wanted, but now it was telling me that time continued its inexorable march, that I shouldn't be wasting this precious few seconds with banter.

I didn't care. Not now. Not with him.

David stroked my hair back from my face, but it kept sliding over my shoulders to rain down around us, a privacy curtain that made the world seem small and perfectly safe. Illusion. But a nice one.

'Most of the Djinn are gone,' he said.

'What?' The illusion was thoroughly shattered. 'What do you mean, gone?'

'Withdrawn from this plane. I sent them to the place where Jonathan kept his house – you remember?'

I remembered. Not precisely where it was, or how to get to it, because it wasn't exactly explicable to mortal brains, but the point was that it was sealed off from the regular plane of our reality. A pocket universe, of a sort. A retreat. A sanctuary, in a sense.

'While they're there, they'll be outside of anyone's control – mine, and hopefully, even the Mother's,' he said. 'It's the best way I know to keep things from escalating out of control between the Djinn and humans, if the worst should happen.'

'If she decides to kill off the human race, you mean?' He didn't answer. He didn't have to. 'You said most of the Djinn were withdrawing. Not all?'

'A few volunteered to stay with the Ma'at,' he said. 'Ten or so. Enough to help them complete their circle. The Ma'at are working to try to stabilise systems – they won't intervene directly, but they can provide a kind of ballast, settle things down.' He paused for a second, and I could tell the next thing wasn't good. 'About twenty Djinn are staying with Ashan. I can't stop them, not without a straight-out fight. The problem is that by withdrawing, I let him have the field of battle.

But if I don't . . . Djinn get hurt. And humans get caught in the middle.'

Not good news. Ashan was a force to be reckoned with, even by David's standards, much less by my own. And with a small army of immortal, arrogant, angry beings . . . twenty was more than enough to destroy everything in his path.

'I think Ashan's counting on you to give up, actually.'

'I can't fight him.'

'Can't – or won't? That was Jonathan's problem. I thought part of the reason he handed things to you was so that you'd be able to . . . act.'

He looked so grave that it chilled the lingering warmth inside me. I slipped off to the side and curled against him; his arm went around me, holding me close.

'I need time,' he said. 'I need *time*, Jo. What you're talking about is the beginning of the end for us. It's what Jonathan was afraid of all along. War. Death. Destruction. I'm not . . .' He hesitated. 'I'm not ready. I'm not sure I can be what he was. Ever.'

'So you're willing to let humans take the heat for you in the meantime while you debate it?'

His hand, which had been stroking my hair, went still. His eyes closed.

'Yes,' he said softly. 'I have to be willing to do that. And so do you. Listen, Jo – you spoke to the Oracle. That's unprecedented. You might have succeeded if the Oracle hadn't been – prevented—'

'Infected.'

'Yes,' he said, and kissed my bare shoulder. 'So we try again. We keep trying. And if it comes to a fight with Ashan, I'll do everything in my power to end it with a minimum of bloodshed.'

I rolled up on my elbow, looking down at him. 'Human bloodshed? Or are you talking about the Djinn?'

He regarded me with absolute steadiness, and there was that shadow in his eyes, the same one that had been in Jonathan's before him. Power. Vast and unknown power. 'I have to be true to my responsibilities, Jo. But you're one of those responsibilities now.'

'I know,' I said, and put my hand on his chest, over his heart. Not really a heart, of course; not really flesh, except by his will. I was touching fire. Touching eternity. 'We're just flying by the seat of our pants, aren't we? But then, we've done that from the first moment we saw each other.'

'Yes.' His burning lips pressed on my forehead for a brief second. 'It's like your forest fire. The old world is burning. It's hard to see the new one that's coming, under all the destruction, but the green always comes, Jo. It always comes.' He kissed my shoulder again, making a slow trail along my collarbone. 'Imara and Sarah's flight touched down in Phoenix without incident, by the way. Safe and sound. Imara's taking Sarah to the Ma'at.'

'Sarah in Vegas,' I sighed. 'I'm not sure that's such a great idea . . .'

'I was thinking the same thing about Imara. I remember how much trouble *you* got into there.'

'Maybe you'd better keep the kid someplace safe,' I said morosely. 'Ashan's going to target her to get to us.'

'I know he'll try.'

'But?'

'But that isn't likely to work,' David said calmly. 'First, like you, she's too unpredictable. He's never going to understand her well enough to use her. Second . . . I won't let him touch my daughter again.'

I shivered. Ashan didn't know it, but he was playing catch with a grenade if he crossed David on that one.

I kissed him with wordless agreement, and he held me, and for the moment, these precious few moments, danger was something that existed outside of the safety of this still, quiet room, and the warmth of this bed.

And wrapped in his warmth, even though urgency still beat war drums in my blood, I slept.

Morning came with a boom of thunder, and I awoke to feel things spiralling out of control again. I stayed in bed and rose up into the aetheric, struggling to keep the reins on the weather, but it was wild and getting worse.

'We should go,' David said. I didn't want to. Being under soft sheets with him, cupped warm against his heat, was the best heaven I could imagine. 'The first flight to Phoenix is in three hours.'

'I don't think anything's flying out of town today,' I said. 'Feel the sky.'

He was already moving, sliding off the bed and standing up naked, facing away from me. I watched as he formed clothing.

He turned to face me, pulling his olive drab coat into place on his shoulders. 'It's only going to get worse.' An infinity of regret in the words. I couldn't read his eyes; they were human, and hidden behind glasses and shadows. 'We'll have to find a way.'

I sighed and looked around. My clothes were neatly folded on the chair next to the bed. I began pulling things on. 'So the Oracle is in Phoenix?'

'Not exactly.' He pulled open the drawer in the small desk and took out the slender phone book. At a tap of his finger, it turned into a road atlas. He flipped pages, then handed it to me.

I glanced at it, blinked, and looked at him in exasperation. 'You're kidding.'

'No.'

'Please tell me you're kidding.'

'I'm not.' He tapped the open map with his forefinger. A spot lit up, golden even in the glow of the lamp. 'I don't make the rules, Jo. This is where the second Oracle can be reached.'

Because the map was of Arizona, all right, but the city that was marked was Sedona. Why had I ever even doubted that sometime, somewhere, I'd have to go there?

'What's so funny?' he asked, frowning. I shook my head, laughing until spots danced in front of my eyes. Waved my hand ineffectively. 'Are you all right?'

'Yeah,' I gasped. 'It's just . . . so New Age-y. What do we do? Meditate in a pyramid? Wear a crystal hat?'

'What are you talking about?'

'Oh, come on. Sedona?'

He shrugged. 'The veil's thinnest there.'

Well, it would be, wouldn't it?

David wanted to head straight for the airport. I wanted to stop for breakfast. It was the worst decision of my life. But even before breakfast, we had a fight about the car.

It started innocently enough. We waited for a letup in the rain. Outside, the air was cooler, cleaner, felt more alive, somehow, because of David's presence. I thought it was my imagination at first, but then I wasn't so sure; it seemed as if the flowers out front of the hotel got brighter, opened wider in his presence. Another sign of his strength and connection to the heart of the Earth.

Or of really great sex.

The Camaro was wedged in between a giant-tired Ford pickup and a van the size of the space shuttle.

David stopped a few feet from the car, looking at it with an expression I couldn't read. 'This is from Lewis, isn't it,' he said. Uh-oh. I unlocked the passenger door for him, then went around to my side.

'Official transportation,' I said, since I didn't want to think about how deeply obligated I was to Lewis right now. 'Warden motor pool.'

He sent me a *drop the bullshit* look, opened the door, and slid inside. I did the same. 'Expensive gift.'

'Yes.' I slid the key into the ignition and fired her up. David ran a contemplative fingertip over the dashboard, seeing who-knew-what with his Djinn senses. 'It's fast. I needed a fast car. It wasn't personal.'

'Oh, yes it is,' he disagreed. 'This is a *very* personal car. A very personal gift.'

'David—'

'You can't see it,' he said. 'You would have, when you were Djinn, but he's in love with you. He's been in love with you for a long, long time. It's all over this car, his feelings for you.'

Oh, dear. It wasn't so much that I didn't see it as I didn't *want* to see it. I'd been careful around Lewis. Not careful enough.

'Well, fine, but I'm not in love with him,' I said, and put the car in gear.

'You are,' David said. There was a hard edge to his voice I couldn't understand. 'Don't lie to yourself.'

I felt that, all right. It hurt. 'David, I'm *not* in love with Lewis!' Except maybe I was. A little. A teeny little traitorous bit of me that still remembered the crush I'd had on him back in the day. And liked it when he crinkled those brown eyes at me and smiled so charmingly. And gave me sexy cars. 'I'm *not*! I'm in love with you! Dammit, why are we fighting?'

'Because he gave you a car, and you took it.'

'I *needed* the goddamn car, David! What was I supposed to do, get Cherise to chauffeur me around to the apocalypse? Don't get me wrong, she'd do it, but it's not exactly the best idea ever!'

He set his jaw and looked out the window. I slammed the car into gear with violence unnecessary to such a sweet ride. 'You don't have to worry. I'm not sleeping with Lewis.'

'No,' he agreed. 'You're not. But you have.'

Oh, ouch. I'd never directly discussed that with him, but I wasn't too surprised that he knew about it. Hard to hide anything from the Badass Head Djinn.

'Can we get over this now? Because frankly, after last night, there's nobody on this earth that I could possibly sleep with except you.'

His eyebrows quirked. 'Only last night?'

'Oh, you're pushing it, pal.'

He let it go. 'You said you wanted breakfast.' He nodded up ahead. There was a huge sign, rotating with dignified deliberation, showed a tasty-looking artist's rendition of a blueberry pie and announced that LOU-ANN'S PIE KITCHEN was open for breakfast.

I saw no reason that pie didn't qualify as breakfast food, anyway.

The parking lot was half full, which wasn't bad for

the oh-my-God hour of the morning; apparently, the place was something of a favoured watering hole. It was pouring rain, and the Camaro hadn't come equipped with either rain slickers or umbrellas. I formed an invisible-air version as David and I walked across the wet pavement towards the entrance to the restaurant, represented by double glass doors in a weather-beaten glass-and-wood oversize log cabin structure. Someone – Louann, maybe, if she wasn't apocryphal – had planted a wide variety of flowers around the building in creative tiers of planters. It looked lush and rather sweet. I ducked under the green awning that sheltered the doorway and swung open the door.

When I did, I glanced back and caught sight of David standing rigid, staring off into the distance. 'What is it?' I asked. He left me and went out to stand in the rain, still staring. 'David?'

'Just a second.'

'What's happening?'

'Don't know,' he said. 'Hang on.'

And he disappeared. I hesitated. I didn't want to go in, if there were innocent bystanders around; the Djinn wouldn't care how many bodies they had to go through to get to me, if it was me they wanted . . .

David reappeared, misting out of the air in mid-stride. He headed straight for me, grabbed me by the neck of my shirt, and marched me inside.

The door slammed shut behind us and locked. And sealed, in some way that I was not immediately familiar with; my ears popped as if we'd suddenly shot up a few hundred feet. David kept hustling me along.

'Hey!' I protested. It dawned on me about three steps later that something was very, very wrong at Lou-ann's Pie Kitchen.

There was nobody inside.

I blinked. The lights were on, but nobody – and I mean *nobody* – was home. Empty kitchen. Empty lunch counter with pots of coffee steaming on burners. Empty booths and tables. Not a sound of human habitation anywhere. I had an ugly second of memory of some crime documentary I'd once seen, about customers and employees herded into a back room and shot, but in that case there'd be some sign, right? Purses left lying around. Chairs tipped over. Maybe even blood . . . This looked perfectly ordered, just . . . empty.

Maybe I was going crazy. Maybe David hadn't been as thorough as he'd thought in cleaning the drugs out of my system, and I was hallucinating. Maybe all of this was a dream. Maybe everything since Eamon had given me the shot had been a dream.

David let go and pushed me into a dull-green leatherette booth, then slid into the other side, facing me.

Oh, bad feelings. Very bad feelings. A fork of lightning suddenly split the clouds outside and cast a harsh white illumination that blanched the warm, homey atmosphere.

And in the flash of lightning, David changed. His body filled out, with broader shoulders, whiter skin. He folded his hands on the table, pale and strong.

When the transformation finished, I was sitting across from Ashan, in his trademark tailored suit. His teal-blue tie looked natty and perfectly tied, his shirt crisp.

When had he taken David's place? Oh *God*, not in the hotel . . . No, that was impossible. Afterward, in the parking lot? Or just now, outside? I had to believe it was just outside the door of this place, and that David had been lured away to give Ashan this chance at me.

I debated my choices. I could either die facing Ashan, or die running away.

I didn't run.

And oddly enough, he didn't kill me. At least, not right off.

'Hungry?' Ashan asked blandly. 'I recommend the strawberry pie.'

He looked down, and he did, indeed, have a plate in front of him with a slice of strawberry pie. The brilliantly red filling was oozing out over the plate like blood over bone. He picked up his fork and took a bite, then took a sip of coffee from a chunky cafe-style cup.

I might mention that each of these things – the plate, the pie, the fork, the cup – appeared just as he reached for them. A flagrant and unnecessary display of his powers, just for my benefit.

'Where's David?'

'Occupied. I'm sure he'll be back soon,' he said smoothly. 'Sure you're not hungry? It may be your last meal.'

I smiled. It felt wrong on my lips, but I hoped it would be good enough to pass his inspection. 'Sure. Mind if I serve myself?'

He shrugged. I went behind the counter and cut myself a slice of coconut meringue pie that looked like just about heaven. I decided against the coffee in favour of a glass of milk. I eased myself into the booth with an annoying squeak of plastic.

If it was a dream, at least I was going to get a piece of pie out of it. And if it wasn't . . . well, dying on a full stomach sounded like a better idea than the alternatives. I was trembling with fear for David, sick with the knowledge that if he managed to make it back here (*occupied*, what did that mean?) Ashan would have the upper hand in every way.

Ashan took another bite of pie, watching me.

'I see you made sure we had privacy,' I said.

'I felt it best.' Another chilling predator's smile. 'I'd hardly want to share you with anyone else.'

From Eamon to this. I was too numbed to be terrified, really; Eamon had done me that favour, at least. Whatever reaction Ashan had been hoping to provoke, this couldn't have been it.

I took a bite of the pie.

If Ashan was disappointed, he hid it well. He

continued to nibble and sip without any hint of homicidal intent. Well, OK, hints, but not actions. I could read the desire to kill me in every look and careful, neat motion.

'Where are they?' I asked. 'The people who were in here.'

'Still here.' He gestured vaguely. 'Out of phase. They won't notice a thing. I've moved us a few seconds back in time, in a kind of bubble. Once we leave, it'll snap back. It's a local phenomenon only.'

That was mildly interesting. 'You can do that?'

'Time is my specialty,' he said. 'It's an interesting thing, time. Fluid. Very tricky. I don't expect you to understand.'

He was positively chatty. Which was odd. Ashan had always treated me like a cockroach. I couldn't imagine him sitting down to a nice, cosy chat with me over pie and coffee. If there was a single burning flame inside Ashan, it was ambition – cold, ruthless, and all-consuming.

So why was he sitting here making nice with me? Was he waiting for word that David had been hurt? Killed?

If Ashan had hurt him, I was going to find a way to make him pay.

Ashan smiled at me over his forkful of strawberry pie. I smiled back and took a bite of coconut. The meringue melted on my tongue. Even in my numbed, tense state, that was nice.

'So,' Ashan said, and I sensed he was ready to circle around to the point. 'What did the Oracle tell you, Joanne?'

'Besides the screaming? Nothing. Good pie, by the way.'

He lost the veneer of affability, and what was left had no interest in dessert. His plate, fork, and mug disappeared. He pressed those large, strong, pale hands palms down on the table. I kept eating, slowly and deliberately. No way was I letting anything this good go to waste. I needed the strength.

'You mock me,' he said. 'You are not my equal. You are nothing. You are less than the lower life forms that spawned you.'

'Oh, you smooth talker,' I said. 'Careful. You're turning me on.'

I'd surprised him. He was used to people cowering and screaming. Even me. Again, my fresh inoculation of terror from Eamon had done me a strange favour.

Surprise made him thoughtful, not angry. He tilted his head and continued to stare at me. 'Why do you say such things to me? Do you want to die?'

'Nope,' I said. 'You'll kill me, or you won't. Your petty little political ambitions are not my concern. You want to be the centre of the Djinn universe? Fine. Take it up with David. I sleep with him; I don't tell him what to do. Speaking of David, you're not exactly facing off with him hand-to-hand, are you? What's the matter, Ashan? He got you scared?'

Ashan put his hands flat on the table, watching me, and his eyes were the eerie colour of deep oceans lit from below. 'Do you have any idea how much I want to destroy every cell of your body? Grind you into paste until all that's left of you is fragments of bone and screams?'

My heart hammered faster, but I kept eating. 'Poetic. You should write that down.'

I had completely nonplussed him this time. He barked out a dry laugh and sat back. 'Do you really think you can defeat me? A weak little creature like you?' I shook my head. His eyes glowed brighter, and the smile grew sharper at the edges. 'Perhaps you have finally lost your mind.'

'That's probably it.' I forked up the last delicious bite of my pie, savouring every bit, and washed it down with a prodigious gulp of milk. Now that was a snack. 'I've gone insane. But at least it came with dessert.'

He steepled his fingers into long, strong columns of flesh and bone. It reminded me of Eamon, fingertips touching his lips, watching me in the motel room. I felt a bolt of sheer terror flash through me, and it made me flinch; that was bad. Numbness was good. Numbness was my only real defence right now.

I compensated the only way I knew how: with sarcasm. 'What are you going to do, Ashan? Glare me to death?'

I'd goaded him a little too far. He reached across the table, knocking my plate off in a wobbling arc to the floor, and grabbed my wrist. He pinned it to the table with crushing force. Probably wasn't even an effort for him to break my bones, shatter the table beneath, bring down the entire restaurant, for that matter. But I just sat still, watching him. Unresisting.

And he didn't exert any more force than he had to, to hold me still.

Like Eamon.

'What do you want?' I asked him breathlessly.

'You keep coming after me. *What do I have that you want*?'

There was a flash of loathing in his eyes so extreme that I swallowed. 'You are of no interest to me at all. You are less than what crawls in the dirt.'

I realised something terribly important. Ashan didn't want to be here. He really didn't, and it wasn't about me. He was just dicking around with me out of some obscure desire to play with his food, like a giant tomcat.

'Let go,' I said. He did. I boggled, but covered it quickly. No sense in letting him know that I was lost, too. 'What do you want to know, Ashan?'

'What did the Oracle say to you?'

'Nothing.'

'You lie.' His hands were flat on the table again, and if anything his eyes were even brighter, incandescently bright in the darkened corner. 'What did the creature say to you?'

'Look,' I said quietly. 'I don't know what you want, but I can only tell you what I know. Which is nothing. The Oracle screamed, and—' I realised what he was getting at. The Oracle hadn't told me, but Ashan had told me himself, with all his paranoia.

He'd had something to do with the Demon Mark breaking through the defences to get to the Oracle. Maybe he'd even done it himself.

He must have seen that I'd figured it out, because he backhanded me.

I saw it coming, and I was able to turn my face with the smack, but even so, it knocked me into the wall. My head impacted wood with a crack, and I felt a hot wave of sickness crawl over me. It didn't hurt immediately, but I had an instant conviction that it was going to hurt later. For now, there was just a high-pitched ringing in my head, and a fire-hot throb on my right temple.

Ashan was standing up. I was about to be ripped to pieces, I could feel it in the raw fury boiling off him. He reached out . . .

And David caught his hand.

They didn't speak. David just stared at him, face set. He looked hard – as hard as the Djinn facing him. Fire and ashes, neither one of them human.

Ashan smiled. 'Took you long enough,' he said. 'I thought I might have to make her scream more to get your attention.'

'You're a fool,' David said. 'And you're the second

fool who's tried this in less than a day. You have no idea—'

He stopped talking, and slowly turned his head off to the side, staring into shadows.

'Fool, you were saying?' Ashan asked. He was still smiling. I liked that smile even less the longer it stayed. 'I'm not so much of one. Though clearly you are, since you continue to come running at her beck and call, even without the bottle forcing you to her will.'

'What have you done?' David let go of Ashan's wrist. 'Ashan—'

'What was necessary,' he said. 'We were gods once. We were worshipped. And we will be again.'

'Yessssss,' whispered a new voice. If it could be called a voice. It was more like flesh being dragged over sandpaper. 'Godsssssssssss.'

And an adult Demon stepped out of the shadows.

It could have been the same one who'd chased me in the forest; all I could identify about it was its wrongness, its essentially *alienness*. The geometry of the thing didn't make sense. Skin that wasn't skin. Terribly wrong, misshapen, bleeding light and shadow like a drug-induced nightmare.

It was speaking.

David took a soundless step back, mouth open, eyes wide. Astonished, for a split second, and then the true horror of the situation snapped in for all of us.

Ashan was in league with the Demon. Betraying the Djinn themselves. Betraying the Mother.

His betrayal of humanity was nothing compared with that.

David lunged for me, and *threw* me over the back of the booth to slide down the lunch counter. I tipped over and slammed to the tile floor on my hands and knees. He didn't have to tell me to get out. I got the message, loud and clear. I scrambled up and ran full speed for the glass doors.

I hit them and bounced.

No time for pain or confusion. I whirled around, grabbed a chair, and whacked the hell out of the glass. Again. And again. The chair came apart on the fourth try in a clatter of loosened screws and aluminium framing.

'An old trick of Jonathan's,' Ashan said. 'Freezing time makes a good refuge. Or prison.'

David was backing away from the Demon, but it was coming, and I didn't think he could stop it. Not with Ashan on its side. He reversed course and lunged, grabbed the Demon by one misshapen limb, and slingshotted it into Ashan.

Who staggered and screamed as the Demon's claws ripped into him for support. I felt that popping in my ears again, painful and deafening, and David spun towards me to scream, 'Now!'

I yanked open the door. 'Come on!'

He tried to reach me.

318   Rachel Caine

The Demon was faster. Horribly fast, faster than anything I'd ever seen. It moved in a blur, and then it stopped in the next fraction of a second, and it had him. Its claws wrapped around him, growing to the size of knives . . . of swords . . .

They punched through his flesh and skewered him in a cage of black steel.

'No!' I screamed.

He reached out with one hand, and I thought he was reaching for me, but then the wind hit me with brutal force, driving me back through the open door.

Outside.

Thunder cracked overhead, and the door snapped shut, almost ripping the skin of my arm with its force. I grabbed the handle and pulled. Tried harder. Tried until I was panting and shaking with effort.

Lightning flared again, and on the other side of the glass I saw a nightmarish vision of Ashan moving towards David, who was slumped in the Demon's claws.

There was a tremendous crash, like the biggest glass pane in the world shattering under a hammer. The door suddenly gave under my pull, and I staggered backward, whipped by the wind, soaked by blowing rain, and lunged back inside the diner. I had just enough time to take in a breath, and something awful went wrong inside me. It felt as if along the way, every cell in my body turned inside out, ripped itself apart, mutated, exploded, and then reformed in a shaky configuration likely to melt at any moment.

I coughed. The breath I'd inhaled felt stale, minutes old. Filthy with toxins. My stomach rolled. There was a sense of a rubber band snapping against my skin, and suddenly a roar of voices, rattle of dishes and glasses and mugs, of footsteps, of cloth rustling, and everything seemed out of focus and nauseatingly loud.

'Sweetie?' A hand under my elbow, a kind woman's voice in my ear. 'Sweetie, are you OK?'

That snap had been Ashan letting go of the time he'd kept frozen. Everything had lurched forward, including me. The diner looked completely normal – patrons chewing and talking, waiters pouring coffee, cooks serving up behind the gleaming steel counters.

I stared at the bare spot of floor where David had been, shuddering. Water pattered off me in a continuous rain.

They were gone. *David* was gone. With him out of commission – I couldn't think he was dead, I couldn't – there was nothing standing in Ashan's way.

Nothing but me.

I straightened up and reached for power. It came in a welcome hot blast of air, drying the moisture from my hair and body. I didn't even try to hide it. The pink-uniformed waitress backed away from me, eyes wide, as I formed the moisture into a tight-packed grey ball, like a round cloud, and pitched it at the nearest industrial sink. It broke into a splash and swirled away.

'Wait!' she yelped as I headed back for the door again. I didn't.

I needed to get to Sedona, and I was going to make it happen.

Driving was out of the question, even in the Camaro. It would mean hauling ass into Ohio and Indiana and all the way down to good old Tulsa, Oklahoma . . . and from there, it would be a mere nine hundred miles or so to Sedona.

I didn't have the time.

I called Lewis. This time, I got him on the first try, and without preliminaries, I said, 'I need the company jet. Right now.'

There was a brief hesitation, and when he responded I heard a smile in his voice. Not much of a smile, granted. 'You want the keys to the Jag, too?'

'I need to get from Boston to Sedona, and I don't have the time to waste taking the scenic route. Send the damn plane, Lewis.'

The smile was no longer in evidence. His voice got lower, tenser. 'Jo, tell me you're kidding.'

'No. David—' I bit my lip to keep the sob at bay. 'David ran into trouble. I have to do this alone now, and I need to get to Sedona. It's – Lewis, if I don't do this, we may not have any kind of a shot.' I had to shoulder the phone as I changed gears to whip around a log-hauling eighteen-wheeler. 'Got a crew who's willing to chance it?'

'The plane's already busy taking Earth and Fire Wardens to new posts.'

'Then I hope the pilots on duty aren't afraid of a little turbulence.'

'A *little*' he repeated. 'Jo, think about what you're saying. You know the protocols. Weather Wardens *do not fly* under Condition Violet. Ever.'

'True,' I agreed. 'That's a good rule. Now we're going to break it.'

'If I put you in a plane right now, with what's going on, it's like shooting fish in a barrel. You know what kind of trouble you're asking for. And how do you know that you need to be in Arizona?'

'I know.'

'No other better ideas than flying?'

'If I was still a Djinn, I'd put my hair in a ponytail, cross my arms, and do a Barbara Eden. Crap, hang on.' I dropped the phone, downshifted, and narrowly avoided rear-ending a sedan that pulled out of a side road and *braked* in front of me. The Camaro growled, and the tires scrabbled for purchase on the damp pavement. I got her straightened out and whipped around the sedan so fast, I think I blew the Yankees cap off the driver. I fumbled one-handed for the phone and got it braced between my shoulder and my ear. 'Sorry.'

'Don't crash. That really would be the end of the world.'

'You're only worried about the car, aren't you.'

'Little bit,' he agreed. He was tapping keys. I hadn't even known he could type. 'Jo, I'm not going to argue with you. You're right. We're losing Wardens every time we engage.' There was a short, telling silence, and then he said, 'I hate to send you out there alone.'

'No choice,' I murmured, half under my breath. 'Listen, when this is over, I want a damn raise, got that? And . . . a nice house, on the beach. And . . . I'll think of something else when I'm not saving our asses.'

He laughed hollowly. 'If we live through this, I'll make sure you get it. I can redirect the plane. Where do you want to meet it?'

'Logan,' I said. 'I'm heading there now.'

No good-byes. Lewis and I were well past good-byes right now. I remembered the fight with David, and struggled again with a massive crushing weight of tears. *I don't love Lewis*, I thought fiercely. *I love you, David. You, damn you.*

I sucked in a deep breath and shook it off. No point in getting killed in a crash because I was teary over my boyfriend.

He wouldn't appreciate the sacrifice.

There was a reason flying was a last resort. Wardens – particularly Weather Wardens – just don't fly in unsettled systems like these, the ones that trigger a Condition Violet emergency. Trapped inside a thin-skinned metal box tens of thousands of feet in the air with a bunch of innocent passengers, you're helpless. And there's something about moving through the atmosphere at airplane speeds that draws attention, especially if you have to pass through clouds or storms. Ever dropped ink into a bowl of water, and watched it swirl and expand? That's what clouds look like around a speeding airplane carrying a Weather Warden when the aetheric's out of control.

The flight crew who staffed the Warden jet were all combat trained, the best of the best. If they couldn't get me through, nobody could.

All I had to do was get there. With the rain and wind so fierce, the roads were terrible; I fought the elements and traffic in equal measure. The Camaro was named Juliet, I decided. Juliet didn't have the brass of Jezebel, or the teasing flirtation of Delilah. Juliet was a pure flame of passion, of dedication, and that was how I felt. The Camaro wasn't going to be turned away from its goals, and neither was I.

The Wardens were having to push hard to save lives, and balance was precarious, up on the aetheric. I could sense the cool vibrations underneath the Warden's bolder moves. The Ma'at were on the case, contributing their subtle countermoves. In this particular instance, what they were doing wasn't undermining the Wardens; it was actually helping. Nice. I wasn't under any illusions that the interfaith cooperation would last long.

As I drove, I scanned the radio. Talk radio stations along the East Coast were chattering about the weird weather, the sudden explosion of natural disasters around the world. People were using words like *global warming* and *apocalypse*, but they were the fringe elements, and people were still laughing it off. Good. The last thing I needed to deal with, in addition to fighting the growing hostility of the world around us, was the general population going nuts.

When I hit clear road, I raced. The police who might normally have been interested in a speeding Camaro were involved in other problems, and my coast stayed clear all the way to the airport. I screeched into a short-term parking spot – if I didn't make it back, I wasn't going to be in a position to worry about fines. If there was anybody left to charge them. I jumped out of the Camaro and nearly got bowled over by a gust of wind; I created a relatively calm space around the car and went to the trunk of the car for my luggage before I remembered that I didn't actually have any.

Except I did. There was a neat little leather rolling bag in the trunk. I unzipped the pockets and found cash, a platinum card embossed with my name and an expiration date some years in the future. In the main compartment, a half-dozen pairs of underwear, a couple of additional sexy lace bras, some lace-topped stockings, two pairs of designer shoes (one the high-heel Manolos that Imara had brought me), and an explosion of outfits, all neatly folded. There was even a pair of snappy sunglasses that made me look as mysterious as a fugitive film star.

David. David and Imara, most likely. I wondered

when they'd had a chance to put this together, and there went the tears again, futile and dangerously sapping my strength.

I stopped off in the first airport bathroom to change clothes. I stripped to the skin – a weird sensation in a public forum – and put on new everything. After the underwear, I donned a hot-pink sleeveless tee with a crisp white shirt worn loose. New black jeans with the Miu Miu flats. My old clothes went into the bag.

As I left the bathroom, I heard my name being called over the intercom, and I headed for a courtesy phone, which directed me to a deserted area of the concourse. People milled around, looking frustrated. All the boards showed delays or cancellations, and from the look of some of them, it had been a long twenty-four hours or more.

I followed the directions and spotted a handsome uniformed man waiting for me with a hand-lettered sign that read WARDENS on it. He had the posture of somebody who'd done military service, and the uniform was still formal – the standard captain's suit of commercial aviation, with a cap to match. I smiled at him and held out my hand, palm towards him. He passed his own close to it and nodded at the stylised sun-symbol that manifested.

'Ms. Baldwin,' he said, and put the sign under his arm to offer me a firm handshake. He was middle-aged, probably in his early fifties, and he had the hard-bodied look of a guy who was enthusiastic about his fitness. Tanned, too. Streaks of silver in his hair that he might have cultivated, they looked so casting-office perfect.

'What's your name?' I asked him. He looked momentarily surprised.

'Captain John Montague, ma'am. My co-pilot is Captain Bernard Klees. No other crew on board for this trip. We try to keep it small, times like these. I understand that you're Weather.'

I nodded. 'That's right. I know it's going to be a challenge for you—'

'Ma'am, we eat challenges for snacks.'

'Don't you mean breakfast?'

'Never found them to be a full meal,' he said, straight-faced, and made a graceful, professional gesture to move me towards the departure doors. We didn't have a Jetway, of course, being a private plane. The captain took charge of my bag as we stepped out into the rain and wind, and trundled it briskly across to a waiting Learjet big enough to carry ten or fifteen passengers. A budget Learjet, if such a thing was possible. Weather Wardens were generally loath to fly, so it usually carried only Fire and Earth Wardens, and only at the highest levels.

He loaded my luggage in a compartment and told me to take any seat, and as my eyes adjusted to the relative gloom, I saw that there were other passengers on the flight. Seven of them, in fact. I didn't recognise most of them, but there was no doubt they were

Wardens; the crew was taking authorised personnel only. It was possible that these unlucky few were being flown in from overseas, as the Wardens redistributed their manpower to meet the crisis.

I knew Yves, an Earth Warden with long dreadlocked hair and a perpetual smile; he winked at me and gestured to an empty seat next to him. I winked back, but before I accepted, I scanned the remaining faces. Nancy Millars – Fire – not my favourite person in the world, not my least favourite. Rory Wilson, also Fire, who rated higher both because he was a better Warden and because he was just, well, cute.

The last two caught me by surprise. They were sitting together, heads down, but then looked up as I took a step down the aisle, and I found myself looking at Kevin and Cherise.

'What the hell?' I blurted, amazed. Cherise shouldn't have been anywhere near this plane. She didn't have the credentials.

Kevin's face was setting itself in stubborn angles – jaw locked and thrust forward, head lowering like a bull about to charge. Man, the kid was defensive. 'We're supposed to be here,' he said. 'Check with Lewis if you don't believe me.'

I stared at him, at the mottled flush on his chin and cheeks and forehead under the lank unevenly cut hair. I couldn't tell what he was thinking. I couldn't even tell if he was lying, but I always allowed for that possibility when it came to Kevin.

I looked at Cherise. She raised an eyebrow, the picture of cool competence. Sometime during our time apart she'd found time to get her look together. She was ready to shoot the cover of *Sports Illustrated*. I had no doubt that there was a bikini somewhere in her bags. She'd never leave home without one.

'Glad to see you, too, Jo,' she said. 'Are you OK? Last time I saw you—'

'Sorry,' I said. She stood up, and we hugged. 'Yeah, I'm OK. I guess. Looks worse than it is.'

She put me at arm's length and studied me. 'Looks pretty bad. That's maybe a seven on the cute scale, but only because it's you in that outfit. And what's up with the bruises?'

'Bad day.'

'No kidding.' She nodded towards Kevin, who was glaring at me resentfully. 'Lewis said I could keep him company.'

Lewis, I reflected mournfully, was *such* a guy. If Cherise wanted to go, she'd have found a way to convince Lewis in about ten seconds flat. It was just her special superpower. I could manipulate weather, she could manipulate men.

'I even have a special identification thingy,' she said, and pulled it out of the pocket of her jeans. On it was a silver metallic printed copy of the stylised sun of the Wardens, with her name and picture below it. 'See? I'm, like, official. I can flash my badge, Jo! Isn't that *cool*?'

She'd always wanted to be one of those people from *The X-Files*, I remembered. Good grief. This was out of hand.

'Miss Baldwin?' That was the cool, firm voice of the captain, coming from behind me. 'We need to get moving. Please take a seat.'

I could exercise my authority – presuming anybody acknowledged it – and toss Cherise off the plane, but that would mean tossing Kevin, as well, and if Lewis had dispatched him for a reason, that was a very bad idea. I pasted on a smile, waved to the captain, and moved past Cherise and Kevin to slide into the seat next to Yves.

'Long time no see,' Yves said, and leant in to kiss my cheek. 'Such a warm greeting! I might think you don't even like me anymore.'

I turned and kissed him, as well, both cheeks, European-style. 'Yves, you know better. But you might have heard, I've been having some, ah, challenges lately.'

'Challenges,' he repeated, and laughed. Yves had a wonderful laugh, bubbly and full-bodied as champagne. 'Yeah, I heard about your challenges. Somebody tried to get me to vote against you, you know. Get you taken in for—' He made a snipping gesture. We tried never to directly refer to getting neutered and having our powers removed, except in gestures and low voices. 'Told 'em to fuck off, I did.'

I squeezed his fingers. Yves had thick, strong

fingers, scarred from years of working outdoors. He was a big guy, solid and comfortable, and I'd always liked him. All Earth Wardens seemed to have a sense of Zen balance to them, but he was one of the best, and I was lucky to have him on my side.

Actually, I supposed I was lucky to even *have* a side at all.

The seats were lush and comfortable. Whoever had chosen the interior had gone with a dark chocolate leather, butter-soft to the touch. The row Yves and I occupied was mid-cabin, over the wing. I was on the aisle, away from the windows. That was fine with me.

The intercom came on. 'Welcome to Hellride Airlines, folks; this is your captain, John Montague. It's not going to be a nice trip, since as you see, we have a Weather Warden flying with us today,' the pilot's electronic voice announced. 'We have no flight attendants on board for this trip, so if you want to eat, help yourself to sandwiches and drinks from the cooler. I do hope you enjoy them. You'll be throwing them up later.'

The co-pilot's voice came on with the same cool competence overlaid with a veneer of humour. He had a British accent. I was instantly reminded of Eamon, with a cold flash and a shiver. 'Also, should we survive this, donations towards our retirement fund are cheerfully accepted, ladies and gentlemen. My name is Bernard Klees – *K-l-e-e-s*, no relation to anyone in

Monty Python, so please don't ask me for a rendition of the dead parrot sketch.'

There was a ripple of laughter. Montague came back on. 'Strap tight and hang on, people. We'll get you there.'

Radio off. I heard a shift in the idling engine noise, and fumbled for my seat belt. My hands were shaking a little. God, I *hated* flying; I'd done it a few times before, but only when the weather was firmly under Warden control, and only when circumstances required it.

Yves covered my fingers with his and gently held them as the plane taxied out onto the runway and picked up speed. 'Relax,' he told me. 'They're the best pilots we have. Maybe the best in the world.'

I didn't have to tell him how little that meant, if circumstances turned against us. Yves knew.

The plane lifted off with a bump and a sudden angular thrust of acceleration, and then it got eerily smooth. The force pressed me back into the leather, and I whimpered a little, thinking about the air around us, the fact that we were moving through it and drawing attention to ourselves. I squeezed my eyes shut and tried to slow my rapid heartbeat.

'I heard you were—' I looked in time to see Yves's eyebrows doing an interpretive dance. 'With a Djinn.'

'Not just any Djinn,' I said. 'And yes. His name is David.'

Yves lost his smile. 'Something wrong?'

'You could say.' I turned my head away and tried closing my eyes again. It didn't really help. I still saw David's face as the Demon's claws closed around him, that desperate, furious intensity.

He'd used power to break me free of the trap when he should have been using it to fight for his life. My fault.

'Hey.' When I opened my eyes, Yves was holding out a copy of a magazine featuring shiny, glossy people doing stupid things for the cameras. 'You used to like these, as I remember.'

I needed to put it away. Bury the pain, and focus on something else. Self-pity wasn't my style.

I forced out a smile as though at gunpoint, took the magazine, and flipped it open to the first photo page. 'Oh my God,' I said, and pointed to the unzipped miniskirt and white stirrup leggings that the misguided pop star was wearing with low-heeled pumps. 'Tell me that's not a sign of the end of the world.'

Yves chuckled, shrugged, and opened his magazine: *Mother Earth News*. I wondered if he knew how funny that was.

For the first hour, at least, the trip was uneventful. Self-pity lingered, but Yves had succeeded in distracting me. The magazine's outrageous fashion mistakes occupied my mind, and I was almost feeling normal when something cold pressed against my arm.

I yelped and tossed the magazine into the air.

It was Cherise, with a can of soda. She offered

it again. I took it, and she perched on the air of the empty seat across from me. 'You OK?' she asked, and popped the top on her own can.

'Sure,' I lied. 'Why?'

She looked me over. 'Jo, honey, you look pretty good, but don't kid a kidder. I saw what you looked like on the way to New York, and I'm pretty sure you've been through hell since then.' She sipped daintily at the sweat-beaded can. Moisture dripped onto her lime-green raw silk capri pants, and she frowned at it, then found a napkin and wrapped the can.

I considered my answer carefully. 'Um . . . yeah. I'm OK. I – you know how Earth Wardens can heal people? Has Kevin told you—?' She nodded. 'Well, I got healed up, so I'm more or less OK. Just tired.' And discouraged, and scared out of my mind. But other than that? Peachy.

She nodded again, looking down, and then suddenly those sky-blue eyes locked on mine. 'I got a phone call. From your sister.'

'*What?*' I didn't mean to yell it. It rang around the interior of the plane, bringing everyone to sharp attention. Even Yves, normally the least excitable of people, put his magazine down to look at me. 'Sorry. Sorry, guys.' I lowered my voice and bent closer to Cherise. 'You got a call from Sarah? When?'

'A couple of hours ago. She couldn't get through to you this morning. She sounded—' Cherise's face turned just a bit pinker. 'OK, this is going to sound bad and all, but does she do anything? Heroin, maybe?'

'No,' I said. I felt sick to my stomach, and it wasn't the altitude, or the overly sweet soda I was automatically sipping. 'No, not Sarah.'

Compassion didn't come naturally to Cherise; it made her look too young. 'Sweetie, the family's usually the last to know. Listen, she sounded really spaced. Orbital. She said to tell you that she was OK, and that everything was going to be fine. She'd met somebody in Las Vegas. I asked her where she was staying, but she said not to worry about it.'

I leant forward, pressing the cold soda can against my forehead, fighting not to laugh. Or cry. 'Yes. Thanks, Cher. That's Sarah all over, isn't it? Rescue her from one madman, she's off to find the next one—'

'She's not OK, is she?'

'No,' I murmured. 'I doubt she is. I really doubt she's going to be, either.'

'She's not with what's-his-name anymore?'

'Eamon? No.'

'Too bad,' Cherise sighed. 'Damn, he was cute. I *loved* his accent.'

'He was an asshole, Cher.'

'They're all assholes. But it's not every day that you find one that's really decorative.'

'He tried to kill me,' I snapped. 'More than once.'

She froze, deer in the headlights. Amazed. And then her face just filled with delight. 'Oh my *God*! You go, Jo! That's so cool!'

'What?' There were times when I really didn't get life on Planet Cherise.

'You're still here,' she said simply, and grinned at me with the unbroken enthusiasm of the truly weird.

I hugged her. Hard. 'Staying here, too,' I said.

'Oh, you'd better. You owe me for scratches on the Mustang.'

She moved away, back to her seat. The gap between her white tank top and the green capri pants showed flawless tanned skin, and a tattoo of a big-headed space alien flashing the peace sign as she bent over to move something out of her way. Probably Kevin's feet. He was snoring.

He stopped snoring as the plane shuddered.

'Damn,' Yves said quietly. 'Here I was starting to think we'd make it without this.'

Turbulence. The plane shuddered again, then dropped, a free fall that seemed to last forever. Outside, clouds were swirling. It was hard to get any sense of what was happening, but I could feel the hot energy consolidating itself out there.

Something had sensed me. A storm, maybe, one big enough to gather some elemental sentience. Or something else, and worse, like one of Ashan's Warden-killing Djinn. This would be a prime target. That was why I hadn't wanted to have others on the plane. My life – sure, I'll risk it. But there were a lot of lives at stake here. And I was the point of danger.

'Everybody hang on!' I yelled. Lightning flashed

outside the windows, and I felt the plane powering up. They were going to try to get above it, looked like. Good strategy. The only problem was that the storm was going to chase them. 'Yves, switch with me.'

We unbuckled and fumbled across each other, mumbling politenesses; he was dressed in a pair of blue jeans and a colourful dashiki-style shirt in yellow, blue, and orange patterns. A blaze of brightness in a world that was rapidly turning the colour of ashes outside. I settled in his empty chair and buckled in, clutched the armrests, and looked out the window.

I didn't really need the view, but it helped; sometimes, focus could be achieved better with a visual cue. I filled up my lungs, let it out, filled them again, and allowed myself to drift free.

I got battered immediately by currents of force on the way up to the aetheric. It was a war zone, with silent colourful explosions of power snapping and popping in a hundred places at once. The cloudscape roiled, black in places, red in others, everything unstable and bizarre. I spotted an area that had taken on the silvery overlay I knew was going to be a huge problem, and concentrated on it. As I did, I felt myself joined by someone else who boosted my concentration and power, bracing me when I faltered. The power signature felt familiar, but I couldn't stop to wonder about it. I just worked, fast and frantic, trying to make sure the space around our airplane remained relatively disaster-free as our pilots arrowed for the safety of the higher sky.

On the mortal level, the turbulence shook us hard, and then the engines howled louder and suddenly, the ride was glass-smooth again. I gasped in air, feeling the shift on the aetheric at the same time, and recognised the power that had helped me.

Imara. My daughter was with me – not physically, not on the plane, but she was watching over me.

'No,' I whispered. My breath fogged the glass of the plane's window on the inside as mist beaded on it outside. 'No, stay with Sarah. Stay out of this.'

Words wouldn't do on the aetheric level, but she understood what I was saying, I think. I felt a pulse of reassurance from her, from that shadowy flicker of presence; I couldn't see her at all clearly, just as I couldn't see any of the Djinn (or Ifrit, for that matter) while we were on the aetheric plane.

'I mean it!' I said to the flicker that was my daughter. 'Stay out of this! Stay with Sarah!' Who, God knew, needed the chaperone.

The flicker moved away from me, but not far. Not far enough. She wasn't minding her mother, clearly; maybe she was under instructions from her father, but I didn't find that too likely. David had been in agreement with me about keeping her out of Ashan's grasp, and yet here she was, hanging about like bait on a hook.

And there was *nothing* I could do about it.

* * *

We stayed high for most of the trip, well above the unsteady clouds; the storms kept forming beneath us, hopscotching across the country. Our passage was causing chaos, no doubt about it, and I had the sick feeling that we were probably causing deaths, as well, but it wouldn't have been better if I'd driven, and it probably would have ended up worse in the end. I couldn't save everyone. Hell, I was no longer sure that I could save anyone.

The speaker gave that distinctive little click, and everyone in the cabin looked up from what they were doing – mostly reading or sleeping. 'Hi, folks. Well, we've run about as far as we can at this altitude, we're going to have to start our descent. As you know, this is going to be rough, so please, try to keep those amusement-park screams to a minimum. It doesn't make us fly with any more confidence. Ah, and Captain Klees would like to remind you that today's movie selection of *Die Hard Two* is now available on your LCD screens. Ah, hell, that was a joke. It's really *Turbulence*, followed by *Con Air*. Anyway, you guys keep cool back there. Let us do the sweating.'

He was off the air about ten seconds when the first shudder came, as the plane began to tilt forward, nose down.

Oh, crap.

We were in for it now.

The shuddering turned into a steady shaking, as if some giant hand had closed around the plane's fragile skin. I swallowed hard and clutched the armrests as outside the pale blue sky went mist grey, and then started a hellish descent towards black. The clouds looked thick enough to walk on. Thick enough to trap us, like spider-webs around a fly. Lightning flashed close, illuminating the interior with a wash of blue-white flame, and in its flare I saw Yves calmly reading his *Mother Earth News*, legs crossed. I couldn't see anyone else, but I doubted they were all so fatalistic about it. Surely some of them must have been as terrified as I was . . .

We shuddered and dropped. Free fall. Ten feet or more, and it seemed to take forever. We hit an updraft with a bang and fishtailed, or tried to; I sensed the pilots correcting up front, adjusting the engines. Keeping us intact.

We dropped again, farther this time, and I felt the plane twisting to the left – and then something hit us from the right side, and we rolled.

Screams. Yves dropped his magazine and grabbed for his armrests as everything went sideways; my empty soda can clattered against the cabin wall in a chittering panic, and I heard a crash from below as bags shifted. The roar of the engines shifted, and then the speakers activated again. Co-pilot Klees made an authentic western-style *yee-haw*. 'Well, you people are *so* lucky,' he said, as if flying sideways, staring down at the ground from the side window, was an everyday occurrence. 'You're about to experience the joy of flight all those U.S. Air Force ads talk about. Hope you're all observing the seat belt sign. Three – two – one—"

The plane rolled left. Rolled completely over so that we were hanging upside down, and I had a brief surreal glimpse of my long black hair shuddering in mid-air like a beaded curtain, and then the world was rolling again, and we came upright again. Steady as a rock once we'd achieved level status.

Maybe people screamed. I don't know – I'm pretty sure I did. I looked over at Yves as I clawed my disordered hair out of my eyes, and his legendary calm was shaken enough for him to cross himself and begin murmuring something I recognised as an Our Father.

We were still descending.

'Hope you enjoyed that,' Klees said. He still sounded absolutely cheerful and unperturbed, as if he did this daily, with two shows in the afternoon. 'If anyone feels the urge to purge, please, avail yourself of the bags. My contract does require me to do cabin cleaning, as well.'

A shaky laugh from someone up front with more intestinal fortitude than me. I was seriously contemplating the aforementioned bag, which looked sturdy and inviting, but I hadn't eaten or drunk enough to need to resort to it. A few grim, sweaty moments, and I was OK.

I grabbed leather as the plane did another unsettling shimmy combined with a bucking motion. Outside the windows, black clouds pressed as close as night. I rested my aching head against the pillowy seat and thought that maybe I ought to try the aetheric again, but I was no longer certain it was a good idea.

Yves took my hand. The warm anchoring of his skin helped keep me from visions of the plane corkscrewing down into the earth and exploding.

I closed my eyes as the plane shuddered and rocked, heeling from one side to the other, slipping violently sideways as if trying to avoid something I couldn't see or sense. My weather senses were overloaded. I was useless up here, with so much happening and focused right on us. If I'd been on the ground, it would have been different, but I felt so helpless up here, so out of control . . .

The plane levelled out in a sudden lurch, as if it had suddenly hit a patch of glass-smooth air. No turbulence, not even the slightest bounce. I opened my eyes, blinked at Yves, and he raised his eyebrows and gave a Gallic shrug.

'Bathroom,' I said, and unfastened my seat belt, climbed over his knees and hustled for the tiny, cramped stall. It was unoccupied, thank God, and I lunged inside, clicked the latch shut, and leant over to splash cold water on my face. The urge to vomit was passing. I dampened a paper towel and used it to blot sweat from my face and neck, then leant over to splash my face again, since it had felt so good the first time.

When I straightened up, there was fog coming out

of the air vent over my head. I blinked at it, thinking wildly about James Bond movies and knockout gas, but I didn't smell anything, and I didn't feel any more light-headed than normal.

It continued drifting down from the vent in thick, cloudy streamers, twisting lazily in the air, tangling together into a denser mist as it fell. I stretched out my hand and felt cool moisture on it.

Even though I didn't fly much, I was pretty sure this didn't qualify as normal.

In seconds, the mist had formed a shape, and that *definitely* wasn't normal. Not even on an airplane full of Wardens.

I felt the hard edge of the sink cabinet digging into my butt, and realised that I was staring when I ought to be fleeing. I reached for the latch on the door –

– and it instantly froze up, covered with ice crystals. When my skin touched it, it burnt like liquid nitrogen, and I yelped and flinched backward.

The shape in the fog wasn't male, and it wasn't female. It wasn't anything, really. Soft edges, curves, a gender-less oval of face, no features on it.

As I watched, the whole door glittered and glistened with forming ice. No way was I going out that way.

Which was the only way, unless I was brave enough to rip out the chemical toilet and go that direction.

Which I wasn't.

I backed away as far as the tiny bathroom would allow, overbalanced, and sat down hard on the toilet's lid. The fog-shape leant towards me, and the air around me began to move and breathe in subtle motions, whispering over my skin and combing through my hair, sliding under my clothes to touch me in places where, well, wind just didn't usually go. I controlled the impulse to self-defence. So far, nothing that had happened was life-threatening, just – weird.

'Um – hi?' I ventured. The air around me stirred up, moving faster, ruffling my hair and fluttering my shirt. There was no sense of heat or cold to it; everything was exactly room temperature, passionless and sensation-free. 'Who are you?'

The figure wrapped in fog bent closer, and suddenly I couldn't breathe. No air. OK, no problem, I was a Weather Warden, I'd dealt with this before . . .

Only I couldn't. I couldn't get a grip on the air at all. Whatever was facing me had absolute control over my native elements.

As soon as I realised it, the air flooded back in, and I took a grateful gasping breath. 'Right,' I said. 'Oracle. There was a Fire Oracle, so you'd be . . . Air and Water.'

I hadn't even thought about it, but of course Oracles would come in threes – Fire, Weather, Earth. Collect the whole set . . . Well, at least it was another opportunity for me to communicate.

Maybe. So far, this one hadn't said a word.

'I'm – I'm supposed to talk to the Mother,' I said. It'd be nice to dress my mission up in fancy talk, but

I didn't think that would come naturally to me under stress, and I didn't think that I'd have the time, either. 'Can you help me with that?'

No answer. Even the subtle currents of air that had been stroking my skin came to a halt. I hoped that wasn't a rude question.

'I'm a Weather Warden,' I said. 'I'm – in a way I'm part of you—'

Mistake. The wind came back, a steady, crushing pressure all over me, pinning me in place. I'd never experienced real g-forces, but this reminded me of the films I'd seen. It was painful in ways I'd never imagined, stressing every muscle and bone to the limit.

Then it stopped. I overcompensated, pitching forward almost to the floor, and sawed in ragged breaths that tasted of blood.

The Oracle didn't like being compared to humans; that much was obvious. I could understand that. We were imperfect creatures, constantly being born and dying. Tied to the earth and sea by gravity, hunger, a thousand invisible strings. The Earth herself saw us as a nuisance. The Oracle hadn't seen anything to change its mind.

'I saved him,' I said, and looked up at the faceless creature floating in the air above me. 'I saved the Fire Oracle. The Demon Mark would have destroyed him, and once it was past him, it would have been in the Mother's blood. So a little respect might be in order here.'

No answer. Man, this was frustrating, not to mention scary. I cast a longing look at the ice-covered bathroom door.

'I saved the life of an Oracle, and I need you to help me now. Just help me talk to the Mother.'

There was a sudden sensation in the air, as if everything in the world had shivered. The Oracle, wreathed in fog, leant closer. As it did, streamers of milk-white mist wrapped around me to lick me like tongues. I shuddered, and as the Oracle's face came closer to mine, I saw its eyes.

Just for a split second, because I turned my face away and closed my eyelids and prayed, *prayed* never to see such a thing again. I remembered that I'd thought Jonathan's eyes had been scary – and they had been, depthless and terrifying – but at least they'd reminded me of something I understood. Something inside my experience.

These were the eyes of eternity itself.

'Help me,' I said. 'Please.'

The air shivered again, more violently this time, with a sound like a million silver bells falling out of a dump truck. Deafening. Was that a voice? Was I supposed to understand it? I didn't. I couldn't. Even the Fire Oracle's screams had made more sense.

'I can't understand you!' I said, and immediately knew that was a mistake. One doesn't correct gods, even minor ones, and if the Djinn bowed to these creatures, that was good enough to qualify them for the name. The air around me curdled and thickened, pressing on me again. Squeezing. I couldn't breathe. Spots danced bright in front of my bulging eyes, and I pitched to my knees on the tiny bathroom floor with the Oracle, bent at some impossibly inhuman angle, following me down. Boring into me with those *eyes*.

I was starting to wish that I was any kind of Warden other than a Weather Warden. If this was my patron saint, I was in real trouble, because I had the sense that it was playing with me. Enjoying my pain. Interested in my panic.

Just when I thought it would crush me like a grape, the air stilled again, completely dead of intention or life. The Oracle hadn't moved away. When I breathed, I was breathing in mist that flowed off its genderless, featureless face.

I avoided looking at it directly.

'I'm not quitting,' I said. 'If you won't help me, I'll go to the Earth Oracle.'

It had a mouth, after all, and teeth made of ice, and it showed them to me. I whimpered, I think, waiting for it to destroy me, and mist wrapped around my neck in a thick, choking rope to pull me closer.

My skin stung with a sudden ice-cold chill.

I focused past the teeth, on the terrifying eyes of the thing, and said, 'I'm not giving up. If I have to give my life to get this done, then I will. Kill me, or let me talk to the Mother.'

The vote seemed to be on the side of killing me, but

it was too late to reconsider, and besides, I meant it. If I had to die, I would. Hell, I'd done it before, and I would again, at least once. Might as well make it count.

Apparently there was a third alternative I hadn't considered, because the rope around my throat suddenly dissolved into cool white fog, and the Oracle's teeth flashed in what could only be interpreted by my brain as a smile, and . . . it simply misted away. Back up through the ventilation system.

Gone.

My gasping breaths hung white on the ice-cold air, and I sat there shivering for a few more minutes before I felt a shudder through the deck.

We were out of the clear air and heading back into turbulence.

I unlocked the bathroom door. It unsealed with a snap-crackle of ice, and I walked on shaky legs back to my row, lurched past Yves, and strapped myself back into my seat.

'*Mon Dieu*, you look as if you've seen a ghost,' he said, and touched the back of my hand with his fingers. 'You're freezing.'

Lightning flashed hot in the sky, changing black to smoke grey, and there was something floating outside the plane in a drift of mist and curves, with the eyes of eternity.

I flattened my hand against the window in a reflexive gesture, trying to reach it, trying to push it away, maybe both, but then the lightning failed and there was nothing there.

Nothing.

I felt my stomach churn and grabbed for the airsickness bag.

Yves, alarmed, pulled away as I retched, and looked relieved when I stopped, wiped my mouth, and closed up the bag. 'OK?' he asked, and patted me awkwardly on my shoulder. I nodded, throat still working. I felt drained and exhausted, as if I'd been through hours of Warden work. 'We're almost down. We're going to make it.'

He was right. Even as he said it, the clouds swirled from black to grey outside the windows, and then there was free air and the sight of desert under us. The rest of the passengers spontaneously applauded. I clutched my airsickness bag in both hands and tried not to weep.

The Learjet touched down with barely a bump – smoothest landing I'd ever seen – and taxied sedately towards a terminal. The engines powered down to a purr. 'Right,' said the co-pilot crisply. 'I won't tell you to stay seated because you won't anyway, passengers never do, so I'll just say that it's your bones – break them if you will. Miss Baldwin, thank you for flying with us, you certainly gave us a nice diversion from the boredom, and you're now on the ground in Phoenix, Arizona. Good luck to you.'

I sucked in deep breaths and managed a weak smile

in return for Yves's delighted grin. I managed to get myself loose from the safety straps and kept the airsick bag because I didn't know what to do with it – they never tell you these things – and air-kissed Yves on the cheeks because I wasn't sure he'd want vomit-mouth on his lips. He hugged me. That was nice.

Cherise hugged me, too. Kevin just gave me his patented too-cool-for-this shrug and waved a limp-wristed good-bye. Everybody else seemed relieved when I made my way to the door.

Nobody else was getting out in Phoenix.

Captain Montague appeared to open the door and let down the steps for me. He looked just as starched and together as he had at the beginning of the flight. I, on the other hand, was trembling, clutching a sloshing airsick bag, and had my shirt plastered to my skin with sweat.

'Good flying,' I said. 'I think I owe you one.'

He lifted his silvery eyebrows and moved his uniform jacket enough to show me damp patches of sweat on his shirt, under the arms.

'Not at all,' he said. 'First time I've broken a sweat in three years. I haven't had so much fun since I flew a planeload of drunk Weather Wardens from a convention in Tahiti in hurricane season.'

I offered him the hand that wasn't holding the sloshing bag. 'I'll never fly with anyone else.'

'I think I'm in love,' he said, and gave me a professional smile to make sure I knew it was a professional sort of rapture. 'Take care, Miss Baldwin. It's nasty out there.' He wasn't talking about the weather in Phoenix; it was cloudy, but seemed stable enough.

I saluted him and retrieved my suitcase, then rolled it down the red carpet towards the entry gate. I resisted the almost overwhelming urge to throw myself to my knees and kiss the tarmac.

There was a trash can at the entrance, and I dropped the evidence of my weakness into it.

My journey was complete.

If the Oracle in the clouds had been my last hope, it was over in more ways than one. But maybe, just maybe . . . there was one more chance.

Chapter Eight

The first rental car agency didn't have a huge selection, and mostly it ran to sedate four-door sedans or cramped little economy cars. When I expressed that to the rental agent, a neat little redhead who was just cute as a bug in her dark blue suit, she looked conspiratorial and leant forward to say, 'You should call these guys.' She handed over a brochure with the underhanded motion of someone completing a drug deal. I glanced down at the name on the glossy paper: *Rent-A-Vette*. Holy crap, I'd actually found somebody who understood. What were the odds?

'Thank you,' I said with heartfelt sincerity. 'You're a lifesaver.'

She winked and moved on to the tourist family behind me, who wanted a boxy four-door sedan.

I went to the phone bank and called the number on the paper. Did I have a driver's license? Sure. Major credit card? No problem. I almost wept over the choices the woman on the other end began to reel off: Viper SRT-10, Mercedes SL-500, Porsche Cabriolet, Corvette C6, Porsche Boxster . . . I stopped her at the BMW Z4, mainly because I'd never driven one and always wanted to. If we were entering the end of days, I might as well indulge myself.

I had a shuttle within fifteen minutes.

Phoenix is pretty. Austere but pretty, in the way that only desert towns can be – the urban part looks pretty much standard, but it's surrounded by rugged country, upthrust hills and mountains, and three hundred days out of the year, it's dry and cloudless.

Unfortunately for the two million residents, I'd flown in dragging one of those not-dry, not-clear days along with me.

The shuttle driver chatted about things to do in Phoenix, which I accepted with a polite smile and a deaf ear. I had deadlines, emphasis on the *dead*. Hiking probably wasn't going to be on the agenda. Neither was a spa day, tempting as that might be.

Rent-A-Vette was a showplace of heart-stopping automotive delights. I could have wept at the gleaming ranks of muscle cars, but I managed to keep my cool and present myself at the rental counter to claim the keys to my Z4. It required me to pull out a driver's license and credit card, which I did, emptying my pockets along the way. While that was getting settled, I turned away and speed-dialled Sarah's cell phone.

A sleepy warm female voice answered. 'Hello?'

'Sarah,' I sighed. I managed to keep my voice low, somehow, although I wanted to shout. 'I heard from Cherise. Are you OK?'

'Of course,' she said, and laughed. It was a drunken, slow laugh, the kind you make right before you succumb to the ansesthesia after counting backwards. 'Yes, silly. I'm fine. Eamon's taking good care of me.'

'Eamon?' I interrupted.

'Didn't I tell you?' Another slow throb of a laugh. 'I forgot to mention him. Silly me. But I know you don't like him—'

How had he found her? Oh *God* . . .'Listen to me, Sarah. Please. Eamon is not a good man. I need you to start paying attention. You need to walk away from him.'

There was a long, long delay, and then she said, 'I don't understand.'

'Look, just tell me where you are!'

Another laugh. 'I can't do that. It's a secret.'

And then the phone changed hands.

Before he even spoke, I said, 'You fucking bastard. How *dare* you?'

'The rules were that I stay away from you and your daughter, Joanne,' Eamon said in that low, pleasant voice that was such a good disguise for him. 'Which I am doing. I love your sister. I told you that. And I'm not willing to give her up just yet. So please, do keep on with your no doubt important crisis, and let us have some time to get better acquainted. I'll see you at the next family picnic.'

'Eamon!' I hissed it, as much as you can hiss something without sibilants. 'You *keep your hands off my sister!*'

'Love, I can't keep *her* hands off *me.*' He laughed, and it sounded utterly unaffected. Villains didn't have the right to laugh like that, so infectiously. I could hear Sarah joining in.

I was glad I'd emptied my stomach on the plane.

I hung up without any good-byes before he could cut me off – a little control on my part, anyway – and went back to the counter. They looked happy. Apparently, my credit limit was stratospheric.

I pulled out of the parking lot in a sky-blue convertible Z4, hit the gas, and almost broke the sound barrier. *Damn.* The thing was little, light, and incredibly manoeuverable. It smelt like rental cars smell, only newer; the interior wasn't roomy, but it seemed to make that an asset by cradling my body in an almost sensuous fashion.

I slipped on my sunglasses at the first stoplight and consulted the free map they'd given me. It looked easy enough – a straight shot up I-17 towards Flagstaff, with a quick jog off to the west at the Highway 179 exit. About a two-hour drive, if you obeyed the speed limit.

I was in a Z4, trying to save the world. Did I intend to obey the speed limit?

Hardly.

I've never really thought about why I like to drive fast, but it probably has to do with control. I like being in control, and I like pushing limits, and the adrenaline rush you get from hurtling down a clean, empty freeway – that's like nothing else. Driving felt especially good after the nauseating, disconnected trip in the plane. Not that I didn't have faith in the pilots, but I never liked being in the backseat. Or the passenger seat, for that matter.

The Z4 throbbed around me like a living thing, and we left the stone-and-glass caverns of Phoenix behind. The sun was a weak brass shadow behind grey clouds, and the rain fell in fits and starts. Not as determined as it had been to wash me away, but spitting its contempt nevertheless. The road looked black and shiny as it stretched out due east, towards Sedona and Flagstaff. I shifted gears as the traffic thinned, and felt something primal in my body relax at last. I might be flying towards disaster, but at least I was controlling the trip.

I felt the hair on my arms stir and come to attention, as if an electrical field had formed around me and I was static-charged. Something dark and shadowy formed slowly in the passenger seat next to me . . . too slowly. Djinn were masters of the now-you-see-them, now-you-don't, and this was *way* too gradual an appearance.

I backed off the gas, saw a scenic turnout up ahead, and took it in a hiss of tires on damp road, then braked fast as details came clear in the figure appearing next to me. Long black hair hanging limp, half-hiding the face. A shredded black leather jacket. Leather pants split in long cuts, showing pale-gold skin and blood.

There was blood on her hands.

'Imara?' I said, and felt my heart freeze solid in my chest. Part of me felt like it was falling backward. 'Imara, what happened?'

Her head slowly tilted back to rest against the leather seat, and I saw the blood spattered on her face. She looked far too pale. Her eyes were colourless, pale and clear.

'Help,' my daughter whispered, and slithered sideways into my arms. 'Mommy, help.'

I screamed, calling her name; she didn't answer. Her eyes were still open, and her chest still rose and fell, but that was all. I couldn't even begin to think what to do. Djinn could have human form, but it wasn't real in the sense of mortal flesh; if they got hurt badly enough, they could let go of it, mist away. Their real injuries were metaphysical ones – energy depletions. Had Imara been attacked by an Ifrit? No, that would show up in other ways, not as physical wounds . . .

I remembered Rahel, coming up out of the surf in Florida not so long ago, looking ragged and half-killed. Who – or what? – had she been fighting? I'd never really had the time to find out. Could it have been a Demon? Imara shouldn't have even tried; our child didn't have the experience of a full-fledged Djinn, or the endurance. Or the powers.

I could barely breathe. When I felt for a pulse I found one, weak and unsteady under my fingertips. Not that a pulse mattered, but as long as she was manifesting physically, it was an indicator of how strong her life force might be.

'Imara, can you hear me? Imara!' It was crazy, but I shook her. Her head lolled. No reaction. She was like a living corpse.

Ashan had allowed this to happen. If he hadn't done it himself. My cold terror turned hot. Incandescent. *If he's laid a hand on my daughter . . .*

I cradled her in my arms – she was heavy and warm and oddly human – and braced her head against my shoulder. I pressed a kiss against her temple, and tried to think what to do. If David was . . . I couldn't let myself really think about David, where he might be, what he might be suffering. Too frightening. If Imara had been human, I could have driven her to a hospital, hooked her up to machines and tubes, let doctors take care of her. But an injured Djinn, even half of one, couldn't be so easily handled. If she couldn't do it on her own, I had no idea how to do it for her.

The Ma'at. The Ma'at had demonstrated some arcane knowledge that the Wardens certainly didn't possess; they'd been able to heal Rahel, for instance, when she'd become an Ifrit. So they had some kind of resources I didn't. The only problem was that, so far as I knew, the Ma'at were off handling things with the rest of the Wardens, or else they'd be hunkered down at their cushy Las Vegas headquarters, safe within the glass and faux-Egyptian sleekness of the Luxor hotel. Probably playing cards. They liked playing cards while things burnt down around their ears.

I reluctantly moved Imara, got her upright in the passenger seat and strapped in place. Blood dripped from her hand in a steady rhythm onto the leather seat, but I had no idea whether it was real blood or metaphorical – if I bound up her wounds, would it make her better? Or would it just not matter, one way or another? Dammit. No signal on the cell phone. I had no way to contact Lewis until I got to the next town.

Or I could turn around, go back to Phoenix . . .

It hit me in a sudden rush of comprehension. I was *meant* to turn back, wasn't I? There was a reason Imara had appeared here, now. She was a vivid, unmissable distraction, an emotional roadblock I couldn't help but consider.

I turned off the engine of the roadster, set the brake, and stepped out onto the crisp gravel of the roadside. The wind was cool and cutting, sharp with the scent of rain in an area that had little of that kind of thing in the normal course of events. I breathed deeper and got an aroma of wet sage. 'You might as well come out. I know you're here.'

Ashan was as grey as the clouds, and he seemed

to just appear out of them, gliding down like some Hong Kong wire artist, landing with perfect poise and walking towards me without hesitation. A perfectly tailored suit around a perfectly proportioned body. Expensive, shined shoes that disdained little things like rain and wet sand. Ashan was twenty feet away, then ten, then five, and he wasn't slowing down.

'You bastard,' I said, and I called the wind. It came as if it was waiting, as if it was more than willing. A hard wall of air hit him hard, shoved him back on his heels and dragged him ten feet. He stayed upright, staring at me with fierce colourless eyes. 'You did this to my daughter.'

He shrugged. 'Don't take that tone with me. I could have ripped her into nothing. She's barely Djinn, and yet she's inherited all your arrogance.'

He waved a hand. That was all it took to turn the wind around, and it hit me with the force of a sandblaster, driving me back against the car. I instinctively shielded my eyes and gasped for breath as pressure tried to compress me flat. He was playing with me. If Ashan really wanted to, he'd introduce my ribs to my backbone with shattering force and leave me a ruptured bag of meat.

The pressure slacked off enough for me to catch my breath. 'How long have you been planning to destroy the Wardens?'

'Not the Wardens,' he corrected. 'Humans. You're killing us. Draining us of magic, and life. Your kind are a revolting perversion of the Djinn, and you think you are the lords of creation. We are *better* than you. We were *first*.'

'Some of you were. Some of you came from humans,' I said. 'That must really piss you off. I mean, how does the inferior create the superior? By your logic, it can't happen. But it does, Ashan. It happens all the time.'

'No,' he said sharply. 'Mongrels came from you, creatures like Jonathan and David. Heavy with humanity. I am not like them. My brothers and sisters are not like them.'

I'd forgotten, but David had made that clear, once upon a time: there were Djinn who were created from humans, like the five hundred born out of the destruction of Atlantis, or like Jonathan and David on the battlefield. And then there were the – nobility, if that was the right term. The pure. The ones who'd been spawned directly from the Earth itself.

Ashan, of course, was one of them. And it appeared he had a whole political party behind him, because I could feel the power crackling around him, the hissing presence of others who didn't choose to show themselves.

Who stood between me and the next – the last – Oracle.

'Turn around,' he said. 'Turn around and go. Die with your people when the Demon turns her mad and wipes your corruption from her skin.'

'If you put a Demon Mark into an Oracle, how do you know it won't destroy *you*?'

'It won't,' he said. 'We are eternal.'

'I thought you said we were killing you. Humans. You can't have it both ways, you know. Eternal, not eternal—'

'I control the Demons.'

'Sure you do. Ashan, you really have mastered all the basic skills of a bad guy, including arrogance and cluelessness. I'm proud of you. Now, if you can just make an empty, impotent threat—'

'Shut up or I'll destroy you!' he roared, right on cue. Oh, he was mad. Really mad. I'd succeeded in royally teeing off the second most powerful Djinn in the world, and all his invisible allies, when I was all that stood between humanity and destruction.

'Do it,' I said quietly, and pushed away from the car to stand in the clear. Facing him with my arms at my sides, hands limp and open. Staring right into his eerie Djinn eyes. 'What are you waiting for? Smash me. Destroy me. Rip me to pieces. I'm just a mortal, I can't stop you. Come on, Ashan, kick my punk human ass.'

He growled. It was a low, primal sound, and his human form distorted under the pressure of his rage. He misted at the feet, then the legs. The suit disappeared. Everything remotely elegant disappeared, and he was pure flame, pure roaring energy, like the centre of a volcano.

He rushed at me. I flinched a little, but I held my ground.

He came to a halt less than two inches from my face. I could feel the burn, the fury, but he didn't touch me.

He *couldn't* touch me.

And he knew that I knew.

I opened my eyes and smiled. 'You said it yourself. Jonathan, Lewis, *me*. She wants to see me. Hear me. Doesn't she? And she's not going to let you kill me.'

He formed himself back into human flesh again, pale and solid as marble, cold as tombstones. His eyes were an unholy shade of teal, glittering with silver. 'I wouldn't smile,' he said, and there was a grave hint of fury in his voice. 'I may not be able to hurt you, but I can take it in trade. Blood for blood. The blood of your lover.'

That meant that David was still alive, oh God . . . Relief made me weak at the knees, but I couldn't let him see it. 'David's willing to die for this if he has to. I don't even have to ask him,'

'Not just him. I'll destroy every one of the Wardens. If you think to play the game with me, you need to know the stakes. Lives will be lost. I will see to it.'

'You already did,' I spat back. 'Hundreds of Wardens are dead. Tens of thousands are in danger, or dying, and for every Warden that dies, more get put in jeopardy. I know what I'm playing for, Ashan. And you're not going to threaten me into giving up.'

I expected him to laugh and bluster – I mean, good villains did, right? – but he just looked at me, and when his comeback came, it was slow and deliberate and scary. 'No,' he said. 'I have never known you to respond to threats against yourself. Or the world at large. And you're quite right about David and his self-sacrifice.'

He was looking behind me. I know, I know, it's the oldest trick in the book, but I didn't think that he was all that up on strategy.

I glanced back. Imara was out of the car and standing mute and somehow *limp* a few feet away. As if she were unconscious, being held up by an invisible hand at the back of her neck. Her head lolled forward, then back, as if someone had tugged hard on her hair.

Her eyes were empty, flat silver.

I turned back to Ashan. His were the same colour.

'She's mine,' he said. 'Until you take her away. Mine to use. Mine to kill, if I want. You can accept your own death. So far as I can tell, you seem to actively seek it out. And like most of humanity, the plight of the distant and faceless doesn't move you. But your daughter is in my hand, Joanne. And I think that means something more.'

I swallowed hard. He was right, of course. Every cell in my body screamed at me to do something, anything, to save my daughter. She was part of me, and I wanted to protect her so badly, it was tearing me to pieces. Ashan might not have human ancestry in his background, but he knew what we feared.

'It does,' I said softly. My eyes filled up with tears suddenly – hot, hard, aching tears that seemed to pour right up from my heart. 'I love my daughter more than my life. But I'm going, Ashan. You do whatever you have to do, but I'm going. I have to.'

I got back in the car. I could barely see it for the tears, but somehow I kept myself from sobbing. The wet trails on my face where they'd streamed felt cold in the sudden blast of the air conditioner as I turned the key and started up the roadster.

Ashan was still watching me, with my daughter clutched in one hand like a broken marionette. I couldn't tell what he was thinking. Hell, I could barely tell what *I* was thinking.

I took a deep, damp gulp of air, pressed the clutch, and put the car in first gear. The engine shifted to a low purring growl, and the car eased forward with a crunch of gravel.

Ashan didn't move. He was ten feet away, with Imara. Around him, I sensed the other Djinn, his twenty companions, the faithful or faithless, depending which side you came down on in this struggle. I could almost see their calm faces, their inhuman eyes.

A jolt of lightning joined sky and earth behind Ashan, a pale pink-and-purple line that unravelled into dozens of thin strings on the way. Beautiful. Alien. Powerful. Terrifying.

I don't know why I said it, but I whispered, 'Please.' It was a sacred prayer, as much as a request.

And then I hit the gas.

At the last minute, he stepped aside as graceful as a matador, using my child for a cape.

I hit the freeway and shifted gears while my soul burnt and crumbled into ruins.

When you give up everything – and I mean everything – there's this eerie sense of calm that comes over you. I didn't have David; I knew now that I couldn't have him. Whatever Ashan had done to him, it was thorough enough that he couldn't be my personal lifesaving God-in-a-bottle anymore. No power on earth could have held him back from coming to Imara's defence, if he'd been able to break free. Ashan had him, and now he had my daughter, too. I'd abdicated the one responsibility that should have been impossible for me to give up: motherhood. I'd turned my back on my own child. I'd let myself count her as a cost of doing business.

It felt like Pompeii on volcano day, and all I could taste was ashes.

I let him have my daughter.

I could hear Lewis's warm, dispassionate voice telling me that I'd made the right choice, the only choice, but it didn't matter. It's written in our DNA somewhere: our children first, the rest of the world second. I couldn't believe I'd done it. Couldn't believe I was that much of a monster.

Ashan was going to kill her, and I was going to let him, and that tore my heart to bloody shreds. I hated this. I hated being strong. I hated understanding that this was the cost of things.

Please. I said it again, with all my heart and soul, letting it fill me up in prayer and desperation. *Please God, take care of her. I don't know how you fit into all this – I don't know whether you're in everything or nothing, whether you're an absentee landlord or watching the flight of every bumblebee. But I beg you, don't let my daughter pay the price. Please. I don't care what it costs, but please, find a way . . .*

God must hate our me-me-me whining; like kids sent off to college, we call only when we need a favour. I wasn't sure if I'd built up any credit in the Bank of Miracles. Probably not, given my history, but maybe the Bank of Mercy didn't have such strict lending rules.

I wiped my eyes and opened up the roadster down the clean, straight road. It seemed to go on forever, and then I took the indicated turnoff, AZ-179, to make the last leg of the journey.

It was beautiful. Really, searingly beautiful, even with the grey cotton of cloud cover obscuring that burnished blue sky – the rocks were ancient and powerfully sculpted, and it was a landscape to conjure the old, old gods of the empty spaces. The road looked alien and out of place here. I was no Earth Warden, but even I could feel the power that whispered through the air and ground; this was a place where the skin between the real and aetheric was paper-thin. No wonder New Agers flocked here, not to mention the religious of all faiths and sects. It had a purity that I'd never felt before, not even in other desert spots.

The clouds, already thinning, broke into haze by the time I reached the town of Oak Creek, which according to the rental agency map was just outside of Sedona proper. Behind them was that limitless sky, the bright unblinking stare of the sun.

It occurred to me, rather stupidly late, that I had no street address for the Oracle, and now, with Imara gone (my heart dried up and died at the thought of that, and I felt another flood of tears burn my eyes) I didn't have a native guide, either. All I had was instinct, and not much of that.

Well, the last Oracle was an Earth spirit, so I didn't figure to find it hanging out at the Old Navy store, but that left a lot of territory.

I kept going, absent any reason to do anything else. Oak Creek passed in a blur of houses and xeriscaped yards, businesses and cars, and was swallowed up again by the desert that outwaited everything. The silence took over again. The sky brightened, and my hands shook on the steering wheel. I kept expecting Ashan to smite me with righteous fury, but he hadn't made a move. I wondered why. Maybe he was still trying to figure out why I'd abandoned my daughter to die . . .

I shook my head violently to clear it of the images.

The sun was molten out here, pouring energy in syrupy waves, and the ground soaked it up. Shadows were sharply drawn and as cold as black holes where they fell. The flora was angular and beautiful in its austerity, and it passed by in a continuous roll until I topped a rise and saw Sedona up ahead.

At the same instant, I felt the same artificial sense of calm and steadiness here that I'd felt in Seacasket. I was in the right place, all right.

I just didn't know where to go from here.

The sense of panic started to set in when I passed the town limits, because I really *didn't* know. I suppose I was expecting some kind of magic guidance – a flashing sign that said THIS WAY TO THE ORACLE TO SAVE THE WORLD! Not that I'd expect anything so crass in this place. Maybe a discreet, hand-carved art nouveau plaque in native woods.

I pulled in at a gas station, trembling all over, and consulted the map again. Nothing. No helpful Djinn-induced sparks of light. No ORACLE marked on it, with a pointing arrow. I'd come all this way, given up my *daughter*, and for what?

Easy, I told myself when I felt the shaking start to get too bad. *You can do this. Ashan wouldn't have tried to stop you if there hadn't been a way to get it done.*

Logical, but not comforting. Hell, Ashan might have been trying to stop me just for the pure joy of seeing me have to choose between duty and child. He struck me as that kind of Djinn.

I wished, illogically, that Jonathan was still around. Lean, angular, sarcastic Jonathan, with his infinite eyes and shallow patience. David was my love, and he was half my soul, but I needed someone with more perspective. Someone who viewed me as a white knight on a chessboard, not the queen, to be protected.

Someone to move me to the right square.

I got out of the BMW and stretched. A couple of guys gassing up stared. Might have been the car they were lusting after, but I smiled wanly at them anyway and walked over to the telephones. After a futile and maddening search for change in my pockets, I went into the gas station and bought one of those phone card things, then came back and dialled the number of Lewis's cell phone from a telephone booth.

I got him on the first ring. 'Jo! I've been trying to find you—'

'Cell phone service is bad,' I said. 'I'm still saving the world for you. I need a favour, and it's a big one.'

Silence for a long few seconds. There was a steady, agitated sound of shouts in the background. All was not quiet on the Warden front. 'Go,' he said.

'First of all, if you've still got any clout with any Free Djinn, use it. Ashan's got Imara. He's trying to use her to stop me. I need help.'

I felt the sudden intake of breath on the other

end of the line, as if I'd gut-punched him across the intervening miles. 'Ah, dammit, Jo, I'm sorry. I was trying to get hold of you to warn you. Rahel showed up in the New York offices about fifteen minutes ago.'

'What?' Oh, I had a bad feeling. Bad, bad, bad.

'It's happening again,' Lewis said. 'They're – turning. Be careful.'

I swallowed hard and angled my back to the rough adobe wall, so that I could squint through the glare at the parking lot. It looked calm. My BMW sat glittering in the sun, sleek and beautiful and just a touch arrogant; beyond it, two big-ass SUVs were drinking the pumps dry. A woman was tossing trash in the courtesy cans. Normal human life, nothing out of the ordinary.

'Did she kill anybody?'

'Let's just say it didn't go well.'

'How many—'

'Stay focused, Jo.' Lewis sounded grim and ragged, very unlike his usual cool self. 'You can't afford to worry about individuals right now. I can't do what you're doing, or I'd be knocking down the doors right now, believe me. I've tried. Even though I've got the right mix of powers, there's something missing in me. Something you've got.'

'Djinn,' I said. 'I have a little bit of Djinn.'

I heard someone yell his name in the background. 'I have to go,' he said. 'We've got wounded. Jo – about Imara—'

'I understand,' I said. The taste of ashes was back in my mouth. 'There's nothing you can do.'

'Nothing anybody can do,' he said. 'We're trying to stay alive – that's it and that's all. Keep as many people breathing as we're able.'

And that, ultimately, was the mission of the Wardens, wasn't it? The greater good.

'Wait,' I said. 'I'm in Sedona. Do you have any idea where to—'

'Find the Ma'at,' he said, and hung up.

Just . . . hung up.

I stared at the receiver in disbelief, because that wasn't exactly what I'd call a red-hot clue. The Ma'at weren't listed in the yellow pages under *World, Saving Of* . . . and I had no idea if there was even one single person, out of the several Ma'at I'd met, who lived in the Sedona area. As far as I knew, they were all strangers. How the hell was I supposed to find them, send up a flare?

A flare . . .

I was still thinking it through when one of the big SUVs pulled away from the pump and out onto the road, and revealed three figures standing there, watching me. Focused on me like hungry wolves.

Rahel. Alice. The male Djinn from back at the forest, the one with the long white ponytail.

Their eyes were crimson, burning like the forests up in Canada, and hell if I knew what I was supposed to do to save myself.

* * *

I swallowed and carefully replaced the receiver in the cradle on the pay phone. I briefly considered running, but that didn't seem so smart. I couldn't outrun Djinn.

So far, they hadn't moved, but I was deeply scared. The three of them together represented a huge amount of firepower – think China in a pissed-off mood – and I was trying to remember all the advice about what to do with wild animals. Move slowly. Avoid eye contact. *Don't run.*

They all moved together. I mean, *together* – not like one started and the others followed, they all just flowed into motion and began walking towards me. Slow steps. Alice had to walk faster, because she was so small, but they were identically eerie.

Clearly, moving slowly and avoiding eye contact wasn't getting me anywhere. I pressed myself against the wall and held up my hands, trying to appear as helpless and pathetic as possible while simultaneously grabbing and gathering up as much power as I could. Not that it would do any good, but I wasn't going down without a fight. Not now. Not after I'd come so far.

If I thought I'd been shaking before, well, this was like standing on a fault line. My heart was hammering. I remembered how many Wardens had already died, and I remembered my name, already carved on that marble wall of the fallen. I'd seen my funeral. It had been nice, but I had no great desire to schedule an encore. At least, not yet. I was fed up with the dying.

I focused on Rahel, looking for some sign – any sign – that she was still even partly in control. Nothing. She was a vessel: Rahel on the outside, and something else entirely on the inside. Did she know? Could she remember how it felt, later, to be so lost to herself?

Would she remember killing me later?

Why was the Earth doing this now? What had I done to piss her off? Anything? Nothing? Who could tell?

They stopped moving just as suddenly as they'd started, facing me. Rahel was on the right side, and I kept watching her, *willing* her to recognise me. The madness hadn't lasted too long last time, had it? Maybe an hour? Lewis had said it had started fifteen minutes ago . . . that left me forty-five minutes to keep the tigers at bay . . .

Their mouths opened, and what came out was noise.

I clapped my hands over my ears and tried to keep it out, but it wasn't sound, really, and it didn't come in through my ears. It was something else, a kind of vibration that used the aetheric and the real world, was part of both, part of neither – it was awful and terrible and it was somehow *sick*, as if I was hearing a physical manifestation of a disease.

The Demon. The Demon had succeeded in getting to another Oracle – probably this one, in Sedona – and the Mother was horribly hurt and angry, unable to strike back in any effective way to protect herself. So she was striking out at anything and everything that moved.

I was like a bacteria trying to talk to Albert Einstein, but I had to try something. Anything. I pried my hands away from my ears and yelled, 'Shut up!'

They did.

Wow.

All three of them stared at me, and I blinked back; all three of their heads tilted slowly sideways, considering me. Crimson eyes flickering with flares of orange and yellow and a hot, pale blue.

'I know,' I said. My stomach was trying to contract itself into a tight little ball of terror, and my knees didn't want to stay firm. I braced myself against the adobe wall and thought madly that of all the hostage negotiations ever conducted, this had to be the biggest. No pressure. 'I know how much it hurts. Can you hear me? Can you understand me?'

Nothing. Their heads stayed tilted. They didn't move, not so much as an inch or a twitch. Frozen, like statues, except for the unsettling, alien furnace in their eyes.

'I can help,' I said. 'If there's a Demon Mark on the Oracle, I can help. Just take me there. Or at least show me the way.'

It wasn't working. They didn't understand me, although they certainly knew I was there – they'd sought me out, which meant she was aware of my existence. Dammit . . . David was the buffer. Imara said that she couldn't find him, which meant that somehow he'd been taken out of his connection to all other Djinn, and without him standing in that place, *no one* stood there.

No buffer between the Djinn and the earth. Nothing to keep them sane.

The trio opened their mouths again, and sang. It was indefinable, but I thought it was a lament. Sorrow, deep and jagged and painful. Loss. Horror. It hurt to hear it, made my knees give way; I cried out at the short stab of agony that bolted up from my kneecaps hitting concrete, then stayed down. I wasn't sure I could get up. Wasn't sure I *wanted* to get up.

I had no way to answer her, except with words. 'I know,' I said. 'I know it hurts. I know you want to stop hurting. So do I.'

Maybe there was a colouring of the same anguish in my voice. Maybe she heard the music of that in the words, even if the words meant nothing.

Rahel's eyes flickered. Red, then pale blue, then that fierce predatory gold I was used to.

For an instant I read everything in her – sheer deep terror at what she was doing, helpless rage at not being able to stop it, despair, a tearing pain that was an echo of the earth's.

She didn't have time to speak, and I could barely draw the breath and form the intention to ask before the Mother had Rahel again, hard in her grasp.

The song came again, soft, almost a whisper, and

in it was something deadly. Like a mother singing a lullaby to a baby she was about to smother, because the world was too harsh a place, too unbearably sharp-edged for such a fragile life . . .

I reacted instinctively. I was terrified beyond all reason because I knew, *knew* my life was about to come to an end, and I had to act or die on my knees.

I wasn't about to die on my knees. I lunged to my feet, crossed the few feet that separated me from Rahel, and slugged her. A strong right cross to the jaw, with as much shoulder behind it as I knew how to commit. And if I may say so myself, it was a hell of a good shot, because I felt every bone in my hand turn to shards of glass, and I was sure I'd broken every damn thing in my body between fingertips and collarbone . . .

. . . but she shut her mouth, rocked back a step, and the other two Djinn followed suit.

'That's enough!' I yelled. '*Enough!* I know it hurts, I know you hurt and it's making you crazy, but dammit, *stop!* This isn't some teenage soap opera! We live here! We're part of you. Humans *matter!* The Djinn *matter!* You can't kill us just because you're – depressed and angry!'

It was an impassioned speech. I don't think she got a word of it. Probably sounded like a fly buzzing in her ear as she sobbed in anguish, but for just a second, the Earth was surprised enough by the simple appearance of the nagging fly that she paused in the act of ripping us to pieces.

And the Djinn all looked at me with their own eyes, in varying stages of worry and disquiet.

'And fucking *ow*!' I yelled, and cradled my right arm. God, that hurt. I mean, really. 'How much time do I have?'

'Not much,' Rahel breathed. Of the three of them, she looked the least concerned, but I wasn't convinced that meant much. Rahel had always been good at hiding her feelings. 'She's waking. It's done, my friend. It's finished. You should let us kill you now, without pain, before the choice is gone for all of us.'

'We can't kill her,' Alice observed. Her voice sounded preoccupied. 'She won't allow it. There's something about this one.'

'Venna,' Rahel said. I looked around, curious, but there were just the four of us. Alice cocked her head attentively. Oh. That was right, her name wasn't Alice, I'd just gotten to thinking of her that way – she'd kept the Alice in Wonderland pinafore and silky blond hair, but she was a very old, very powerful Djinn. And her name, apparently, was Venna. 'Can you sense David?'

'No,' she said. 'Although part of him is in this plane.'

'Part of him?' For a breathless second I thought she meant an arm, a leg, a disembodied spirit . . .

'The child,' she clarified. 'Ashan has her.'

'Go and get her,' Rahel said. 'Now.'

'He'll resist.'

'Yes,' she agreed. 'Enjoy yourself.'

Venna raised one eyebrow – a very odd expression for an Alice look-alike – and smiled coolly. 'How much?'

'Until you stop enjoying yourself.'

She nodded once, folded her hands primly, and vanished. My hand was starting to feel normal again, though incredibly hot, as if I'd stuck it in an oven to bake all the bones back together. I tried not to move it. As if he felt my pain, the big Djinn reached out to touch my hand. His fingers stroked up and down over the aching cracked or broken bones.

'You shouldn't put your thumb in your fist when you punch someone,' he said. My broken thumb reset with a snap, and I yelped. 'That's to help you remember.'

'Good enough,' Rahel said. 'Give us a minute.'

The big Djinn didn't comment, just shrugged and walked away, around the corner of the convenience store. Maybe he was going to buy a Slurpee. Anything was possible, at the moment.

My legs just flat stopped working, and all of a sudden I was pitching forward, helpless to prevent it, and the asphalt parking lot was coming up fast and straight for my nose.

Rahel grabbed me and hoisted me upright, then leant me back against the wall. I gave a deep-throated moan, let my head rest against the rough adobe, and closed my eyes for a few seconds. Stars. I was seeing stars, and they were moving fast. Too fast for me to keep up.

'It's all happening,' I said. 'Right? I'm too late.'

'A few minutes left,' Rahel said. 'Not so many, though.' She accompanied that with a shake of my arm. 'You must finish it,' she said. 'She won't listen to us, but she hears you. She doesn't understand you, but there's something about you that . . . sings. Finish it. Make her understand. Go.'

'I can't.'

'You have to.'

'Rahel, I *can't*!' I wanted to stay here. I wanted to wait to see Imara's face again. I wanted –

I just wanted to be like the rest of the world, filling up my car, buying my Slurpee, unaware I was half an hour or less away from dying.

There was no forgiveness or mercy in her expression. 'You will,' she said. 'Because it's who you are. I have seen this in you from the first moment I saw you.'

'Bullshit!' I burst out. 'I don't even know where—'

'Get in your car and drive.'

'Did you hear me? *I don't know where I'm going!*'

'*Drive!*' she snarled, and practically threw me across the parking lot towards the BMW. My legs worked fine this time, holding me upright as I braked my forward momentum against the side of the car. I whirled to face her, and the fear turned white-hot with rage.

'Don't you *ever* do that again!' I shouted. 'Ever! I swear to God, Rahel—'

'Yes,' she said, walking towards me with fast, choppy steps. Her hair, intricately braided with beads, swirled and twisted in a sudden hot wind rushing over the parking lot. I felt the patter of sand against my skin. 'Swear to God. Pray. *Pray.*'

She was terrifying now, and it wasn't the Earth inside her, it was purely and wholly Rahel.

'Pray,' she said again, as if it really meant something, and put her hands together and gave me a full, formal bow.

I blinked against a stinging rush of blown sand, and then . . . she was gone. Nothing there but discarded paper cups rattling around on the ground, making pointless circles in the wind.

I scrabbled for the door and threw myself inside the car, fastened both hands tight on the steering wheel for a second, and then started up the car.

Pray.

Well, it was a start.

I pulled out onto the highway, still heading through Sedona, looking for . . . a sign. Overhead, the sky seemed to be getting darker, although it wasn't anywhere near dusk; the cerulean blue was taking on ocean colours. The sun blazed on, brassy-bright, but it didn't seem to be giving any warmth.

I paid no attention to the traffic, and let my instincts and peripheral vision take care of it while I frantically scanned the horizon. Jagged rocks all around, ringing us, and I had no idea what she'd meant except that she'd meant something specific.

And then, up ahead, I saw a sign. A literal exit sign. It said, CHAPEL ROAD, and in a smaller size type, CHAPEL OF THE HOLY CROSS.

Pray.

I took the exit fast, with tires squealing, and followed the winding road.

Chapter Nine

There was a parking lot at the top of the hill, and a sign told visitors that it was a steep climb up to the Chapel of the Holy Cross. I closed the car door and stood there, shivering in the suddenly cold breeze, staring up at the place. It was . . . beautiful. Built into the rocks, organic, angular. Strikingly memorable. The shape was oblong, the sides sloping in with a short line connecting them at the top – all plain grey concrete, contrasting sharply with the red sandstone around it. The front was all glass, reflecting the sun and the beautiful eternity of the desert around it. It wasn't as large as I'd have expected, but then it was a chapel, not a church. It was a place pilgrims came to ask for favours, and to leave a gift of worship.

There were a few other cars in the parking lot. I was hoping there wouldn't be unsuspecting visitors caught up in this, but it was too late to worry. Everybody was in the crossfire now. Six billion potential innocent bystanders.

I took the steep stairs towards the chapel at a run.

Sweat dried on my skin as I pounded up the steps, and I was about halfway up when I realised that somebody was right behind me, and gaining. I glanced back.

It was Ashan, feral and bloodied, and as I looked, he changed himself to mist and flew at me. He surrounded me, and coalesced, yanking my head back by the hair and catching me off-balance. It would be a long, bruising fall. A broken neck, at best.

But he didn't fling me over the edge, or down the steps. Again, I got the weird sense that he just couldn't, no matter how much he might have wanted it. Something prevented him. While he was fighting against that instinct, something hit him like a small pinafore-wearing freight train, and he went sailing over the edge of the drop, with little Alice/Venna on his back and riding him like a struggling surfboard towards the rocks. He had time to mist. So did she. They reappeared at ground level, and I had the sense that Ashan was trying to get free to come after me, but she circled to counter him at every turn.

It was fun for her. There was a terrible tiger's smile on her innocent little face that made my stomach lurch.

'Go!' she called to me, and extended a little-girl hand towards Ashan.

And blew him past five parked cars to slam up against a concrete retaining wall. He bounced off and came back at her like a man-eating rubber ball.

I turned my attention back to the steps, taking them two and three at a time. My calf muscles screamed in protest. I hadn't run stairs in . . . well, years. Since evil Coach Hawkins in high school, who'd made it the start to every PE class. I'd never been all that good at it then, come to think of it . . .

The stairs shouldn't have been this tall. It felt as if I were trying to run the stairs at Chichen Itza, not just a few dozen up to the local chapel. I couldn't see the top. I couldn't tell that there *was* a top.

And then I felt it . . . a whispering sense of presence. Something vast and powerful and not like me, not at all.

Not even like the Djinn.

I stopped on the stairs, grabbed the railing in one hand, and listened.

It was . . . whispering. I couldn't tell what it was saying, but I heard the voices. Lots of voices. Male, female, neither, all swirling. All questioning.

All crying out in pain.

'Let me in!' I yelled. My voice echoed from the rocks, from those lovely, silent, patient rocks. They'd heard it all, those rocks. Listened to lovers whispering, to warriors killing and dying, to speeches and preachers and songs. It was just noise. It didn't last.

I slipped under the railing on the side away from the drop and clambered drunkenly up a pitch, my shoes unsteady on the footing. I put my hands directly on the blood-warm stones. They felt rough as sandpaper, and flecks of mica glittered in them like flecks of gold.

Please, I prayed. *Please let me in.*

It wasn't going to work. I was just too small, too frail, too temporary . . .

'Venna!' I yelled. 'Quit messing around and *get up here!*'

She didn't respond. When I looked down – risking a broken neck in the process – there was no sign of any Djinn at all in the parking lot. *Dammit.*

'Rahel! Dammit!' I yelled it without any hope at all. 'David!' The echoes mocked me, ringing off into the distance. Losing his name in the empty spaces.

It was all going to be lost because I couldn't get up the damn stairs. I took two more steps, but it was like forcing myself through molasses, then drying concrete.

I froze in place, sweating, trembling, and clawed at the stone for another few inches.

Something pushed me back. I half slid, half fell back to the railing, skidded underneath, and began pounding up the steps again. No barrier this time. Two steps at a time, a regular, even rhythm. If the spirit of this place needed sacrifice, I'd give it. I'd run until my feet bled, if I had to. Until my heart burst. Until it damn well saw that I wasn't going to quit.

There was nothing in the world for me but the steps, and that simple stone landing at the top of them, with the enamel-blue sky heavy overhead.

Ashan was standing at the top, waiting for me. He wasn't Mr Neat anymore. His suit was rags, his tie missing. Alabaster skin and fresh road blood showed through the rents in the fabric. It was just representation, I knew that, but he looked bruised and trashed and thoroughly pissed off. He'd defeated Venna, then. Probably Rahel as well. And David, David, oh God . . .

I put my head down and kept running. Screw Ashan. He was just another obstacle, and I *would* get past him. I could feel things changing in the air, feel polarities shifting. There was something coming alive in the Earth, and there could be no fighting that. The Wardens were useless. The Djinn were – or would be – hers. And human beings were just a resource-consuming problem, like an overpopulation of wood lice and just about as important to her.

And there was a corruption in it, too. A black, spreading, cold corruption that meant the Oracle had been infected, and the infection was spreading.

Please.

I sent my prayer up, up into the sky. Up to a heaven I wasn't sure even existed. Wardens were literal. Scientific. We weren't into the spiritual, and our theology tended to start and stop with the idea that nobody really knew what the hell was going on, beyond the aetheric level.

But if God was out there, if he cared, this was the moment for that hands-off policy to be rescinded.

I ran my heart out. Ran until my leg muscles felt like overcooked noodles. Until my heart was hammering so fast, it felt like one continuous long reverberation in my chest. Until I was soaked with sweat and spots danced in front of my eyes.

Until I could barely lift my feet for each endless step.

And then, I couldn't.

I tried, made it halfway, and tripped. I instinctively put my hands out to break my fall . . . and someone grabbed my wrist. I still banged a bruised knee painfully against a stone step, but the pain barely registered as I looked up to see who had hold of me.

Imara. Bruised, bloodied, but not beaten.

My daughter gave me a slow, lovely smile, and reached down to take my other hand in hers. 'One more step, Mom,' she said. 'Just one more.'

There was always one more.

I raised my foot, trembling, and set it on the step. Imara pulled, and with her help, I raised myself up.

One last step.

And then I was at the top.

Ashan stood between me and the door. Imara

still had hold of my hands, and she was smiling so sweetly, so luminously, that tears flooded my eyes. Oh *God* she was lovely. She was all that was good about me, about David, and I barely knew her, I wanted to have time to understand her, who she was, what she meant . . .

'I love you, Mom,' she said, and let go.

Ashan lunged at her from behind. He took her in both hands, snarling with raw fury, and snapped her neck with a dry, terrible crackle. I saw it happen, right in front of me, and I saw her eyes go wide, the pupils spreading.

I saw my daughter die.

He threw her down the steps as if she was *nothing*. As if she wasn't worthy of respect and love and devotion. A broken doll thudding down those steep concrete stairs to flop limp and shattered at the bottom, small and human and mortal after all.

I didn't scream. I had nothing left to scream with. I stared at Ashan. He was primal. He'd defeated everything and everyone who'd come against him, from David to Venna to Rahel.

But none of that mattered now. He'd *killed my daughter.* And I was not backing down.

'No allies?' he said, and grinned. 'No Djinn to rescue you? No Wardens to fight on your side?'

'No,' I said raggedly. 'No one.'

He'd kill me if he could. If there was even the slightest chink in whatever was holding him back, it would break now, and my blood would soak into these thirsty, eternal stones, and it would be over.

Just . . . over.

I extended my right hand and walked towards him with deliberate steps. He snarled, and it was such a low, vicious sound that if I'd still cared about living or dying, I'd have stopped. But it was all or nothing, now. David had put my feet on the path. Rahel and Venna had defended me. Imara had pulled me when I couldn't make the last effort, and she'd – she'd—

My turn to sacrifice all, if I had to.

My hand was in his space. I waited for the blow that would snap my neck and send me to my death, but it didn't come. My fingers reached, moving forward, then flattened against his chest. His shirt was ripped, and my fingertips registered the difference between hot skin and cool fabric.

We were close enough to be kissing.

'You don't understand,' he said, and suddenly I was talking to a man – an entity, anyway – not just a force of nature. Someone with flaws and fears and longings. I heard them trembling in his voice. I saw them in his inhuman eyes. 'We were *gods*. We were kings of this world. Then *you* came, and we were slaves, slaves to you. You took our birthright. You took away our place.'

As if he wanted me to *understand*. Forgive. Wind blew cold over us, swirling the rags covering him, tossing my hair back in a banner. The Chapel of the

Holy Cross was ten steps behind him, and the doors were open.

'The Mother forgot us,' he said softly. 'Heat. Pain. Birth. A slow and quiet cooling. We were her children, but she forgot us.'

'She remembers you now.' I looked over his shoulder at the open doors, the glow of light through the huge expanse of glass window at the far end of the chapel. It was a simple place, with polished wood benches, a plain altar. I could hear the whispering again, stronger now. A union of voices. The Oracle was within. 'You've killed your own, right in front of her. I don't think she'll ever forget you again.'

He couldn't get paler, but I think he might have, at that. 'Nature is selfish,' he said. 'Sacrifice is meaningless. Only survival matters.'

I couldn't think about Imara, about sacrifice. 'I'm not fighting you anymore.'

His eyes filled with a silver sheen of tears, and he pulled in a sudden breath. 'No,' he said. 'I choose this. I choose to stop you, now, here.'

'Don't.'

'*I choose!*' He screamed it, and reached out with all the power that was inside of him to destroy me.

Stop.

It was a pulse of intention, not a word, and the world froze between one pulse beat and the next, waiting breathlessly. I thought it was Ashan's doing for a second, but I saw the wild fury and fear in his eyes, and I knew.

I turned. The air dragged at me, slow and thick as molasses.

The Oracle was doing this. She was giving me a chance, and I knew it was my very last one.

I walked into the chapel.

Chapter Ten

The Oracle was sitting on a bench, facing the glorious sweep of glass that looked out on the stunning vista. It really was one of the most beautiful things I'd ever seen. I'd looked into the eye of more than one storm, and seen the complex, mathematical beauty of it; I'd seen most of the most savage, gorgeous, violent faces of nature.

But this was different. Deep and slow and silent. There was no math to it, no science. Only spirit.

Unlike the other Oracles, this one looked ... normal. A woman, with generous curves and a lived-in face, with lines at the corners of her eyes and mouth. She was wearing a dress the colour of the rocks outside of the window, brick red, with a subtle patterning to it, like the creases and shadows and textures of the sandstone. It had flowing sleeves and a loose drape, and it pooled around her feet, into shadow.

She was no race I could identify – coffee-and-cream skin, with a faint golden glow underneath; slightly upturned eyes, but not enough to make her distinctly Asian. Full lips. Beautiful bone structure under a soft mask of flesh. Her hair was dark, shot through with wide swathes of grey, and her eyes reflected back the light from the chapel's windows so strongly, I couldn't tell what colour they were, at least not from a side-on view.

She was sitting with her hands neatly folded in her lap. Rough, scarred hands. Hands that had seen a lot of work, and little gentleness. She looked tired, poised on the knife-edge between middle age and growing old.

Her head slowly turned, and then she was looking at me. *Seeing* me. I can't describe what that felt like, except to say that it was beyond terrifying. As if the stars had come alive in the sky and were weighing me, judging me, finding me wanting. I felt small and dirty and ridiculous, a clumsy freak of nature with no business here, no business at all. The Oracles barely recognised the Djinn. Humans were beneath contempt.

And yet, she was looking at me.

I got to my knees. I did it instantly, without thinking, because I knew I was very close to something greater than the furious energy of the Fire Oracle, or the menace of the Air Oracle.

The Earth Oracle was closest of all to the Mother.

She tilted her head slowly to one side, considering

me like a particularly interesting piece of abstract art.

'Please,' I said. The sound washed over us both, meaningless in this place. Talking wasn't going to get me anywhere. The Earth didn't use words. It spoke in the whisper of leaves, the hiss of grass, the groaning of rocks buried deep. Communication was something very different here, and I was completely unprepared, completely unworthy to try it. Not even an Earth Warden, which at least would have been *something*, some connection, however slight and fragile.

I was just dirt on the floor in this place. No, less than that. She'd at least understand dirt.

Her gaze slowly shifted away, towards the altar, the flickering banks of candles on either side in their red glass holders, and the astonishingly beautiful vista stretching out before us.

She wanted something from me, and I had no idea what it was, or how to provide it.

I felt the gradual withdrawal of her presence from me.

I was being dismissed.

'No!' I said, and held up my hands. 'Please! Please listen to me, I need you to understand—'

No answer. She didn't even blink. It was as if I didn't even exist to her anymore. Maybe I didn't. Time was different in her world. Geologic. Human lives came and went faster than the ticks on a clock.

'Please!' This time, I shouted it, and I did something that was either very, very brave or abysmally stupid:

I reached out to her, and took her hand. It felt warm and rough, more like sandstone than flesh. '*Please listen.*'

Not a flicker. Not a tremor. I'd come so far, fought so hard, run so fast . . . and she was ignoring me. Unlike Rahel, this wasn't someone I could give a hard right cross to the chin to get her attention. There was a strong sense of deep holiness here. Respect was required.

Respect was demanded.

Outside of the glass windows, I saw the sky . . . change. It had been getting darker, but now it curdled, like ink dropped in clear water – a sense of something wrong, something desperately and fatally wrong. I felt it happen inside of myself, too. I felt the deathclock we all carried, all mortal things, speed up.

Oh God. Was she going to just wipe everything clean? All life? Destroy it all and wait that long eternity for things to grow again? Or would the Djinn step back into their place as firstborn, best loved?

I went up into the aetheric, and there I saw it for what it was. A storm coming. A storm that showed blood-red, full of fury and power. I felt a tethering tug, and looked down at my aetheric form to see that there was a line, a thin, unbreakable line stretching from the centre of my being up into that storm.

It was connected to me, and as I looked around, I saw hundreds of lines. Thousands. Millions. Like solid raindrops, each leading down to a human life. A human who'd just felt an instant of shadow, of doubt in his or her own immortality.

Who'd had the sensation of someone walking over their graves. Six billion graves, and only one entity walking, but it only took the one.

It was starting.

'Please,' I said. 'Please don't do this. We don't deserve this. We *can't* deserve this! Dammit! *What do you want me to say?*'

The Oracle trembled, a sudden all-over shake, and I felt the Earth itself groan in response. What the hell—?

Her eyes closed, and the hand I was holding suddenly turned and took hold of me. Hard, hot, unyielding. I felt the tremors continue, both through my knees and where she was clutching my fingers. Something was wrong. Terrifyingly wrong.

Oh no.

I took an aching breath and reached forward to move the neck of the Oracle's robes aside, and there, battened on her like a black nest of worms, was the Demon Mark. The skin around it was drained white, leached of life, and I could see the black writhing tentacles bulging under the skin. It was burrowing.

I was too late. It already had a firm grip on her.

I reached out and put both hands on the Demon Mark, willing it to come to me. It ignored me, burrowing for the rich, burning source of power that was the Oracle. I was insignificant. There was no way I had enough power to make it come to me.

There was something coming towards us, digging through stone and concrete. Something dark and terrible. The adult Demon was on its way here, following me or drawn to the immense outpouring of power that was going on – no telling. But we didn't have long.

None of us did. I could feel the terrible pull inside of my life being dragged away.

The Oracle's power was compromised as it tried to fight the infection of the Demon Mark, but even so, it was channelling the intention of the Mother to wipe humanity out of her way.

I couldn't stop it. I couldn't even heal the Oracle, which was the only way I could even begin to make things right.

'Take my hand.' A rusty, exhausted voice. I looked aside and saw Rahel, holding out a trembling, blood-stained hand on which the claws had raggedly broken. When I took it, it felt cold.

She extended her hand to Alice – Venna – who was equally damaged. The line stretched on. Djinn after Djinn after Djinn. And with them, humans. I recognised a few Wardens. A few members of the Ma'at.

A chain of hands, joined one to the other, building a circuit of power that, while it couldn't possible be as huge as the potential of the Oracle, was a much easier target.

Come on, I begged the Demon Mark. *Come on, you sick little freak. Take us. You know you want it.*

It wasn't coming. I hissed in frustration, grabbed hold of it, and *pulled* with all the fury and grief and rage in me. Felt it spiral through the circuit of hands, rebound, and come back again, stronger. Stronger still.

They poured their power into me, and the Demon Mark moved in my hand, turned, and struck. It was enraged, and my skin was nothing like the barrier of the Oracle's; it tore into me with full force, already bloated to twice its original size, and ripped towards my heart.

I let go of Rand's hand just as the adult Demon erupted from the stone beneath my feet, scattering razor-edged shards like thrown knives. I felt the hot cuts of the debris, and hit the floor, panting, gagging on the sensation of the Demon Mark.

I don't know why I thought it might work. Don't know why it did work, except that I knew that two Demon Marks couldn't touch without fighting. Destroying each other. I knew that because having two of them inside me had killed me, once.

I turned and threw myself directly on the Demon, wrapping my arms around it.

It didn't feel like I'd expected it to feel. I'd thought it would be cold, ice-cold, and sharp to the touch, but it was lukewarm, and its flesh – if that was flesh – was only semi-solid, sickeningly fragile. I felt its talons dig into my shoulders to push me away, but I pressed harder against it, driving my hand into its chest.

And I felt the Demon Mark stop its burrowing, stir, and turn. It raced down my trembling, bloody arm, distending the skin as it went, sliding like a bundle of worms.

It didn't care what kind of damage it did, and it felt like being set on fire from the inside. Like having every muscle ruptured, every bone shattered on the way. I screamed, but I didn't let myself pull away.

The Demon Mark erupted out of the palm of my hand, the one bearing the mark of the Wardens, and slammed into the centre of the adult Demon.

I looked up at it, but there was no face, no sense of any sort of humanity to it. I couldn't tell if it felt pain, or fear, or even disappointment.

And then it screamed, a high thin metal sound, and plunged back through the hole and into the dark.

Gone.

Maybe dead, maybe not, but it was in trouble.

I collapsed to my knees, bleeding, whimpering, exhausted. The death clock inside of me was ticking slowly, inexorably down.

'Please,' I whispered. 'We saved you. Please stop this.'

The Oracle hadn't moved from where she sat on the bench, but now, her head turned. I don't know what she saw, because her eyes were white. Pure white, with a tiny dot of black for pupil. Eerie and totally inhuman.

She said nothing. Did nothing else. But at least I had her attention.

'We're not invaders,' I gasped. 'Maybe we're greedy, and selfish, and stupid, but that's our nature. That's *all* nature. Weeds strangle wheat. Bees go to war against each other. Humans are just . . . better at it.'

Nothing. But she didn't turn away, either. I felt tears break free, and I didn't try to stop them. So much to cry for, right now.

'Please,' I whispered, out of strength. I leant forward and rested my forehead on her lap. Soft fabric rustled around me as she shifted, and her scarred right hand slowly moved to rest on top of my hair.

I felt something tug inside and heard my deathclock tick faster. Faster. Years running out of me with every exhaled, terrified breath. It was going to end quietly after all. Not in blood and fire and storm, but in silence.

When there was nothing left, I collapsed in a heap at her feet, on top of the pooled brick-red fabric of her dress. It wasn't fabric. It felt like sun-warmed stone. It smelt like the empty, quiet places, and clean wind, and for a few seconds, it didn't seem to matter so much, that everything would be gone that I knew. That I loved.

She was offering me peace.

The hell with that. Peace was overrated.

I reached out with one flailing hand, grabbed hold of the bench beside me, and pulled myself into an awkward sitting position. Staring up at her. 'No,' I said. 'Hear me. *Hear me*. Listen. We're a part of you. *Hear us!*'

Millions of voices, talking. Babbling.

—scared, honey, there's nothing to be afraid of—

—Ayudame, padre—

—Jag inte den så goda känselförnimmelsen—

A storm of languages, of voices. Merging into one sound.

Into a jagged, discordant human chorus, six billion strong.

The Oracle slowly tilted her head, listening. I clapped my hands over my ears, but it wasn't enough; the din was enough to beat right through the barrier, billions of voices shouting in my ears. Howling. Scared.

And one of them said – *Listen*.

I knew that voice. That low, calm voice, with its blur of warmth and assurance.

Lewis was speaking, too. Lewis, who was like Jonathan had been, who had the keys to power. Once I'd opened up the line, it was like creating a network, and all he had to do was tap in.

I felt him, as if he was actually in the room with me. Maybe he was, in a sense. I saw the Oracle's blind stare go away from me, to some empty spot in the chapel.

The Oracle's head turned back towards me. One of her hands raised in a graceful, slow motion, and the babble of voices ceased.

And I heard a voice speak, a single voice, and it was vast and huge and unknowable.

Something broke with a sharp tug in my chest, and for a second I thought, *This is it, we're all dying*, but then I felt – heard? – the clock that had been speeding along inside slow down.

Then wind backward.

Now *that* was a weird sensation. I gasped and held on to the bench for dear life, gulping down nausea, and then, with a subtle and whispered pulse, everything just . . .

. . . went back to normal.

All over the world, human beings stopped feeling bad, paused in the act of dialling 911 or their local equivalents. Stopped clinging to each other in fear. Felt vaguely embarrassed by that sense of sheer terror that had gripped them for thirty long seconds of eternity.

The Mother had stopped in mid-house-cleaning.

The Oracle considered me, and then extended a single pointing finger.

I felt something stir inside, and then grow. Waves of heat and sensation coursing through me, beating like wings. Each one more intense than the last, shaking me free of the flesh. Hot golden pressure bursting through my mind, dissolving me in showers and waves and pulses of ecstasy. I let go and floated on wave after wave of incandescent glory.

The Oracle smiled, and dropped her hand back to her side, and I slowly drifted back into my body.

When it was over, there was something left behind. A slow, rich, deep pulse of power. Connection. Rhythms that I'd never felt before, or had any idea existed within my own body.

The Oracle turned away and took her seat again, contemplating the bright red rocks outside, the washed blue sky, the molten sun.

She looked peaceful. So peaceful.

I turned to go back out into the world.

Ashan was standing in the chapel. Staring at me with murderous, bloody fury. I backed up a step and shot a look at the Oracle, but she was sealed in that silent contemplation again. Might as well have been a thousand miles away from the confrontation going on three feet from her.

'It's over,' I said. 'Back off, Ashan.'

'No,' he growled. He was far from the polished, self-contained Djinn I'd come to know and fear – this one was primal, reduced to his most basic instincts to inflict pain and terror. 'Not you. I won't be your slave!'

I'm not asking you to . . .

I would have said it, but he didn't give me the chance. He lunged forward, exactly as he'd lunged at Imara, and I was glad to see him come for me, glad, because I wanted this monster dead more than I'd ever wanted anyone dead in my life.

I reached for power, intending to finish this once and for all, but I wasn't fast enough. He grabbed my head and held it between his hands, and I knew I was one millisecond from a broken neck, dead like my child, oh God, Imara . . .

Instead, he held me still and stared into my eyes, and I felt something happening. I fought to get free, but he was too strong, and whatever it was, he was doing it up on the aetheric levels, too –

Something in me ripped away, something vital and irreplaceable, and I felt a liquid heat race through my head, burning, erasing, taking me away from the world . . .

No.

The Oracle *moved*. Impossible, that something so composed of stillness could move so fast, but Ashan was in her hands and being pulled back and down, still snarling and fighting.

Whatever he'd done to me, it was still happening. I swayed, gasping, and grabbed for a bench. Missed. Thumped hard to my hands and knees.

Ashan was on the floor, too, and something was happening to him, something bad . . . the woman, the thing, she was bending over him and there was a pure white light and screaming, so much screaming . . .

. . . and when it was over, she was sitting on a

bench, staring straight ahead as if she'd never moved. Never would.

The grey-haired man with the pale, young face rolled over on his side, still screaming. Something different about him now. He was weeping, gagging on every breath.

Not a Djinn at all now. Just a man. Human.

Cast out from the angels.

. . . what was a Djinn?

I'd known his name once, hadn't I? And this place, I knew it, too . . . there was a haunting feeling of déjà vu, but I couldn't remember . . .

Couldn't remember.

There was a popping sound, like thin glass dropped on stone, and without any more warning than that a naked man was lying on the floor near the altar. Golden skin, auburn hair. When his eyes opened, they were the colour of melting brass, fierce and hot and inhuman.

I flinched and scrambled out of his way. Towards the other man, who was at least human.

'No—' The metallic one reached out, trying to grab hold of me, and I pulled away. 'Jo, what's happened to—?'

I had no idea who he was, but he frightened me. Scenes flickered in front of my eyes, people I didn't know, a life I'd never lived. Terrifyingly vivid, but they had nothing to do with me, did they? I didn't know these people, these places. I didn't know . . . it was all so confusing . . .

The grey-haired man screamed and charged up from the floor, hands outstretched for my throat.

The woman on the bench turned her head towards me and made the tiniest gesture, the smallest little lift of a finger, and I was spinning into the darkness.

My last sight was of the auburn-haired man lunging for me, trying to hold on. There was torment on his face, and for a second . . . for a second I thought I knew him.

Then I was gone.

Chapter Eleven

I was lying on something cold and wet, and I was naked and shivering. Afraid. Something was very, very wrong with me.

I reflexively curled in on myself, protecting as much of myself as I could, as awareness of the world washed over me in hot, pulsing waves.

Biting, frigid wind. Ice-cold sleet trailing languid fingers over my bare skin. I forced my eyes open and saw my arm lying on the ground in front of my eyes, hand outstretched, and my skin was a pallid, blue-tinged white, red at the fingertips. Frostbite.

I ached all over, so fiercely that I felt tears well up in my eyes. And I felt *empty*, cored out and thrown out like an old orange peel.

I forced myself to look beyond my own hand, and saw that I was lying in a mound of cold, slimy leaf-litter. Overhead, fall-coloured trees swayed and scratched the sky, and what little could be seen between the skeletal branches was grey, flocked with low clouds. The air tasted thin in my mouth.

I tried to think where I was, how I'd gotten here, but it was a blank. Worse, it terrified me to even try to think of it. I shuddered with more than the cold, gasping, and squeezed my eyes shut again.

Get up, I told myself. *Up.* I'd die if I stayed here, naked and freezing. But when I tried to uncurl myself from the embryonic position I'd assumed, I couldn't get anything to work right. My muscles jittered and spasmed and protested wildly, and the best I managed was to roll myself up to my hands and knees and not quite fall flat on my face again.

I heard a voice yelling somewhere off in the woods. Sticks cracking, as something large moved through the underbrush. *Run!* something told me, and I was immediately drenched in cold terror. I lunged up to my feet, biting back a shriek of agony as muscles trembled and threatened to tear. I fell against the rough bark of a tree and clung to it as cramps rippled through my back and legs, like giant hands giving me the worst massage in the world. I saw sparks and stars, bit my lip until I tasted blood. My hair was blowing wildly in the wind where it wasn't stuck to my damp, cold skin or matted with mud and leaves.

I let go of the tree and lurched away. My legs didn't want to move, but I forced them, one step at a time. My arms were wrapped around my breasts to preserve a warmth that I couldn't find, either within me or without.

My feet were too cold to feel pain, but when I looked back I saw I was leaving smears of blood behind on the fallen leaves. Cuts had already opened on the soles.

I kept moving. It was more of a lurching not-quite-falling than running, but I was too frightened to wait for any kind of improvement. *Had to keep moving.*

More shouting behind me. Voices, more than one. The hammer of blood in my ears kept me from focusing on the words. *Someone did this to me*, I thought. *Put me out here to die.* I didn't want them to find that they'd failed.

Not that they really *had* failed, yet.

Up ahead was a tangle of underbrush. My body was already covered with whip-scratches and a lacework of blood against cold white skin. Even numb as I was at the moment, I couldn't throw myself into a thorn thicket. I needed a way around . . . I turned right, holding to a massive tree trunk for support, and clambered up a short rise.

Just as I reached the summit, a shadow appeared at the top of it. I gasped and started to fall backward, but the shadow reached down and grabbed my forearm, pulling me up the rest of the way and then wrapping me in sudden warmth as his arms closed around me.

I fought, startled and scared, but he was a big man, tall, and he managed to pin my arms to my side in a bear hug. 'Jo!' he shouted in my ear. 'Joanne, stop! It's me! It's Lewis!'

He smelt like woodsmoke and sweat, leaves and damp fabric, but he was warm, oh God, warm as heaven itself, and against my own will I felt myself go limp and stop fighting. For the moment.

'Jo?' He slowly let his arms loosen, and pulled back to look down at me. He was taller than I was by half a head, with shaggy-cut brown hair, and a long patrician face with big, dark eyes. A three-day growth of beard coming in heavy on his cheeks and chin. 'We've been looking for you for days. What the hell happened to you? Are you—?' He stopped himself with an impatient shake of his head. 'Never mind, stupid question, you're not OK or you'd have contacted us. Listen, we're in trouble. Bad trouble. We need you. Things have gone wrong.'

I realised, with a terrible sinking feeling, that I had no idea who he was. And then the sinking turned to free fall.

He must have known something was wrong, because he frowned at me and passed his hand in front of my eyes. 'Jo? Are you listening to me?'

I had no idea who I was.

Soundtrack

Yep, once again, I had a soundtrack to help me stay focused, and boy, it was *huge* this time. (It was a big challenge. What can I say?) If you can't afford a gazillion CDs, hey, do what I do: Download them from iTunes or one of the other fine music services where the artists receive compensation per song. Please don't steal. Mother Nature doesn't like it when you steal, and I think we've established what happens when you make her mad . . .

'Battleflag'	Lo Fidelity Allstars
'Extreme Way'	Moby
'Come Undone'	Duran Duran
'Objection (Tango)'	Shakira
'Push It'	Garbage
'Let's Get It Started (Spike Mix)'	Black Eyed Peas
'Goodnight Moon'	Shivaree
'Virtual Insanity'	Jamiroquai
'Stop Don't Panic'	Jamiroquai
'Superstition'	Stevie Wonder
'You Haven't Done Nothing'	Stevie Wonder
'Angry Johnny'	Poe
'Molly's Chamber'	Kings of Leon
'Red Rain'	Peter Gabriel

'Twilight Zone'	Golden Earring
'(The System of) Dr Tarr and Professor Fether'	Alan Parsons Project
'Pretty Fly (For a White Guy)'	The Offspring
'Mustang Sally'	The Commitments
'Vertigo'	U2
'No Sugar Tonight/New Mother Nature'	The Guess Who
'Thunder'	Prince
'Tusk'	Fleetwood Mac
'S.A.L.T'	The Orb
'Shiver'	Maroon 5
'Gel'	Collective Soul
'Where the River Flows'	Collective Soul
'Angel'	Sarah McLachlan
'Oh, Berta, Berta'	Tony Furtado
'Passive'	A Perfect Circle
'The River'	Joe Bonamassa
'Bodies'	Drowning Pool

Acknowledgments

The author wishes to thank the following:

My absolutely incredible editor, Liz Scheier, for her patience and help during my personal crisis that fell right across the deadline for this book.

My equally incredible agent, Lucienne Diver, without whose support and encouragement none of this would be happening (or ever would have, for that matter).

The Stormchasers, all five hundred-plus of them, who are some of the most enthusiastic and wonderful folks I could ever hope to know.

My LJ friends, nearly as numerous as the Stormchasers, every single one of them a gem.

Kelley, Marla, Claire, Laurie, Katy, and Becky: the Time Turners. Goddesses all.

Independent booksellers Edge Books and Bakka-Phoenix.

ORAC, especially P. N. Elrod, Joanne Madge, and Jackie Leaf.

My husband, Cat, for supporting me at every step of the process, and being my cheering section.

Tory Fuller, who has given me immense help by vetting the weather content of these books . . . Mistakes are all mine, mine, mine.

And as always, the great Joe Bonamassa, who makes this writing process so much more fun by turning out incredible music. Come back to Texas more often. We love you.

DON'T MISS THE NEXT BOOK IN

The Weather Warden series

'The forecast calls for . . . a fun read'
Jim Butcher, author of the Dresden Files

'Another powerhouse urban fantasy'
SFRevu

'The Weather Warden series is fun reading . . .
more engaging than most TV'
Booklist

ALSO BY RACHEL CAINE

The Morganville Vampires series

Check out our website for free tasters and exclusive discounts, competitions and giveaways, and sign up to our monthly newsletter to keep up-to-date on our latest releases, news and upcoming events.

www.allisonandbusby.com